I'm Frankie Sterne

I'm Frankie Sterne

a novel by Dave Margoshes

Canadian Cataloguing in Publication Data

Margoshes, Dave, 1941
  I'm Frankie Sterne

ISBN 1-896300-23-5

I. Title.
PS8576.A647I42 2000   C813'.54   C00-910687-1
PR9199.3.M354I42 2000

Editors for the Press: Robert Kroetsch and Thomas Wharton
Cover and interior design: Ruth Linka
Cover image: Johwanna Alleyne
Author photograph: Bryan Schlosser

Author's acknowledgements: Much of this novel has appeared, often in different form, as stories in various magazines. Chapter 1, "Frankie on Frankie," and Chapter 4, "Music and Art," appeared, in very different form, under the title "Frankie on Frankie" in *Dandelion*. Chapter 2, "Uptown A," was in *The Gaspereau Review* and Chapter 3, "Radio Silence," in *Canadian Forum*. Chapter 6, "Summer-time Blues," and Chapter 12, "Push Comes to Shove," appeared separately in *The New Quarterly*. Chapter 9, "The Edge of the World," appeared in *The University of Windsor Review* and Chapter 10, "Buddy Holly Died Here," in *Grain*. Chapter 13, "Another Woman," was in *The Wascana Review*. Chapter 15, "Montana," was the co-winner of the 1996 *Prairie Fire* long short story contest and appeared in the magazine and subsequently in *1998: Best Canadian Stories* (Oberon). My thanks to the various editors of these publications for their support.

  My thanks also to Alberta Culture, the Saskatchewan Arts Board and the Canada Council for the Arts for financial assistance during the writing of this book.

THE CANADA COUNCIL   LE CONSEIL DES ARTS
FOR THE ARTS   DU CANADA
SINCE 1957   DEPUIS 1957

🍁 Canadian   Patrimoine
   Heritage   canadien

NeWest Press acknowledges the support of the Canada Council for the Arts and the Alberta Foundation for the Arts for our publishing program. We also acknowledge the financial support of the Government of Canada through the Book Publishing Industry Development Program (BPIDP) for our publishing activities.

NeWest Press
201-8540-109 Street
Edmonton, Alberta T6G 1E6
(780) 432-9427
www.newestpress.com

00 01 02 03 04 4 3 2 1

PRINTED AND BOUND IN CANADA

This book is dedicated to the memories
of Ted White and Phil Ochs,
who paused to rest, just for a minute, in the snow.

"A moment passes, and then from the woods comes the sound of mourning. They are always mourning, those doves. In the mornings and in the evenings they mourn, and sometimes in the late afternoon. They are not mourning death, you understand. It is life that is making them mourn."

—Merle Miller, *A Gay and Melancholy Sound.*

"It is over too soon."

—Joseph Stein (1871-1949)
from *his memoirs, privately published.*

Contents

My name is François Sterne. If you don't believe me, take a look at this driver's license. You can buy anything—hell, I can't even drive. Even passports, more expensive, though. I don't have a need for one. Every place I'm likely to want to go I've already been.

I have a new life and an old one. I'm still figuring out the new, so it's the old one I'll tell you about.

1. Frankie on Frankie

I was conceived, if you must know, on the first night of spring in 1941, "a night"—my father used to tell me, the gold in his teeth flashing with delight—"when the stars outshone the lights on 125th Street and covered the sky with a soft white sheen like snowflakes and it was so warm windows sprung open all over Harlem for the first time in months, like the mouths of small boys up way past their bedtime." This is the way he speaks sometimes, as if he were reciting the poetry of Lorca, who is one of his gods, along with Charlie Parker, Langston Hughes and Eugene Debs.

It was the opening of one such window, my father said, that awoke him, somewhere along three in the morning. "The groaning of the sash in its frame was like a finger rubbing its knobby way up my spine and I blinked in the darkness, listening, my skin tight"—tight, though he didn't say this, as, years later, when circumstances and inclination would lead him to that way of making a living, the mailbag's strap across his shoulder would be when he began his rounds in the morning—"until the sound came again, this time like a baby's nagging cry, and I could place it. My shoulders settled against the pillow, brought by my mother from Russia"—and one of the last remaining vestiges of her in his life, though he didn't say that—"squashing the ancient feathers like the last gasps of air in a deflated inner tube, and my eyes closed, but I was awake, and so much trouble washed over my mind it forced me out of the bed and to my own window, which I creaked open"—and I can imagine him sticking his lion's head on its chicken neck out into the warm, soft night, letting the stardust trickle over it like tepid wine from the goatskin bag he had worn over his shoulder in Spain, foreshadowing the mailbag yet to come. "It was very still," my father said, "quiet"—which was unusual for Harlem, even at that hour, even in those days. "The combination of it all, the warm honey air and the soft milky sky, the stillness, made the skin on the back of my neck get up and march toward my scalp like the buglers at the Four Square Gospel Missionary Church on Sunday afternoon, just the way it always did on those nights in Spain in the hours before battle."

Thinking of Spain, as always, turned his mind to the woman who would be my mother, though I would never know her, and he padded softly back to the bed and, as he put it, "roused her."

That was the way my father liked to tell *that* story. He has a fitful memory, and sometimes—these days—can't seem to even remember his own name, which he's changed a number of times over the years, just as I have, but he has total recall, like he was reading from this morning's newspaper, for what he likes to call the "religious experiences" of his life: a dozen or so moments spaced out over largely the first half of his sixty-some-odd years during which, for a moment or an hour or half a day, the clock stopped and eternity stepped back to watch. The first time he picked up a horn, that's one of them, etched like Egyptian hieroglyphics on the face of a tomb, readable for all time for anyone who knows the language. The moment he was wounded, his first sight of the Statue of Liberty ... for most of us, things that seemed dreadfully important once lose their snap with the passage of time, but not for my father. For him it is quite the reverse, the further away things are, the more important they become, the more precious, all the more clear, so his first acknowledged orgasm—which he had when he was thirteen, standing on trembling legs in the dark hole of an immigrant ship, his arms twined around a railing to steady him and his stomach lurching beneath his rope belt like a drunken peddler while the blonde curly head of a Polish girl he'd met only that morning bobbed just below his line of vision, all of this illuminated in his memory by the kind of stark, naked white light the police are known to shine in the eyes of suspects as they question them. That first piercing sweetness washes away for the rest of his life like saltwater waves crashing down on a spilled glass of skim milk all the other moments of passion and heat and trembling— with a few notable exceptions, of course, that first night of spring 1941 one of them. A religious experience.

Pressed, he can never remember, however, whether the day past was that notable vernal equinox, or the day approaching. Three in the morning is a confusing time at the best of times, and, at any rate, he doesn't like to tell that particular story anymore.

———

I never knew my mother, except through my father's ramblings and a handful of other trinkets, scraps and clues I've managed to assemble over the years. She was, my father always said, not quite as black as Ebeneezer's tooth and spoke no English to speak of, which is to say, I suppose, that she spoke enough to get along on Harlem's rough streets but no more. Some men, to spite their Jewish parents, might marry a black woman or a Puerto Rican woman; my father managed to combine the two. I sometimes wonder if she was really as unilingual as he claims she was. As a boy, I often dreamed of her, and in the dream she would sing to me, whisper to me, but when I awoke, I could never remember if it had been in Spanish or English. My father, who is a linguist as well as a scholar and a musician, speaks Spanish impeccably, which is what always gave him away when he was trying to pass for Puerto Rican or Cuban, of course. Dark as he is, bushy as his mustache used to be, Madrid University grammar was always

3

suspect in the third trumpet of a machambo band. That in itself was not his undoing, but it helped.

In the one photograph of her that survives, my mother is standing tense and awkward behind an overstuffed chair, one hand on its back, the other on the arm, in a posture that must have tired her. Her body is slightly twisted but there is no hiding the slimness of it, nor the ill fit of the dress, a narrow-waisted, full-skirted, floral-patterned arrangement of stiff-looking cloth that must have been heavy and hot. Women don't wear dresses like that anymore, and they're wise not to—my mother's life, as far as I can see, revolved around them, or they around her. There is a smile on her lips—African lips, though not much thicker than mine—but it appears forced, pained, as if the starch in the dress's bodice is pressing uncomfortably against her breasts, as if the weight of it all—the dress, the thick black hair piled upon her head like rope, the awkward pose, the dusty, slightly sour smell of the chair, the orders and cajoling of the photographer—is becoming almost too much for her to bear. That is what life with my father, who took the photograph, must have been like.

It is impossible, since the photograph is black and white, and faded, to tell the exact tone of her skin, but it's certainly darker than mine and I choose to think of it as ebony, and it does appear to give off light, much the way polished pieces of that remarkable wood will do. Her eyes too are dark, brooding and hurt, but luminous, like the crushed velvet pillows on my Aunt Ida's settee. They were, my father would say, black as the underarms of the fallen angel. He is given to hyperbole.

She is wearing a ring—I don't mean a wedding band. Her left hand, on the back of the chair, is tilted slightly so the fingers are not completely visible. But her right hand, on the chair's arm, is relaxed and splay-fingered, and there is a ring on the small finger, a ring with a stone that catches a ray of light and sets a thin, sharp glitter forever into the photograph, something so insignificant and yet as sharp and impermeable as my father's tumescent memories, undecipherable but forever. I've asked my father about the ring, of course, numerous times, but he denies memory or knowledge of it; the first is believable, considering the general quality of his memory, but the second not so. How could he not have known about the ring on the finger of his beloved, whether he put it there or not? As to the wedding band, of course there was one, a plain gold ring unadorned by design, and my father himself wears that, on a silver chain around his neck, and always has, in all my own memory, which is excellent. Whether he leaves it on or takes it off when he gets into bed with his ladyfriend Ruth is something I choose not to speculate on.

That photograph raises but doesn't answer so many questions about my mother—for example, why should a woman so young, so apparently strong, so fine-boned and firm-chinned, with skin so lustrous, be dead within two years? That, I suppose, is the central question I've asked about my mother all my life, although there have been dozens, hundreds of others. Very few answers. My father claims he doesn't know, or doesn't remember, simple things like when and where she was born, *exactly*, how many there were in her family, any brothers and sisters, what her parents did, that sort of thing, and I can believe that he never did know at least some of those things. My father approaches people the way a bee does a flower—it's the sweet juice at the heart he's interested in, not the flower or the leaf or the stem or the roots. And the other things—things more personal, things about *her*, like what her laugh sounded like and did she display it often, did she paint her nails (there is no sign of it in the photograph), could she play the piano, things he couldn't possibly *not* have known and I don't believe even *he* could have forgotten—he shrugs my questions off, always has.

"What was my mother like?" I might ask, and he will shrug, "Like a woman, what else? Like a peach, all fruit and pit." He won't say any more. If I press him, he's likely to leave the room. My father never gets angry.

My relatives, in their uncomfortable, helpless way, are even vaguer.

"She was a very fine woman, you should be proud of her and behave so that she could be proud of you," my Aunt Ida told me the summer I stayed with her and Uncle Nate in the Catskills, while my father enjoyed his first steady gig in years, playing second trumpet in a dance band at one of the resorts across the mountains. I was twelve and my Aunt Ida was a new experience—up until less than a year before, I hadn't even known she existed, she or Uncle Hy or Uncle Ira or any of the aunts and uncles by marriage, cousins and second cousins, including my best cousin Rhoda, who is also my good dear friend, all members of a world belonging to my father he had sought to shut himself and, therefore, me, out of. It had taken me most of July to get used to Aunt Ida and the others, who were always around, either living there in the cottage with us or trooping in on weekends, their arms filled with baskets, folded blankets and bulging bags of fruit and bagels and rye bread. But when I had, when I was beginning to feel comfortable, like an orphan learning a new language or a cat taken in from the pound to a household where the milk is always warm and feet are for curling up against, not dodging, I took the occasion one afternoon, when I had a slight cold and had been confined to the cottage while the other children went off swimming, and asked her if she had known my mother.

My Aunt Ida, you must understand, is a slow woman—not slow-witted but slow in movement and speech. She continued with her sewing, her head partially inclined, her glasses halfway down her nose—the same oddly arched fleshy protuberance as my father's—as her fingers flashed over the needle and the sock or whatever it was she was mending. She said nothing, as if she hadn't heard my question, but I knew she had and I continued to look at her from my curled-up place on the sofa across the fruit-laden coffee table from her chair. After a few minutes, she finished a seam and looked up. Her hair was gray even then, and she brushed aside a fallen curl.

"Yes," she said solemnly, "I knew your mother." And then, without being prompted or coaxed, she delivered herself of the pronouncement mentioned above—"...a very fine woman ... proud of her ... proud of you..."—although she made it sound like several sentences. That was her last word on the subject. "It's not for *me* to say," was the defense she offered when I began to let fly with dozens of small questions aimed at the details of my mother's life I hungered so deeply to know. "Hasn't your father told you that? Shame on him. Well"—and here, if I remember correctly, the slow speech ground almost to a crawl, and was punctuated by a deep sigh, Aunt Ida's favorite rhetorical device—"he has his reasons, I suppose." There was no point in pressing further.

The others were no more helpful. The most I could glean from my uncles and aunts—these are all my *father's* kin, as must be clear—is that she was a very fine woman, a very lovely woman, a very lovely *person*, but that they hadn't, unfortunately, known her long or well before, God rest her, her sudden demise; and, this last from my Uncle Nate, the magician who can pull pennies from small children's ears, that I, thank God, look like *her*, not *him*. Only my cousin Rhoda, one year younger than me and linked to me somehow, if not by the stars than by what we were to become to each other, was able to offer something of real value, although I hated her for it then.

It was Rhoda who gave me my first good experience with sex. I already knew quite a bit about sex at this point, but mostly it was penis-oriented. I had been masturbating for awhile, and I had put it *into* things, including the damp, rotten-smelling swamp of a fifteen-year-old girl whose running pimples had made me feel sick and who charged me a chocolate Coke for the favor. But I had never *felt*, with my hands or mouth or chest or belly, the softnesses and smoothnesses and electricity of another person. I had felt excitement rising through me like a taut wire, but I had never laughed in sex, never pressed my fingertips to my mouth afterwards to taste the tingling. Rhoda gave me all that, all the subtleties and finesses of sex—an *introduction*, I'm talking about—without the main act.

Behind the cluster of cottages which lay like a fringe of algae around the small, almost perfectly round lake, were mostly woods, but on one side there was a farm, its fields tilled and ripe but its buildings deserted and falling back into the land. We used to go for walks through the woods, Rhoda and I—me almost thirteen, she almost twelve—and chase each other across those fields until we'd wind up in the barn, up the creaky, cracked ladder to the hayloft where, finally alone and secret in the rich darkness slatted with shafts of sunlight knifing in through the tattered roof, we would lie in the thick, sweet-sour damp hay and wrestle, feeling each other through our clothes, groping under our clothes, showing each other things, kissing. We laughed, grew to know each other, grew to be friends. Girls, I think, are satisfied with just that, and why shouldn't they be? That much is so much. But boys are never satisfied, and I was always pressing her for more. She was patient and kind but firm, and frightened, I suppose, and still largely ignorant, surely far more ignorant than me—of *specifics*, that is; far wiser than me in every other way. But still I pressed, too far one day, until I felt her skin grow cold with fear and there was no laughter in me, only the taut wire, ringing in my ears, and then her voice, shrill and frightened, spinning out like the point of a knife to hurt me. She had been saying "no" and "don't" repeatedly and I had been ignoring her words. Now she said, "No, I don't want to be a whore like your mother."

It was like a kick in the belly or lower. I sat up, rolling her away from me. I stood up, my chest heaving, and looked down at her with something like revulsion. *She* was a whore. And ugly and foul-smelling and diseased. I put my hand on a beam above my head to steady myself. There was a story that the farm had been abandoned after the farmer had opened the barn door one morning to find his fourteen-year-old son hanging by a rope from the rafters, his slim body swaying slowly, the rafters creaking. It was a story only the children of the cottages told, dismissed by the adults as nonsense, and Rhoda and I had forced ourselves to believe it couldn't be true before we'd dared venture into the barn the first time, but as I looked down from the loft now I could imagine a body swinging there, my own body, the purple welt around my neck vivid and ugly, as vivid and ugly as Rhoda's word. I didn't have to ask her what she meant, although already she was standing beside me, stroking my shoulder, telling me she didn't mean it, that it didn't mean *anything*, it was just something she had heard, something mean her brothers had said to tease her, she didn't know why she had said it, it was only because I was hurting her....

There was a small, triangular window at the end of the hayloft, and I stood staring through it for a long time, waiting for her to leave. She takes something from her mother, from Aunt Ida, and she was slow in realizing what I wanted, but eventually she retreated down the ladder. I heard her say, "I'm so sorry, Frankie. I'm so sorry, so stupid," and then her creaking steps descended, and she was gone, I was alone. I cleared my eyes and forced them to focus. Way across the farm field was a clump of trees and then a winding blacktop road, like a ribbon dropped onto the countryside by a careless girl. The road led deeper into the mountains. Somewhere in that direction it led to a hotel where, that evening, my father would be playing his trumpet while women in straw hats danced with pleasure.

2. Uptown A

Strange things are happening, just like Red Buttons says.

Pops came home with his nose all out of joint the other night and he's been like a cat on a fence ever since.

He don't talk directly. Getting stuff out of him is like prying the lid off an old paint can, you have to nibble at the edge with your screwdriver, a little here, a little there, or you don't get *anywhere*. Keep working at it, eventually you get something out of him—sideways, always sideways.

It seems he was down at Times Square, on the subway platform. He'd been down to the Village with his ax, on his own as always, just shaking around to see if there might be a gig for him, and there wasn't, which is usual for him down there, and he'd hopped the subway back uptown but got off after a few stops, on a hunch, he said, and lurked around Broadway and 42nd Street for awhile. Don't know why—there's no bars with bands along that stretch of Broadway—but Pops is always prowling around. Who knows what he's looking for? Sometimes I think he's waiting to bump into Bird or Basie or Ellington or someone who'll recognize him and lead him by the hand, save him from his dead-end life in the post office.

"Hey, man, I heard you last year at Birdland during that session, remember? You wuz *good*, man. Didn't catch your name so I didn't know how to look you up. How'd you like to play in my band?" That sort of thing.

Or maybe a Hollywood producer—I can just see Pops in 3-D, his trumpet sticking out into the audience like those spears in *Bwana Devil*, the spit spraying your face. Naw, Pops don't give a shit for the movies, calls 'em plastic bubbles.

Anyway, who he did bump into wasn't no Count or Duke, it was his brother.

Not Duke Ellington's brother, his own, *Pops'* brother.

"You have a brother?" I say the next day, when I pry it out of him, my mouth hanging open just the way his must have, and he gives me one of his looks—*the* look, like I'm no smarter than the cockroaches in our kitchen, though they're smart enough to stay out of his way, so maybe he's got a point.

"You got wax in your ears, Frankie?" he says. "I talk just to keep the walls from falling down?"

Okay, okay, he's right, I *did* know he had a brother, all sorts of family. He talks about them all the time, his family, but that's about when they were kids in Russia, or greenhorns just over on the boat and living on the Lower East Side or someplace, Pops not much older than I am now. He never talks about family like they was *real* people, I mean alive and kicking *now*. You ask him, hey, whatever happened to Uncle Whatshisname, you know, the dopey brother who ate the green apples and almost died, you ask him something like that and his eyes go that cloudy gray and he gets up and moves away, like some dumb whale edging out to sea, not because it's *afraid* of the harpoon ship but just can't be bothered. All the other kids I know, they got relatives up to their asses, but I don't have anybody, not even a mother. Just Pops.

But there it was, *he* was—Pops' brother Ira, *Uncle Ira*. And I do mean bump. Pops had given up his prowling and was heading home, he says. Down on the IRT platform waiting for the train, about ten at night, a Friday, so the platform's crowded. He turns around, and bam, he bumps into this guy, big guy, suit and tie. *Why don'tcha look where you're going?* the guy must of hollered, and

Pops, never no trouble, he probably just snuffles out a *'scuse me* and starts to sidle away, head down, clutching his horn case the way he always does when he's in a crowd, afraid someone will snatch it away, like tearing out his heart with a bloody hand.

Then he hears: *"Moishe!"*

The word must have paralyzed him; the name itself, almost forgotten but instantly familiar, the sound of it, and the deep, raspy voice carrying it, together they must have nailed him to the platform as if a spike had been driven down through his spine, right through him and into the floor; the hair on the back of his neck must have stood on end, the skin crawled; the lid of his left eye must have begun to rattle like a Venetian blind in the wind, the way it does when he gets nervous.

Then: *"Murray!"* I can practically hear the voice behind him, sliding out this other sound like a dot on an i, one last knot in a rope already tight around his neck. But it must have broken the grip the subway platform had on his legs and he spun around, bumping into the man again, this time right into his open arms.

"Ira!" Pops said. The name must have sounded like a sob.

They embraced—I can see it clearly—their arms around each other, heads on each other's shoulders, eyes brimming, like lovers on a dock after a troop ship comes in. An Uptown A roared in, opened its doors with a vacuum *whoosh*, loaded, closed its hissing doors, lurched out of the station and, for a few moments, they were alone on the platform, until, like water sifting into a hole dug in the sand, people began to trickle down the steps. They stood back at arms' length finally, hands on each other's arms, and gazed fondly at each other, Pops biting his lower lip.

Ira is a tall man, taller than Pops, and half again as thick, dressed well in a gray fall topcoat and shiny cordovans, a gray hat—this is the way I see him, anyway. His graying hair was trimmed close to his rounded head and his face was plump, fresh-ly shaven, pink on the cheeks from health and food but dark around the eyes as if he never gets enough sleep. He's a doctor, a surgeon at Columbia Presbyterian, and I imagine him with the wrong kind of hands for the work: fat, clumsy-looking, with stubby fingers and square nails, hands like Pops'.

"Thank God," he says.

"I don't understand," Pops says.

"Thank God I couldn't get a taxi."

"I don't understand," Pops says again. He's still dazed, and the hand clutching the trumpet case is starting to hurt, the knuckles angel-wing white.

Ira laughs, his face opening up like one of those folding leather satchels. "May is ready to kill me. It happens like clockwork, every time we go out to dinner or the theater, there's an emergency. But what am I supposed to do? I'm a physician, not a plumber. Some things can't wait. Don't tell them where you're going, she says, but it can't be done, it just can't be done. So, sure enough, we just finish with the roast beef and the dessert is about to be served—something so full of calories the medical association would have me on the carpet if they knew—and the waiter comes with the message. And off I go—thank God, I'm spared those calories, at least. And, thank God, it's Friday and I can't find a cab anywhere. I was running through the streets—*downtown*, like a fool, when it's uptown I want to go—yelling *taxi, taxi, cab, cabbie,* people are starting to look, not that I care about that, but it isn't getting me anywhere anyway. So I find myself in front of the IRT and come down. What the hell? At this time of night, on a Friday, if there's a train right away, this will be faster, just as fast. And thank God for that, because here you are, Moishe, Moushie, Murray, baby brother, like a long-lost child returned from the desert."

All of this must have come out of Ira's wide mouth with the speed and force of an express roaring through a local station, and it made Pops breathless just to listen. His eyes were still glistening with tears, but he had put his hands down and was starting to edge away uncertainly. "I don't understand," he repeated, stupidly. There was something about a taxi, not being able to find a taxi, but he himself always takes the subway and his experience with cabs is limited. All at once, he must have wanted to flee, like at the end of one of those demonstrations he goes to, when the cops start pressing in. He turned and began to run, lopsidedly, the old wound in his hip betraying him.

Ira caught Pops with a tackle that knocked him over, his shoulder banging against a salted peanut machine, the trumpet case clattering to the filthy platform, the stench of piss and chewing gum sharp in his nostrils. He scrambled after it, on his knees. Ira stood over him, panting, shoulders hunched, a gray, red-faced bear.

"You should of seen us, Frankie," Pops tells me. "Two grown men, like idiots."

"You won't get away from us again, Murray," he says Uncle Ira said.

A woman with a face like an old apple stuck her umbrella between them. "Should I call a policeman?" she asked Pops. "Decent people don't have to be molested in public places. It only happens if we let it happen."

"He, he ..." Pops stuttered. He clutched the trumpet case to his chest, raising one knee. "My...."

"I'll pursue you," Ira said, ignoring the woman. "I'll follow you on the subway, uptown or downtown, it doesn't make any difference to me. My patient can die, I don't care, God forgive me. I'll chase you from car to car."

"I'll call a policeman," the apple woman said. She turned to Ira, the tip of her umbrella pointing menacingly at him. "I'm going to call a policeman. Don't you harm this young man, don't you *touch* his suitcase."

Ira didn't take his eyes off Pops, who was pulling himself to his feet, but he wriggled his eyebrows with authority. "Madam, I *happen* to be a physician. This young man, as you call him, *happens* to be my patient. Now, he is not completely in control of himself, but I can assure you that *I* am. If you would be so good as to remove your umbrella from my face, I could continue with my treatment of this poor, unfortunate fellow."

Pops says he was laughing, doubling over, and the apple woman retreated, her face even more wrinkled than before. People were watching, but Ira didn't care about that.

"You know it's true, Murray, I'll pursue you, I'll follow you, chase you car to car. I've been kicking myself for ten years for not chasing you when I had the chance. Now that I've got you again, you think I'm going to lose you?"

"No, Ira," Pops said. The laughter had subsided and so had the fear. He was forty-eight years old, had just been sent sprawling in a subway station, had been defended by a woman probably little older than himself who called him a young man, and now a comical image of his older brother flashed through his mind: Ira groping through a subway car like a blind man with a cup and an accordion, pursuing the scent of coins. He must have wanted to crawl into the other man's arms and stay there. "No, I know you won't let go this time."

"Let go?" Ira said. He was brushing off his trousers, shrugging his shoulders more smoothly into the topcoat. "We don't want to grab you by the throat, you know. We just want to touch."

The two men stood gazing at each other for a moment, listening to the approaching roar of an uptown train. "Mama died," Ira said just before the train pulled into the station. "Just this year."

"I didn't know," Pops said. He had to shout to be heard, and a tear began to trickle down his cheek, catching itself in the groove above his mustache.

"It's okay, it's okay," Ira said. "She was old, sick, past her time. The last few years, she didn't know me, wouldn't have recognized you even if...." He let his voice trail off. "I thought maybe you'd see the notice in the *Times*, that it would bring you out of hiding. You don't have to be a stranger you know, what's in the past is past. But this is just as good. God works his wonders...." He shrugged. "And your boy?"

"Boy! He's twelve."

"Almost a man," Ira said, shaking his head. "We missed his whole life." His own children are grown, out in the world, he told Pops.

"Don't worry, you didn't miss so much," Pops said, winking. That *is* what he'd say about me.

They rode uptown together, sitting on a backward seat with their shoulders rubbing, shouting at each other over the roar of the tracks. They got off at the same station and Pops walked his brother to the hospital, then went on home himself, the long way, sticking his head into the dives to see what was happening.

———

I was still up, all by my lonesome as usual, reading comics and listening to the radio and wishing we had a TV so I could watch Uncle Miltie or Gorgeous George on the wrestling, and I could see right away he was jumpy about something. Right off the bat, he yelled at me, how come I wasn't in bed?

"No school tomorrow, Pops. It's Saturday. Anyway, I'm twelve, I don't need curfew anymore."

"Eleven," he snaps back. "Don't push it, Frankie, two months to go."

Usually he doesn't pay any attention to me, and when he does it's just like a barometer telling you it's going to rain.

"What's up, Daddy-o?" I ask him. "Got a gig? Play a good jam?" Or a bad one? I think, but I don't say that.

"Up? Nothin'. Why do things always have to be *up* with you? And don't call me that. How many times I gotta tell you?"

"It's just an expression, Pops. Both of 'em. Like you say

'Wha's happenen', man?' when people come over."

"And don't call me Pops, either. I'm your father, for Chrissake." He's shouting and I back off, let him be. I go to bed with my flashlight and a *Mad* comic. What, me worry?—that's my motto. He's been moody as hell, much worse than usual, since spring when they fried those people he was always marching for, those Rosenbergs, and I don't know what else is eating him because something is and tonight he's extra spooky. I can hear him clattering around in the kitchen for a long time, slamming the icebox door, chipping slivers of ice off the block, rattling them in a glass, squirting seltzer—a regular Alfred E. Neuman, just like there wasn't anybody in the whole *fershluginer* block, let alone the building or the next room, trying to sleep. After awhile, he quiets down and when he thinks I'm asleep he comes in and stands by the bed for a minute or two. I keep my eyes closed and breathe deep, and in a little bit he puts his hand on my head and tousles my hair, then creeps out to his own room.

The next day, while we're doing our weekend chores, cleaning up the apartment with the *Make Believe Ballroom* on the radio and Pops scowling like his ears are being bitten off by Patti Page and rabid bats, I start working on him, prying it out like pulling teeth. At first he's worse than usual, denying that the day before even existed, let alone that he lived through it and something out of the ordinary happened to him. But, bit by bit, I get it out, enough detail for me to fill in the blanks myself.

"I'm sorry about your mother," I say when he tells me that part. I've always wondered about my grandparents on my mother's side, if they were alive and where they might be, but I guess I just assumed Pops' mother and father were dead, just like it didn't occur to me his brothers and sisters might actually be alive, and living in the same city we do. Turns out his father did die a few years ago, but somehow he'd already known about that, just hadn't mentioned it. "Now you're an orphan like me."

I'm not sure if I mean that to be funny or serious, and Pops gives me a look like he's wondering the same thing. "Another thing we have in common," he says finally, with a shrug and a face like that thought doesn't especially thrill him.

Later, the phone rings and it's Uncle Ira himself, wanting to make sure the number Pops gave him was kosher, that's the word he uses, wanting to hear Pops' voice again, make sure it was real, that he didn't dream the whole thing, mesmerized by the roar of the subway.

"Moishe?" this voice asks when I pick up the phone. I know from his stories that's Pops' name, his name as a kid, I mean, but it doesn't click.

"What?" I say.

And then the voice hits me right in the gut: "Francesco?" it says. "Is that you? This is your Uncle Ira. You don't know me, but you're going to."

So I know Pops didn't make this up, that he wasn't dreaming either—and neither am I.

I can hardly believe it, though. There's not only Uncle Ira, who sounds kinda cool, but another brother, Uncle Hy, and a sister, Aunt Ida, all living right here, in the city, with wives and husbands and children, *cousins*, my cousins. There's another brother, too, George, that's what they call him though his name's really Isaiah, and he lives in Los Angeles. He may come in. There's going to be a big reunion, all of them and us, me too. I ask Pops again and again why we haven't seen these people all this time, but he just ignores me. I figure it has something to do with me, maybe—me being born, my mother dying, my mother being black, Pops being a Red—I don't know, something. But I'm going to meet all these people I barely knew existed, that's the important thing, and they're going to meet me.

And all of this because Uncle Ira couldn't find a cab. And because there was an emergency at his hospital. And because he and his wife, Aunt May, went to Manhattan to eat dinner out at a restaurant—they live in the Bronx somewhere. And because he told them at the hospital where he was going to be so they could reach him in an emergency. And because Pops went out prowling and shaking Friday night just as if there was some real reason to do it.

I keep turning those things over in my head, all those "just becauses," and marveling at them, like a handful of fireflies. And Pops is doing the same thing, I think, turning those "becauses" over in his head, wondering about them.

Something else funny, we don't even have the same last name as these people. I found out because, just thinking about it all yesterday after he called, and getting excited, I looked up Uncle Ira in the phone book, or tried to. But no luck.

"What gives?" I ask Pops.

He sort of smiles—the first time all day, except for when he was telling me about the apple-faced lady and the tackle—so I figure it must be gas. "Oh, yeah," he says, like he's just remembering, sure. "Look under Stein."

And sure enough, there it is when I check: Dr. Ira Stein, physician and surgeon. So, naturally, first I think it's just him, that *he* must have changed his name for some reason, but no, when I ask Pops about it he comes out finally and says that's the family name, Stein, that we're the only ones who are different. Can you dig it? Francesco *Stein*, that's me, not Stern, and I never even knew it! Pops just shrugs it off when I press him about this, says there's lots of families where one branch has a different spelling than the rest, and maybe he's right, because Stein and Stern *are* pretty close, although they don't sound anything like each other. My own guess is that Pops changed his name so his family couldn't find him. Or my mother's family.

He ain't so crazy about getting back with his people now that they have found him, I know that, and he ain't so crazy about me getting to meet them either, or them getting to meet me. This morning, I was smiling, I guess, while I ate my Wheaties, sort of humming to myself, like you do when you're feeling happy but you aren't even thinking right that minute about what it is that's making you feel that way, you're just *feeling* happy, and he looked up from Walter Winchell in the *Mirror* and his coffee and made that little quacking noise of his.

"Don't let yourself get too wrapped up in this relative business, Francesco," he says. "Family is like a suit of clothes. It only feels warm and good if it fits right. If it gets too tight, it can choke you, just like last year's collar."

That many words at one time from Pops is like Lincoln delivering the Gettysburg Address. I look right at him. He likes to spoil things for me. He *does*, he really likes to. And I'm not going to let him spoil this.

"Okay then, so this is like a brand new shirt, a brand new suit of clothes. It fits me fine." I look away so he can't see my face.

When I look back, he's smiling, that crooked little half smile of his that makes his mustache crawl like a caterpillar over the scar on his upper lip.

"Okay, wise guy, just remember you haven't tried this suit on yet. When you do, maybe you'll need an old tailor to tell you what it looks like in the back."

That's where we left it. I don't know for sure when this reunion will be, but Uncle Ira has our number and address and knows Pops' last name is Stern and everything, so I don't think he can wriggle out of it, no matter how tight *his* collar may be.

Me, I'm tired of hand-me-downs.

3. Radio Silence

The other night, it was past dark and I was in my room with the lights out, lying on my bed listening to the radio, when Pops came in and we actually had a talk. If you can call it that. I'd been doing my homework—math, ugh!—with the radio on, Alan Freed, this new guy on WINS, and when I finished the last problem I switched off the light and lay back, my head on the pillow, staring up at the ceiling. I was thinking about something Miss Schwartz said in class that day, talking about degrees, that if the train tracks that go from New York to San Francisco, the city they named after me, had been off just one lousy degree—ONE DEGREE!—they would have wound up in Los Angeles instead.

There's just enough light coming in from the street that I can see the ceiling and shadows that go sliding across it, ricocheting against the bulb and into the corners. Cars passing by in the street below cast shadows that start like rabbits and then pounce across the ceiling like bears chasing after the rabbits—at least, that's the way it looks to me. I like to lie there and watch them, the radio on, and imagine that I'm out in the woods somewhere, lying by a flickering campfire, the way my cousin Rhoda and I did last summer at her folks' cottage in the Catskills, looking up at the trees and the stars caught in the branches like little fish in a huge net. It's nice to lie on a bed in the darkness when you're wide awake and not trying to go to sleep. A few hours later, I'm always in the same spot but under the covers, staring up at the same ceiling and surrounded by the same darkness, but the radio's off, I'm in my pajamas and I'm supposed to be asleep, and the thoughts that come then are different.

Pops tapped at the door. It used to be that he would just come in whenever he felt like it but we had such a fight one time last year that he doesn't dare do that anymore. He taps now all the time, and, of course, what can you do but say "Come in."

"Whatcha doin', boy?"

"Nothin'. Just list'nin' to the radio."

"In the dark?"

"Sure, why not?"

"No reason."

He moves with such softness he's across the room and beside the bed before I notice. Usually, he stands in the doorway, in his undershirt and baggy uniform pants, the seat drooping and stretched, sticking his head in like a stray dog pawing around garbage cans in an alley, smelling the air. He sniffs around, wagging his shaggy head, says the usual things which I answer in the usual way and then he retreats, sliding backwards like a shadow across the floor. "In the dark?" "Sure, why not?" We've had that exchange a dozen times, maybe a hundred. Then the door clicks softly shut and I hear him shuffling back to the front room or the kitchen, where he sits at the table, his naked elbows on the faded Formica, listening to *his* radio, the Harlem station, tinny jazz, with the lights *on*.

This time, though, he comes in, silently sliding across the floor in his socks, his bony ass perching itself on the foot of the bed like a flesh-eating bird. In the darkness, I can't quite make out his features, but the contours of his lion's head are illuminated by the soft glow of streetlight coming in through the window behind him, and there is a flash of light from the center of that blurry darkness, his one gold tooth, when he opens his mouth, but he doesn't speak right away. A song ends on the radio—it's Rosie Cootie, "Hey, there, you with your head up your ass"—and there is a moment, just half a moment, before the deejay's voice comes stabbing in, when there is silence, a grating, metallic silence, filled with electricity and the sucking hiss of vacuum tubes, and above that flash of silence I can hear the moist hum of his breath, like the vibration of an animal transfixed by light on a night-time road. Together, we listen to Freed, then the jingle commercial he plays. His voice rattles at us like a key chain.

"How can you stand that?" Pops says finally. I know what he means because it is the one thing I can't stand, the grating noise between the songs.

"It's okay. You don't have to listen to it."

Immediately, I know he's misunderstood what I said, and that it's my fault. I've caught myself at that lots lately, saying things that can be taken two ways and leaving myself open to the chilly draft that springs off him like steam off ice when he draws in, hurt, like a caterpillar bending itself into a hairpin when you poke it with a stick. This is something new, something I haven't seen or felt or known before—that *I* can hurt *him*.

"I mean, you don't have to *listen* to it. You can just blank it out. I do. I keep on listening to the song that's just finished until the next one starts. In my head, I mean."

"I know," he says. His voice isn't convincing and I don't believe I've undone the damage, however slight it might have been. At the same time, there is something in the way he says it that makes me feel I've impressed him, as if I'd said something he never would have expected to come from me.

He nods his head. "It isn't all that bad, the music you play. I've been listening more. That one was shit, but some of it's not too bad."

That surprises me. We've had words about it, if not exactly fights, and he's made it clear he thinks it's crap. "Tin Pan Alley junk," he calls it. "Listen to it," I've told him, "it's different. It isn't all white anymore. *Listen.*" The worst thing he can say about music is that it's *white.*

"It's *good,*" I say sharply, wishing I was defending something other than Rosemary Clooney. He can budge, maybe, but I won't, not an inch.

"I *said* it ain't bad, Francesco." He stirs, as if to get up, and I clam up so as not to spook him, but he settles down again, like a big bird shaking out its wings. Another song comes on and we listen to it. It's "Sh-Boom," the Chords' version, not the one by the white guys the other stations have been playing, and I grin, feel like I won that point, but I don't say anything and neither does he. We listen in silence, me humming in my head, "Life can be a dream, life can be a dream, sweetheart," but I can see his knee moving as he taps his foot. In the darkness, I uncross my legs, cross them again.

He has been morose this evening, silent and sighing at dinner, and whatever it is that was dragging him is percolating now, like water under a rock, working its way to the top where it can spill out to relieve the pressure. There was a letter this afternoon, one of the few we ever get that isn't a bill or an ad or something sent to a wrong address. This is one of the few small jokes between us, the mailman who himself never gets mail, and it's even funnier now that he's driving a bus instead of working for the post office. When a letter does come—a real letter, not just junk—one of us will invariably say "busman's holiday," though my father was saying that for years before I knew what it meant, long before he was driving a bus himself. This afternoon, when I came home from school, I thought that as I thumbed through the folded paper in our box: a bill, something from the musicians' union, a circular from a linoleum store, and this letter. I looked it over, natch, but I couldn't tell much. It was thin, in a long white envelope with frayed edges, like it had been turned over and over in someone's hands before being dropped into a mailbox. There was no return name or address but the postmark was Cleveland. That means nothing to me, I don't know anybody there and Pops has never mentioned the place. I only know it's a city, somewhere in Ohio, out west, in the direction those railroad tracks to Frisco head, but it could just as well be in China. I was always heading that way, out west, I mean, whenever I used to run away, back when I was a kid, but I never got as far as Ohio.

When he came home, I said "busman's holiday" and pointed with my chin to the pathetic little pile of mail on the kitchen table, but I turned my back and busied myself with supper, heating up the mutton stew he'd made on the weekend, so he could look at it in peace. When I turned around, he was seated at the table, his peaked cap in front of him, gloves neatly folded on top of it, empty coin changer on one side of it, the torn envelope on the other side, the unfolded letter in his hands, white on white. His mouth was grim and there was something like pain flickering over his eyes, the way a small cloud will whisk back and forth across the sun.

I think about all this and ask him suddenly, when the song is almost over, "Who's in Cleveland?"

He has been watching the lights and shadows darting around the window frame like cats and mice and his head turns now, his eyes falling on me. There is shadow on his face but I can almost see those eyes, I know them so well: wide mud puddles floating on off-white sand, ridged with tiny veins like animal tracks.

"A friend." He says this casually, as if he has friends all over the place, friends to spare. His shoulders rise slightly, involuntarily, in a shrug.

"I didn't know you had a friend in Cleveland."

"Neither did I." He makes a noise intended to be a laugh but it falls into the empty air between us more like a sob.

I bite my lip. He has come into the room on impulse, I guess, spurred by a need to be near me—someone—and to talk, to tell me—someone—about the news that is churning around in his

25

belly and head. But when I open myself for him, give him the chance, he pushes me aside with a feeble joke. He will joke his own chance away if I let him, and soon, in the silence and the crackling from the radio, there will be nothing left for him to do but rise and shuffle away, hurt and sour, the thing that's bothering him still festering, adding another layer to the wall between us. But it's me, damn it, who has to pull him through, because he won't, he won't lift one finger to reach out, all he'll do is shuffle into the room, sit on the bed, stare at the darkness and cough, as he does now, as if to remind me of his presence, of his waiting.

After a bit, the Aimless Brothers come on crooning about "The Naugahyde Lady of Shitty Lane," all the proof Pops could need about the junk on the radio. He does his ritual groan and I make a face to show him I agree. Then I push on, like someone seeing how far he can slide onto ice before it cracks beneath him.

"What'd your friend in Cleveland you didn't know you had have to say?"

"Oh, I knew I had the friend," he says quickly—he has already figured out the way this will go. Our habits are old and rigid, built on great ceremony, and it is only recently that I have learned they can be broken.

"Just not that he was in Cleveland?"

"How do you know it's a he?"

I smile despite myself. "I looked at the handwriting on the envelope. It's a man's."

"How can you tell?"

"Like you told me once. The ink is dark, written with a heavy hand. Women's hands are light." Having delivered millions of letters, Pops is an expert on such matters.

"Very good, Watson."

I should say now, "Elementary, my dear Holmes," or merely "Elementary," as he expects, but I don't, to short-circuit the game, to let him know I'm not playing it tonight. He coughs in the awkward silence and I say: "What did Cleveland say?" The question is reduced now to its essentials, and there's no more room. He'll either say now, or he won't.

The room is very quiet somehow, still, despite the radio. The wall of sound behind us has blended into one long white pulse of noise neither of us hears, the music and Freed's chatter indistinguishable, as if it had faded into muted static. No cars pass in the street below and the shadows stand stationary, like sentinels on the edge of a dark woods. The room is bathed in a white-walled hush, like the cushion of air a fly floats on to keep it from being swatted.

"Somebody died," my father says.

Immediately, there is the sound of traffic below the window, a car squealing its tires around the corner, a receding engine. The word "died" hangs in the air between us like some fragile winged insect caught in a spider's web and I'm suddenly engulfed by a great sadness, not for myself but for him. Death, this is something I can barely comprehend—nobody *I* know has ever died, only people I *don't* know, never did, like my mother, her people, *his* people. But death is something he must wear around his shoulders all the time, like his mailbag used to, weighing down one shoulder so that even now he still walks with a stoop. Everyone around him, it suddenly strikes me, everyone but me, has died—at least in a way. My mother, who really died, and her people, who went out of his life; and his own people, who for so many years he pretended had died or at least weren't alive. I remember, last year when he came home after running into Uncle Ira and I pried out of him what had happened, the first real thought that came into my mind was this: But I thought they were all supposed to be dead. And that made me think something else: What of my mother? Was *she* not really dead either, merely left behind somewhere, like a wounded soldier left to die and therefore as good as dead? Is that what my father had learned in Spain, in that soldier time he never talks about? How to leave his wounded for dead?

And now, I think, his deaths are catching up with him, just like Uncle Ira with the whole Stein family in tow has done, except that this particular one, today's, is a real death: something real falling away, leaving a scar the way a branch pulled away from a tree will leave an open, oozing wound.

I want to ask Pops more, find out who died and what this person meant to him, but I can't think of a way to proceed and I know he won't tell me on his own. What that small confession has already cost him I can only imagine. Already, I can feel that the moment is going, that the moment in which, if I could only find the way, I could reach out and touch him is hovering above the bed in the darkness like an angel, its face turned away, wings fluttering. I open my mouth to speak but words don't come and heat sears across my eyes but they stay dry. Instead of tears, I have a sudden clear vision: there are only two ways this can ever end, this tangle between us—with his leaving me behind as he's left all else, or me leaving him, with my death or his. And I know something, suddenly, with a clarity that startles me, as if the light in the room had abruptly been snapped on, something I have never known before: he will die.

I know the moment has passed because I can hear the deejay's voice, I can actually hear the words he's saying: "Pimples making your life miserable? There's a new way to clear up that skin problem, kids...."

"I'm sorry," I say. My voice sounds cold to me, as if I didn't really care, but the words are out and there isn't anything I can do about that. Simultaneously, I wonder what it is I mean I'm sorry about.

"That's all right," he says. He too knows the moment has passed and he's stirring, shifting his weight uneasily on the bed.

"Somebody in Cleveland?" I ask, trying to hold on.

A pause, as if he's considering, then, "No, not in Cleveland, somewhere else." I can hear from the way the words bend around in his mouth that he's smiling now, his crooked smile. He says it as if he has somebodies dying all over the place, somebodies to spare, but I know he isn't going to tell me about them, the one who died, the one who wrote to pass the news, the comrades-in-arms from Spain, the beboppers from roadside clubs, the immigrants on the swaying ship that brought him here from Russia, not any of them—not tonight. He gets up suddenly, the bed rising with him to its usual level.

"A friend?" One last try.

Another pause, then a shrug, a surrender to habit. "No, not a friend, really, just somebody I know. *Knew* ... back in the old days," as if that last bit explains everything. Even he must know how unsatisfactory an answer that is and, after a moment, he adds, haltingly, "...in Spain." His voice has changed, though, the kind of subtle change the light goes through before a rain comes up, and I know it's over. In a moment, he'll say something else, about the music, maybe—it's Kitty Kallen now, "Little Things Like Hundred Dollar Bills Mean a Lot," and it isn't very good. Then he'll shuffle out of the room and down the hallway to the kitchen or the front room, somewhere *away*, where I won't be able to touch him. He'll be *there*, I'll be *here*. I might as well be in Cleveland. Already, he's spit it out of his craw, turned his back.

"You through with your homework?" he says abruptly.

"Yup."

"Sure now?"

"Sure, Pops."

He hesitates. He doesn't like me to call him that and we fight over it sometimes, but it's up to him to start. "I don't see how you can stand that," he says awkwardly, his chin lifting slightly to indicate the radio. Freed is blaring at us, his voice clanging like tin cans chasing a wedding car.

"You don't have to listen," I say. He can take it any way he wants.

29

He shuffles to the door, the limp just barely noticeable. The light from the hall knifes into the room and I see him standing in the doorway, his hand on the knob, his great shaggy head bobbing on his spindly shoulders like a buoy in the water, and I realize he's crying, silently and without tears, the way I had, a minute or two before. I wonder, with shame, if he had seen.

"I'm going out for awhile, boy," he says. I had known that would be coming.

"Okay."

"You'll be okay." As usual, the question mark is blurred.

"Sure," I say. He turns, his shoulder blades rising like the wings of a chicken. The door swings shut behind him, closing off the light. I hear him padding across the hall to his room. I reach out my hand and turn down the radio so I can hear better. There is a shuffling from his room, a chair scraping across the floor, the rustling of cloth and the jingling of change in his pockets as he slides off the uniform pants, pulls on the gray gabardine slacks he'll wear out, into the street. The strange certainty of his death washes over me again, then the image of his death: the bristling hair and drooping mustache, relaxed for once, the big muddy eyes closed. I wonder if they'll bury him in his bus driver's uniform, his coin changer beside him, or in his old mailman's uniform, maybe, with his old bag, the faded letters spelling out *US Mail*—or in the gabardine suit, with his horn.

Then I hear music that excites my ear and I turn the radio up again—it's Bill Haley, "Dim, Dim the Lights," a *real* song, with something almost like jazz in its wildness, something even Pops might like.

4. Music and Art

My father was a story-teller with a limited repertoire. He told the same stories over and over again, their basic structure always the same but, with each retelling, added embellishments to keep the listener's attention. In this way, and through his refusal to acknowledge hints, polite and otherwise, he maintained an audience, even me, who, through my childhood, heard some of his stories hundreds of times. What he wouldn't tell, almost never, were things I wanted to know.

Those I learned on my own.

One of his favorite stories was how, or at least why, he became a musician.

He was, as far as he knew, tone deaf for all his early life, the result, he thought, of a cuff on the ear from his father. Music, he always said, was no different to him than noise, and he could no more follow a melody than a theological argument. Attempts to teach him to dance, in the crowded kitchen at home by his sister Ida and on the polished wood floor in the gymnasium of PS 17 on Delancy Street, were failures. The popular music of the day—the streets of the Lower East Side were flooded with music, he always said, just as they were with noise and a cacophony of aromas—was lost on him. Later, as a young man, if, in a barroom, he did join in on a song, he was usually hooted down by the other revelers, so lamely did he carry the tune.

None of this caused him any grief. "What you never had, you

don't miss," he would say philosophically, occasionally citing, as an example, the difference between a person born blind and those unfortunates who lose their sight.

He became a trumpet player, he would say, the way the temporary blind regain their eyes—with a painful shock of new recognition.

One evening when he was nineteen or twenty, which would have been around 1925, he stopped in at a tavern on Orchard Street, as he usually did, on his way home from the silversmith shop where he worked. He had dropped out of school after the sixth grade, no more able to conform to the requirements of the classroom than he would to anything else in his life, and he'd had a succession of jobs, but those that involved working with metal were always the most satisfying. By chance, my father would say, he found himself standing at the bar next to a man wearing a derby hat and carrying a black leather case. The case, which was on the bar by the man's elbow, lay between them.

"That's a nice case," my father said, admiring its polished brass hinges and silver clasp. "What've you got in it?"

"In here?" the man said, looking at the case, then around him, as if my father might have been referring to something else.

"In the case," my father said, nodding his head and wiping a mustache of beery foam from his upper lip.

"Oh, this," the man said—he must have been thick-headed as a mule, my father would always comment at this point in the story. "A trumpet."

"A trumpet?" my father said.

"Sure, I'll show you." And the man, suddenly becoming friendlier, thumbed open the silver clasp, lifted the case's lid and withdrew the shining silvery contraption of tubes and valves. My father's eyes grew wide with interest.

"That's a trumpet?" he said. "That's some trumpet." He reached over, intending merely to rub a finger against the polished gloss.

"Keep your hands off it, you filthy kike," the man said.

My father, telling the story, would always comment that the man said this with neither anger nor rancor in his voice—he said "you filthy kike" in the same tone that someone else might use to say "fellow" or "buddy." Just the same, my father said, he took offense, and he hit the man in the mouth, so hard, he said, that the man fell down, his lips blossoming with bloody froth. And then, almost out of spite, my father picked the trumpet up from where it had clattered to the bar after its owner fell, placed it to his own mouth and blew one short, sharp note.

"It was the sweetest sound I ever heard," my father would say. "I didn't know how sour it could be sometimes. I didn't know how sour...." Here, he paused. "I didn't know what I had done, but I knew *I* had done it. And I was hooked. It was like St. Peter opening the gates of heaven to someone who had never had any such expectations."

I'd heard that story dozens of times, probably, by the time I was thirteen, but my father had just discovered a whole new audience, eager to hear almost any words from his lips. After years of being estranged from them, he—and I—had been pulled back into the bosom of his family, where we soon became wary visitors. They were happy to hear my father's stories, and, after thirteen years of being virtually unaware of my existence, they were eager to play a role in my life. That's how I came to go to the Bronx High School of Music and Art, though it wasn't without a struggle.

My own introduction to music was considerably less dramatic than my father's. On the streets of Spanish Harlem, there was music all around me, always, but it was music for the ear, not the eye, so I didn't learn anything about it, how to read it or how it worked, until I was in high school. But radios and scratchy record players were always braying, through every open window on the street, from open-door stores, at the newsstand on the corner, and people were always singing, the older boys sitting on the stoops doing harmony imitations of radio songs or just fooling around, making tunes up as they went along. My friend Otis, who lived one flight up in our creaky tenement and whose father, Lester—lately home from Korea with an arm missing—was my father's drinking pal, had a falsetto voice just as good as Little Anthony's or Frankie Lymon's, though he was soon to grow out of it. I was just starting to really get into music then, when I was thirteen and rock and roll were two words people were just starting to put together. There were some groups making hits who weren't much older than Otis and me and a few years later we'd be part of one of those groups, sixteen-year-old black and spic kids making more money in one night than my father ever did from music, try as he did.

My father had given me a guitar, for my birthday or Christmas, when I was seven or eight, and I'd fooled around with it a little bit and learned some chords. But things weren't so great between me and my father during those years and I was always trying to run away, so I hated everything he gave me and I dropped the guitar after awhile. But that year, when I was starting to feel like a real Puerto Rican, I picked it up again, because it seemed like some kind of a link between me and my mother, who I had never known.

I'd always known my mother was Puerto Rican, but I only learned that summer I spent with my relatives in the Catskills when I was thirteen that I'd been born on the island. Like so much else I got that year, this news came from my cousin Rhoda. Aunt Ida and Uncle Nate whispered about me all the time, she said, but in Yiddish mostly, which they used whenever they wanted to talk about something without the children understanding. Rhoda, who had been a favorite of her grandfather—Nate's father—had learned a bit of Yiddish from him, enough to catch phrases and splinters of meaning from her parents' conversations, an ability she shrewdly guarded, telling not even her brothers.

"Better watch out or the big, bad PR will get you," I said, with a wink.

We were sitting on the dock, in our swim suits, me skinny and brown as a nut from the sun, Rhoda pale and still stuck in that awkward stage between girl and woman, her body beginning to blossom and I don't know who was more conscious of it, her or me.

"Just you try!" She reached down and skimmed her open palm quickly through the water to splash me.

It was a couple weeks after she had hurt me with that unforgivable comment about my mother and we were still trying to regain our equilibrium, tiptoeing around each other. Unforgivable, except that I *had* forgiven her. She'd tried to explain, that it was her goofy young brothers, Bernie and Bret, who she'd heard the word she'd thrown at me from, but I didn't want to know, didn't want to think of where *they'd* gotten the idea. I told her to forget it, and I tried to.

"I'll eat you up," I said, kicking water and stretching out my arms Frankenstein style.

"You'll have to put hot sauce on me, Frankie. I'm too bland for someone like you," Rhoda laughed.

Someone like me! The Puerto Rican reference was a great prize for her, like a fantastically glittering nugget of information, something of immense value come upon by accident. By contrast, it was only of mild interest to me, at least at first, and in some ways didn't surprise me at all. I had always sensed my foreignness, always felt that I *was* a foreigner. Learning that I was one, in fact, by virtue of birth and geography if nothing else, was only confirmation of something deeper I felt I had always known. As for

Rhoda, this knowledge cast me in an even more mysterious light than I already had been and gave me an even sharper allure. I noticed this right away and was puzzled by it. I was already aware that she liked the idea of my dark skin, and now this new, exotic dimension in me excited her more. If anything, I thought, she should be frightened, not attracted, by it.

I had come from out of nowhere, a cousin she hadn't known she had in a family that seemed to put great stock on family ties, the mysterious son of a black sheep father who'd disappeared from the face of his family's earth for almost a dozen years, only to resurface full blown—a *working* man, a *jazz* musician, living in *Harlem*, filled with *incredible* stories—and now this, this foreignness, something else to set me apart. Rhoda, despite her limits, was transfixed, but I wasn't even thirteen, not quite yet a man in the reckoning of the religion my father's family seemed quite absorbed in, though my father himself had long ago turned his back on it, and I knew very little about women and girls.

When I told my father what I'd learned, he seemed genuinely surprised, not that I knew, although he frowned at that, but at the truth of it. It was another one of those things he had forgotten.

"Is that right, Frankie?" he asked, and not disingenuously.

With coaxing, he was able to recall that he and my mother had moved to the island the summer she was pregnant. They had lived with her parents and he had worked in a band at a hotel in San Juan until the war and I came, simultaneously, on December 7, 1941, the roar of bombs on one American island all but drowning out the newborn cries on another.

"So she did have a family," I interjected. This was one of the questions to which my father had always professed ignorance.

He waved his hand in a gesture of annoyance. "Of course she had a family. Did you think she was washed up on shore, like Moses from out of the bulrushes?"

"Then what were they like?" I pressed. I wanted to know their names and what they did. Were there brothers, sisters—uncles and aunts for me? Are any of them alive? In New York? Could I...?

The wave of a hand, a snort. "They were people, gnats like all others. Who can remember? Who paid any *attention*? And why should you care anyway?"

That was something guaranteed to stop me cold. "Care? Who cares? Who gives a fuck? I was just making conversation."

My father looked away, so as not to have to see my face. This business of my searching after my past was one he either didn't understand or took delight in thwarting. Either explanation would be believable to me. My father himself refers to the past as toilet paper, something soiled and crumpled, a useful thing handy for wiping off the ass of the present but then to be discarded, flushed away, surely not treasured or sought after. If you think I'm making sophomoric imagery, don't blame me—those are my father's images, his words.

But my inclination to look over my shoulder was too strong to be shunted aside. And now it got stronger.

Growing up in East Harlem, I spoke Spanish, of course. We spoke English in the apartment, my father and I, but he spoke Spanish on the streets he plied by day—first with his mailsack and later, thanks to Mr. Eisenhower and Mr. McCarthy, driving his bus, the smaller government apparently willing to tolerate what the larger wouldn't—and in the bars he occasionally played in at night. As for me, English was spoken in school, but Spanish just as much in the playground and the hallways. So naturally, I knew it, but I had never paid any serious attention to it. Spanish was like slang to me, street talk, not something that serious people would speak to each other, not if they had something of *meaning* to convey. I had always resented my father's aping of Spanish, his futile attempts to pass as Puerto Rican or Cuban or even, on one occasion, Mexican, his rejection of his Jewishness, his denial of *that* language and culture. After a certain age, I made a point of staying out of school on

Jewish holidays, even though that made me conspicuous and vulnerable. I had seized, like a young fish nibbling at corn on the water, at the strands of Jewishness dangling from the newfound relatives I was thrown in with that summer.

My father had been dubious—no, that's too mild a word, he'd been absolutely horror-stricken—when he literally bumped into Uncle Ira on the subway at Times Square the fall before. He hadn't seen his brother or any other of his family for a dozen years, not since before I was born, and now, like a door bursting open behind him, they had found him again, and he was caught in their orbit. Gradually, like fishermen on a shore, they pulled us toward them. My father would always swim just on the periphery of their pool, but me, I was hooked, there wasn't any escaping that. My father watched this with a frown, a dark face and a jumping eyelid, always a sure clue to his agitation. When the invitation for the summer in the mountains came, he said no at first, then maybe, he would think about it. Ira and Ida pressed him—"Why not, Murray? It'll be good for the boy, how can it hurt him?"—and I pressed him, alternating between pouting and pleading, but he remained noncommittal. Then came his own invitation, the work of Uncle Ira, I always assumed, though there was no proving it: a job playing all summer at a Catskills hotel rich as borscht and sour cream. It was a chance he would be crazy to turn down, and, coming as it did soon after he'd lost his job, caught up in the McCarthy frenzy, one even he couldn't hide from. No excuses. He would have to get on with his life, whether he wanted to or not. But he would have to live in a dormitory; there would be no room for me. There were lights in his eyes for many nights as he sat brooding at the kitchen table, picking up the coffee spoon, turning it over in his fingers, examining it, putting it down. For several years, I'd been aware of the shutting off his own life had gone through, and now, I believe, he was becoming aware of it himself. And here was an open door. Finally, he took a deep breath and we went off to our separate mountains.

What it all meant, of course, was that doors were opening all around us. I was only dimly aware of this, but for me there was the door Rhoda stood in, the door to my Jewishness that my other relatives held open, which was intriguing, and finally, open just a crack, the door—or doors—to my mother and to myself. It was that one which I chose.

I was a goddamn Puerto Rican for real. Not a pretender, like my father, not just somebody the lousy old Italian lady who ran the grocery store on our corner could call a dumb spic kid, but a genuine Puerto Rican, an inhabitant of a place, an heir.

I felt my shoulders widen, my hips slim, my walk loosen, my biceps grow. My hair was blacker now, straighter, my nose was straighter. Skin was growing at the end of my cock.

And I took Spanish as my own.

Rock and blues and jazz and folk and all those other forms can be played on the guitar—and I have—but it is really a Spanish instrument, Segovia's the only *real* guitarist, and playing the guitar, no matter what kind of music I was playing, was like a secret way of talking to my mother. Everything came easy to me when I had that thing in my hands, my fingers finding their way through the tangles of notes and chords and rhythms like magicians with lives and minds of their own. I would sit in my room in the afternoon when I came home from school, crosslegged on my bed, my bare feet looking dark and clumsy against the pale-blue crinoline of the bedspread, the guitar cradled in my arms, picking out "The Streets of Laredo" or "Greensleeves" or some blues or flamenco, and it was like *I* was cradled in *her* arms, my head against the soft flesh just above her breast where the arm met the shoulder, her gentle voice—*my* voice—crooning in my ear. Sometimes I would cry, but more often not. I felt glad sitting alone in my room, alone with her, making music. Years later, I read a book about spiritualists who make contact with spirits through some sort of medium, a crystal ball, perhaps, but often something else, some thing which has meaning for the departed spirit. I didn't know about that then, but that's what I was doing. The guitar was my medium, like a conduit through which the spirit of my mother came into my room to visit me, to listen to me sing, to sing with me, to tell me she loved me.

I only practiced my guitar when I had our cockroachy little apartment, filled with its second-hand-store furniture, to myself. I didn't want to give my father the satisfaction of knowing I was taking after him, even if only in that small way.

Down 125th Street, at the Apollo, I used to see Bobby Bland and B.B. King and people like that on Saturday afternoons and, if my father was away, I'd go home and play blues licks on the guitar all evening. There was a radio station uptown and another one across the river in Newark that played R&B, and I listened to them all the time, in the evening when I was doing my homework, on the weekends. I had a good ear and knew lots of chords so I could pick up on almost anything I heard on the radio, and I could match Chuck Berry solo runs note for note, though maybe not *quite* as fast as him and, of course, on my old acoustic box—it wasn't a romantic old Gibson or National, just a cheapie from Japan—it didn't *sound* quite as good. There were a couple of Latin stations uptown too, playing rumbas and cha-chas and pachangas, and even though that's what my father listened to mostly, I started paying attention, learning some of the tunes. He was only pretending, after all, only wishing he could be, but I really *was* a Latin, that was *my* music. On the street, on our block, that's mostly what came streaming out of the windows and the store doors, the blaring trumpets that always sounded red, like blood translated into music through a brass pipe that squeezed it, like liquid turning into gas in a beaker above a Bunsen burner at school, and drums, pounding like heartbeats and the vein in your temple when you've run a long way or taken the three flights of stairs to our apartment two steps at a time, without stop, the way the seltzer man always did, the single case for us slung over his back like it was filled with bottles of air or feathers.

That was the kind of musical education I had, for the ear—not for the eye or the brain.

Rhoda wanted to change that. She and I had been writing to each other regularly since the summer, trading jokes and stories. We got to see each other every couple of months when my father and I would take the subway for the long ride downtown and into Brooklyn and all the way down to Brighton Beach and the swell house where she lived, an old brownstone that Uncle Nate had had completely stripped out and renovated. Aunt Ida would cook brisket and *kugel*, or stewed chicken and dumplings, and there'd always be others there too, either Uncle Ira and his family or Uncle Hy and his, or all of them. At first, my father wouldn't say much and would look annoyed, as if, somehow, he'd been trapped into this visit, forced against his will. He would stand in the corner of Uncle Nate's study in the hour before dinner, pretending to be reading the titles of books on the dark walnut shelves behind the glass doors while the other men would chatter and gossip and solve the problems of the world and the women would cluster in the kitchen like conspirators and we kids would be on the other side of the house, in the playroom, my cousins Bernie and Bret trying to bait me into the plastic-edged world of cards they inhabited, or Rhoda and I would be outside, bundled up and walking along the tree-lined street to the pavement promenade that skirted the sea.

Often, what Rhoda and I talked about would be Music and Art, the specialized high school she wanted to go to, and where she was urging me to apply. I did want to go there, more than anything, though I wouldn't admit that to her, or even to myself. Certainly not to my father.

On our walks, Rhoda would recite her latest poems. Reading between the lines, I could make out the shadow of myself in some of them. But I would never sing her the songs I wrote in my head or say much about the anger towards my father or any of the other things churning up inside me. I wanted to, I tried, but somehow I never could.

"He's such a strange man," Rhoda said. Even though I agreed completely, I must have reacted defensively because immediately she added, "I don't mean in a bad way, in a *nice* way."

I shrugged. "You were right the first time. I guess he's nice enough as an uncle. You can keep him as a father."

That was as far as I'd go—mild as the criticism was, somehow it seemed disloyal.

Sometimes, once we were out of sight of the house, Rhoda and I would hold hands, her pale fingers in my darker grip, and when we stood at the low railing, looking out at the chattering gulls wheeling over the rocks, diving into the furious white water to seize a flashing fish, I would put my arm around her thin shoulders and kiss her, each time new and fresh, like we had never done it before. Her lips were soft as the raspberries we had picked behind the cottage, and I never pressed her, the way I had once that summer to my regret, never would again.

It was at one of these family dinners, in the spring, that the subject of my going to Music and Art came up at the table. Rhoda, who could see through my protestations, had all but given up trying to cajole me into making a case to my father and now, with just a few weeks left to decide, she had given the chore to her mother, who was happy to oblige.

When we came back from our walk, dinner was already on the table, steam rising over the dumplings like haze over the East River at dawn, and my father had drunk several *schnapps* and had loosened up, his face going red, the twitch over his eye gone. The first time we'd had such a gathering—just weeks after the accidental meeting of Pops and Uncle Ira that brought him back into the family fold—he surprised us all, me especially, by taking it upon himself to tell a story of childhood, one of half a dozen or so of his frozen religious moments that had forced all other memory of his early years out of his mind by their weight and strength, like the strongest puppies at the mother's belly. And the story-telling at the table, after the *schnapps* had taken its effect, became a ritual of our visits, like the ceremonial opening of a window in a *shul* to allow into the dark heart of that secret temple one brief arrow of illumination, the opening of a window into a portion of his life that, at all other times, he kept closed and guarded even from himself.

The story he was most fond of telling, one I'd already heard dozens of times, was about the young rabbi his father hired to tutor the children in the years just before they'd fled Russia, and how he'd been caught in the barn screwing the cow—"having his way," my father would say, in deference to the ladies, if not necessarily the children, in his audience. Hauled before my grandfather, who he described to us children as a towering, stern man with lightning flashes in his eyes and sparks pouring from his nostrils above his beard, the terrified young rabbi had fallen to his knees, cowering, saliva dripping down his own spindly beard, teeth chattering—and here my father would leave his chair and fall to his own knees. "My dear master, my dear master, you don't understand, you don't understand," my father mimicked, his voice rising and falling like a saw—but in English, pointedly, whereas Uncle Ira or Aunt Ida, telling a story of childhood, would have delivered the juicier parts in Yiddish—and his eyes leaping from face to face around the table. "It's not what you think. Are not all of God's creatures equal in the eyes of their Creator?"

With that, he would burst into laughter, and the whole table would laugh, including the children, our eyes aglow with the story's sexual resonance, even though we had heard it the last time at dinner, and perhaps the time before that. There had not yet been that many times for it to become boring, and each time, though he claimed not to remember having told it before, my father would add new details—the frayed knees of the rabbi's pants or the ragged ends of his *peyes* where he had chewed them—some nuance to make the story seem fresh. Even Aunt Ida laughed, although she shook her head and frowned, pretending to be cross. "Please Murray, such stories at the table? And in front of the children?"

"The children, what's to keep from the children?" my father shot back. "These children these days, ah, you should hear the language the children use on my bus, right in front of me, the other passengers, even a copper, you think they care?" There was a pause here that suddenly blossomed into an awkward silence, and I knew everyone was thinking, yes, of course, but those are Puerto Rican and Negro children, what can you expect?

"My own little Frankie," my father said abruptly, frowning at me with something like pride in his eyes, enough to make me look down at my plate in embarrassment, "what he knows about the world already is like a master's degree compared to what I knew when I was his age. Or even"—here he turned his attention to his older brother—"such a wise child as you, Ira."

This was a surprise to me, this imparting of wisdom on my head. At home, he was forever telling me how dumb I was, how, compared to him when he was my age, I was merely a child, and a backward one at that. My father must have realized the contradiction because now he mumbled, "Kids these days, they're all regular Einsteins," as if to take the burden off me.

There was one more twist to the story of the rabbi and the cow, and we all waited, holding our breaths, for him to remember and go on, but my Aunt Ida, who liked the last part least, understandably, and whose plump cheeks would flush with blood like those of a teased schoolgirl when she heard it, caught hold of the tangent he'd just tossed aside like a fish snapping at a piece of bait thrown overboard.

"You know, Murray, you're not just making noises like a proud parent when you talk how smart Frankie is. That boy...."

My father held up his hand, a napkin pressed against his chest with the other. "Wait, I'm not through with the story, as maybe you remember, Ida?" His face was solemn but there was a glint in his mud-puddle eyes that made us children look furtively at each other and giggle softly over the noodles.

"They've heard it already, Pops," I whined at him, still in the grip of my own embarrassment, but he merely cast me a killing glance and forged on.

"Papa, despite his reputation, was a realist," my father said, raising his hands, palms upward, shrugging. He turned to Rhoda and her brothers, explaining, confiding: "Your grandfather wanted us children to have an education, the schools were not friendly to us, and rabbis who would undertake such a job, out in the country on a farm like ours where the life was sometimes hard and the pleasures few, such rabbis were hard to find. Papa snorted at the young teacher, gave him a kick, just to let him know he wasn't getting away with something, and shrugged."

My father put his elbows on the table and leaned forward, peering narrowly down the table at Aunt Ida, who rolled her eyes toward the chandelier and emitted a soft sound of exasperation. Under the cover of the tablecloth, Uncle Nate was patting her wrist. "'Better the cows than Ida,' Papa said," and now my father's face expanded again, his eyes and teeth gleaming, as if he had divested himself of a secret no one had ever known or heard or dreamed of before.

Out of the awkward laughter that followed rose a silence, and from that my Aunt Ida seized her chance.

"You know, Murray, speaking of how smart children are, our Rhoda is going to be going to the High School of Music and Art in the Bronx next year."

I had my eyes fastened on my father's reddened face and I saw his jaws tighten, then form themselves into an appreciative expression. He had picked up his fork to resume eating but now he returned it to his plate.

"Frankie could go there too, you know," Aunt Ida said slowly. "I think he should."

My father looked up, as if to reassure himself that it was he who was being addressed, and poked me on the forehead with the knuckle of his thumb.

"This dumbbell? No, no. He may be smart, but he ain't *smart*, if you know what I mean."

There were murmurs of dissent from around the table.

"Murray, is that any way to talk about your son?" Aunt May said crossly. "And in front of him." Like Aunt Ida, Aunt May was plump, but her face was disproportionately thin, the cheekbones prominent, which gave her an air of elegance I thought appropriate for a doctor's wife.

"Between Frankie and me, there ain't no secrets," my father said, which made me look up with surprise.

"In front of him or behind his back is neither here nor there," Aunt Ida said in her slow, even voice. "It's not true. Things that aren't true don't get any less false when you say them to somebody's face."

My father looked at her sharply, but he didn't say anything.

"The boy's got a real head on his shoulders, Murray. You're kidding yourself if you don't think so," Uncle Ira said. He was a large man with a head as shaggy as my father's and stubby fingers that should have kept him out of medical school, surely out of any operating theater.

"That's very true," my cousin Becky said primly, turning her blonde head to give me a thrilling smile. She was Uncle Ira's and Aunt May's pride and joy, a brain who had gone to Barnard and was now in graduate school at NYU, in economics. She rarely came to the family dinners, but when she did her few pronouncements were given the respect usually reserved for oracles. "All right, all right, already," Pops retreated. "I don't mean to make him out to be a dumbhead. But Abraham Lincoln is a good school. It'll be plenty good enough for him, right, Frankie?" He jabbed at me with his fork, a forced smile on his lips, which glistened with chicken fat. I looked down at my plate and bit my tongue to keep from swearing, but my father had already looked away.

"Abraham Lincoln is a *very* good school," Aunt Ida said deliberately. "But it can't compare to Music and Art. Young people these days, when there's so much specialization in the world, should go where they're best suited for, where the school is best suited for them."

Pops sniffed. He was chewing on the word specialization, I could tell, and a moment later he spit it out: "So what's so special about my Frankie?" He raised his hand quickly to ward off the torrent that would have erupted. "I don't mean to say he isn't *special*, but what's *so* special?"

"*Oh!*" Aunt May said crossly, frowning, her elegance wearing thin.

Uncle Ira patted her hand. "The boy's a fine musician," he said. He was looking down at his fingers, perhaps visualizing them working over a severed abdomen, the fingers sleekly coated with thin, slippery rubber, gleaming steel instruments flashing between them.

"A musician, oh ho," my father said, glancing at me slyly. "I see. A *musician*. He makes a few sour notes on a guitar and that makes him a musician. *I* must be Dizzy Gillespie."

The word musician rasped against my ear as much as it did my father's. If anyone had asked me even a year earlier whether I'd like to be a musician, I'd have laughed. Only creeps were musicians! But since the summer, a little bug of an idea was scurrying around under the carpet at the back of my brain: maybe I *would* like to be one. *What? A creep?* Well, maybe they aren't *all* creeps. Maybe it was possible—just *possible*—to be a musician and still be a decent human being, though you sure as hell couldn't prove it by my father, not the way I saw it. But the more I played my guitar—and especially *while* I was playing—the more I thought, yeah, it *can* be done. I went even further: maybe being a lousy human being has something to do with being a lousy musician, rather than the other way around, in which case I was sure as hell going to try real hard to be kind and considerate and nice and truthful. It should be easy for me, I thought. All I'd have to do is pay close attention to my father and do everything exactly the opposite.

Thinking like that always churned me up all the more because I knew I wasn't being fair. I knew it wasn't easy for him, raising me on his own, knew how much it hurt when the few gigs he got never turned into anything else, knew how much he'd hated the drudgery of the post office and now his bus route. Sometimes everything Pops said was stupid and I hated him, but it wasn't always that way. Sometimes, like when he was telling a story, he was *almost* human. But it seemed to me it was hard for him to be human, hard for him to be even decent, like there was something big standing between him and what he wanted to be, something so big that it was even hard for him to see what it was on the other side, let alone reach it.

"Murray, you are such a dumbhead yourself, you should talk," Uncle Nate said suddenly. He was a thin man finding himself going fat in his middle years, and the success of his umbrella factory—which he had begun to work in as an apprentice and now owned—had given him a quiet confidence. Usually, in matters of his wife's family, he stayed silent, but now he was agitated. That summer, I had played Woodie Guthrie folk songs for him on the porch under the pines and he had nodded his head in satisfaction, thinking back to a younger life I couldn't even imagine. Rhoda told me he had been a communist, but that word was murky for me then, muddled up with things my father had said about himself, in

Spain and during the war, about the post office and organizing, that seemed to double back on themselves, like a cat chasing its tail, and there was no sign of it on Uncle Nate, as if he had completely stripped himself of that life, the way a butterfly casts off the worm it once was. "The boy can really play that guitar. You talk like you've never listened to him."

Pops looked at his brother-in-law and blinked slowly, an idea forming behind his muddy eyes. This wasn't just talk, he was realizing, there really was something here—he *hadn't* listened. Or, rather, the sounds had not been meant for him. His head shifted on his shoulders like the gun atop a tank seeking its target and his eyes came to rest on me, the irises wide and damp, as if seeing something in me for the first time. I knew there'd be plenty to talk about on the long subway ride home and I shrank in my seat.

"Sure, sure he can play," my father said slowly. "It takes more than playing to be a musician."

"Of course, that's exactly why he should be going to Music and Art," Aunt Ida said. "So he can *learn*." She smiled, pleased at her point, and began to gather up the plates closest to her, signifying that the conversation was over.

Pops wasn't letting go, though.

"You think they don't have music classes at Abraham Lincoln?" he said sharply. He was like a cornered animal, lashing out in fear at larger creatures that had already turned their back on him, but it was *my* neck and cheeks that were reddening.

"Sure, they have music classes there," Aunt Ida said, her hands filled with plates. "But not like at Music and Art. That's not their specialty. At Music and Art, it is." She gave my father a defiant look, bolstered by the force of her logic.

"Special, special, what's so special about special?" My father's voice was rising, but he paused to grin stupidly at the inadvertent play on words. "We live three blocks away from Abraham Lincoln, a perfectly good high school supported by the very same tax dollars, yours and mine, ladies and gentlemen, that go to the high falutin' Music and Art, and named after a quite prominent personage in American history, the man who *freed the slaves*." Here Pops' voice quavered, and he paused for effect. "He should ride the subway for an hour, morning and night, just to go to some fancy-ass, excuse me ladies, some fancy school where music is so special? Music is *always* special. It can be just as special at Abraham Lincoln, three blocks away." He threw his bunched napkin onto his plate, a look of satisfaction on his darkening face.

"And I suppose you don't care what the boy wants?"

Uncle Ira had his thumbs hooked under the straps of his suspenders at armpit level and was leaning back in his chair with the self-satisfied look of a physician who had just made a particularly difficult diagnosis. Beside him, my cousin Becky, who had a mole on her pale cheek from which three small hairs grew, nodded her pretty head vehemently.

"What the *boy* wants?" my father said, a crooked smile flitting across his mouth. "Papa should hear you say that, Ira."

"This is America, Murray," Aunt Ida said. She hadn't moved from the archway between the dining room and the kitchen, a stack of plates still balanced in her large, white hands. "It's 1954."

"You don't have to remind me," he said with enough bitterness in his voice to bring my eyes up. He was frowning, his mouth pursed.

He turned to me. "Francesco, you want to go to Music and Art?"

"S'okay," I mumbled, as much surprised by the question as by his unaccustomed use of my full name. I could feel Rhoda's disappointed eyes on me from across the table.

"What's that? Speak up, don't mumble."

"It's okay," I said, breaking the words up into stiff syllables.

"Okay, is that all? What about Abraham Lincoln? Isn't that okay too?"

"Sure, that's okay," I whispered. I was scrunched down as far

50

as I could go into my chair without slithering out of it onto the floor, which I was wishing I could do.

"See? Hear that?" my father said petulantly. "Abraham Lincoln is just as okay with Frankie as Music and Art."

"Murray, for goodness sake, you're browbeating the boy," Aunt Ida said. There were round spots of red in the center of her white cheeks, like bloodstains on a pillow the morning after you've had a nosebleed.

"Browbeating the boy? What about me? *You're* browbeating *me*."

Uncle Ira and Uncle Nate both pushed their chairs back, looking at each other meaningfully across the table, and Aunt May and Becky began to gather up the plates. We kids squirmed, Bernie and Bret nudging each other with their elbows. Rhoda had her head bowed, avoiding my eyes.

"Okay, Murray, enough for today. No need to get excited," Uncle Ira said. He was reaching into his vest pocket, fishing for one of the wooden matches he favored.

"Excited? Who's getting excited? I'm just trying to find out what's so special about Music and Art that makes it worth an hour's ride on the subway before it's even light out in the winter when a perfectly good high school is only three blocks away, three short blocks. That's all I'm trying to find out."

"All right, all right, Abraham Lincoln is a fine school, nobody's saying it isn't. Now, how about a cigar? Nate, you have any of that plum brandy left?"

"You children can be excused," Aunt Ida said and the boys leaped up, scattering. Rhoda burst past her mother into the kitchen, her eyes streaming. Only my father and I were left sitting, as if the argument had burned us fast to our chairs like electricity through a faulty wire.

"Isn't somebody going to say it's because Abraham Lincoln is full of niggers and spics?" my father said defiantly.

"No, nobody's going to say that, Moishe," Uncle Ira said wearily. Aunt Ida turned on her heels, an exasperated expression on her wide face, and went into the kitchen, clattering dishes. Aunt May followed, raising her eyebrows at Ira, and then Becky, glaring at my father. Just four of us were left in the dining room, four men—my two uncles, my father and me.

"That's what you all mean, though, isn't it?" my father growled.

"No, that *isn't* what we mean," Ira said. He had stuffed a cigar into his mouth but hadn't yet lit it, and his eyes were examining with weary interest the glittering glass of the chandelier.

"Because if it is, let me remind you that Frankie here is a nigger and a spic, too," my father said coldly. He pushed back his chair and got to his feet slowly, glancing at his brother. He raised his hand, as if to ward off a blow, but there was no blow coming, just stunned silence in the dining room, the heavy clattering of dishes from the kitchen. "And let me remind you," my father said, his hand coming to rest on my shoulder, "that I say those words with *respect*."

On the long subway ride home, the musical whine of the wheels on the rails singing in my ears, I made up my mind that I *would* ask my father if I could go to high school in the Bronx, and I expected, hearing the request from me, that he would say yes. It had been a long time, if ever, since I'd known how much he loved me.

5. Consolation

I have just lived through the absolute worst, most horrible day of my life, no exceptions.

The world is about to go to war and blow itself all to shit, but what do I care about that?

No, it's Irene who's torturing me, fucking me up all the way to Sunday and back. Something has been brewing with her and me since her main squeeze Fartie Artie broke half the bones in his worthless body falling off a truck a few weeks back, in answer to my vengeful prayers.

She and I have been *consoling* each other—that's *her* word for it. She consoles me because of the scam the band's been suckered into this summer. I do the same for her because Fartie's up in the city, making love to himself with his arms wrapped in a permanent hug and his head up his asshole, though how he manages to keep every hair of his bear-greased duck's ass in place in that position is beyond me. More and more, this consolation has been edging toward something else—we've been playing the game that only, my pal Otis says, ends one way.

"Nook-eyyyyy!" he shouts, the white of his bulging eyes and teeth flashing like the third-string Al Jolson imitator he is at heart.

Otis, who claims to be irresistible to women, ought to know. Or so he says.

But, ha! I say. Bull-sheet! To me, the game looks endless.

Before Irene, there were some other chicks I fooled around

with here, but *nada*! So here I am, sixteen getting on to seventeen fucking years old, at the peak of my powers, a fucking *star* on the musical horizon, for Chrissake, but my balls blue as the sky.

I don't know, maybe I got a hangup or something. Rhoda says I do, and my kissin' cousin's pretty smart about that sort of thing. She says it's my Jewish blood that keeps stopping me. She says if I was all Puerto Rican or all African I'd've been screwing my teachers since kindergarten and they'd be begging for more, I'm so sexy and all. Of course, Rhoda says all this from the well-known safety of theory, not experience, but her point is this: that one side of me, my mother's side, is uninhibited and free, dark and muscular and beautiful, like a wild horse running free, but my Jewish blood gets in the way because it wants me to suffer, or at least to worry.

Sounds wild, but maybe she's right. I can believe that if something's going wrong inside me it would have to be Pops' genes at work, and *something* ain't working right, that's for sure.

Me and Irene, we're two of a kind. She's sweet sixteen, and she *says* she's a virgin, though I don't believe her. It just couldn't be possible.

She's a half-breed like me, too: her father is Jewish but her mother is Polish Catholic, which is the next best thing to being Jewish, Irene says, except that you get a temper instead of a big nose. But Polish is one thing and Puerto Rican is another. "My fatha would kill me if he knew I was datin' you, Frankie," she says, "so don't you tell him 'cause I sure as hell won't."

Every evening these past few weeks, after I get through in the dining room, toiling away as an indentured servant, we wander back to the staff cabins so she can change. Me, I like to get out of my sweaty busboy monkeysuit quick as possible, taking off the jacket, with "Blaaberg's Fabulous Resort" sewn over the heart in stylized red letters, and walking around in my undershirt and black pants with the satin stripes, but Irene is fussy as hell about her clothes.

She's a counselor in the tiny camp the hotel operates for the few guests who have young kids in tow, and she glides through her days there like Elizabeth Taylor floating around that Southern mansion in *Cat on a Hot Tin Roof*—head erect, slanted yellow eyes cool and distant, her mouth open just the tiniest bit to let out the heat which must always be steaming up inside her. At the camp, she wears loose white shorts and a sweatshirt and floppy white hat to keep the blistering sun off her nose, which always has a reddish-brown burn going along the smooth, straight bridge—that's her own body chemistry's doing, not a surgeon's. She keeps her hair, which is honey brown with lighter streaks in it, in a ponytail.

She takes a shower before dinner and puts on another pair of those loose shorts and a different sweatshirt, usually a red or blue one that says "Bronx Science and Art" on it over her tits. The thought that we both go to high school in the Bronx gives me a thrill, not that the kids from Music and Art would have anything to do with those Science and Art shmucks. Later, when it's cooler, she lets her hair hang loose and fluffy around her shoulders and puts on shorts that don't have any air between them and her ass, short ones usually but sometimes Bermudas, and a soft sweater that makes her chest look like a topographical map of the Catskills. No, must be the Adirondacks. They're bigger. I wait in the hallway or the porch while she's changing, then come in to button up the back of her sweater, static arcing from her hair to my fingers as I brush it aside, or watch while she's bent over tying her sneakers, the leg openings of her shorts riding up the soft, sweet lip of her ass.

Then I put my arms around her and everything goes hazy. She's small—*petite* is the word she likes, *pint-sized* is what I'd say—her head coming just about halfway up my chest, and if we kiss for more than a minute standing like this my neck starts to hurt. Her skin is so tight my hands draw sparks as I run them up and down her sleek, tanned legs and over her shorts and all along the outside of her sweater. She won't let me go any further.

"This way, Artie can't say I'm cheating on him," she says, jutting out her lower lip like a slice of peach I'd like to take a bite of. "He says my boobs are just for him."

Then we go out for a walk down by the lake and wind up at the soda shop, where the woman who runs the place, an Auschwitz survivor with a tattoo on her arm, gives us a mournful smile, or hitch a ride into town, this one-horse jerkwater called Bushnelsville a couple of miles down the road, and see a movie and have a burger. A couple of times we went to the lobby late and slowdanced to the music of Moe Leader and his Fabulous Band (pat me on the back here, I'm choking), half a dozen tired-looking, middle-aged guys in wrinkled tuxes, the trumpet a little off tempo (not half the trumpet my father plays, I have to admit), Moe beaming at us like some sort of squashed Paul Whiteman, his teeth gleaming and regular, like an extension of the shiny white keys on his accordion.

"I think I love you," I whisper in Irene's ear as we dance, for no good reason, since I don't really love her, or think so, and I'm not really sure what effect that might have on her, although it's more likely to be good than bad—no *real* reason, I just feel like it. Her face is pressed against my chest, a crystal of ice, tiny and clear and perfect, her pointy tits sticking into my belly like a holdup man's pistols.

"I think I love you, too," she says, and I don't know if she's saying it for any better reason than I had but there's a magical glow surrounding us, I can tell that. Even Moe's accordion sounds sweet and lyrical, the whole band drowning in syrup as they slosh through "Oh, My Pa-Pa."

"But I can't cheat on Artie," she says, after a minute.

The Fart, I should say, just finished his first year at City College, taking commerce, whatever the hell that is, and he's one slick prick. He's got no ass to speak of, which is amazing because he's *all* asshole, and hair running down his chest to his stomach, which is flat and hard as a schoolhouse wall. He was assistant bell captain here, one of the cocks of the walk and a pretty good looker until he fell off the luggage truck. Now he's in two casts, his elbows sticking out like a parody of Charlie Chaplin duckwalking down the street, and he don't look too hot. There's a bandage on his head and the skin is just starting to grow back over the scabs on his cheek and beak. Couldn't have happened to a nicer cat. He's back in the city, but he came out for a visit last weekend, strutting around like a peacock, his arms tied around himself and his fingers sticking out of the casts like those white-glove sausages Mickey Mouse wears.

Irene was back at his side, feeding him in the staff dining room and cooing over him just as if I didn't exist, as if all that consolation hadn't ever happened. "Does she hold his pecker for him when he has to whizz?" Otis asks and the boys all laugh. Yeah, very funny. Ha ha. But come Sunday, I got the laugh. Artie powders and Irene is all smiles for me again. I don't understand it, but that doesn't surprise me. I don't think I was cut out to understand women, something I must have inherited from Pops, who treats them like they're an entirely different species.

When this weekend rolls around, I know things are going to be different. For some reason, Artie isn't coming up. I take a deep swallow and resolve that this is it, no more stalling, no excuses. This time I won't take Artie for an answer.

Friday night, I walk back to the cabin with Irene after dinner, earlier than usual, because I don't have to work tables. That's the deal the boys have with Blaaberg: if we behave ourselves bussing tables all week, on weekends we get to take off our uniforms and play, which is what we thought we were coming up to do all the time.

I wait while she changes, we embrace, we murmur, I insist, she protests, then we're off to see the movie—it's a Jerry Lewis, about this goofy GI who keeps tripping over things, fouling things up. And finally I'm up there on stage, hips thrashing, fingers strong on the guitar strings, voice husky, certain, singing just for her. Who, after all, can resist the plaintive, sensual strains of Frankie and the Runabouts when we're playing at the peak of our form?

Most of the time, Blaaberg's is more like an old-age home than a resort and the loudest sounds outside of the kitchen during the day are the snores coming from the beachfront and the occasional thud when someone keels over, the lonely whistle of a shuffleboard rock crawling toward its target. But on weekends, the children come to visit momma and poppa, and they bring *their* kids along, and they're just about the right age to dig us.

At nine, right after the movie, Moe puts on his white dinner jacket one more time and, before striking up the band in the lobby for the old folks to waltz to, he comes down to the shuffleboard court to introduce us, slurring into the microphone, "Ladies an' Gennelmen" (though there ain't too many of *them* around), "goys an' berls" (and this is what we came for, right? the berls?) "an' anybody else who might have wandered in by mistake, tonight, Blaaberg's Fabulous Resort Hotel takes great pride in presenting, right here, for your list'ning an' dancing enjoyment, *di*rect from the Brooklyn Paramount stage" (and that ain't no lie, we were there, even if it was only for that one night, those two songs, and even if only because those other cats were throwing up backstage), "Gee Records recording artists" (*artists*, that's us, not singers or musicians or even a band, but *artists*) "Frankie and the *Runabouts*. Let's give them a nice hand, let's *hear* it for them." The lights that rim the shuffleboard court go down and the spotlights come on, splashing all over us, and Reno starts in with his falsetto: "I hear a heartbeat," and Mel thumps on his bass, first one thump, then another, then a string of them like bubbles breaking through the water, and Reno sings: "I hear a footstep, someone running close," and Juan hits his cymbals with the brushes, then taps the ridge of his top drum with a stick, first slow, then a little faster, then real fast, like the spark of high heels running on pavement, and Reno sings: "I hear the falling of tears," and I open my hand across the strings with a G chord that fills the court with sound and hangs there in the night air, and then Otis's guitar joins in and he and I begin to sing: "You are the one, baby, you are the one who does it, you are the one who does it to me," and we're off, we're goddamn *off*, we're doing what we come to do.

And the kids are dancing, the ones who came dragging along to visit *Bubba* and *Zaida*, and the few who were here all week long anyway, waiting for this, and the waiters and waitresses and the guys who are busboys *six* days a week, not just three or four like us, and the maids, and the college kids who work the front desk, and the bellhops and the lifeguards, and the counselors from the camp down the road, and kids from the hotels nearby who come over on weekends, just to hear us, they're all dancing, and bopping up the path to the soda shop or the bar on the terrace above it, or sneaking down the winding path to the lake, with its dark canoe house, pier and swimming raft, and the moon so bright behind the clouds it stops your heart—that's what we come to do.

Irene dances a couple of the faster songs with her roommate, Lyn, who's chubby and cheerful, but mostly she's standing by the side of the court, just watching and smoking her cigarettes that taste like after-dinner mints, bopping her head to the beat, cool slanted eyes on me, tits rising and falling, and she is melting, I know it—I can feel the heat rising off her, can actually see the waves radiating into the fuzzy light above her head.

But Saturday is a big day at the camp and Irene needs her beauty sleep, she says, so right after the dance she heads for bed, with me walking her and settling for a goodnight kiss. "Just one, so you won't forget about me," she says. As if I could.

Next day, we do it again. Dinner, the walk back to the cabin, hands entwined. She hesitates at the door—she's been funny all weekend and I don't know if she's pissed off at Fartie for not coming up, or as jumpy as I am because of it. There's a sort of electric charge spritzing off her skin, but I don't know if it's positive or negative. "I guess you can come in," she says, almost shyly. I stand just inside the door, mouth hanging open, as she takes off her sweatshirt and shorts, the sight of the bra and panties, white as neon against her tan, stealing my breath. She's got her back to me, looking over her shoulder, the ponytail bouncing, exactly like that Elizabeth Ann Whatsername, the teenage Playmate, just sixteen like Irene, who bopped through my dreams all winter, except that I have to imagine Irene's ass under the panties, not that there's all that much imagining to do. "It can't hurt if you just look," she says. I guess she doesn't know how much it does hurt.

I'm paralyzed, my feet rooted to the bare wooden floor, and she's into her red shorts and fluffy pink sweater before I can break free. "Be a doll and button me up, Frankie, will ya?"

"Oh, God," I say, "I can't stand it." I have my arms around her, my hands all over her as she tries to brush her hair.

"Neither can I," Irene says, dropping the brush and lifting her face, fragrant from powder and gum. "Artie wouldn't mind if we do it just a little."

We kiss and I start to undo the buttons I've just done up but she slaps at my hands, laughing. "Not now, silly, I'm all dressed. And don't you have to play tonight? Or did you forget about that?"

Saturday night's a rerun of Friday, but the next day is perfect. The bellhops and desk clerks run their asses off Sundays but there's a buffet so most of the dining room staff have the day off. There's camp in the morning, but it's shut in the afternoon. The Runabouts don't play, so we have the whole day to ourselves. Sometimes Mel and Juan grab a ride into the city but today's even better than I could have hoped for—there's room in somebody's station wagon and they're all going.

"How 'bout you, Frankie?" Otis asks.

"Naw, I'm gonna hang around here, work on some new songs."

That doesn't surprise anybody—they all know there's no great love lost between me and Pops. They split first thing, won't be back till tomorrow morning. The whole fucking cabin is empty, deserted—even Chip, the little faggot who bunks in with Reno, is gone for the weekend.

I sleep late, for strength, but not too late, not to waste the day away. And, as a precaution, I close my eyes and see the blazing white of Irene's bra and panties against her taut brown skin—so long, Lizzy Ann, it's been nice to know ya—and whack off, just so I won't be *too* eager. Everything in working order.

Then I shower, dress carefully, scrutinize my face for pimples, find one and demolish it, comb my hair, brush it, brush my teeth a second time, brush my hair again. And I'm ready.

We meet at lunch, which is grilled cheese sandwiches and soggy fries, then wander up to the lobby, where Irene stops at the newsstand to buy a pack of butts. The Sunday papers are filled with Lebanon, Egypt, Iraq, a grinning marine sticking a rifle big as an elephant's trunk toward the camera on the front page of the *Telegram*. Ike's bland old puss is splashed across the *Times*, stern and thin-lipped, like Irene's father's would be if he'd just come across his sweet little girl and yours truly coiled up with each other on the living room sofa.

It's been spooky here all week. Most of the guests are Jewish, and they get a little panicky anytime anything happens anywhere in the world that might have even the remotest effect on Israel. People have been talking about it all the time, crowding around the TV set in the lobby in the evening to watch the news. None of this mess has anything to do with Israel, as far as I can tell, but people are nervous anyway. But the whole thing is a puzzle to me—I don't even know where the hell Lebanon is. I mean, I always thought it was a kind of bologna. Some of the older guys, though, like Mel and Reno, who are eighteen and already have their draft cards, man, they're shitting their pants thinking about slicing that particular bologna.

"I worry about Artie," Irene says, her face peering around my shoulder. "He's old enough to be drafted."

"He's okay, he's in college, right?"

"What if he flunks out?"

"Yeah, what if?" I say, grinning, and she bats at me with an open hand.

"Don't talk that way, Frankie. I *love* Artie."

"I thought you loved me?"

"I love you *too*.

"You can love two people at the same time?"

"Sure," she says, giving me that cool-eyed look of hers. "Why not?"

Then we stroll back to the cabins, hand in hand, not saying much, me worrying like crazy I've fouled it somehow. The grounds around the staff quarters are deserted, most of the kids who haven't gone into town or the city down at the lake now, the afternoon still and hot, only birds and squirrels chasing each other in the trees like rabid rats and the steady drone of cicadas to break the sweltering silence.

All the staff live in a hollow near the marshy end of the lake, where the mosquitoes are fierce and about as far from the guest cottages as they could get us. There are two big bunkhouses for the dining room and kitchen staff and the bellhops, but the boys and I and some other privileged characters are in a bunch of dilapidated old cabins that smell of pine cones and mothballs and old sweat. We're in one that's part of a cluster of three set off a little ways by itself, out of sight and almost out of normal sound range from the bunkhouses, reserved for people who work funny hours, the bakers and watchmen and Moe and his merry men. That poor bastard, Chip, he's odd man out and he wound up with us. He works the graveyard behind the desk and he suffers because we keep regular hours four days a week while his days are always standing on their heads, him going to bed just as we're getting up, trying to sleep while we're banging in and out, but that's what he gets for being a queer, Reno says. He don't complain and he don't bug us, we don't bug him. Reno showed him his shiv the first day and that was that. He says it's an "hona and a priv'ledge bein' aroun' beautiful, talented boys like you." But he gets away most days off, and he's not around that much anyway. When he is, he sits in his room or on the porch knitting. No shit, knitting.

We go past Irene's cabin, looking over our shoulders, and slip into ours, and into the room I share with Otis, my hand trembling on the door knob. I turn on the radio to fill the awkward silence and it's the Everlys, "All I Have to Do Is Dream," Don or Phil, whichever one has the high sweet voice, going "dream, dream, dream," and we look at each other and laugh.

"I should go change," Irene says, "take a shower. I'm still all sweaty from this morning."

"I like you sweaty," I say, my fingers sliding along the soft, tight skin of her cheek. Her face is covered with millions of tiny blonde hairs, each one glistening, not with sweat but scented oil from some Arabian nights story. There are specks of dark brown in her yellow eyes.

"I'm a virgin," Irene says, startling me. "You'll have to do everything, okay? And be gentle?"

I don't believe her for a minute. How could it be? "Don't worry," I tell her. "I know what I'm doing."

But I don't know, not *really*, and *I'm* worried.

"And you got one of those things?" Irene is asking.

"Don't *worry*," I tell her and shut her up.

And then—oh, God—then we're naked and lying on my bed and I *really* don't know what I'm doing. I'm so hard I'm afraid I'll poke a hole in her, like a finger through fresh white bread, but when I climb on top she doesn't open up the way I expect her to, and the angle seems wrong—I curve up where it seems like I should be going straight out—and I'm jabbing at unyielding flesh. It's good I took precautions.

"Shouldn't you put it on?" Irene asks. "Maybe that helps."

"I've got one, don't worry, but I think I should, you know, get it started first. I'll put it on later."

I poke away, grabbing at what I can. "Maybe we should kiss some more," Irene suggests. "I think I have to get wet."

I don't see the connection right away. "Oh, yeah. I've got some stuff for that. I'll try it in a minute."

I'm almost limp but when we embrace I bounce right back, like a faithful dog with a stick. I kiss her mouth, all sharp and licoricey from Sen-Sen, her ears, her eyes, feel the incredible soft push of her tits—which are BEAUTIFUL!—against my chest, let my hand wander down her back to where the swelling begins, and when I'm so hard it hurts I roll over, lift up and scrunch into position. But nothing happens. I can't find the way in.

"Kiss me more," Irene says.

"Okay, but don't touch me there," I tell her.

We lie next to each, my eyes glassy with the richness of her, the swellings and the mysterious dark dips, and run our hands over each other. I kiss her mouth and ears and eyes, and then I tilt my head down and kiss her nipples—*God, I can't believe it*—and she makes a sound deep in her throat that makes me think the moment has come, must have. But again there is nothing there where I know there has to be something. Has to be. And I'm cursing myself, my stupidity, my cowardice all the other times I've had the chance and muffed it. Even once, in the dark, and I'd know what I was doing now, I'd know *something*.

"Jesus, are you sure you *have* one?" I say, too sharply.

"That's not very funny, Frankie Stern, Stein, whatever your

name is. I know what *I* have. Let's try some of that stuff."

I roll off the bed, my body feeling like it weighs five hundred pounds. The Vaseline is in a dresser drawer. My back is to her and I stick my fingers into it and rub it on. I'm still hard as a rock and the stuff is cool and slippery—and a mistake.

"Oh, Christ."

"I think you're supposed to put it on *me*," she says.

"Now you tell me." On the radio, Pricky Nelson is singing about some "Poor Little Fool." I know just how he feels.

We sit on the edge of the bed and Irene lights a cigarette, puffing sweet-and-sour smoke into the small room. She puts her arm around me, one sweaty tit rubbing up against me like a friendly puppy. "Hey, it's not a big deal, Frankie," she says. For the cherry she says she is, she sounds like she knows a hell of a lot.

"Yeah, that's what it's turning out to be, all right."

"Hey, that's no way to talk. I'm flattered I make you so excited." She giggles, then we sit silent for a minute while I think that over. Irene runs her hand along the inside of her thigh, where the skin is white as snow under the fine tan hairs, then up past her muff to her belly and midriff, that narrow band between her belly button and the bottom of her tits, where it's brown as I always am, then to her tit, white again, jiggling it. "You like me?"

"Sure I like you. What a dumb question."

"No, you know, do you like ... *it*?" She jiggles it again.

"Sure I do."

"Well, show me."

I put my hand on her, and then my mouth, and she slides her hand between my legs. She seems to know what she's doing. After awhile, I'm hard again and Irene lies down.

"Give me that jar. Look the other way."

65

I turn to the door, my ears straining for any sound that'll give me a clue, *anything.*

"Okay."

I climb on top of her. "Maybe it would help if you'd spread your legs a little more."

"I do that, you'll fall right through."

"There's a fucking bed underneath us, Irene, for Chrissake. I'm not going to fall through. I can't get through *you.*"

"That's not *my* fault."

I slam my eyes shut and grit my teeth, jabbing at her. She moves her legs but it's no use. Now she's too slippery, the hair dark and glistening with petroleum jelly, like the fur on a drowned kitten.

"You used too much of that damned stuff, it's clogged up the works."

"Oh, shit, Frankie."

"Maybe I should use, you know, the other way," I say hopefully. "At least I can see that."

"Don't you dare." She reaches up and slaps my hand lightly. "Don't even *talk* like that. Who d'ya think I am?"

I roll off her and sit on the edge of the bed to catch my breath. I'm soft again, and starting to hurt from battering against that unyielding wall. "I don't know *who* you are. I don't know who the fuck *I* am anymore."

"Frankie!" She rolls over and buries her face in the pillow. The room is so quiet, all I can hear is her breathing, short and fierce, louder than mine for some reason. After a minute, she says softly, "Maybe you should use those talented fingers of yours, you know, sort of get it started. Make like I'm a guitar."

That turns out to be a good idea. I find what I'd been looking for right away. "Oh, there. It's lower than I thought."

"You sure you've done this before, Frankie?"

"Sure I have." I try to make my voice sound angry, and that

comes surprisingly easy. I *am* angry, but don't ask me who at.

"You're just built a little funny."

"I am *not*."

"No, really, Reenie, on most girls it's up a little higher."

"Oh, big man, been with so many girls you're an *expert* already. And I told you not to call me Reenie."

"I know where some things are," I say, reaching up with my slippery hands to tickle her belly. Then we're rolling together on the bed, laughing and kissing, and she puts her hands on me, which always seems to work. I roll onto her and scrunch up—and batter against that wall again, slippery and wet and where it ought to be now but still impenetrable.

"It closed up again, damn it."

"It is not, Frankie, I can feel it."

"Well, maybe you could help a little, you know. You like holding it so much, why don't you sort of steer it in?"

She grabs me so hard it hurts and pulls me down. "Oh, God, it's in, I can feel it."

"Push, damn it, Frankie, *push*."

That's what I'm trying to do, but I hesitate a moment too long and I slip out. I'd only been in a little bit.

"Oh, shit. You're too fucking slippery now."

"Right, it's *my* fault again."

I sit up and Irene rolls over, putting her face in the pillow, pounding the bed with her little fists. She's covered with sweat, and beginning to give off a sour smell. When I put a hand on her back, she shakes her shoulders, kicking her feet.

"Well, I apologize for one thing," I say after awhile.

"What's *that*?"

"I didn't really believe you were a cherry, but you must be. There's *something* there I couldn't get through."

She gives me a look. "Yeah, it got toughened up from all the horseback riding I do."

"I thought it worked the other way."

"It *does*, stupid."

"Oh." I think about that for a minute. I don't think she's ever been on a horse anyway. They don't have any here, and there aren't any in the Bronx that I know of.

"Well, anyway, I apologize for thinking that."

"Thanks a lot." She sits up and reaches for me, but this time, nothing.

"I'm exhausted, Irene."

"Me too. Let's get out of here for awhile, okay?"

We put on our clothes and go out for a walk. We go through the woods and down to the lake the back way, passing nobody and winding up on a stretch of pebbly beach far from the sandy roped-off area where people swim. We hold hands, just like nothing's happened. Well, nothing *has*. We sit down on a rock and let the sun soak into us.

"You must think I'm a real idiot," I say. It's exactly how I feel.

"Aw, Frankie, don't be silly. This probably happens with everybody." She laughs and wiggles her shoulder against my arm. "That's why people are always so nervous about it. I don't blame them." She looks up at me, her face solemn, and squeezes my arm. "And why it's so memorable afterwards."

But I don't believe her. I feel as miserable as I ever have in my short, miserable life.

"And besides," Irene says, giggling, "it's *funny*, you have to admit *that*."

"Funny as death," I say.

"Maybe..." she starts, but lets her voice trail off.

"What?"

"Maybe God's punishing me for being unfaithful to Artie. "

"*Reenie!*"

"Well, I was just wondering. And don't call me that."

Walking back on the path along the lake, we run across two of the musicians from the regular band, a couple of Italian cats in their thirties, with matching neat short haircuts, sunbathing city style on a sandy spot by the water, in open-necked golf shirts and slacks with creases sharp as one of Pops' dirty looks. One of them has taken off his shoes and socks and has the cuffs of his slacks rolled up to reveal pasty white ankles. They've got a portable radio and they're passing a bottle of booze back and forth, drinking straight from it the way the boys on 125th Street do except they aren't hiding it in a paper bag, although they give us a guilty, furtive look, and they're nodding their heads the same way they do on the bandstand when they're laying back, listening to a solo. They make me think of those pictures in the papers of the marines on the beach in Lebanon—there was one showing a bunch of girls in bikinis throwing flowers at them. Yeah, war is hell!

Something about these hipsters makes me think too of Pops, of that summer when I went off with my aunt and uncle in the country and he had a job in a band like that, at a place like this, although I think the band Pops was in probably had a little more swing to it than Moe's dozy little Mouseketeers, and I don't really know if the hotel was like this one or not.

When we got this gig—our goofy manager-agent-whatever Stockman so proud of himself for putting together a deal that turned out so lousy—that was the first thing I'd thought of. "Hey, my old man played a gig at a place like that and had a blast," I told the boys, although, in fact, all he'd ever said about it was "fine, fine," just like he always does. But I don't think I had ever *really* thought about it, made the connection between him and me— like, wow, I'm doing the same damn thing he did, though I got to it at sixteen, not forty-whatever-he-was-then—until now, eyeing these two coolcats leaning back in the sand. I suddenly have a flash of Pops, in his gabardine slacks and shades and that porkpie hat of his, out in the woods someplace with a bottle in his hand, drinking straight from it. I mean, I've *never* seen Pops drink from a bottle, and I guess I've never thought about it one way or the other, do he or don't he? But I bet he do, I bet a million he did that summer, when I wasn't around to cramp his style, when he was *free*, and I have the sharpest feeling, just like a fucking ice pick stuck in my gut, of the loneliness he must have felt, not just that night, if there even was such a night, and not just that summer, either, but all the goddamned time when I was growing up and I was his prisoner and he was mine.

"See those bastards grinning?" Irene says, soon as we're out of earshot. "The whole band'll hear what we been doing."

"You're crazy. How could those queers know?"

"They could smell it," she says, giving me an evil, sexy grin herself. "They could smell what we've been doing."

"What we *ain't* been doing," I say, but I kiss her and everything seems okay again, don't ask me why.

We go back and try again, pretending we're starting brand new, like what's happened *hasn't* happened, but it doesn't help. The angle's just wrong. We take showers in the tiny stall in the cabin's one bathroom, even try to do it in there, soaking wet, with the water streaming over our heads, cascading over us like a waterfall, standing up, soapy and slippery. Almost make it, too, but she's too short and I have to bend so low my knees get in the way and all that happens is I slip on a piece of soap and almost break my neck.

"Maybe this just isn't destined to be, Frankie," Irene says.

I've been thinking the same thing but the soap gives me an idea, and after we towel off I take the bar back to the room, along with a wet washcloth, and we lather her good. "That fucking Vaseline probably did more harm than good," I tell her.

"It *was* pretty sticky."

I kiss her all over to get myself good and hard, then make her spread her legs good, and I kneel down between them and find her with my fingers. I *am* learning. She's open and wet, no doubt about it, and I make certain I have a good fix on the location. I put one finger a little way in and there's nothing in the way.

"Oh, God, Frankie, *do* it, for Chrissake, put it in," Irene cries out, and there's something so wild and plaintive in her voice that I know this time is it for real, no shitting around this time, she wants it, I'm strong, I'm sure, my aim is true—this time I can't fail. Just for insurance, I ram the pillow under her ass, to improve the angle.

But I do. Fail. I don't believe that chick *has* a goddamned pussy. I think I almost have it when she grabs me and pushes me in, but I slip out, and she pushes her hips up hard chasing me just as I come down again and bounce off her, and when she reaches for me again it's too late, my hips are churning and my breath is rattling in my open mouth like nails in a rusty can. "Oh, God," I say, slumping forward like a load of wet laundry in Irene's arms. She gets quiet and folds those arms around me, placing a hand on each of my ears, as if to shelter me from something awful I might hear.

I cry. "I must be sick or something. I've had too much sun, or I picked up a bug, maybe. Something in the lousy water. I swear, Irene, this has never happened before." That part's true.

Irene moves a little under me, shifting her shoulders and head so she can see me better, but not letting go. Her body, slick again, feels rubbery. "It's okay, Frankie, it'll be okay."

"*Okay?* Jesus, you must hate me."

"No, I *don't.*" She makes it sound like she means it, but I don't believe her. How can I?

"Maybe God *is* punishing me," Irene says after a while. I lift my head and look sideways at her.

"For cheating on Artie." She turns her yellow eyes on me. She lets go and slides onto her side, propping herself up on one arm, tits bobbing against me like soft, rubber beach balls.

"But I guess I didn't, did I? I didn't cheat on him."

She stands up and walks across the room to the chair where her clothes are folded. She looks funny without them on, without the sweater and shorts, her skin sweaty and marked from the sheets, loose looking. She glances over her shoulder at me and, for a second, she looks just like Elizabeth Ann, her ass shining white between the tan above and below it, but she doesn't look sexy, not at all, and I look away.

She gets dressed, gives me a kiss and some more consoling talk and splits. I lie naked on the bed, staring at the ceiling, the plaster cracked and water-marked where the rain has leaked through. I'm thinking of something Pops always says, that things have a funny way of coming around in the end and working out the way they should. So maybe Irene's right, in a lopsided way, and it is all God's doing—not that God was stopping *her* from cheating on Artie, but maybe He is saving *me* for someone else.

I stare at those shapes on the ceiling for a long time, then I close my eyes. I just want to sleep, to let it all wash away, but I can't. The bed's too wet.

I get up and strip off the sheets and wrap them around me like Julius Caesar and take a shower, standing under the water with the sheets on me, then off. After I get dressed, I hang the sheets on a line strung up between trees outside and sit down on the porch with the half-full bottle of Jim Beam that Mel and Juan keep hidden in their room.

I'm still sitting there, pretty drunk, I guess, when Chip, the night clerk guy, comes home. It's way past dinner and starting to be dark, pale points of stars just coming into focus in the sky and I've been staring at one, wondering if it's Sputnik 3, wondering if *it* can see *me*. Chip stands in the grass just below the porch and stares up at me.

"What the fuck you lookin' at, faggot?"

Chip smiles. I don't think I've ever talked to him before, just "Hi, Chip," "Hi, Frankie," that sort of stuff. He comes up on the porch and looks at me hard, and even though my eyes are blurry I can see he doesn't look as different as I thought, just a smallish, skinny guy in his early twenties, I guess, but looking not much older than me, with a sleek blond mop he must spend a hell of a lot of time combing and a sharp foxy kind of face like two flat planes joined together at an angle.

"Whasamattah, Frankie, you got gull problems?"

I have to laugh at his stinking Brooklyn accent, but I squirm backwards against the porch wall, out of reach of the touch his voice implies.

"What's it to *you*, fuckin' queer? At least girl problems is somethin' I *can* have."

I thought he'd cry at that, or get pissed and rap me one, which I wouldn't be able to do much about, since I can barely lift my arms by now, but all he does is laugh, flipping back a tongue of the honey-blond hair from his forehead. "Sweetie, you are certainly right about *that*. But you really think one kinda juice is all that different from the otha kind? Sweeta? Or one kinda heart?"

He goes past me and I can hear him moving around in his room while I think about that. After awhile, he comes out again with his knitting and sits down in one of the crumbling wicker chairs. "Go ahead, Frankie, you tawk, I'll lissun."

I'd have liked to, too, you know? It would have been like this, just talking and talking into a wind, no face or voice or breath to contend with, no memory. But my tongue's too thick, my head too filled with Irene, those cats on the beach, Pops, cotton candy swirling around the May pole. I feel ashamed, somehow, but I don't know if it's for him or myself, or both of us.

"*You* talk, Chip," I say. "You talk, *I'll* listen."

And he does, telling me about his boyfriend—his "lovva," he says—a marine, one of those poor bastards who got shipped to Lebanon, shows me his hands, the nails at the ends of long, pale slender fingers bitten to the quick, ragged and bloody, talks on long past dark, his thin, reedy voice spinning on like Rapunzel's wheel, pouring out all sorts of stories of the heart, but I swear, I don't remember a one, not a friggin' word.

6.   Summertime Blues

I guess we were just about the jinx-iest bunch of musicians you could ever hope to meet, not that anything particularly bad happened to us on the tour—Otis fractured his elbow in Dayton, Ohio, where the show broke up, but that was about all. But look at who was there: Valens, dead within a couple of months, in that airplane crash with Buddy Holly. Cochrane, dead in a year or so, in a car crash. I don't know what became of the people in the other groups along with us, so maybe not dead in the flesh but certainly dead as acts. And us—can you believe I'm the only one of Frankie and the Runabouts to survive?

Nothing very mysterious about it—I mean, no curse of the mummy on us, far as I can tell. Otis and Reno both killed in Vietnam. Crazy Juan, who always had a temper and liked his knife too much, killed a guy in a robbery and then was killed himself in prison, poetic justice, stabbed with the sharpened end of a toothbrush. His father had died in prison too, in Nicaragua, where he'd gotten into some kind of trouble with Somoza, when Juan was still a little boy. Mel, who had gotten really good on the bass, stuck with it, drifting into jazz, playing around New York for years—he's on a couple of records with Bill Evans. Good, clean, strong lines, not one of the best but pretty good. Dead of a heroin overdose, couple of years ago. Someone sent me the obit from *Variety*.

When I think of those days, which I don't very often, it's usually Mel who comes into sharpest focus in my mind, standing next to me behind stage at the Apollo Labor Day weekend, after we came back from our crazy summer in the Catskills. "Look at 'em all," Mel says in his artesian-well voice, wiping his hands on the curtain he's peering around as we're being introduced. He rolls his eyes, doing his Alfalfa imitation. "We's gonna get *creamed.*"

We'd played the Paramount that spring, and all those shuffle-board court sock hops at Blaaberg's, but none of that, nor all the places we played later, compared to the Apollo. We were Harlem kids, and the Apollo was *ours*—hell, Reno always claimed he'd been conceived in the air-conditioned balcony one hot summer afternoon, that he was named after the cowboy on the screen that day. Even my father was impressed, in a way that the record and the hotel job had failed to move him. Of course, any good will I earned that night blew right out the window the next week when I told him I was dropping out of school.

The last time I ran into Mel was '67 or '68. I was still on the road with my folkie act then and used to get into the city once in awhile, either passing through from south to north or vice versa, or to see Armand Mitterand, my agent. This time, I'd been at Armand's office but he was out and I went into the Automat on Broadway to kill half an hour and there was Mel, bearded but still the gangly lead pencil he'd been when we were kids, sitting with a high-yellow woman in her thirties with brilliantly white buck teeth, a singer, I think, and a cat with an incredibly bad complexion who didn't say a word for the twenty minutes or so we sat over coffee. Mel was part of a band that had just come back from Tokyo and other points east and he seemed prosperous, if a little hollow-cheeked, and content, still jiving and clowning.

"Hey, man, you don't gotta worry about ol' Otis stealin' yo' licks no mo," he cracked—that was the first I heard of his death, just a few weeks before, blown apart by a grenade. Otis and I had been good friends once, but we hadn't been in touch since the band broke up.

Reno was still alive, but had been wounded once, shot in the shoulder, and was back over there, Mel told me. He was a pugnacious half-pint with the typical tough, short guy's outlook on life— no big bastard was gonna get on top of *him*. Juan was already in jail then.

"Hey, bro, I was right all along, now, weren't I?" Mel said. "We *did* get creamed, just like Ol' Mel say."

I'm not spooky about it. I don't look over my shoulder. And what happened to the guys, obviously didn't have anything to do with rock 'n' roll, but I'm glad I got out of it, just the same. It was too hard on the body.

We were all still alive and healthy, though, when we got to Dayton. It was December already, a few days before my seventeenth birthday, and we were laughing about it having been just about a year exactly since we cut "Don't Leave, Baby," the record that had made us mini-stars and landed us a spot with Alan Freed's autumn tour. It was a big one, fourteen acts, with Paul Anka and Jerry Lee Lewis as the headliners, Jackie Wilson, Danny and the Juniors, the Del-Vikings, Joanne Campbell, Eddie Cochrane, Ritchie Valens, a whole slew of others, and a full orchestra led by Sam "The Man" Taylor, a great sax player who could really honk. We were supposed to hit twenty-seven cities in I don't remember how many days, about six weeks' worth, and wind up in New York for Thanksgiving, but after the Boston riot all the other dates canceled out and we were stuck in Montréal—the first time I'd been in Canada, and with no reason to guess I'd be living there not all that many years later. Most of the acts went back to New York but a few of us hooked onto this new tour, covering much of the territory we'd already been through, but smaller cities.

"Look how far we come in jus' a year," Otis said, straight faced, "all the way to Dayton," and we all cracked up laughing.

In my memory, the tours—both of them—were an endless stream of days, nights, rooms, glare in my eyes, steady applause tapering out to a drone, like that of a receding motorcycle. Being the crumpled roadmap that the tours were, the only time I was ever nonstop, never-any-doubt excited, turned on, was when we were on stage. That's why we had come along, to play. The bus was a constant, our home, and the hotel rooms, the restaurants, the stages were all the same, even the music we performed was always the same, so there was nothing to distinguish one day from the one before, one week from another, except, I guess, for changes in the weather. It had still been high bright autumn when we pulled out of New York, the days warm, the trees just starting to change. The Yankees had just wrapped up the World Series, avenging themselves on Milwaukee for the year before in the seventh game, and us guys were still hashing it over—that and the Martin Luther King stabbing in Harlem a couple of weeks before, because one of the guys in the orchestra had been there, had seen it—as the bus headed out of the city, feeling like we were part of the flat blue sky as we crossed the George Washington to Jersey. As the tour went on, heading west to Philly and Pittsburgh and north and east and north again, the days got shorter, the trees erupted into flames of orange and gold and crimson, then began to shed, and the air got colder. At night, the heater in the Greyhound hummed and sometimes, if you fell asleep with your head against the window, there'd be frost on the glass when you woke up, "where yaw breath kissed it," Joanne Campbell told me.

She and I had become regular seatmates on the bus and she liked to cuddle up, big sister style, while I grinned and tried to bear my hard-on and sweat. She was protective, frowning over my excesses, which were few enough, and praising my virtues, which were also few, I thought, but seemed to grow daily in her eyes. "You wa' *won*daful tonight, Fwankie," she'd lisp in my ear after I collapsed against her creamy shoulder, the scent of her powder and perfume lifting my heart to heaven, and it was always clear it was *me* she meant, not Frankie and the Runabouts, just Frankie.

She was *my* fan, and for the first time in months I started to think about myself as an individual again, not just a piece of a greater whole.

After Boston, it was a much smaller show, Cochrane as the headliner, Valens, who had a small hit on the radio right then, "Come On, Let's Go," plus a couple of groups that hadn't been with us on the big show, and us. I tried to talk Joanne into joining us but her manager said no, and I really missed her. It was pretty punk stuff after Freed and his Greyhounds and good hotels. We traveled in a converted school bus, stayed in real dives, rooming houses sometimes, played in small theaters, union halls, once, in Ithica, New York, in a Masonic temple.

"Alan would have liked this," Eddie said, and we all felt bad, because from what we were hearing he was getting into deeper and deeper shit, but we laughed because it seemed so true.

"Fuckin' A," Otis said, flashing his gap-toothed grin.

"Yeah, the whole world is watching," I said, "except in Ithaca, where the Masons are sleeping."

We all looked up at the crest at the back of the hall, that all-seeing eye peering out of the pyramid, and we started laughing. "Hey, man, the fuckin' thing *blinked*," Mel said.

The streets of the towns we were passing through were decorated for Christmas, and snow was falling endlessly against the clicking windshield wipers of the bus as we slept from town to town. We'd been on the road for almost two months and it seemed a lot longer, we were that bone-tired. Homesick and sick of the lousy beds and rotten food, the crummy money we were pulling in on this end of it. More, Eddie's hit "Summertime Blues," which he'd released just before the Freed tour began, had turned into a million-seller and offers were coming for all sorts of things. The same was happening with Ritchie—"Donna" and "La Bamba" had just come out, both were instant smashes and his manager wanted him back in L.A. right away. Both those cats were too big for this kind of third-rate tour. Our second record, "Cryin' Time," had long since peaked and disappeared from the charts, though I guess a few copies were still selling in cities where we played, and we were expecting a new one out any day and had our fingers crossed that it would be the big one. It was an exciting time for all of us, coming to a head a few days before we got to Dayton with a screaming call from Ritchie's manager. Commitments had been made so we agreed to go that far, then no further.

We did our Dayton show in one of those dreary, all-purpose civic auditoriums, a concrete block square, with a rounded roof topped by what I guess was a Grecian-style cupola, that took up half a block next to the public library and across the street from the city hall. The show was sponsored by one of the local radio stations and, because we didn't have any girl groups traveling with us, they had arranged for a Dayton act to join us for a few numbers. This particular group was three sweet black girls calling themselves the Robins. They'd won a talent contest put on by the station and had a couple of records that had sold all right around Dayton but hadn't done anything anywhere else. They were okay, but their material was lousy.

"We call them the Robins 'cause they got red breasts," the deejay who was emceeing the show told us. He was their manager as well as their songwriter. "I read them all several times, cover to cover, right girls? *Real* bestsellers."

He was a big, bear-shaped man with bad teeth and a crooked grin that tended to lapse into a leer and a large, meaty hand that always seemed to be touching someone. He was called Doctor Dan. No last name.

"Hey, hey, Doctah Dan's the man, the man's got the cure, he'll fix your ills, won't send no bills," he'd rattle off between songs on his show, which ran in the prime evening hours, and he greeted the audience at the auditorium with it, warming them up. They were all his fans and they dug that jive, his rap spreading over them like a warm, safe blanket. "Hey, hey, you wanna rock? You wanna roll? Doctah Dan's the man gonna satisfy your soul. *Yeah*. Now you kids apply the south end of your epidermis to the upper side of those seats and open your mouths and say *ah*, 'cause the show is *ah*-bout to begin. From New Yawk City, what they call the Big Apple only 'cause they *never* seen Dayton, Gee recording artists whose big hit 'Cryin' Time' Doctah Dan was the first and the fastes' in the central Ohio valley to spin ... Frankie and the Runabouts, toot toot, c'mon, c'mon."

We did the standard show in Dayton, no surprises and no frills. The only thing different was having the Robins on the lineup, but we often had local groups pad out the show, so that was nothing special. It was our last performance—the end of the tour and, as it turned out, the last time the Runabouts ever played together—but the audience didn't know that and we didn't put any extra spin on the ball because of it. We did our set, which went over well, and then, because we were also the tour band, we stayed on stage for the Hi-Glows, a black quintet that did Drifters sort of material, and the Robins, with whom we'd done about an hour of rehearsal before the show. They did a couple of their own songs—that is to say garbage Doctor Dan had written for them—which the audience knew and really cheered for, and a thing the Chantels had made into a hit called "Maybe," with that great hook on the end, "maybe baby, you'll love me some day," and something else I don't remember.

Ritchie was next, working with his own guitar and Eddie's drummer and bassist backing him up. He started with "Come On, Let's Go," and that got the kids up on their feet, clapping and cheering, and they didn't sit down again till he was halfway into "Donna." He did something else and finished off with "Bamba," which had everybody hanging from the fixtures, natch. Ritchie, if he'd lived, he'd have been ruined, probably, smothered in show biz the way so many of the others were, either smothered by it or ground down by it, but the way he was then, that night and all through the tour, both legs of it, he was still untouched, raw, filled with sex and toughness. Eddie was like that, too, of course, except he'd been around for some time already and was a pro. They were both young, not a hell of a lot older than we were—though *everybody* was older than me—but somehow Cochrane seemed like a grown man, like a cat who'd been around and seen a hell of a lot. Ritchie was closer to us, somehow, just a kid, with a big hurt.

We came back on stage to back up the next act, the Bar-Keys, a stomping, hand-clapping white group modeled on Danny and the Juniors. They did some Juniors stuff and a Del-Vikings song, none of which was a shade on the original, and one tune of their own which had a good hook but nothing else. Then Cochrane came on, with his own backups, and we split. Eddie always picked the audience up in his hands, spun them around and blew them away. That's the kind of act he did. They were up on their feet through it all, clapping, pounding their feet, yelling. Between songs, Doctor Dan scooted out on stage like a fat water beetle, waving his arms in the air and bellowing into the mike, "Doctah Dan knows what ails ya, he knows what's *good* for ya, too. Open your mouths now and say *AH*."

Eddie was the only one on the show who ever did an encore but sometimes, if the vibes were good, he'd call Ritchie out to join him. They were good this night and he did, and, I guess because it was the last night, he called us out too, so there were four guitars, two basses and two drum sets on stage, plus a piano, a hell of a lot of noise, and, though Eddie hadn't asked them, Doctor Dan pulled the Robins out with him and they stood on the side, the three girls looking embarrassed and the big bear with arms like horrible caterpillars in the red plaid sleeves of his sports jacket around two of them, bellowing along as we did a souped up "Summertime Blues."

It was a great way to end the show, to end the tour, and we were all feeling good backstage. "Party at the station, party at the station," Doctor Dan was yelling. "Come on, the Doctah knows what's good for ya, ain't that right, girls? Cool sailin' ahead, daddy-os."

We all piled into the school bus and followed his big, bright red wagon with the station's call letters emblazoned on its doors across downtown Dayton, the Doctor occasionally leaning on his horn, a brassy beacon for us to follow through the deserted, dark streets.

The station had its offices and studios on the ground floor of an old but spiffy looking brick building with a glassy lobby that seemed to have been designed especially for raucous music and bleating deejays, their jingles and hype spilling out from behind wide polished wood double doors bearing the letters WDAY in foot-high, gleaming black metal. On the rest of the building's six storeys, according to the directory between the elevators, were an insurance agency, a bunch of doctors and dentists, a wholesale jeweler, an architect and a handful of mysterious sounding companies with names that offered no clue as to their business or purpose: Acorn Associates, Birnbaum & Co., Day-Cal Industries.

Inside the big doors off the lobby, the party was already going full tilt when we arrived. A clutch of shiny-faced men congregated around a girl with bright red hair and zebra-striped pedal pushers as she languidly rotated a hula hoop on her hips. More than a dozen chattering people with drinks in their hands perched on the edges of desks or on a couple of scrawny sofas set against walls papered with gaudy concert posters: station managers and accountants in gray flannel suits, deejays in open screaming shirts, office girls and secretaries with short curly hair and wide red mouths in tight skirts and blouses open to the third button, a couple of middle-aged women with elegant hairdos in evening dresses and expressions on their flushed faces that alternated between excitement and embarrassment. Music and jive from the late shift deejay working in a studio behind a padded door poured

83

through a tinny speaker and, above the door, red electric letters spelled out "on the air."

"Hey, hey, the *doc*tah's here, let the festivities com*mence*," Dan bellowed, and into this group, which just comfortably filled the office, we crashed, about three dozen sweaty musicians and hangers-on, already high from the show. "Let me at those oarsy durveys. Now you take your medicine like men, men," he ordered, gesturing to a long table laid out with a good spread of food, the station's reward to us for having made it a bundle of money: cold meats and shrimp on ice, salads, trays of pungent canapés and bowls of sweet pickles and the kind of tasteless, airy rolls you find throughout the Midwest. And lots to drink, cases of beer and a row of liquor and mixer bottles.

"Aw *right*," Reno said, flinging his jacket on a chair and rolling his shoulders like he was in the ring getting ready for a Golden Gloves fight. "Take cover, girls, we has arrived." Within minutes, the noise level was almost what it had been at the auditorium.

The party went on for a couple of hours, not unlike a bunch of others we'd been to in other cities. The deejays always liked to show off, letting the acts see what great guys they were, letting the station managers and other bosses see how tight they were with the acts. It didn't cost the station much and it might pay off in the future, the next time a tour came through. And everybody had a good time.

A little after 1 AM, Doctor Dan jumped on a desk, doubled his big fists in front of his mouth and sang a trumpet fanfare that silenced the room and drew everyone to him. "This party is *lif*eless, good folks, lifeless an' gettin' *terminal*. What the good Doctah pre-scribes is *el*evator races." The girls squealed with delight, clapping their hands, and the other deejays gathered around, grinning. Most of the suits had gone home and everybody who was left was pretty drunk or close to it.

"Elevator races? Man, you crazy," Valens said, somberly,

unwrapping himself from a sofa where he and one of the skirts had been getting to know each other better. In his soft-collared sports shirt and maroon velour jacket, bulging over those shoulders of his, he looked more like the high school football player he'd been than the star he was becoming. He was seventeen, just a few months older than me but about twice as wide. He had taken to wearing a sort of Bill Haley curl on his forehead and in the last hour it had gone limp, trailing down toward his right eye like a fern frond.

"Naw, c'mon, man, trust the old doctah. This is the real thing, this gonna be *fun*, you watch now."

Most of us trooped out into the brassy lobby behind Doctor Dan, the noise of the party spilling out of the station with us. The old building had been given a pretty thorough facelift, but nothing had been done to the elevators other than polishing the brass. They were the old-fashioned kind, two of them side by side with small triangular glass windows on the outer doors and inner doors that were like folding cages. They had hand controls so you could make them go slower or faster and stop at each floor, and little wooden folding seats where the elderly black men who operated them during the day sat in their baggy uniforms.

The idea of the race was that two people or teams, as long as the weight was more or less equal, would start at the basement and zoom up to the top floor, quick as they could, then down again, the first one through the course the winner, obviously. Doctor Dan and the other deejays had played this game before and thought it was great fun, and Dan himself boasted of being the champion, holder of the record, something less than two minutes, which we all had to admit seemed pretty fast for those kind of clunkers, which always take forever when you're waiting for one.

People took turns going up and down, some of them several times but once was plenty for me. I'd been drinking beer all evening and when I came down I felt like my stomach was full of mud sandwiches, my head full of butterflies. Besides, I was getting on famously by this time with one of the Robins, not the lead singer but one of the others, a mulatto called Renee with skin not much darker than mine. She was wearing gold earrings with double hoops that jangled when she moved her head, and one of those little sundresses with petticoats under the skirt and flounces along the bosom—the hell with the weather outside, she was dressing summer. The neckline swooped down to just below her hair and bent into a smooth curve like the hull of a boat across her upper breasts, which pressed tight against it, making my throat close up every time my eyes strayed in that direction. She was probably a couple of years older than me but because I was so tall nobody ever seemed to guess how young I really was, and the air was getting thick and steamy around us, the way it does before a lightning storm. We were giving each other meaningful looks, though it wasn't clear what they meant, and I kept thinking about Doctor Dan's thick hands and what he'd said about the best-sellers. That made me excited, because I'd think about my own hands running over her breasts, then I'd think of his again, those big sweaty-palmed paws, and feel a little sick.

Everybody who'd come out to the lobby took a turn, and most drifted off, back into the station, but Dan and another deejay, a skinny cat with a bad complexion called Bobby B., were still going strong, and so were Otis and Reno and Eddie, who could be pretty wild when he got drunk. The three of them were about equal in weight to the two deejays, and the two elevators kept whizzing back and forth, up and down, first one team winning, then the other. Renee and I, because we were practically the only ones left in the lobby, were the judges.

"Man, these dudes are *weird*," she said, giving me one of her looks, and I didn't know whether she was including me, or excluding me, which could be worse.

"Two months on the road, it'll do it to ya," I said.

"Yeah, but what's *Dan's* excuse?"

"I don't think he needs one."

"That's no lie."

The two elevators came to a thumping halt, the one with the deejays in it slightly ahead of the other, and they came stumbling out, yelling at the top of their lungs, "We *did* it, we're the champs, can't *nobody* beat the doctah." The skinny guy's eyes were popping and his face was sweating and red, the acne scars a vivid white.

From the other elevator there was a thumping noise, as if someone had been sent flying, and when the doors folded open Otis was lying on the floor, nursing his elbow. "Ow, man, I've had enough of this fuckin' shit."

We helped him up and out of the elevator and he seemed okay, just bruised along the elbow, wincing when we touched it. As it turned out, it was cracked, though he didn't know that until a couple of days later, when he was back in New York and had it x-rayed. He had to wear a cast for a month or more, and I suppose that had a lot to do with him drifting away from music, not that Otis was ever all that great a hand. He played decent rhythm, sometimes sounding like he had mittens on, but mostly he liked to sing. By the time he could play again, the band was all shot to hell and gone.

"My fuckin' funny bone's fuckin' wrecked," he kept saying, tears streaming down his cheeks, which were puffed up with a mixture of pain and laughter.

"C'mon, man, you need some med'cine to dull the pain," Reno said, steering him back to the party.

"Yeah, man, *med'*cine," Dan called after them. "Doctah Dan'll cure his ills. Gave'm some *chills*, din I?"

"Shut the fuck up, man, or I'll take away your fuckin' license," Reno shot back, glaring.

Dan shrugged his shoulders, raising his big hands in a gesture of innocence and surprise, the crooked teeth flashing in his gaping mouth. Eddie was leaning against the wall opposite the elevators and let his feet slide out from under him on the slick tile floor. "I don' need no fuckin' elevator to go up 'n down. See how easy I go down?" He winked and his wide, pegged pants billowed up like parachutes as he sank. He settled down with his back against the wall, legs stretched out, laughing, a beer bottle in one waving hand. "Hey, who won that las' fuckin' race, anyways?"

"We won, the good doctah won," Dan said.

"Like hell. We were *miles* ahead of you."

"Like hell yourself." The deejay stuck out his chest belligerently. He'd taken off his sports jacket and tufts of sandy hair curled aggressively from the front of his electric blue velvet shirt, which was stained maroon under the arms. "What about it, timekeeper? Who won that las' heat?"

"It was a tie," I said. Suddenly, I felt really tired: drunk, bored and tired of the whole thing. Renee's hand was on my arm, and that's all it was, just *on*, but it felt like it was tugging, pulling me away, to someplace I couldn't imagine.

"Tie like hell," Doctor Dan bellowed. "Hey, timekeeper, you been keepin' time?"

"Nope."

"Nope? Why the fuck not?"

"I don't even have a watch."

"Aw, shit." He turned to the other deejay, who had flopped into the frayed leather chair between the elevator doors and was staring at his shoes with a dazed expression. He poked his shoulder. "Bobby, you got your watch. C'mon, man, you time me, the old doc's goin' for a new record."

He wobbled uncertainly in front of the elevators, which hung open like the beckoning caverns in that story about the lady and the tiger, then lurched into one of them, propping the weight of his back against the rear wall. "Now watch, daddy-o, watch this. I'm gonna go down, down to the basement, right? Then up, all the way, then back down here, okay? You got that? You got the watch, Bobby? Okay, when I say go, you start timin', right, dad?"

"Right, right." The skinny guy's eyes were closed, but he had his arm raised, the watch on his wrist cocked toward his face.

I took Renee by the arm and started steering her back toward the party, but she resisted. "Wait, I wanna see *this*."

Doctor Dan hunched his shoulders and blew on his fingertips, like Ollie Hardy preparing to crack a safe. He hunched over the hand controls. "Okay, man ... GO!"

The outer door stuttered shut and the elevator lurched to a start, went down, where it paused, then up past us and we could see Dan's big face grinning at us through the small glass windows. The car went up and we watched the brass needle pointing out the floors as it went, faster now with only one passenger than it had gone before, up, to the top. The brass needle quivered for a moment before the elevator started its quick slide down, slowing just a fraction between the second and first floors. Then it thumped to a halt and the door jerked open.

"Wha' was it? How'd the doctah do, daddy-o?"

Bobby peered at his watch, his mousey face screwed. "Le's see, wait a second ... one minute, forty-seven seconds. 'Xactly."

"You call that fast?" Eddie taunted from his spot on the floor. A shadow falling on his face turned the dimple in his chin into a dark hollow filled with danger and promise.

"Aw, shit, tha's just two friggin' seconds slower'n the god-damn record," Dan whined. He waved a beefy hand at Bobby, who was starting to walk away. "Wait a secon', dad, will ya? I'm gonna do it one more time, okay? I know how to get more speed outta this friggin' thing." He hunched over again. "I'll show you fast, Mr. Coch-sucker-rane." He grinned to show he was kidding. "Okay, Bobby, you ready, man? GO!"

Renee and I gave each other a look and this time she nodded.

Dave Margoshes

As we walked toward the station, we could hear the elevator car settle into the basement with a lurch, then whiz past on its way up. We were just opening the doors when we heard a kind of *zzzzzzzz*, a sick whining, immediately followed by a rushing sound like that of a vacuum cleaner being turned on. We ran back but there wasn't anything we could do—the cable had broken and the elevator was falling. We just stood there as it went by, but we could see Dan's face, sick and pathetic, through the little windows as he zoomed past us. The control lever had come off in his hand.

"Jeezuz," Bobby whispered.

"Call *me* a cocksucker," Eddie mumbled. "Ha!"

There was a terrific crash when the car hit bottom and a cloud of dust came pouring out from the edges of the door into the lobby. We all went running down to the basement, Renee and I and a bunch of others drawn from the party by the noise, the skinny deejay leading the way, even Eddie, ambling along at his own pace and grinning like the whole thing was his personal doing. The outer elevator door had sprung open from the impact and the inner door of the cage was crumpled, the car itself sitting sort of lopsided. Dan was sprawled inside like a collapsed Jack-in-the-box, his body a parody of his own crooked grin, his legs crumpled up beneath him, in a puddle of plaster and shattered glass and his own urine, his face red as a thumb that's been jammed in a door, singing at the top of his lungs, "Hey, hey, Doctah Dan's the man, the man's got the cure, the cure for sure, he'll fix your ills, won' send no bills." His legs were both busted, but he was so far out of his mind I don't think he was feeling a thing. When they got him to stop singing, all he was interested in was how fast he'd gone and he was really pissed off at Bobby for losing track of the time in the commotion. "That was a record run for friggin' sure, ain' that right, daddy-o? Ain' that right?"

"The fucker's got heart," Eddie said, turning toward the stairs. "Give him that."

We stood around in the crumpled elevator trying to keep Dan

still until the ambulance came, listening to him raving on, and I looked up and saw the trap door on the roof of the car had come off and you could see straight up the shaft. The light at the bottom, where we were, cast its glow only to about the first floor; after that, the shaft was a corridor of blackness broken only by cracks of light slivering in around the doors of each landing like rimes of thin neon, and one lonely, naked lightbulb hanging like an aloof star at the very top, where the pulleys were. I could imagine the cables now swinging idly. For some reason, it made me think of that night in Boston, the cold, wavering light outside the theater as we left after the show, people still milling around as we trooped out to the buses, not just girls wanting autographs but tough-faced boys in leather jackets with long greasy hair slicked back, eyeing us like we were cattle at a show, flashing cold, fishy smiles. Joanne and I had looked at each other for a second, without any real meaning, but then she squeezed my hand and I put my seat back and crapped out. I didn't wake up until we got into Montréal, and we didn't hear about what happened until morning when we came down for breakfast, the headline on the stack of papers outside the coffee shop screaming "Boston Riot: Rock 'n' Roll Show Kills."

The ambulance came and the medics hustled Dan onto a stretcher, ignoring his mumbling and chanting, and had him out of there quickly. Two firemen who came with them glanced around and one of them, a tall, red-haired man who looked like John Wayne, whistled through his teeth. "That fucker's lucky to be alive."

They asked a few questions, then went up to the top floor in the other elevator to check out the cables, and everybody else seemed to drift away. Renee and I stood there in the lopsided elevator car, looking around us, then at each other.

"He's a crazy man," Renee said simply.

I waited a beat. I didn't want to ask but I couldn't stop myself. "I guess he's a real cocksman, though, that right?"

Renee laughed. "If he is, *I* wouldn't know about it. That what's botherin' you, Frankie? Lord, he's a *disc* jockey, honey, mouthin' is his *biz*ness, he's *all* mouth."

I took hold of her and we kissed, first soft and nuzzly, then hard, all tongues and teeth and breath. When our lips got tired we stopped but kept standing there with our arms around each other, and I craned my neck and stared up the shaft with its flickering light at the top and tried to imagine what it would be like if the car had gone the other way, torn loose from its controls and the cables that held it *down*, tied to the earth, and had shot up the shaft, like a rocket being launched, like one of those Sputniks or Explorers being sent up into space. The elevator would have shattered the roof of that old building and kept going up and up, through the atmosphere and stratosphere, until the lights of Dayton faded and all Ohio was just a dark green smudge on the face of the spinning earth, out into outer space, Doctor Dan the first man in space, singing his stupid head off as he went, "open your mouth an say ah, *ah*, AH, AHHHHHH...." We stood there in the clutter and dust, Renee and I, holding onto each other for dear life, until my neck was stiff, and I imagined I could see all the way up that elevator shaft clear to heaven, the sky a clear, naked window in the house of God. There was the face of God, a meaningful look on it just like Renee's, the meaning just as unclear. Beneath my feet, I could feel the earth turning, the long, deep, gentle rhythm of the earth's breathing, the vast, impenetrable earth upon which I was merely a breath. Then I excused myself and went behind the elevator and was sick.

I went home with Renee, but this wasn't one of those notorious rock 'n' roll orgies. I was too sick and she lived with her mother and a bunch of brothers and sisters. She made a bed for me on the sofa in the living room and I zonked out as soon as my head hit the pillow. The next day, everybody seemed to be flying off, Ritchie to L.A., Eddie to New York, the other acts back to wherever they'd come from, the black group to Montréal, I think. The Runabouts went back to New York, too, though on a bus, not a plane, and I gave my guitar to Otis to bring home for me. I didn't want to go back there, not just yet. I was two days away from turning seventeen, and I guess I wanted to see, if I just sort of stuck out my thumb and headed with the breeze, where I'd be on that day. As it turned out, it was New Orleans.

It's funny the way things turn out. The boys went home and Reno had a draft notice waiting for him. While we'd been away, he'd turned eighteen and registered by mail, scared and a little proud, the way boys used to be. I don't know why, maybe it had something to do with his sailor daddy, who went down with one of those battleships at Pearl Harbor, but he raced down to join the Marines before the army could grab him. I only saw him once more, when he was home on leave at Christmas time a few years later, it must have been 1963. He hadn't touched a piano for years, he said, all that natural talent just tossed down the drain. Otis went back to school and had to make up a whole year because of the two lousy months he'd missed, then tried a year at City College before dropping out to look for a job and getting scooped up by the draft, found he liked it too and wound up an officer with the paratroops. Juan never had any draft troubles, whether it was his arrest record or his father's politics I don't know, and Mel had flat feet, or so he used to say—"feets, don't fail me nowwwwwwww," grinning and winking as if he'd had something to do with the defects in his bones.

As for me, a few weeks later I was in Cuba, drafting myself, just about getting my ass shot off. My worries with the draft board didn't come till later. I stayed in music—and look at me now, Doctor, wherever you are—but never back to rock 'n' roll. I can't say I really know why, except that, standing in that elevator shaft, I had a different vision of heaven.

7.   A Boat Ride

"**Y**ou get seasick, Francesco?" Guillermo asks me, and old Coney Island hand that I am, not to mention general all around cool cat, fazed by *nada*, naturally I reply in the negative. But this ain't exactly Coney Island. All the Nathan's hot-dogs and frozen custard in the world never made me throw up. The last time I got seasick was on the Staten Island ferry, when I was seven or eight, but this ain't the Staten Island ferry either, not by a long shot.

Our boat—it looks exactly like the fishy old tub Humpty Bogart drives around in *To Have and Have Not*—is breaking its neck against the fearsome sea somewhere in the Gulf of Mexico, chugging south through thin late afternoon haze on its way to Cuba, and I've taken refuge in the dimly lit cabin, wiping the spray from my face. I was outside, watching the gray salty world go by (and up and down) when I felt my stomach buy a ticket on the Cyclone and I figured I'd better have something other than just my feet beneath me or I was gonna be in trouble real quick. The heavy reek of engine oil and dead fish may wind up being worse but for the moment things are under control.

I'm sitting on a filthy, splintery crate of rifles—M1s and other nasty pea-shooters—my elbows propped up on another crate, this one filled with ammunition and grenades left over from Korea and even older disagreements. Who knows, some of them may even still work. The crates have the words "Lucky Louisiana Dried Fish" stenciled on them. They're bigger than coffins, of course, but I can't help noticing they're of the same general shape.

It still knocks me out how I got here. There haven't been any romantic sea voyages in my fortune cookies lately.

Since the band split up, though, I've been on the move, via thumb power, and, once, for a short ways, hopped freight. I've always wanted to see the South, where so much of Harlem seems to have sprung from, and now I have. They can keep it, thanks. Harlem's bad 'nuff. But there are a few bright spots, and New Orleans is one of them, especially in the dead of December.

I rolled into the town four days ago, all bright-eyed and ready for a walk on the wild side, just another hillbilly boy in from the bayous eager for the bright lights and painted ladies of the big city, which was all lit up like Broadway in honor of some pagan rite I didn't quite catch the drift of. I beat it on down to the Quarter, as they say here, checked into what must be the seediest hotel in the world, on a street called Ursulines, and after the sun went down and the moon came up went on out to let the sin seep into me.

The jazz down here is so thick you can smell it, you can *cut* it, if'n it don't cut you first. Pops would say he'd died and gone to heaven (which I devoutly pray is not what's gonna happen to *me* in the next day or two).

But nothing ever happens the way you expect, that's what Pops always says.

I walk into a bar, thinking *spades, Creole, jazz, bourbon, chittlins*, and wind up drinking rum and trading Spanish dozens with a Cuban cat no older than me and half his damn body blown away.

I'm sitting at the bar, wrapped around a beer and listening to chatter, because the sweet music that'd been blowing in my ear when I walked down the street and pulled me in this place quit the second I sat down. "Takin' a wee break," the trumpet player says, this thin gray-faced cat who must eat horse for breakfast and where he gets his wind I don't know. "Back in five or dime."

Okay. The beer tastes good, the bartender, who is big as a house and black as a coal box with teeth like piano keys, there's that many and they're that big, doesn't seem to mind that I'm a few years shy of legal age here, and the place *smells* like nothin' I've run into this side of 125th Street, except even sweeter, and there are some *exceptionally* attractive young ladies around and about, brushing up against each other and anybody else that's moving— including me—it's that crowded in the place, and I must confess I'm seriously eyeballing one of them and not paying attention to much else when I hear this squeaky *"Que pasa, amigo?"* and feel this warm breath on my ear.

I turn around and here's this kid, skinnier than me, which is going some, but as tall, with moist-looking olive skin, tangled black hair tufted over his ears and neck and the right sleeve of his shirt pinned up from elbow to shoulder where everything below the elbow is missing.

"Hey, man," I say.

The scarecrow gives me a serious look, like that wasn't the answer he expected but it isn't *completely* wrong. "You Carlos?"

"No, man," I say, "Frankie." And then, because he's clearly a spic of some kind, I add: "Francesco." It's been so long since I've used that name or been called it by anybody other than Pops, it sounds funny, but it makes the kid break into a grin.

"Sorry, *amigo*, thought you wuz somebody else. Francesco." He extends his left hand, which confuses me for a second, but I finally grab it with my right and we do an awkward shake. "I'm Guillermo. You Cuban? Now I look close, you don't *look* Cuban."

I laugh. "PR. Puerto Rican. From New York."

"Oh, yeah? You one a those crazy *separatistas* that machine-gunned Congress? *Muy cojones*, those guys." He breaks into a wild, sort of syncopated laugh.

We jive some more, English and Spanish, and when we see some people get up from a table across the room we head over there and I see Guillermo is limping. I look down and he seems to have feet at the end of both legs, but he's walking like one of these windup mechanical men that funny old guy hawks around Times Square sometimes, listing first to one side, then the other. He's wearing this frilly white shirt that's got half his breakfast and whatever he had to eat yesterday on it, shapeless khaki pants and pointy-toed shoes that must pinch like hell, and it occurs to me maybe it's the shoes that make him limp, they would me. When we sit down, a waitress comes over, transfixing me with her breasts bulging against the low neckline of her tee-shirt when she leans over, and before I can say anything, he's ordering a couple of rums. "White rum," he tells her strictly, "*Cuban* rum."

We chitchat away like a couple of old *amigos* and have a couple of these sensational rums, which is like nothing I've ever had before and is making me dizzy, my face hot, and Guillermo laughs, saying something to the effect that my *padre* must have had weak lead in his pencil—he should see Pops! Either that or I got skimmed milk from my *madre's* breasts, he says, and even though any kind of talk about mothers always hurts I swallow it and shoot back that at least my folks taught me how to dress myself and even—this rum really is getting to me—not to misplace pieces of my body. We're having a jolly old time when this other cat joins us, this *is* Carlos, and I can see why Guillermo might have mistaken me for him since, as it turns out, they haven't met but have been described to each other. Carlos is about my height and build and coloring, but his hair is slicked back with bear-grease into a slushy duck's ass and he's dressed like a Times Square pimp, with shiny black shoes, the toes even pointier than Guillermo's, pin-striped draped and pegged pants like Pops used to wear when he had an uptown gig, and the same kind of frilly white shirt as Guillermo's. In Cuba, they tell me, everybody wears these things, which are called *guayaberas*—except his is white as an Ipana smile. He flashes us a black-toothed grin, sits down and he and Guillermo promptly ignore me and begin talking machine-gun fast in Cuban Spanish I can't follow except for a word here and there.

After awhile, still another cat comes over to the table, this one a friend of Guillermo's, just as scrawny and young looking, even though he's got this wispy beard that makes his face look like a peach, wearing the same kind of khaki pants but heavy, dusty boots, bright red and blue sports shirt and a white cowboy hat over his long greasy hair, which is almost shoulder length. Guillermo introduces him as *El Vaquerito*, the little cowboy, and after everybody has shaken hands, which they spend just a couple seconds on before tearing back into the breakneck conversation, the new cat included but me still ignored, it strikes me for the first time that nobody uses last names. Suddenly, through the rummy fog, it comes to me that these guys are *fidelistas*, and that the topic of the conversation I am only getting bits and pieces of is guns.

Then something very funny happens, one of those moments when the world seems to stop spinning, know what I mean? Just for a fraction of a second, everything seems to stop, there's dead silence—I mean, everybody stops talking to take a breath every once in awhile, and the odds against it happening to everybody in a room at the same time are astronomical, but still it *can* happen, and that's what must have happened here, in this crowded bar-room on Bourbon Street where the band, after cooking away through most of our powwow, is taking another wee break. Dead silence, the world motionless on its axis, and everyone's heart—I mean everyone at our table—skipping a beat. Then, just as suddenly, everyone around us is yapping away again, their lungs refilled with air, even the friggin' jukebox is blaring away, but everybody at our table is silent, and these three sets of eyes are suddenly on me, Guillermo's and *El Vaquerito*'s both a little bloodshot, Carlos' sharp and glittering as shark's teeth.

"Who *is* this guy?" Carlos asks, in Spanish, slow enough I can make out every word.

There's a pause just long enough for me to conjure up a vision of a knife slitting my throat, my body being dumped in some smelly, jazz-smelling Quarter back alley, then Guillermo says: "Oh, this here's my cousin, Francesco. From New York. It's okay, he's one of us."

One of us. I don't even know who *us* is, but I is one of them, and I can't explain it but a thrill runs up my spine and over my shoulders like the cool fingertips of some sexy lady were sliding down my back. I don't know why Guillermo has included me, but I don't correct him.

Then the machine-gun chatter starts back up, the eyes go back to business and I'm ignored again. The waitress goes by and I order more rums. Somebody, I think it's Carlos, but I could be wrong because things are already starting to go hazy, produces cigars, big fat Havanas, natch, and everybody lights up, including yours truly, who's never had anything thicker than a little white lie between his lips.

Things get really hazy after this, so I can't say exactly how it happens, but the money I'd put down in advance on my flophouse room is wasted 'cause I wake up the next morning on the floor of a kitchen that is southern US cockroach breeding central. My head is the size of a watermelon, one that's just about to split open, it's that ripe, and when I move my arm to reach up and hold it, about a thousand of the awful motherfuckers scurry across the floor. The thought that some of them must have been *under* me makes me feel like puking, and I would except I don't know where to do it and I've got just enough control to stop it. Gritting my teeth makes me conscious of the fur growing on them and turning my attention to how that could have happened makes my head all that much riper. I'm a fuckin' mess.

There's a few other people on the floor—we each have a blanket and a rolled-up towel or jacket for a pillow—and they start to stir when I get up, complete with moans and groans, and stumble out in search of a bathroom. On my way, I pass through a living room, where I see a few more sleeping bodies scattered about—Guillermo on a sofa, his sad, twisted body looking like a question mark, others on the bare floor—and past the open door of a bedroom, where at least two people are crammed together on a mattress on the floor. There is no other furniture in the place, which, as it turns out, I've completely explored now that I've come to a bathroom door, which is slightly sprung from its hinges but I'm able to wedge shut so I can throw up in peace. The fact that it is the morning of the day before Christmas, which I remember when I see the scrawny tree propped up in the living room waiting to be tinseled, doesn't make me feel any better.

I feel, in fact, about the way I do now as the boat takes a wave and lurches under me, the naked light bulb swinging over my head flickering and hissing. The soft murmur of Guillermo's and Vaccy's voices drift down to me here in the cabin where the stench of dead fish is becoming unbearable, and I swallow back the bile in my throat and focus my eyes on the words stenciled on these gun coffins I'm sitting on, "Lucky Louisiana Dried Fish," reading them over and over.

I've been thinking about my cousin Rhoda and her pal Slimy Sid back at good old Music and Art expounding on Cuba and Castro. "This is the *future*, babes," I remember Sid saying at one of those Trot meetings Rhoda used to drag me to, and we all nodded gravely, as if we had just encountered the Revealed Word. The future—wow, and I'm part of it! Thinking too about Pops in Spain, the little he's ever talked about it. His face flashes into my mind, but it's blank and I can't tell what kind of expression he'll have when he hears the news that I'm in Cuba, fighting with the rebels, or gunrunning for them, at least. It might be pride and satisfaction but it could just as easily be disgust. With Pops, you never can tell.

That pad I woke up in turned out to be rented by Guillermo and about half the Cubans in New Orleans, which is sizable, though *El Vaquerito* isn't one of them. Later in the morning, Guillermo and I took a city bus across town to a place by the docks to meet the little cowboy and he filled me in. He—Guillermo, that is—is a lieutenant in the 26th of July Movement, which is Castro's bunch.

"Kind of young to be a lieutenant, ain't you, *amigo?*" I ask him, but he just laughs, showing me this mouthful of greenish teeth.

"In Cuba, all the *old* lieutenants are *batistianos*," he says.

He got shot up pretty bad about a year ago and has been out of action since then, working in Havana and elsewhere organizing underground. A couple of months ago, he was sent to New Orleans to arrange shipments of guns—Miami has been the main source of supply but, with victory near, he says, the US coast guard has tightened its grip around that city. He's already sent a couple of boatloads over and on this foggy hangover day he's making final arrangements for another load, which will be leaving in a couple of days. Carlos is some wheel in the Miami exile community and is part of the group that's supplying the stuff—God only knows where it comes from and neither he nor Carlos is saying. *El Vaquerito*, who is also a lieutenant in the Castro bunch, Guillermo says, came over from Cuba the night before to deliver some money and lend a hand. Both of them are eighteen, just a year older than me. Guillermo took to the hills when he was sixteen; the cowboy's been at it since he was fifteen.

"And you, Francesco, *amigo*, you like to come along?" Guillermo asks me as we stroll down a tough-looking street at the end of which a pier studded with shrimp boats juts into the oily Mississippi. Guillermo "strolls" just like somebody doing a parody of Popeye the sailor man, his upper body dipping with each step of his bum leg, the pinned-up arm jerking with the motion.

"Me? Sure," I say, without really thinking, an invitation like that the last thing I was expecting.

"It's dangerous," Guillermo says with understatement, as if the pretzel his body's been turned into is just an inconvenience, but he raises the stump of his right arm as a reminder. "People get killed."

"Not me," I grin, all mouth and balls, no brains. "Shit don't stick to me, I'm that slick."

He puts his hand on my shoulder and gives a little squeeze, and a shiver of fright races through me. "Even when you shit your pants, Francesco?"

The cowboy, he's not so hot on me coming along but Guillermo outranks him somehow.

"*Loco*," Vaccy says, spitting a big gob of phlegm speckled with what looks like blood on the wooden planks of the pier. Vaccy is what I privately call him, though doing that to his face would risk the loss of my balls. "The *yanqui* will just be in the way," he complains in Spanish.

Guillermo shakes his head, insisting—for reasons better known to him than me—that I'm *un americano con cojones* who will be useful as a translator should we run afoul of the coast guard. The thought of this both scares and thrills me.

Vaccy spits again and offers the opinion that Guillermo is a *bobo*, a moron, but that he is helpless against such stupidity. The three of us walk to the end of the pier where an old man with a white beard is sitting in the sun fishing, his legs dangling beneath the railing.

This old man looks more Chinese than Cuban, he's that small and yellow-skinned, all wrinkled up like hands that have been in water way too long, his eyes narrow slits from gazing at the sun. Guillermo asks him what's biting and the old man mumbles something, gesturing toward a plastic bucket filled with nothing but holes. Vaccy asks him what he's using for bait and the old man gestures again, this time toward a tackle box. The three of us squat around the box and open it. Inside, wrapped in musty newspaper, is a hand grenade.

"Holy shit," I say, but Vaccy gives me a dirty look and Guillermo shushes me with a finger to his lips. The two of them handle it in turn, like jewelers eyeballing a diamond. A few yards away, a for-real Chinese man and a couple of skinny kids are tossing their lines off the pier, yapping a mile a minute. Guillermo and Vaccy are careful to shield the object of their inspection with their bodies.

"*Bueno*," Guillermo says, pounding the old man on the back and giving him a wink. The old man ignores us and, after a few minutes, we amble off.

"How do you know it'll work?" I ask when we're far from anyone's earshot.

"Don't worry, Francesco, we know," Guillermo says. "We're *soldatos*." But I notice Vaccy giving me an appraising glance, as if impressed that I would have thought of such a thing.

Three days have passed and I am practically an old N'Orleans hand, having spent quite a bit of time prowling around it while Guillermo and the cowboy took care of the skullduggery. I had a Cuban Christmas at Guillermo's place, bare surroundings but a feast just the same, roast pork and yams and other good stuff, and a jolly good time, just as prescribed by all the ads. The next day there was some hocus pocus with Carlos that I didn't fully dig and don't *want* to, and now here we are, halfway to Cuba, I would guess.

If all goes well, we'll be in Cuba tonight, landing on the northern coast at a place called Pinar Del Rio, which is west of Havana, a couple of hours drive away but in the mountains and somewhat remote. M-26-J is in control of the area and the idea is for us to land at the dock of a sugar plantation that the rebels have free run of at night. If we're stopped by the coast guard, I'm to say I'm a rich New Yorker on vacation and I've chartered the boat and its crew—Guillermo, Vaccy and the captain—for fishing. The hope is they'll hear my New York accent and be satisfied with that and won't insist on boarding, where they'd get too close a look at lop-sided Guillermo to buy him as a fisherman. If it's the Cuban navy, that'll be something else again, but Guillermo says that's unlikely to happen. He says the war will be over soon and lots of soldiers and sailors are shifting their sympathies.

The *plan* is for me to go back to New Orleans in the boat with Ricky, the guy who owns it, who is a genuine fisherman when he isn't making pleasure excursions like this one, but I've been work-ing on Guillermo to let me stay with him. I like this idea of me being a rich New Yorker on vacation from some fancy-ass college or boarding school—me, Frankie!—I've been telling him that if that story could fool the coast guard maybe it could be handy in Havana too, for a little while at least.

Guillermo has just stuck his head in the cabin to see how I'm doing and I pull on an oilskin and drag my ass up on deck to shoot the shit with my *companaros*, which is prudent. Vaccy always gives me shifty looks if I'm out of sight for too long. He's still not crazy about having me along, but at least he treats me civilly. Like a lot of young Cubans, he's nuts about rock and roll and when he heard about the band, when he heard the name "Alan Freed," whose show they can get in Havana if the wind is right, he tells me, he began showing me some respect. He also seems to get a kick out of the jiving Guillermo and I do, though he doesn't lower himself to join in.

"Miami," he says solemnly, lifting his fuzzy chin toward the smudge of lights just visible far in the distance as we churn out of the gulf around the hook at the bottom of Florida and into open sea where, to my surprise, the waves are calmer, but the chance of running into the coast guard greater.

I grit my teeth and tell my stomach to be cool and settle in, slumped against a soaking wet bulkhead, my shipmates' soft voices and cigarette smoke spinning around my head like cotton candy. And sure enough, within minutes the lights of a boat come into sight and Ricky kills the motor, plunging us into complete darkness.

"Coast guard," Vaccy hisses.

"Maybe it's just a fishing boat," I suggest, "or a rich *americano*, like me."

Vaccy doesn't bother replying—it's almost pitch dark, but I can still make out the look of disdain on his face. We all but hold our breaths until the lights of the other boat disappear, and, a few minutes later, our engine coughs to a start and we get underway again, this time running dark. "Too bad, Francesco, no chance to be brave," Guillermo whispers beside me, touching my arm lightly.

Sitting on a hatch cover and watching the furry, receding lights of Miami, I find myself thinking about the one other memorable time I've been on a boat: the good old Staten Island ferry, still only a nickel and worth every penny.

I've been on the ferry more than once, of course. Pops used to like to ride it just for cheap kicks, and the boys and I played a gig on the island last year. And there was that time I threw up over the rail, Pops laughing and holding my head, when I was just a kid. But the time I'm thinking about—the *memorable* time—was half a dozen years ago, when I was ten or eleven, and I ran into my "pal" Peter Coonkicker.

Peter's real name is Cooney, one of the small gang of Irish kids—Micks, we called them, or Micmacs; for mackerel snappers—from north of 125th up toward St. Nick's Park who went to P.S. 43 in those days. The Micks were tough, even though they

were outnumbered, and Cooney was called Coonkicker because
"coon" was his favorite word, "kike" coming second only because
there weren't many Jews at 43. Peter was so big and tough, even
at nine and ten and eleven, and so dumb he didn't *care* that calling someone a coon could wind up in him getting his ass kicked
by the kid's big brother and pals. That dumb, but smart enough,
somehow, to dope out I was some kind of Jew, even though I never
stayed home for holidays and I sure don't *look* Jewish, and I sure
never volunteered the information to anybody. Truth is, I look
more like a coon than a kike, but, maybe because he got so few
chances at Jew-baiting, he liked to emphasize that.

He and his potato-eater pals had a corner of the playground
staked out where they'd mill around during recess, glaring at any
teacher who yelled at them to get their asses moving, and taunt-
ing any kids chasing a loose ball that rolled their way. "Hey, kike,
this area's for *real* white people," Peter Coonkicker would yell at
me if I got too close, "not coon spic kikes."

Any one of those words would hurt, but all three of them really made me see red and sometimes there'd be pushing and shov-
ing, and, since Peter outweighed me by twenty pounds or so, I'd
usually be the one who wound up on the ground with my elbows
and knees chewed up.

Then one day, when I was in fourth or fifth grade, the Micks
pushed around the *wrong* coon—a skinny little runt with buckteeth
and a stutter, a sweet boy called David Brown. David went home at
lunchtime with a bloody nose and told his brother about it, his
brother Jimmie, who was just home for a few days on his way from
reform school to out-of-town. That afternoon after school someone
who may have been Jimmie Brown and another guy roared into the
schoolyard in a stolen black Buick boat. Waving shotguns, they
zoomed right up to the potato-eaters' corner, knocking a couple of
them down and scattering the rest. A load of buckshot was blasted
against the school wall, sending a red spray of brick chips and dust

flying, and later there was a crowd of kids around it picking up the shot. The next morning, Mr. Little, the janitor, cleaned up the debris from the blasted bricks but you could see the blackened, chewed-away spot for months afterwards, until the rain washed the gun-powder or whatever it was away, or maybe we just stopped noticing it. None of the Micks was hurt too bad, but most of them didn't come back to 43, transferring to a parochial school. Once, walking up on 8th Avenue near the park, I ran into Peter and a couple of his pals and they chased me halfway through the park, but they could-n't catch me—they were tougher than me, but I was faster. And other than that, I didn't see any of them again.

But a year or two later, on one of the first nice weekends in spring, I was on the Staten Island ferry with Pops, going I don't know where. Pops was inside, having coffee, and I was walking around on the deck, the wind pounding against me like I was a flag, and I came around a corner and there was this kid up against the rail, a white kid about my size in jeans and a brown leather wind-breaker with the fur collar up, a neat windbreaker like I wished I had—I had this plaid mackinaw thing that was okay but wasn't cool. I walked up to the rail and I was so intent on that jacket that I didn't notice until it was too late that the kid wearing it was Peter Coonkicker.

"Hey, shithead," he said.

"Hi," I said, but I didn't return the compliment. Up close now, I could see he was not really about my size—he was two or three inches taller and about half again as thick. Even though it was bit-ing cold up there in the wind, he wore the windbreaker unzipped and I could see the little bit of neck he had extending over his shoulders out of the scooped collar of his polo shirt. He was, I realized, less muscular than I had remembered, but chunkier, his smooth cheeks bright red from the wind, padded with babyfat. I braced myself for what I was certain what come next, a curse of some sort, and then, most likely, a cuff or a grab.

But that didn't happen.

"Where ya goin'?" Peter asked, but it was more of a curious question, like any human being might ask another, than a demand or a challenge.

"Nowheres. Just across and back. My dad and his friends like to ride." There were no friends along but I thought the idea of them might give me some protection. I glanced over my shoulder. "They're right in there."

Peter didn't seem to pay attention. "I'm goin' to visit my gran," he said, his voice dark with dejection. "My folks go *every* Sunday. I don't hafta go every time, my brother and me take turns. This time's my turn." His tone was so unhostile, *almost* friendly, that I realized the ruse about my father and his friends hadn't been necessary. "My gran's got a cat with kittens," he said, brightening, and, to my surprise, began telling me about this cat, a calico, and the neat kittens it had the last time, one of them all black. He said that like being all black was about the best thing a kitten could be.

We stood there on the deck, the wind sucking tears out of our eyes, talking about all sorts of things, not just kittens, until the ferry slowed down and we could see the landing up ahead. Peter even asked about old 43, how was the old place and did Mr. Goldfarb, the vice principal—Gold*fart*, we called him—still fart during assembly.

Then the loudspeaker squawked and a tinny voice said we'd be there in five minutes, that people should get ready to disembark, and Peter said "Gotta go, see ya," and gave me a chummy slap on the shoulder as he turned to leave. I stood there for a second, watching his broad back in that windbreaker retreating down the deck to the stairs, a clumsy fat boy rolling a little from the ferry's motion, and I don't think I was thinking anything, I was that dazed. It wasn't until later, on the ride back when I told Pops about it and he laughed and said "neutral ground," that I began to see what had happened.

"Sure," Pops said. "No turf to protect, no buddies to impress, out here he's got no *reason* to hate you. You're both in the same boat." He laughed again, pleased with himself, and blew smoke from one of his fat French cigarettes over my shoulder.

I nodded my head over my hot cocoa, I could see that, but it seemed to me there was more to it. There weren't just all those "no"s—no this and no that—but something else, something going the other way. There was a connection between us I hadn't known about before, one that hadn't ever had a chance to mean anything. I was someone he *knew*, a *friend* almost, if you stretch the meaning of the word far enough, and, for whatever it was worth, there was something *between* us, a bond so fragile neither of us could have named it or, until that day, guessed at its existence.

All that, and the feeling in me I remember so well from that day on the ferry, comes back to me now, sitting on the deck here with Guillermo and the cowboy, not because of them, really, just because of the salt spray and the wind in my face. Tough guys, both of them, and I don't really know either of them, though we all like each other, Guillermo and me especially, but there is a link between us just like the one there's been for the last few years between the boys in the band, Otis and Juan and Mel and Reno and me, like what's between my cousin Rhoda and me even—*Pops* and me even—this thread of tenderness that not only joins us but wraps around us, not keeping us safe from harm, really, but giving us that illusion. Something that lets us ignore being afraid.

"We be there soon, Francesco," *El Vaquerito* says. He fists one hand and brushes it lightly against my jaw, where a light fuzz has taken root—I haven't shaved for almost a week now and I'm looking more like him all the time. "Our friends on shore will think you're one of us, a *barbudo*"—that's one of the nicknames for the 26 of July rebels, who I guess all have beards. Even though he's said out loud a dozen times he thinks my coming along is a stupid idea, that if there's trouble of any kind I'll be the weak link that could sink them all—and I know he's right—there is something in his voice that tells me he's glad I'm here.

Damned if I know why, but I cling to it.

8. A Freedom Ride

Oh, send me a letter
Send me some mail
Send it in care
Of Burlington Jail

How's that sound? I'd like to be able to sing *Birmingham* Jail, the way the song's supposed to go, but this is Vermont, not Alabama, and I guess I'll have to write a song about it myself.

There isn't anything poetic about the place, but nothing harsh or brutal, either. The walls are no more institutional than the ones we used to deface with graffiti back at good old Music and Art in the Bronx. The bed is more comfortable than some I've slept on lately, and the food is certainly no worse than at the lunch counter that brought me here. I wouldn't be surprised if Woolworth's does the catering for this luxury lockup—now that *would* be poetry. And there's no discrimination in here, either. Fact is, everybody's damn friendly. And I've always heard these New England Yankees are cold and suspicious! Well, *some* are. Yesterday, on the streets of this old city where freedom used to ring (there was a Revolutionary War battle fought not too far from here, I'm told), an old woman with a shopping bag and an umbrella and a pair of fancy-ass poodles on a leash called me a "nigger." But in here, the cops and turnkeys are too polite to even *think* of hurting the feelings of a guest. That didn't stop them from tossing me in a cell, but that was because I had hurt *their* feelings. At least that's the way *they* see it.

Anyway, I've been in worse places and I guess what's bothering me as I sit here cross-legged on an upper bunk, my battered old guitar in my lap and a tin cup of lukewarm coffee by my knee, is that I'm not in a worse place now. I mean, down in Greensboro and those places, people are getting their heads staved in and fired from their jobs, and here I sit, barefoot and burping the taste of the scrambled eggs I had for breakfast. I don't mean I want to be a martyr, but what's right is right, right? That's what the cop said when he took me in. I was crossing the street, alone and innocent, guitar case in one hand, knapsack in the other, heading north toward the outskirts of town and the highway. The crowds were gone and everything *bad* I might have done, anything *illegal*, was behind me, goodness and sanctity clung to me like fuzz on a peach, visible and radiating.

"You know you just jaywalked, dontcha?" the cop said. I hadn't noticed him standing there on the curb until he spoke. He was the same big flatfoot, all belly and shoulders, who'd been giving us the eagle-eye, a noncommittal smile on his face.

"No, I didn't know it, but I guess I did," I said. "I won't do it again."

The cop shook his head, which was round as a melon. "You know I have to take you in, dontcha?"

"For jaywalking? You're shitting me, man."

"Yep. That's illegal here. I know you're not from up about here, so mebbe you didn't know. 'Tis, though. People think it's funny, but we had three pedestrian fatalities last year, that's people killed." He paused and a pair of eyes small and black as watermelon seeds looked me up and down, as if to give me time to make the connection. "Pedestrians doing just like you. It's the motorist's fault, a course, when somebody gets hit, that's what people always *think*, but it's not *really* his fault, now is it? When somebody walks right in front of him?"

"I can see that." I put my stuff down. "But there's no cars coming. I know. I looked both ways, like they teach in school." I smiled.

Big, marshmallowy teeth flashed back in the cop's mouth. "Well, you can't always see everything now, son. Can't see the unexpected. Didn't see *me* now, didja?"

I shook my head. "You got a point there, you surely do." We were getting so folksy, I felt like putting my foot up on a rail and taking a chaw a tobaccy, but there wasn't any rail.

"It's dangerous," my friend said. "Have to make people realize that, dontcha think?"

"I do, for sure, man. I'm glad you pointed it out. I travel a lot— I'm just heading out of town now—and I don't see that kind of concern too often. It's a good thing, makes you *feel* good." I reached down and picked up the guitar. "Thanks again."

He just looked at me like I was some kind of new species. When I reached down for the knapsack, he shook his big head. "You *know* I have to take you in, dontcha?"

I hadn't heard a Vermonter talk until a few days ago and I get a kick out of it. It's not like southern, nothing like New York. Closest I've heard is the way Jack Kennedy and his people talk, like someone squeezed their noses so hard they still haven't opened up. My friend's nose was squeezed even harder. In North Carolina and Alabama, people are getting their teeth spit back at them by big bulldogs drawling tobacco juice and molasses and here I am making polite chatter with this squeeze-nose who keeps smiling and smiling, showing me those marshmallows and trying not to hurt my feelings too much.

"You can't just give me a ticket?" I asked hopefully, my grip tightening on the knapsack strap.

The cop's head bobbed forward and back. "Under some circumstances, I might be able to, sure." Hs eyes cast themselves down on my pack and the guitar. "But seeing as how you're not from around here, and might just not *honor* a ticket. Not that I'm saying you'd actually *do* that, unnerstand, but we have our procedures. No, I guess I have to take you in, let you talk about it to the judge. It's just till Monday."

My heart sank. "Monday? Hey, man, it's Saturday. That's two days away." I guess my voice raised a teensy weensy bit because my friend frowned.

"Judge don't sit Sundays," he said flatly, the smile gone. "You unnerstand, dontcha?"

"Not really," I said. "For jaywalking?"

The cop bit his lower lip. I could see he was stuck.

"Or maybe it's something else," I said.

"What else could it be?" His head bobbed on his shoulders as he gestured me to the end of the street and around the corner, where a black-and-white was parked. When I was in, the guitar case between my knees, he slammed the door and came around and slid in beside me. There was a faint smell of licorice in the car. "You did what you had to do, now we're doing what *we* have to do." He saw the look I gave him. "What's right is right, right?"

So here I am, saving the price of a couple of meals, saving my ribs from the springs of some lumpy motel bed. I had a good sleep, a good enough breakfast and a pleasant enough morning, lying on my bunk all alone in this two-man cell listening to church bells and watching sunlight filtering through the bars—bars!—of my window. Now I'm fooling around on the box, thinking there must be a song in all this. Later I'll do some reading—I always carry some paperbacks in my pack. I'm woofing my way through *Lolita* now, and I've got a crumbling copy of *On the Road* I plan to jump into again. In the morning, they'll take me before a judge who'll wink at the bailiff, tell me about the dangers of jaywalking and fine me twenty bucks. Then I'll pick up where I left off, except that I'll be further from the edge of town and a day and a half of my life will have spun down the drain, like the cigarette butt I flushed down the open crapper in the corner here a minute ago.

Maybe I'll head west after this.

The drunk in the next cell has a hangover. "What in the hell *you* in for?" he asks after giving me a once-over, his voice incredulous.

"Lunch," I tell him, and that's the end of the conversation.

I came up here, I should have told him, to help liberate the edible enumerator of a certain well-known five-and-dime chain store, which is to say integrate the Woolworth's lunch counter. Make no nevermind that there's only as many Negroes in Burlington, Vermont, as you can count on the fingers of your hands. Make no nevermind that those few Negroes that are here can munch at Woolworth's as free and openly as the next guy, get just as much mayonnaise on their collars as they want, long as their dollars are as green as the next guy's. Make no nevermind that in these parts discrimination means knowing what kind of wine to order at restaurants fancier than Woolworth's, bias means the angle on which a seamstress cuts, segregate and integrate are words that rhyme with disintegrate. Make no nevermind about all that. The point is that somewhere in the world, and not *all* that far away, the cousins of Burlington's well-fed Negroes *aren't* able to have a chicken salad sandwich and an orange drink along wif da good ol' white folks, not at no Woolfuckingworth's.

And why should Frankie Stein be worrying his pretty little head about their misfortune? After all, ain't he the one who turned his back on politics, ain't he the one who said *anybody* can make it if they try, ain't he the one who said who wants to eat their shitty chicken salad anyway?

Guilty on all counts, your honor, I'se da one. But, ya know, wha's right is right, right? A man gotta *do* what a man gotta do.

A couple of days ago, I was doin' it at Goddard. It's a little free verse college up the road about fifty miles where they serve red wine in the cafeteria, the girls all wear black tights to gym and the school anthem was written by Thoreau. Sid Marvel and Louise Stink, old high school buddies, both go there.

I'd been hustling around the Village for months, but the folkies were so thick you could braid them together and lay a rug from Bleeker Street to the White Horse, and out in the boondocks, I'd been told, they actually like it better when you're slightly out of tune. So I've been hightailing it, highwaying it, moonlighting it, carrying the word into the countryside, bringing the message to Mary, laying it on the line, making like Johnny Appleseed.

As soon as the leaves started to turn and the air began to take on that heavy, sharp smell that always makes me think of the mother I never knew, I bought a red mackinaw and a sleeping bag and pack at an army surplus on Fulton Street and stuck my thumb out, following my nose, like my Uncle Ira used to prescribe. I had no idea how many colleges there are in New England, little mouse-box places on hills and in valleys where people still talk with their mouths instead of through their noses and their grammar is always correct. They have student unions where you can buy coffee for a dime and donuts for a nickel, and courtyards or plazas where a cat can play his guitar and sing and people will gather around and listen. There's always one in every crowd, an *entrepreneur*, who'll come up with the idea of charging admission.

"Hey, you're good enough to play for money," this cat will say. He's an earnest guy with a wide open face and hair just a little longer than a crewcut. His father runs a hardware store or sells insurance and this cat has told the old man to fuck himself because he doesn't have any principles but there's enough of dad's genes in him to make him smell a buck when there's one within whiffing distance—no, I do him a disservice, not a *buck*, an *opportunity*. But not selling hardware or insurance, not this cat. Me, I'm different. I'm soft, I'm an *idea*, a sellable one. "I know it, man," I tell him. "But I'm shy. You set it up." That's usually all it takes. That evening, I'm playing on a stage in a little theater, or in a frat house rumpus room or an improvised coffee house in a church basement, kids are paying a buck or two to get in, and the hardware man's son is collecting. Later, he gets twenty-five or thirty per cent, out of which he coughs for the room and the beer.

If all else fails, there's always the streets of these college towns, where an enterprising fellow such as myself can make an honest bit of change by sitting cross-legged, as I am now, in front of a bookstore, or a bar, or, if I'm feeling perverse, a bank, playing and singing, the guitar case open beside me so people can toss in a coin if they feel like it. Meal money.

Hard to believe, but I actually make more money than I spend, maybe because I don't spend too much, and every couple of weeks I stop at a post office and buy a money order and send it to Pops to put in the bank for me. And there's other rewards. Sunshine, fresh air. Hell, I get lots of it. Now that spring's here, I spend quite a few nights under the stars—*me*, who was afraid to take off his shoes and go barefoot the first few days that summer I spent at my Aunt Ida's Catskills cottage when I was a kid. But it's rare that I have to waste my pennies on a bed for the night regardless of the weather. More often than not, there's some beer-drinking after the gig and someone will offer to put me up. If I'm lucky, some wide-eyed girl with hair like a silk sheet will ask me where I come from, I'll tell her Saturn and damn if that doesn't do the trick.

But none of that has anything to do with me whiling away a couple of days in Burlington jail except that the Johnny Appleseed trail led me this week to Goddard. And it was there that I got roped into helping to liberate Woolworth's.

Well, *roped into* is putting it a bit too strongly. Asked along. The rope notion comes from the color of the hair—yellow as the kind of twine they use to bundle newspapers—of the girl who was asking.

But first there was Sid and Louise, my advance team. They were pretty much the same as the last time I'd seen them, over a year ago, except Sid had grown a Fu Manchu-style moustache and Louise's hair was even longer, clear down to her ass, which was still cute as hell. To tell the truth, I never cared all that much for either of them. They were my cousin Rhoda's friends, though, so we used to hang around together. Sid always had that holier-than-thou attitude I associate with Trotskyites, at least the ones who seemed to be swarming over Music and Art, and those few I've run into since, with the exception of the ones I met in Cuba, but that was different, I guess, because it was real. Stink was more or less the same, with the added attraction that she thought she was the sexiest morsel on God's green earth. But, cute ass or not, she did have that mysterious foul breath. Still, like them or not, there they were, and I had been in touch with Sid and he'd arranged a gig for me, with some local pickers, some of them not too bad, as it turned out.

During the course of the evening, I made the acquaintance of a certain young lady named Molly, "after Molly Bloom," she said. She's the one with hair the color of yellow twine. Her cheeks are ruddy as a peach and glow with fuzz, her eyes green as a spring leaf. She's the only woman I've ever met who doesn't shave her legs—which are covered with more of that peach fuzz—and she hasn't worn underwear of any kind, she tells me, for three years, because "it upsets the body's natural balance." That's what she says. There is the smell of moist earth to her skin, the smell of new-mown grass to her hair, and her eyebrows are thick as caterpillars. She is positively the healthiest, most wholesome human being I've ever met. She isn't anything at all like Rhoda, but still she reminds me of her all to hell.

In short, she made an impression on me. We stayed up all night talking, just that, and when daylight came she packed a lunch of fresh rolls she got from the dormitory kitchen, fruit and beef she'd dried herself in her windowbox and a bottle of awful wine made by a friend of hers, and we went out into the countryside and tramped through the wildflowers along a stream till we came to a cabin the Goddard kids use as a kind of overland ski lodge. We got a fire going in the nice stone fireplace and we ate the lunch, part of it, and fell asleep. When I woke up, my head was in her lap and the first thing I saw were her long, shimmering legs, and all I wanted to do was reach out and stroke them like a cat.

"Some of us are going to Burlington tomorrow to picket the Woolworth store," she said. We were eating oranges and her voice was thick with the juice.

I had already written a song about what's happening down south so I didn't have to ask her what it was all about. But Burlington? Vermont?

"It's all the same thing," she shrugged. "We can't turn our backs to what they're doing, just because they aren't doing it here, or to us. It's all one long lunch counter." She said this with great seriousness, and when I smiled at the image, she frowned. "That's why it can happen," she said, wiping her mouth and placing her hand on the rug next to mine. "That's why they think they can get away with it. Because you're smiling."

"Okay," I said. "I can dig that. I'll stop smiling."

"Everyone has to stop."

"I'm not everyone."

"No, but you can help pass the word." Again, this was delivered with such seriousness I didn't dare smile. We looked at each other and her gaze was so intense I had to look away.

"Okay, I can do that."

She frowned. When she got up, her skirt rustled like leaves before a storm. She was facing the window, her back to me, and I couldn't help notice how broad her shoulders were. "My father was born in Ireland," she said with bitterness, as if it was him she was about to assail, or the curse of the Irish. "Can you imagine what it's like to pick potatoes until your fingers are bloody?"

Having been in Rhode Island in the fall, where I saw Mexicans with backs shaped like harps in beet fields, I could well imagine. I was about to say so, but she went on so fast I didn't have a chance.

"To work your fingers so numb, your eyes so filled with sweat and tears you pick stones instead of potatoes and cannot tell the difference?" She said that, *cannot*, as if she were reciting at a school play. "To suck on stones when you're hungry and there's nothing else to eat? To stand in front of a factory streaming with men carrying lunchbuckets—in *this* country—and stare at a sign saying Men Wanted, Irish Need Not Apply?"

"At least he could read," I said quickly.

Her back stiffened. "*What?*"

"Your father," I said. "At least he could read."

She wheeled around, her upper lip curled and teeth bared. Her hair swarmed around her head like a beehive.

"Hey, don't lay all that on me," I said. "I'm half Jewish, for Chrissake, if you'll excuse the pun, *and* part Negro. And I grew up in Harlem. My people wrote the book on suffering but I don't go around quoting from it all the time."

"You're not really Jewish," she said.

I laughed. "That's my line. But seriously, the name *is* Stein."

Molly looked at me hard, like she was trying to tell if I was potato or stone. "You don't *look* Jewish," she said, but she wasn't being funny.

"My mother was Puerto Rican." That usually makes a hit—all of *those* people's sufferings combined with all those *other* people's, it's too much for some people to bear, especially some women. I could see it was doing its thing on Molly.

"You don't look Puerto Rican either," she said finally. All the starch had washed from her voice, the way it does from boiled potatoes.

"Well, my *father* is Jewish." I shrugged and laughed. Explanations like that make the world almost seem to make sense. She laughed too and came close, dropping to her knees beside me.

"I thought you made that up, you know, your name."

"Stein? Why would I do that?" I must have looked at her blankly, because she started to giggle.

"You know, for the effect. Sid said...." Her teeth were bared again, but not in anger. She tasted of oranges, and I knew I was staying.

We left next morning a little after nine, in a VW microbus with a JFK bumpersticker on the front, another saying "Let Chessman Live" on the back, driven by an English prof at the college named Horsting. There were eight of us in all, including a girl in the race for the world's plainest and a boy with buckteeth a mule would drool over. Horsting was a tall, lean cat built like a mathematical equation that didn't work, with a face like Charlie Van Doren's, that TV quiz guy who cheated. He was clearly unhappy about something but didn't say what, or much of anything else. Just about his only comments were to caution Sid, Plain Jane and me—I guess I looked Jewish to *him*—to be wary on the picket line because there were anti-Semites *everywhere*.

In the back of the microbus, an argument raged over whether it was good politics to support a guy like Kennedy, who Louise Stink said is a fascist in sheep's clothing, whatever the fuck that means, but some of the others liked. Before the fists started to fly, and when Louise got too close, I hauled out my ax and we sang Pete Seeger songs. Molly has a clear alto sweet as Coltrane's and there was a very intense cat from Boston called Tick, constantly quoting Trotsky and Lenin when he wasn't singing, who had a serviceable bass. Turned out that the lot of them were Trots, including the professor, though he didn't say so himself, and that they constituted the entire Goddard Yipsel chapter. I was the sole dissenter, though I've mellowed a lot and they didn't bother me. Molly is smart enough to know better, I think, but was quite caught in the sway. So was the plain girl, whose father, she confessed, was an unrepentant Stalinist. The boy with the buck teeth, who was actually called Buck, was from somewhere in the South and was sulky with guilt.

By the time we'd parked the bus and gotten ourselves together, it was almost noon and the streets downtown were already lunchtime thick. There was a picket line with maybe a dozen people carrying signs and looking self-conscious weaving back and forth in front of the Woolworth's. Their signs said things like "No More Jim Crow," "Hunger Has No Color" and "The North Is Not Without Sin." The picketers cheered when they saw us. Most of them were students from the University of Vermont, which is here, but one guy had hitchhiked up from a college called Middlebury, and there were a couple of older people including a very with-it, white-haired Unitarian minister who was in charge, along with a black UV chick named Tracy, off of whom sparks were flying as if a flint was being rubbed against her steel edge.

We newcomers picked up signs from a stack and joined the line, trudging back and forth in front of the store, about half a block's length. We were quiet and sheepish at first, eyes to the ground and our free hands stuffed in our pockets, almost as if we were ashamed of ourselves. I had a sudden flash of a demonstration I went to with my father when I was a kid, the awkward shape of the signs the pickets had carried and the funny feeling I'd had that I'd get hit on the head by one of those signs as a picketer wheeled around on the sidewalk.

If Woolworth's was losing any business because of us, it didn't show. People elbowed their way in and out of the store, eyeing us warily as they crossed our line, though the lunch counter, which we could see for a few steps each rotation of the picket, *was* only half full, and people sitting at it kept their heads straight, their eyes away from us, as if they were ashamed too. The big cop who would so amiably bust me later in the day stood by the door, making sure we didn't block it, but smiling amiably at us, as if he was doing duty at a Fourth of July picnic. People gathered across the street to watch us, but they too were amiable, occasionally throwing wisecracks that landed with the softness of feathery snowballs, and whistling at a few of the girls.

After awhile, we picked up some of their mood and relaxed, raising our heads and shaking them at people streaming into the store, making little comments. "Enjoy your lunch," Molly said to everyone who brushed past us. The phrase came slithering out of her mouth at first, like acid from a cracked battery, but soon she was saying it nicely. A woman with a red bandana around her head smiled at her. "Thank you, dear, I will," she said, and despite ourselves we all laughed, even Professor Horsting. The sun shone brightly. We were starting to have a good time. I put my "No More Jim Crow" sign back on the stack and got my guitar and Tracy started to sing, "Ain't nobody gonna turn us around, turn us around, turn us around, ain't nobody gonna turn us around, dear Lord, we're on our way."

It was almost 1 PM when I stopped for a smoke. In more than an hour, the only black face I'd seen was Tracy's sparky one, and I was starting to wonder if we weren't wasting our time. Alabama was one thing, so was Mississippi. This was Vermont and a whole world away from there. It seemed like being mad at the weather in Tahiti because some cold got dumped on Alaska.

What I was thinking must have been readable in my face because a man with a baseball cap shading his eyes came and stood beside the lamppost I was leaning against. There was a patch with the word "Case" on the front of the cap. "What a wasta time," he said in a grousing tone. I had put the guitar back in the bus and hadn't yet picked up my sign, so he must not have known whose side I was on. "What the hell do they think they're proving?"

"Why do you say that?" I asked, innocent as could be.

"Whole thing's phony as a three-dollar bill," he said. "There ain't no problem here, this ain't the South." He peered at me closely, as if to see whether I might question that. He had a thin Yankee face, with no spare flesh on his cheeks and deep-set steel-gray eyes. The only excess was in his mouth, where his lips puckered out, almost like Tracy's did.

He hadn't said anything yet that I disagreed with, but I thought I'd play along, just for fun. "Don't you think it's *everybody's* problem, though? I mean, like, even if it don't happen here, Woolworth's is a national store, and in *some* places it won't let Negroes sit down and eat."

The man tilted the baseball cap off his head, wiped his forehead with the back of his hand and replaced the cap, all in one swift motion that was remarkable for its economy of movement. The hair under the cap was black with gray streaks. He had the good solid look of a husband and father, a good provider, and he talked with the same sort of squeeze-nosed twang as the cop whose acquaintance I was soon to make. "No, that don't figger attall," he whined. "What Woolworth does someplace else is nonna our business. Ain't nonna our business what people who don't like it do about it someplace else, neither."

"You don't think it would be a waste of time marching like this down in Alabama, say, that it?"

"That's another fish altogether." He poked me in the chest with a finger. "Look here, I sell farm machinery, see? Case sends me a batcha tractors, say, don't work right? It's my ass goes on the line, right? If I sell 'em. So I don't sell 'em, and I get on the phone right quick to Case and raise hell. That's 'cause it's all happening to *me*. But lemme tell you, mister, I get wind of some dealer down in Brattleboro, say, having trouble with a shipment of lemons, that sure don't stop me from doing *my* business. I don't get all heated up and sore at my Cases, just 'cause somebody else is having trouble with his. See my point?"

I did and it seemed like a good one to me, and I told him so. "Trouble is, though, we're not talking about tractors here, it's people, and people are different because they got feelings."

A woman with two tiny white poodles on leashes squeezed past, between us and the marchers. She smiled at my companion, nodding her head in recognition, and gave me a puzzled look.

"That don't make no nevermind," the Case man said. "Machinery, people, hell, it could be potatoes we're talking about." I smiled at that and looked down the line at Molly, who was walking arm-in-arm with Buck. "What it all comes down to," my friend said, poking me in the chest again, "is that it just don't apply here. We don't even have hardly any niggers here, and those we do have can do and go as they please. See my point?"

I've been regretting ever since that I didn't say something—I have a fantasy of whomping him with a karate chop or something—but I didn't and I guess I just shook my head and backed away. Deliberately as I could, feeling like not only his eyes but those of every man, woman and child in Burlington, Vermont, were on me, I got back on the line, pausing when I passed the stack of signs to pick one up, and maybe that was as strong as if I *had* said something. But if it meant anything to him I don't know because when the line came around again to the corner, he was gone. I found myself next to Tracy, who looked as gritty as she had earlier. She was just a tiny girl, the top of her head coming up to about the middle of my chest, and I had to tilt my head in her direction to talk to her.

"You from this town?" I asked.

"Born and raised." I could have guessed she was from somewhere hereabouts by the way she didn't waste any words.

"I was just talking to one of your fellow citizens. Hell of a nice fellow, except for one small flaw in his character."

"I can guess what that was," Tracy said. Her face was bigger than it should have been for her body, and her eyes, black and lustrous, were enormous. Eyes like my mother's, in the one photograph of her I have. I couldn't keep my eyes off them.

We walked one full round without saying anything else, but I couldn't keep quiet. That farm machinery man was eating at me. "Hard growing up here?"

"What's that?" she cocked her head up. I don't know if she really didn't hear, but I asked it again.

She shrugged. "Hard as you let it be, tha's all."

"There many of you here?" I asked, a little timidly.

"What you mean, *you*?" she snapped back.

"You know...." I began, but I didn't know where I was going. I'd almost said *us*, and now I wished I had.

"No, I *don't* know. You mean how many of you snappy-assed young chicks with flirt in your eye? Or you mean how many of you po' mis'able, picked-on, stepped-on cooked-over *black* folks? I don't know *which* one you mean. Which one *do* you mean?"

"Hey, take it easy," I said, smarting. "I'm on your side."

"Oh yeah?" Sparks were flying off her, but she smiled despite herself, a big wide smile with nice neat lips that earlier I had thought were painted a little too red but now seemed just right. Maybe I looked as miserable as I felt.

I remembered the family tree spiel I'd rattled off for Molly and wanted to say, "Hey, listen, you think *you* got problems, I been called every name you ever were and then some, nigger and spade and spook and boo, along with spic and grease and kike and sheenie. Hell, I even been called a *wop* a few times, and, listen, that ain't all, I was in Cuba, I *fought* for freedom, I ain't no dimestore democrat, the N-double-A-C-fucking-P don't have *nuthin'* on me," but I didn't, I didn't say anything, except

"Yeah," in a voice tough as hers that made her laugh.

"Okay, don't get sore," she said. "Maybe I just wanted to make sure. Gets hard to tell with everyone milling around."

"I know what you mean exactly," I said. "Sometimes it takes more'n a baseball cap to know what team a body's on. But don't take it out on me, hey? I'm here to help."

The smile slid off Tracy's face like water being soaked up by sand. "Help *who*? *Who* you here to help?"

She took me off guard and I wasn't thinking fast enough. "You, I guess, and anybody else who has a hard time growing up in this town, or living in it, period."

She shook her head. Up ahead, the minister or someone must have called a halt, though we hadn't heard it, because the line suddenly stopped, and people began to peel off to the sides, like petals falling from a flower in a gust of wind, but Tracy and I kept walking, our faces turned to each other, intent on each other. We came to the corner, wheeled around and headed the other way, lone soldiers without a column. "Uh, uh, buddy, that ain't the way it works," she said, leaning toward me. "You making a big mistake if that's what you think, an' you better think again, because this is just the beginning, honey, this little walk is just *kind*ergarten, an' you see if I ain't right."

"I don't get you," I said. We came to the middle of the block, where the store ended, and wheeled around. At the corner, the picket signs were being stacked. The lunch crowd was gone but there were still people on the street, looking at us curiously. Across the street, in front of a bank, the woman with the poodles was watching in bewilderment. We gritted our teeth and walked on.

"You ain't here to help me, honey. Don't kid yourself that you are. You ain't here for *me*, you here for *yourself*, tha's all, tha's it. I'm glad we together, but don't come telling me how you're doing all this for *me*, big brother. Uh uh. You here for *you*, an' tha's the way it is."

We stopped when we reached the corner. Tracy put down her sign and shrugged. The smile crept back to her face. "Been nice walkin' with you, honey."

I found myself standing alone like an idiot, a picket sign hoisted above my shoulder. Someone came and took it from me. People were drifting away.

I walked back to the microbus with the Goddard crew to get my gear. They were pumped up, laughing and topping each other with stories of encounters on the line. "Did you hear that big mother tellin' me I should get back to Russia where I come from?" Sid whooped. "You shoulda seen his face when I started talking Russian to him."

Somebody had a portable radio and they all quieted down when the news came on, everybody holding their fingers to their noses and hushing each other in hopes of hearing something about the picketing, but it was tuned to a Boston station. The first item was about the Russians catching the pilot of that plane of ours they shot down the other day, some guy named Powers, that they're going to try him as a spy.

"They should've executed that bastard instead of Chessman," Sid said bitterly.

Horsting gave him a sharp look. "Very sensible, Sidney," he said, sarcasm oozing from his lips like drool. He raked us all over with his eyes, as if we had somehow been responsible for his worst fears coming true. "Capital punishment is fine for capitalists, is that it? Let the punishment fit the crime?" He nodded slowly, a small, satisfied smile seeping into his thin lips. I knew damn well Sid *did* think that, but he didn't say a word.

Molly and I had a clinch while the rest of them were piling into the microbus. She was excited from the afternoon and didn't seem to mind that I hadn't spent much time with her. She wanted me to come back with them, though, and I was tempted, but I didn't want to go anywhere I'd already been.

"You coming this way again?" she asked.

"Maybe. I'd like to. Not for a while, though. I get around." I shrugged, laughing, at myself, not her, but I saw her eyes darken a shade. I kissed her again. That felt so good I almost changed my mind. "I'll try, that's a promise."

I watched them drive away, feeling glad to be alone for the first time in several days. I guess that's why it was so easy for the coppers to pick on me—everybody else went back to their schools or churches and I was left standing on a corner, flapping in the breeze like the last leaf. I was hungry and thirsty from walking around in sunshiny circles through lunch hour and I had a crazy notion, so I turned around and walked back to Woolworth's. The big cop was still there, as if nobody had bothered to tell him it was all over, and he gave me a hard look as I went past him.

I sat at the deserted counter and looked at the menu. "Ain't you one of those that was out there before?" the waitress asked suspiciously. She had the same high whine as my friend with the baseball cap but she was closer to my age than his, probably no more than a year or two older, out of high school and behind the lunch counter just like that.

"Yeah," I said, without making a fuss about it. "All that walking made me hungry." I ordered a cheeseburger and a soda. If I'd known I'd be eating supper in a jail cell for free the rest of this weekend, I'd have saved the buck it cost me. While I was waiting, I amused myself by swiveling on my stool and watching the locals at their shopping. Some of them were watching me back. An old Negro man in gray coveralls came out of a door at the rear pushing a cart loaded with boxes. I watched his progress as he wheeled it from aisle to aisle, making deliveries.

"See that old colored feller?" the waitress asked. She had seen me watching him. "That colored girl who was out on the picket line with you all before? That Tracy? That's her daddy."

The waitress had a complexion like a battlefield, and her nose was snubbed, so you couldn't help but look up her nostrils when you faced her. I felt like punching her, she was so ugly and mean, but maybe she wasn't, maybe she didn't mean it that way.

"Is that right?" I said. I hate that expression, but I couldn't think of anything else to say.

"Ain't that sumpthin'?" the waitress said. She shrugged and shook her head like the world had suddenly grown too much for her. A woman with her hair in curlers under a red and white kerchief sat down at the other end of the counter and blew her nose with a napkin, and the waitress moved away. I ate my cheeseburger but it tasted like cardboard, and the root beer was flat. I wanted to pour it on the counter and walk out, but I knew that wouldn't prove anything, just get people mad. *Prove anything.* Wasn't that the expression the baseball cap man had used? What I really wanted to do was buy another soda—one with bubbles in it, hopefully—and offer it to Tracy's father. Don't ask me why but I wanted to give him something, do something for him. But the best I could do, for myself and for him, was just to leave, without doing anything at all. I even left the waitress a quarter for a tip.

9. The Edge of the World

Yuri Gagarin says the world is round, that he *saw* it, with his own eyes, and it's irrefutable, but I'm still not so sure.

I'm sitting cross-legged in the sand of a little strip of beach at a place called Long Beach on the west side of Vancouver Island, watching for whales, which they say come by here this time of year. I haven't been north of here much but this guy I was talking to says the island, which is a big mother, veers westerly for a couple hundred miles. And that a group of islands further north, the Queen Charlottes, stick even further out into the ocean. And even the California-Oregon bulge down south of here sticks further out on my ragged, much-folded Imperial Oil map, which I've been studying, trying to decide where to go next, though that's supposedly an illusion, that bulge, I mean, created by representing a curved object—the earth—on a flat surface and, so the claim goes, it's not really further west, if you look at the longitude lines, which are supposed to prove something. But north of us is the westward-sloping mainland of Canada, not to mention Alaska, so I'm not at the westernmost point of the continent by any means. But the sky is clear, blue as a robin's egg, blue as anything, anyway, and the horizon stretches out forever out there at the other end of a windy, restless ocean that doesn't seem to want to admit there's any trace of land violating its spirit on either side of where it's had the courtesy and good grace to permit *me*, and the spit of land I'm sitting on, so it

131

seems to me that that's where I am, at the edge of the world, the very end of the known world, not merely a continent, with everything known to man, everything *old*, behind me, and everything you could possibly imagine and everything you *couldn't*, everything *new*, out there, at that hazy line where water and sky blend into each other.

I've been out of touch with kith and kin for months and they probably think I've wandered off that edge and fallen *plop* into the mouth of one of those famous sea monsters. Sit here for awhile, gazing out at that endless sea, its ragged edges constantly curling back like licks of flame on the sides of a fire, and it's easy to see why people thought the world was flat, easy to imagine unspeakable horrors out *there*, just beyond where the eye can see. If the world is round, you can't prove it by me.

I've been working as a faller (*lumberjack*, they told me, is an old-fashioned word, a romantic relic, and, hell, we don't want any romance dusting this tough number), and the folks back home wouldn't recognize this skinny old brown boy. I ain't so skinny anymore—in fact, I'm huge. Gained twenty pounds, most of it muscle, I'm pleased to say, and there's even more of me if you count the beard and shaggy hair.

"Dis'll make a man outta ya, or kill ya, one or da odder," that's what my friend Rogie says, laughing his big, thick-as-pudding bray. That's what the army's supposed to do for a fella, but, thank God, I've found more socially acceptable means of body building. At least here I'm only killing trees, rather than rehearsing for killing people.

I've been living what you might call a nonverbal life, so I don't usually go into those details with Rogie. The people I hang around with laugh a lot, they grunt, nod their heads, grin like crazy men, belch, fart and make other rude noises, but they don't do a lot of what you would call *talking*. And the closest they do come to it is telling dirty jokes or describing women they've known, done something with. And, of course, when in Rome do as the Romans do, if you don't want to be thrown to the barbarians. Or, as Pops used to say, "Blend in, man, blend *in*, so you don't stick *out*. Tha's the way to stay alive."

Amen to that. Good advice, and I'm trying to follow it, best I can.

Fact is, I'm where I am, doing what I am, because I had suddenly begun to feel like I was sticking out.

I am, after all, only nineteen fucking years old, and I felt like I was maybe cramming too much stuff into my still tender young frame. They say life goes in cycles but that's bullshit, if you ask me. It goes in fits, pops, explosions. For the first fifteen years of my life, nothing much happened to me at all. I grew. I got up, went to school, came home, saw my friends, ate dinner with Pops, did homework, listened to the radio, went to bed. That was it, one year after another, indistinguishable—and undistinguished, which is okay, I guess. No reason a child should expect different. But then, just like that, I was a fucking rock and roll star, touring the country with a circusload of crazies and listening to people bang their hands together making a noise like that ocean roaring out there on the rocks. And then people were *shooting* at me, which is another kind of noise altogether, and then I was on the road again, all by my little lonesome, maybe not a star exactly but still somebody who other somebodies put their hands together for in that silly, noisy gesture that I never could get enough of—applause, that was it, man, I mean, there was too much of it, all too loud. Guitars, saxes, mikes crackling, crowds roaring, shooting, bombs going off, applause—it's all too fucking *noisy*, you can't hear yourself think in the middle of it. And there I was, sixteen, seventeen, eighteen years old and right in the *middle* of it, sticking out.

And you know what else? I was tired of traveling around the country, lugging my ax, but only seeing it from one side of the stage. I wanted to hear the sound of just *one* hand clapping, as the smart kids say. I wanted to hear the sound of that famous tree that falls in the forest when there's no one there to hear it. A little education is a dangerous thing, ain't dat da trut'?

I brought my guitar home and left it with Pops and I took off and all of a sudden I felt like I'd shed five hundred pounds, like I'd gotten rid of some terrible load or an incredibly precious cargo I'd been carrying around, worrying about. All of a sudden there wasn't anybody applauding, I wasn't hustling, nobody was paying attention. All of a sudden, I was *nobody* again, doing nothing, invisible, blending *in*.

I headed west, fooled around Chicago for a few days, hanging around some of those South Side bars listening to blues because I couldn't resist, but keeping cool, *anonymous*, then kept going, stopping in eastern Colorado, with the mountains still a blue blur in the distance, to work as a field hand picking sugar beets for a while, along with a mob of Mexican migrants who sort of adopted me, like a mascot. They'd never seen a Puerto Rican before, and their Spanish and mine was not exactly on the same wave length, but after a few days I was picking up on their idioms and it was okay, just the way it'd been in Cuba. They thought I was a little crazy, actually *wanting* to do the work they're trapped into, and maybe I was, and the work almost killed me, but it was good. I liked the smells and the feel of real earth on my hands and the taste of the endless stews the women made after work and the way I fell asleep *this second*, as soon as my head hit the pillow, and even the aching in my muscles that never really goes away completely but stops being a pain after awhile and becomes instead a way for your body to talk to you, to tell you everything's working and doing okay. I liked feeling like I was part of something, the way I was just starting to in Cuba before everything went black and I never have before, not even in the band, not ever.

When the season ended, my friends moved south and I pushed on west, fooling around with some Beatnik types I met in the mountains, then on to San Francisco, where I sent my cousin Rhoda a postcard with a North Beach scene: "Having a wonderful time. Wish I were queer." I figured after all that stooping in the fields my back was strong enough for the docks, something I'd daydreamed about ever since I saw Brando in *Waterfront*, but the union there is too tough. I spent a couple of weeks hanging around the hiring hall and getting half a day's work now and then, but it's tough to break in and I lost interest.

But I met a guy down there who'd been a logger in Oregon and was going back. He wrote his address on the back of a "today's special" card off the menu of a greasy spoon where the long-shoremen hang out, and when I got up there, a few weeks later, I looked him up, in a place called Coos Bay, a pretty little town on the coast that stinks of the wood pulp cooking twenty-four hours a day in yards overlooking the water. It's sad, really. You get out there into the woods and cut down these big mother trees that have been growing since Jesus was in short pants, thick, tall cocks that climb straight up to heaven, pines and spruces, and in your mind's eye you see them stripped and smooth, fitting together like a giant jigsaw puzzle into some huge log mansion, or up on their feet again, creosoted into honest utility poles, or sliced down the middle like bologna into good thick boards, but, uh uh, it's pulp they're after, crumbly sawdust stuff for particle board, pulp to make newsprint for the lousy papers to print their bullshit on. That's what it's all about. It makes me sick to think about it, makes me think of the Nazis burning Jews up in their ovens to get fat for candle wax. I like it better up here, where I'm working for a real lumber company and the trees I cut down at least are going to be used to *build* something, something solid that keeps on going. I like the smell of fresh lumber, the sight of stacks and stacks of boards waiting to be trucked away. I hate the smell of pulp.

I liked the work, so I stuck with it, and now I find myself up here, in another country, though that don't seem to matter much.

In Coos Bay, I fell under the wing of my friend and guardian angel Rogie, and when he split up here I followed.

Rogie, now *he* is a lumberjack, no matter what they call the job we do. He's tall and broad as Paul Bunyan, but he wears cowboy shirts and a baseball cap instead of the plaid flannel shirts and wool toques some of the other guys around here like. He's got French and Indian blood flowing in his veins—though no ennobling African blood like mine, of course—and he's lived all over the country and into Washington and Oregon, too. He don't pay much attention to borders. "The woods is my country, Frankie," he says, pronouncing my name "Fran-kee" in his flat, broad voice that sounds more Indian than French to me.

I like Rogie because he's so elemental. I mean, he doesn't have a lot of extraneous crap floating around in his head to confuse him, neither politics nor religion nor "education," at least not the kind people put value on, the kind Pops always put so much store on me getting. He operates on common sense, that great blind engine of the brain. In his case, though, it's a little off its track.

The camp we work from, which is about thirty miles from here, north and inland, has about fifty-sixty guys and, as of about a month ago, when the weather started getting nice, one woman, a slant-eyed, high-yellow skirt who arrived in a battered old Henry J with two cats you wouldn't want to tangle with unless you were carrying something heavy. I didn't see them arrive myself, but the guys say—true or not I don't know—the car pulled into the compound one evening, just after supper, and stopped in front of one of the bunkhouses, the girl got out, wearing a short yellow sundress that must have been bought for the occasion, and one of the creeps with her said to her, loud enough so that any of the boys lounging nearby, their eyes big and tongues already starting to water, could hear: "Now get in there and don't come out till you've got a thousand dollars."

I haven't had anything to do with her but I'm told the fare is as low as $5 for a quick blow job, $10 for a straight fuck, naked and in the sack, $15 to go up her ass, which Rogie tells me is incomparable, and $25 for a couple of hours, the works, so it shouldn't take her all that long to raise her poke from this crew. Rogie, who's been to the well three times already, kids me about abstaining, saying it's something a man needs to keep working right, just like he needs grub.

"Da fuckin' company, it feeds us but we gotta pay oudda our own fuckin' pocket for sweet stuff," he complains, setting off ripples of laughter in the cook shack at dinner, where the conversation often drifts to the girl, her two companions, who are camped, silent but watchful, on a hill within sight of our camp, and the evening's activities. "Dat ain' fair, eh? We got Cookie," he says, gesturing in the direction of our cook, a tall, skinny man with warts who seems not to benefit from his own talents, which are considerable. "We got Cookie, but no nookie."

Rogie, who tends to take things at face value, would have real doubts about me were it not for a weekend we spent together in Vancouver, but I'm disgusted by what's going on with this girl— though I'm careful not to make that disgust too loud, to avoid getting my head staved in—and he just doesn't understand it.

"Dat girl, she's a whore in your eyes only 'cause you see her dat way," Rogie tells me. "Me, I see her as a sweet liddle girl tryin' to earn her livin' doin' what she does best. I don' see her as no fuckin' whore. It's you puts da label on her, not us guys who do bus'ness wid her."

I just shake my head at this. "Jesus, Rogie, you amaze me." From someone I didn't already like a lot, this kind of reasoning would drive me blind. "I guess you don't see those two motherfuckers camped up the road who'd as soon kill her as kiss her on the cheek if she crossed them or held back a dollar."

"Dey're her bus'ness pardners," Rogie offers cheerfully, "or

like her foremen, maybe you'd unnerstand dat one better, *foremen*,
like we got tellin' us whadda do."

"Jesus, Rogie. Foremen, my ass. Pimps, you mean."

"Whaddever you call it."

"And I guess you don't give a shit about this *sweet liddle girl's*
feelings, taking on one mangy cock after another in that godfor-
saken bunkhouse?"

"Feelin's?" Rogie looks hurt, as if I've unfairly wounded him.
"Sure I care 'bout her feelin's. Lemme tell you sompt'in', Fran-kee...."

"Oh, shit, Rogie, you don't understand shit."

Now he really looks hurt, but the cloud passes over his eyes in
a moment and he shrugs, clucking his tongue philosophically.

"You say *I* don't unnerstand, eh, Fran-kee? I tell you, dere's
sompt'in *you* don' unnerstand. Dat girl? She got a muscle she's
usin' to earn her livin', just like you and me usin' some of our muscles. Dat make us whores to da company 'cause we ain' in love wid
da fuckin' trees? 'Cause we just cut 'em down for da fuckin'
money? Shit, no. We just earnin' a livin', usin' whad muscles God
give us to do it wid. An' dat girl? She doin' da same fuckin' t'ing.
Dat girl? She clean, and she knows lotsa things lotsa wimmin don'
even dream aboud. An' she *cheerful*. She ain' no goddamn whore
anymore'n you an' me. A woman only a whore when she don' give
a shit no more, Fran-kee. Man too."

Another time, he notices me limping, which I do sometimes,
not because of the work but from the dampness, when the weather sets in, and asks what's wrong with my leg.

"An old war wound," I tell him simply.

"Oh, yeah? Whad war wuz you in, Fran-kee?"

"Cuba," I say, keeping it simple, not particularly anxious to talk
about it.

"Oh, yeah?" We're taking our lunch break and we're sprawled
out on the ground in a clearing with sandwiches and mugs of hot
soup that Cookie's delivered, a little distance apart from the rest

of the men. We can hear the murmur of their voices, as they can, no doubt, from us, but no words. Rogie purses his lips, indicating he's thinking, then they twist into a grin. "You don' look old enough, Fran-kee."

I laugh at that, but then, as we talk more, it turns out he's thinking of the Spanish-American War, though his knowledge of it is limited to a movie he saw once, Teddy Roosevelt and the Rough Riders charging up San Juan Hill. He has no notion of when that was, what it was about, who Roosevelt was, anything, and he has no surface knowledge of the revolution in Cuba, of Castro, nothing at all until I prod him a little.

"Oh, yeah," he says, turning thoughtful. "Ain' dem communis?"

"No," I say flatly.

"I t'ought I heard sompt'in' dey wuz."

"Nope. You heard wrong."

Rogie nods solemnly, taking my word for it, although a few weeks later, when the Bay of Pigs is in the papers from Vancouver that get up here a few days late, and everybody's talking about it, he's confused. We have what barely passes for a political discussion but, despite my readiness to brawl, he's receptive to practically everything I have to say. He can understand revenge and betrayal, and the anger of the powerful. "Sure," he shrugs, "like when da bastard companies try ta bust da union." He grins broadly, just as if this was a union camp, which it isn't, and he gives a shit one way or another. "We give'm a bay of pigs too."

But his interest in my wound is revived by this talk, and finally, after a few weeks of him pestering me, I feel compelled to give him an abbreviated version of what happened that day, though it's embarrassing to remember it all again, the first day into battle and the wound in the hip, of all places. It doesn't occur to me to just bluff him off with jokes and evasiveness. Rogie and I try to be straight with each other.

He listens solemnly, not interrupting—we're at lunch again, once more slightly apart from the other men, from whom snatches of a song, laughter, drift toward us—and laughs only once, his deep, hearty guffaw, at the appropriate time.

"Jees," he says when I've finished, "only a kid. I t'ought I wuz young, but nothin' like dat. You wuz one brave kid, eh, Fran-kee?"

I shake my head to that, but I'm confused by his reference to himself.

"You were in a war, Rogie?"

"Me? Sure. Kor-ee-ah," he says precisely. "You hear 'bout dat one, Fran-kee?"

"Sure, don't be dumb, man, everybody knows about Korea."

"Well..." He grins sheepishly. "I din' know 'bout dat Cuba stuff."

I wave that off. "You were in the Canadian army?"

Rogie laughs, shaking his big, closely cropped head. "Hell, no, Fran-kee, da marines, US marines. You din' know I wuz a fuckin' ledderneck, eh?" He starts to sing the anthem that used to thrill me so much as a kid at Saturday matinee war movie double bills, "from the halls of Montezuma to the shores of Tripoli," or however the hell it goes, except Rogie has a tin ear and he mangles the tune.

I stare at him, wide-eyed, absorbing this new information about my friend. Korea makes him be at least thirty, and, while I knew Rogie was older than me, it surprises me, perhaps because he's so childlike in so many ways, to realize that he's half again as old as I am. But, even more than that, he is, despite his size, which is huge, and his rough manner of speaking, a gentle person, a man I've seen back off gracefully from barroom brawls and campfire beefs, dignity intact. A marine? I think about the drill camps they say break so many tough guys, of the shaved heads, and the storming of beaches in the movies. That experience is so foreign from mine that I find it hard to imagine.

"You fucking asshole, you never told me that," I say, punching him on the shoulder. "You never tell any war stories. And I didn't realize you were such a moldy, ancient piece of shit."

"Hey, I ain' so fuckin' old," Rogie complains, grinning. "I wuz just a fuckin' kid, like you, in the war, eighteen when I join up, nineteen when I wuz over there. An' dat was only nine, ten years ago, eh? I ain' so fuckin' *ancien'*, like you say."

"Pretty fucking moth-eaten, man. No wonder you gotta go to that camp girl, that Lou. No real girl would waste time on an old fart like you, probably can't even get it up without help, eh?"

He jumps on me and we're rolling around in the soft pine needle and moss floor of the forest, our noses and mouths—well, *mine*—filled with that sweet-smelling debris, until I'm exhausted and crying out truce, uncle, help, anything.

"Who's da fuckin' old man?" Rogie grins at me. "Who can' get id up?"

The whistle blows and I don't get to hear any more, but through the afternoon, as work tosses us together, we seem to grin at each other in a new way, some new secret bond between us now, veterans of distant wars who keep our wounds to ourselves.

As it turns out, Rogie wasn't wounded, but did kill people, something I know with certainty I didn't. He knows with equal certainty that he did, having done it by hand, half a dozen times or more. He is, again despite his size, a limber, athletic man who, maybe because of his years in the woods, knows how to move quietly, how to crawl on his belly, how to be silent, how to listen and really *hear*, how to blend in. So he was sent on patrols into enemy territory, not *specifically* to kill, he says, but to gather information on their locations, strengths, activity and so on, and to kill, incidentally, if he got the chance.

"Dat firs' time, Fran-kee, she was sompt'in'," he tells me that evening, sitting on the steps of our bunkhouse, smoking his stubby, blackened pipe in the dull light of sunset while behind us Lou the campgirl is at work and voices drift across the compound from the cookshack. A radio is on somewhere and I can hear faint snatches of Ricky Nelson's squeaky "Hello, Mary Lou" through the static. It's late May now and the days have been hot, the lengthening evenings balmy until the sun goes down and cold makes a brave comeback for a few hours. We're in our shirtsleeves, rolled up flannel sleeves with thermal undershirt sleeves sticking out like a second skin. I've been bugging him since dinner for more. "I'd been on a coupla patrols already but I hadn' come up close ta anybody. Me an' a coupla odder guys, we'd go over sometime after dark, in dat damn camouflage gear an' our faces black as a nigger's asshole—hey, don' get sore, okay?—black wid dat cork stuff, and we'd look aroun', den dey'd set up a position an' me, I was da point man, whad dey call. I'd go up a liddle furder, see what I could see, den head back. Dese odder times, I'd see stuff and head back, dat was all, 'cept you always hadda be on your toes for maybe a patrol from *dere* side, doin' da same t'ing you're doin', see whad I mean?

"Dis time, dat's whad happen. My buddies set up, I move ahead, do my lookin' around, an' I'm headin' back, I hear a sound, so I freeze. It's quiet as hell, not a fuckin' sound, an' dark as anyt'in', Fran-kee, I'm tellin' you, deat' n' da grave won' be any darker or more quiet den dat Korea night, I'm sure as hell a' dat. I wait, one, two, t'ree minutes, nuttin', an' dere's no reason why I shouldn't move, get goin', 'cept I *know* dere's somebody out dere, I can *smell* him. An' sure enough, after awhile dere's a sound, somebody movin' out dere, somebody doin' da same t'ing I'm doin', but for dere side, an' maybe dat one heard me too an' he's sittin' an' waitin' and list'nin' but maybe—maybe—dat one's nose don' work good as mine. So I just sit dere, holdin' my breat' hopin' he'll go around me, but if he don', all I gotta do is wait till he comes to me, dat one. Which is what he does, Fran-kee."

Rogie stops to suck on his pipe, which has gone dead, stir the tobacco with the end of a wooden match, fire it up again. The radio has faded out and, behind us, we can hear a bunk creaking, and, from the cookhouse or one of the bunkhouses beyond it, a voice singing: "Hi ho, hi ho, it's off to the girly show, we'll pay two bits to see two tits, hi ho, hi ho."

Rogie's mouth forms a sour grin around the pipe stem. He blinks and I sense that he is not so much here, with me, as he is there, back in Korea, with the man who will be his victim.

"Just a boy," he says suddenly. "Da's all he is, dat one, a fuckin' kid, younger dan me even, like whad you wuz in Cuba. He has black on his face, like me, a knife in his teet', he's crawlin', like a weasel after sumpt'in', crawl a foot or two, lift his head, sniff da wind, crawl some more. I jus' wait till he's almost in my arms, den I grab him." Rogie's eyes snap into focus and he shifts them to me. "Jesus, Fran-kee, Jesus. It was just like holdin' a girl in your arms, see whad I mean? Just da smallest quiver when I cut his t'roat, but no sound, 'cause I got my hand on his mout'. Den just da smallest tremble in my arms as he dies, his eyes wide open an' starin' at me, like a girl doin' it for the first time, surprised at how easy it is, after all."

We sit silently for a moment, Rogie puffing on his pipe, me staring at the rounded, scuffed toe of my boot. The thick rubber sole is starting to come loose at the front, a gap has formed and tiny pebbles have gathered in the V. I reach down to brush at them and leave my finger there under the pressure of my foot. The sun has set behind the pine ridge and the sky has taken on the filmy gray quality of gruel. The voice from the other bunkhouse is singing: "Hi ho, hi ho, it's off to the burlesque show, we'll sit up front to see some cunt, hi ho, hi ho."

"Da worse fuckin' part," Rogie says, his cheeks rising into a weak smile, "is dat he shits his pants just den, and da stink, it's terrible. I roll him away an' start crawlin' back ta where da odder guys are, but dat stink, it follows me, don't seem to be gettin' any furder away, any weaker, an' I feel like pukin' from it. But here, lissen ta dis, Fran-kee, when I get dere, da odder guys say, Jesus, Rogie, you stink, wha's a madder wid you, and I realize den, Jesus, Fran-kee, dat it's *me* shit my pants, all along, or maybe bot' of us, I don' know. But *me, I* done it, da stink is all over *me*."

Behind us, a door swings open, slams shut, and a man comes out onto the steps. It's Patryluk, Patsy, he's called, a solidly built faller from Saskatchewan who likes to tell stories. A nice guy. "God *damn*," he says. He's buckling up his belt, his unlaced boots flopping loosely around his feet. "God *damn*," he says again, a grin spreading across his wide face. "Any you sorry mutts got a butt?"

I shrug. "Sorry." Rogie gestures with his pipe.

Patsy clatters past us down the steps, pausing at the bottom to bend over and half lace up his boots, then strolls toward the cookhouse, whistling. An engine coughs, then roars to vibrant life somewhere, out of sight. On the pine ridge, where clumps of dirty, crusted snow are still visible between the straggling trees, smoke is rising from a small fire where Lou's two protectors are camped. I imagine them scanning us now with binoculars, shaking their heads over the deserted compound. It's Friday and many of the men have taken the trucks and gone into Ucluelet, won't be back till Sunday or when their money runs out, whichever comes first.

Rogie gets to his feet. "Damn, Fran-kee, I need to get drunk now, wash dat smell away." He stretches, his long arms beating the sky like blades of a windmill. "You come to town wid me? Just tonight, I swear. We come back tomorrow."

"No, you go ahead." I think I should, I should be with him, I should wash away the smell, too, but the night is closing in, and the last thing I want is lights, noise, the stink of other people.

Rogie goes up to his room to get his jacket and his wallet and I stand guard to stop the last truck should it start to leave before he gets back. A few minutes later, he's gone and I'm sitting on the steps again, my eyes focused on the small fire on the ridge. There is no thought in my mind. My fingers keep moving on their own to the gap at the front of my boot but all I'm doing is making it worse. After awhile, I hear a door swing open behind me and I sense it's the girl, Lou. I can *smell* it's her, not because she has a scent I could identify, but the men do, sweat and grease, and it's absent. I hear the sputter of a match, smell the acrid smoke of tobacco, hear the creak of wood as she leans against the railing above me.

"Whadabout you?" she asks presently. "Don't you want some of me, honey?"

I don't turn my head, keeping my eyes on the tiny licking flames of that distant fire. Her voice is flat, Negro-sounding but without any regional accent. I take a deep breath and now I *can* smell her, soap and perfume and cum that the other two haven't completely washed away or masked. "No, thanks."

"Suit yourself," the girl says, with no interest. She smokes in silence punctuated by an occasional sigh, a sharp drawing in of breath, a slow release. I sit below her, wondering if eyes are on me, through binoculars, from the ridge.

"Your friends over there, they're going to think you've lost your touch," I say suddenly, without having thought it through. "They're watching us, I bet, wondering why we're wasting time." I attempt a laugh, to show her I'm just kidding, but it comes out sounding more like a sob.

"My friends," she says, in that same bored voice. "They can go fuck themselves. I hope it rains and they freeze their asses off tonight. I hope it fucking snows."

She delivers herself of this without any trace of bitterness and the violence of the words themselves seems deflated, like a dead snake at the side of the road, coiled and deadly looking but harmless. Nevertheless, I'm surprised by the outburst, if that's what it is, and I turn to look at her, for the first time.

She's a short girl, big breasted but otherwise slender, skin the color of coffee with light cream, hair straightened and shoulder length, dirty black. She's wearing a short-sleeved yellow dress splashed with a pattern of small red flowers and she's draped a blue cardigan across her thin shoulders. Her feet are bare. I stand up and take a step toward her, again without thought, and she leans toward me, extending her face as if to examine some object of interest. I'm struck, suddenly, by how young she is, really a girl, no older than I am, probably younger.

"Jesus, aren't you ashamed of yourself?" I say suddenly. I feel repelled, like someone who has caught a whiff of something foul, but I don't step back.

The girl looks at me curiously, making a face halfway between a smile and a frown. "Shit, no," she says, but then, after a moment: "Sure I am. Ain't you?"

That was a couple of weeks ago, and, as I sit here now, communing with nature at the very edge of the world, half believing in sea monsters, it's hard to remember exactly what happened after that. Blood rushed to my face, I remember that—I was confused, angry, but speechless. I lurched down the steps and around the bunkhouse, that same laugh sounding like a sob coming out of my mouth, and made my way across the compound and into the woods, where the darkness had already settled. I remember I stumbled, fell, bruised my knee, got up and lurched on, blindly.

I've just now gotten around to actually leaving, but it was then, that night, that I realized it was time to go, that I was out of my place, not blending in at all but sticking out like the sorest of sore thumbs. Stumbling through those dark woods, without anything to hold onto or give me direction, I realized I *did* have something—my music, the actual physical reality of my guitar—but that I had left it behind. There wasn't any splash of color, a blinding light, no ringing chords of heavenly music reverberating in my ears, but I suddenly knew, with as much certainty as I can bring now to the statement that there's land *here*, water out *there*, that I was a musician, for better or worse, that that was my life, one way or another. Turning my back on it was just a way of not giving a shit anymore. And that wasn't true.

I came into a clearing and stopped to catch my breath. I was disoriented, all sense of geography gone, and there was no sign of the compound, with its electric lights and familiar shapes of buildings and vehicles, but there was the pine ridge, the tiny, flickering fire tended by the two watching men. In the darkness, they were hunkered there by their fire, shotguns across their laps like guerrillas in the hills, drinking beer or whiskey from bottles probably, laughing perhaps, their faces drawn, their eyes tired from staring endlessly down at the lights below, waiting for the realization of some goal.

I *was* ashamed, of course, of so many things. The campfire on the ridge took me back to Cuba, to the camp where I'd spent my few days in the Pinar del Rio, where the smell of frying pork and plantain drifted without end from the fire, like earth lifting its perfumed breast to heaven, but, in truth, I was already back there, had been since I'd stumbled away from the steps into the woods. There, there *had* been blinding light, the deafening roar of mortar. We were marching in a column up the ridge of a hill, bringing up the flank of the attack, but something had gone wrong, there'd been a miscalculation of timing and the *batistianos* had been alerted and they were attacking *us*. "Keep together, keep together and keep going," Pepe was shouting, but shells were exploding all around us and his voice was all but drowned out. There was a flash of light and I turned, I turned ... and then darkness, nothing, not even pain. Later, it was over and, inexplicably, we had won, not only here, in our small battle, but everywhere, they said. The *batistianos* were on the run throughout the country, it really *was* over. I was in a tent hospital, numb and floating on morphine, but it was hard to believe I hadn't been a coward, that I hadn't run—the wound in my ass was practically a badge to that—but Pepe and the others who had been there insisted that wasn't so.

"You weren't where you were supposed to be, that's all," Pepe said, his eyes crinkling behind the tangled fur of his beard. "That is no thing to be ashamed of. If you hadn't moved, no more would have been gained, but you surely would have been killed, and what value would that have been?"

Still, Valdez, the man who'd been in front of me in the line, *was* dead, and if I'd been behind him perhaps he would have been shielded, perhaps he would have been saved. Valdez, a peasant, a veteran of the hills of over eighteen months, a valued man, someone who would be needed now, now that it was over.

Perhaps, Pepe agreed. It wasn't clear from which way the shell had come, ahead of the column or behind, so there was no way of knowing if my movement had made any difference. War, Pepe said, is full of perhapses. So is life, he said. "Don't be bitter that you are alive, Francesco."

It's good advice, of course—great advice, the best. Sitting here, at the edge of the world, it all makes sense, too. Life is filled with shame, and regret, just as it is with pride and honor and satisfaction, just as the day is filled with darkness and light. There isn't one time of day that's *better* than another, just various parts, different, each with its own value, making up the whole. The important thing, as Rogie would say, I think, is to give a shit about the differences.

And that's easy enough to say, even to believe, sitting at the edge of the world gazing out at a herd of sea monsters swimming by, swimming back from the other side of eternity where the world ceases and only nothingness begins—easy enough to say at the edge of the world, where nothing is ever exactly what it seems and sea monsters, after all, are only whales.

10. Buddy Holly Died Here

I make fun of my father's mystical moments, but I've had a few of my own.

The girl in the river, say.

I tell people about her, they laugh, but she was real, all right.

The winter I got back from Cuba, all shot up and some of the piss kicked out of me, they wouldn't let me back into school in the middle of the year and by spring I was going stir-crazy hanging around the house. The band was pretty much broken up and the other kids I used to hang around with were in school. Soon as the weather got decent, around April, I said good-bye to Pops and hung out my thumb, heading west.

When I was a kid and convinced my father hated me, I'd run away from home a bunch of times, always heading west, but never got very far. I crossed the Hudson and the Delaware rivers, but the Mississippi was as far away as China. And that whole tour the band had been on in the fall of '58, which was the most traveling I'd ever done, we'd gone through Ohio and Indiana but, for some reason, never made it to Chicago. Now I was there, and about to make it all the way to what, geography aside, I thought of as the center of the country, the dividing line between *back there* and *out here*.

I stayed in a real skid row hotel, complete with bedbugs and roaches—man, what romance!—and had a long talk with some bums and hookers stationed right outside, made like a real walk-on-the-wild-side tourist, took in all the blues I could eat down on

63rd Street Saturday night and then, next morning, with a fog
hanging over the city, I took a rattling El as far west as I could go,
then hiked a bit to a freeway, and started thumbing.

Oh, man, this was it. The open road, freedom, me and the sky.
I'd just read *On the Road*, was fresh back from the wars and even
had a little limp to make me feel romantic about it. It was spring
and I was on my way toward Ol' Man Ribber.

I had a couple of rides, short ones, and then I was picked up
by a plump salesman in a sharkskin suit and driving a salmon-
pink, shark-finned Plymouth convertible heading for Des Moines.
My head was full of cotton batting and I told him if I dozed off to
please wake me when we were approaching the river. Next thing I
know, this guy is nudging me and I'm pushing away the fog and—
I swear—I can smell the river, smell the water, and I open my eyes
and she's the first thing I see, like a vision one of those medieval
saints might have had.

"Stop the car!" I holler.

"What?"

"Stop the car, come on, I've got to get out here."

"You crazy? I can't stop here," the salesman says, and it's true,
we're on an old-fashioned metal bridge with two narrow lanes, a
steady stream of traffic behind us. I crane my neck out the window
and I can just see a glimpse of her now, and in a second she's
gone, out of sight behind a steel girder. But I have the image of her
burned on my retinas, burned in my mind.

She was a young girl, I think, although I didn't actually see her
face. She was standing in the water, at the edge, a foot or so from
the grassy bank. There was a little dog on the grass, its front legs
stretched out and its rear in the air, barking at her, and she was
leaning over the water and reaching down with one hand, splashing the dog. Her other hand was holding the hem of her skirt up
around her thighs. The tails of her shirt were tied around her waist
and the buttons were open at her throat, which was very white, like

her thighs. She looked up as we passed, maybe because my shout startled her, but her dark hair tumbled over her face and I couldn't see it. There was a fog along the river but there were patches of sunlight every hundred yards or so, wherever there was a break in the clouds flickering overhead, and she was standing in a puddle of sun, like a sigh in the middle of a storm.

When we got to the other side of the bridge, Muscatine, Iowa, my salesman pulled over and gave me a funny look. "You okay?"

I felt a little silly but I thanked him and got out of the car and walked back on the bridge, on a narrow pedestrian shoulder that seemed to have been an afterthought, toward Rock Island. The river's wide there and it took me a few minutes just to get to the middle, where I should have been able to see her. But I couldn't. And, as I got closer to the Illinois side, my heart was sinking, because it was clear she was gone. I scrambled down to the bank and walked along it to where I was pretty sure she had been, but there wasn't any trace of her, just some dog shit that may have been fresh, maybe not.

I sat on the grass and watched the muddy river flow by for awhile, a little surprised, I think, by how dirty it was. There'd never been anything in Mark Twain to prepare me for that, and the girl had been so clean, so shining. I leaned over and reached into the water for some pebbles and tossed them back, one at a time, watching the circles they made grow wider and wider. I felt immensely sad, as if I had lost something of incredible value, but I also felt good because I had come so close to finding something. And I felt a little foolish, too, thinking about how I had yelled to stop the car, and jumped out and ran back, and now was sitting stranded on the riverbank with evening coming down around me. What the hell would I have said to her if she had been there? "Excuse me, miss, but you're America, aren't you? Just the way old Huck said we'd find you, your skirts lifted, your face hidden, your head lifted toward the sun."

Now I look for her whenever I cross the river, at Rock Island or Moline, or anyplace else, and I did again last week, riding in a stripped down red '54 Chevy with Neil Cassady himself at the wheel. Well, if it wasn't Neil, it was his third cousin by marriage. Soul mate. He was all that was left of a crew of Dharma Bums I'd been partying with, just him and the world's biggest hangover to remind me of the dope we smoked, the beer we drank.

The tour I'm on—a real tour, with actual dates and places, someone else making the arrangements, and tickets sold at the door, not a passing hat to be seen—had me headed to a place called Iowa City, where I had a gig that night in a little folkie bar, "a real cool dive," that's what Redbed said, he'd been there, and I had to take his word for it, since I hadn't.

I'd met up with these guys in the Chevy in Wisconsin, where I was working the college towns. After that, it's all pretty much a blur. I wound up in Chicago in this crash pad on the near north side, a few blocks in from the lake and not far from Old Town. There's some nice clubs there, and I've worked in a couple of them, but not this time around. Four years later, Chicago isn't the kick it was the first time. Now it was the next day, Friday, early, and I had this incredible headache and the freezing November wind was slicing us to ribbons, me and this cat called Redbed, as we zoomed through Illinois in his fabulous beast, not a convertible but its windows broken and no heater to speak of, its Hollywood muffler announcing our every move to the world, headed toward the Mississippi, and Iowa, lying beyond like some sort of pastoral virgin, her green corn thighs spread to welcome us. More like a mousetrap, as it turned out.

Redbed—they call him that, he tells me, because he's a Red, but lazy. He laughs like a maniac when he tells me this, showing me a set of tobacco-stained teeth smooth and even as kernels of corn on a cob. Naturally, I tell him about the girl in the river, the girl with the sky in her eyes, but she isn't there. "Tha's okay,"

Redbed shrugs philosophically. "I'll catch her on the run back." But I'm disappointed, the way I always seem to be when I enter Iowa, maybe always will. I've crossed the river, but I'm still not where I'm going, wherever the hell that is.

We wheeled into Iowa City a little past noon. I could still have been sleeping, letting my hangover seep its way into the pillow, if Redbed hadn't been so accommodating. He'd offered to drive me, but then it turned out he had to be somewhere that evening and he wouldn't be talked out of his promise. So instead of sleeping in and then taking a snoozing bus ride in the afternoon, here I was in Iowa City in broad daylight, my head splitting, and hours to go before I'd be playing.

Redbed dropped me at the bus depot, which was at the rear of a crummy hotel with a cafe, and then he split. I was out on the street in my jeans and a denim jacket, carrying a duffel bag and my guitar in its case, feeling rotten from the headache but good at being out and about in the brilliant sunshine, dry leaves crackling under my feet and still a few of them, red and yellow, over my head on the trees along the street and across it, where the campus and the university began, and feeling sad, too.

I stepped into the cafe and had the special, a Number 3: two eggs (I took them over easy, the yolks just barely coated with skin), hash browns, except the sign on the wall called them American fries, toast dripping with butter, and battery-acid coffee. The guy sitting next to me at the counter was a used-up character in his fifties, wearing a brown suit frayed at the lapels and shiny at the elbows and knees, and a limp white shirt transparent with age and washing.

"Name's Homer Brittle, just like Peanut Brittle," he told me, flashing an eggy grin. "That's what they called me when I wuz a kid, but I ain't been a kid in years. Ain't worked in three years, not since I hurt my back. Don't have no home no more, neither, not since the wife kicked me out."

I wiped up egg with toast and commiserated.

"Ain't no bum, though," he said, gesturing at his clothes. "Clean and neat, that gives you pride. You got pride, you ain't no bum, no matter what."

He'd come in on a bus from St. Louis an hour before and was heading to Kansas City.

"Long way around, ain't it?" I asked him.

"Sure, but what the hell, I got plenty of time." He gave me a wink. I didn't ask him how he afforded the bus fare, and he didn't say.

He left to catch his bus and I went back onto the street, thinking maybe there was a song in the old guy. In fact, there was, and I got it down just yesterday, a nice folksy thing I call "79 Cents," which is what the Number 3 at the Campus Grill in Iowa City costs. I walked down the street with the sun in my face, my jacket open, eyeing the coeds. When I got to the corner, I looked down the cross street and saw a beer sign and headed for it. The place was so dark inside, I had to stand at the door for a moment to adjust my eyes, breathing in the sour, yeasty smell. I had a dark tap beer and ordered another, beginning to feel a touch more human.

I looked around me at the bar. It was oak, nicely carved and heavily polished, with a brass rail at the bottom for a foot rest, but I was the only one sitting at it. The plump, gray-haired woman who had poured the beer was drying a glass and ignoring me. A couple of cats and a big, high-cheekboned girl with hair the color of a boiled lobster in a long braid were sitting in a booth against the wall, sharing a pitcher of beer and a bag of nuts. Down at the end of the room, there were a few other faceless people sitting at a table, and a cat with a bald head was playing pinball. Except for the soft murmur of voices and the occasional bells from the pinball machine, the place was Sunday morning quiet. I sipped my beer and thought about the old dude at the bus stop cafe, the first snatches of lyric and melody of his song starting to elbow their way through the fog in my head, and watched, through the mirror above the bar, the people in the booth behind me, my eyes mostly on the girl. I must have looked down for a minute, though, because I didn't notice this cat get up and sidle next to me till he was there.

"Hey, man."

His face was a thick tangle of dark hair, the intensity of his hazel eyes burning through the mop startling. He leaned against the bar with the loose-jointed ease of a cowboy setting his weight against a corral fence. "Hey, you Frankie Stein?"

"Sure," I said. It really is a kick being recognized, not that it happens all that often.

"Your picture's on a poster all over the place," he said, maybe reading my thoughts. "Just like the wozard of iz."

"All over? No shit."

"Well, one or two I seen, mostly at the pest office." He laughed, pleased that I'd set him up. I didn't mind. He told me his name, which was Jim Eisenhower, "and call me Ike, just like the verdant old war mule," raising his hand Indian style. I did the same. "C'mon over and have hopsoup with us."

It turned out that Eisenhower was from Davenport or Moline or one of those river towns along the Iowa-Illinois border—he had a practiced vagueness in his speech that made it tough to pin him down. "Up around Mopyport, Davengaline, that part of the big shiny world, Kit Carson country," he said when I asked them where they were from, "where the river runs sweet as molasses and catfish leap out of the stew to bare their hearts for tomorrow's secrets." So was the other guy, whose name was also Jim, but he didn't say much. The Irishy-looking girl was Ike's wife. She reminded me of a girl I knew a few years ago, in New England someplace. Up close, she was pale and not as good looking as I'd thought, eyeing her through the mirror, with a horsy jaw and startlingly long teeth when she smiled, which she did a lot. Her name was Dorcas, which made *me* smile, never having heard it before.

"That's a good Irish name," she said, showing her big teeth and her cheeks coloring slightly.

Ike was an ugly little guy with a dark brown beard growing all up his face and hair coming down to meet it, with only those bright eyes and a big W.C. Field nose sticking out of all that fur to identify his face as a human's, like one of those mountain characters in *Li'l Abner*. He talked with a Midwestern-southern twang more Missouri than Iowa, and half of what he had to say was overblown poetry, the other half slang he made up himself, on the fly, and he talked a mile a minute, once he got going. There was a sheaf of typewritten pages on the table, along with puddles of beer and peanut skins, and they turned out to be the latest chapter from this novel Ike's writing, has been working on, he said, for years, "since Noah's flood wasted its tears down to the banks of the Great Salt Lake." He started to tell me about it, reading aloud whole paragraphs at a time from the manuscript. It sounded crazy but good, about a magician who lives on a raft on the Mississippi, floating downstream and running across all sorts of crazy characters. This magician lives forever, and whenever he gets too far down the river he turns the raft around and floats upstream for a while, "like fresh blood racing toward the heart," Ike said.

"So he never gets anywhere," I said.

"That's it, nowhere and everywhere, round and expound, through the middle. Like a grasshopper omelet."

Ike's molasses-slush voice washed over me and I closed my eyes, sleepy. My headache had eased off, the beer was starting to do the right things to me and I had the nice crunchy, oily taste of peanuts in my teeth and under my tongue. Naturally, I told them about the girl in the river.

"Tha's my sister, Springtime," Ike said, teeth flashing white and gold through the fur. "Great girl, Springtime, goddess of the river, raises phoenixes in her spare time. Great girl, but, you know, a little ... taitched." He tapped his forehead with a blunt finger, the nail bitten down to the quick.

We ordered another pitcher—I paid for it, being, as it turned out, the only one among the four of us who had anything remotely resembling a regular income—and after awhile I got up to take a leak. I walked back through the semi-darkness of the room to the toilet, which was surprisingly clean, and when I came out, adjusting my eyes again from bright to dark, I noticed a phone booth in the corner, just behind the pinball machine. The cat with the bald head—he didn't look any older than me—was hovering there, not playing, just swaying above the machine, his hands loose along its sides, like some kind of a zealot at a bloodthirsty shrine. Seeing the phone booth reminded me that I needed to call my agent. After Iowa City, I had this other gig in a couple of days in Grinnell, but I didn't know what was coming after that, if anything, and Armand was supposed to be working on it, setting some things up.

So I step into the phone booth and call him, collect. I can see a clock above the bar, a big round yellow face with the word BUD-WEISER across it and a cutout of those big horses and a beer-wagon beneath it, and it's saying a quarter to one, which means it's a quarter to two in New York and, if I'm lucky, Armand will be back from lunch.

The phone rings for what seems like a long time and I'm just about to hang up, my hand already starting to direct the receiver back to its hook, when I hear a tinny "Hello."

"Mr. Stein calling from Iowa City," the operator says, her voice Midwestern flat and static. "Will you accept the charges?"

A pause, then a woman's voice. "Mr. Stein? I...."

"Frankie," I say.

Another pause. Then the same voice, Armand's secretary, Lisa, "Oh, Frankie."

But she doesn't say anything else and the operator repeats after a moment, "Will you accept the charges?"

It sounds like Lisa's crying and there's a clatter at the other end of the line, as if the phone has been dropped, and another pause, and then Armand's phony French accent is accepting the charges and saying "Ah, Frankee, I can't believe it."

"Armand, I told you I'd call. You told me to."

"Not that, Frankee. I can't believe it. I just can't."

"Can't believe what, Armand?"

"Oh, you don't know? No, of course not. They've got radios in Iowa?"

"I guess, but...."

"Kennedy, they just shot Kennedy," Armand said. "We just heard it on the radio. There was a bulletin."

For a moment, I wasn't sure who he meant, then everything, his words, the brittle tone of his voice, the secretary's odd behavior, all fell into place, like soldiers' feet in a long, grim line. "Aw, come on. You're crazy."

"No, I'm not, Frankee, I wish I were. We were listening to OR, there's a group I'm handling, they were going to play their record today but I didn't know when, so we've been listening all day. There was a bulletin."

"Armand, you're kidding, right? You're shitting me."

"No, I'm not, Frankee. They broke in. I swear, it was just a minute ago. Someplace in Texas. It was just ten seconds on the radio and then the phone rang. It was you. That's why we're so rattled, Lisa and I."

I didn't say anything, letting it sink in, and Armand said: "They got him, the bastards. They killed the president. They killed Kennedy." He sounded old and bitter, like a father talking about his son, dead in a war neither of them had understood.

"Who's 'they,' Armand?"

"I don't know. *You* know, the bastards, the creeps, the Commies, the Nazis, one of them. What difference does it make? *They.* They got him."

In the silence that followed, I listened to the crackle of the long distance line for long seconds until I became aware of another sound that I couldn't place at first, then realized it was Armand, sobbing into the mouthpiece. He is a funny guy, somewhere in the vague thirties or forties, and in the third rank of agents. He was born in Coeur D'Alene, Idaho, or French Lick, Indiana, or some place like that—Des Moines, Iowa, most likely—that inspired him to call himself Armand, and put on that phony accent. He's as French as the salad dressing that comes in bottles, but he's got a Gallic soul, honest enough. But I wasn't thinking of him then. I was thinking of the river, the Mississippi, the water lapping up on the green shore, little curly clouds swaying overhead like question marks, and the girl who wasn't there, was never there, was never there.

"Frankee, I can't talk anymore," Armand said. "I got a couple of other dates for you in Iowa, and some other things, but I can't talk now. Call Monday, okay, kid?"

"Sure, Armand." I said good-bye and hung up. Then, for no good reason, I picked up the phone again and held it to my ear, listening to the abrasive buzz. But it didn't tell me anything.

I went back to the booth. Ike and Dorcas and the cat called Jim were still sitting there, and another guy, with long hair and a slightly crooked nose, was sitting next to Jim, where I'd been. And there were two guys in jeans and beards and dark jackets leaning against the bar, facing the booth, and the gray-haired woman behind the bar was standing next to the taps, listening to the conversation. So it could have been any of them, the informer, any one of those seven people—although it seems pretty unlikely that it was either of the Eisenhowers—or maybe someone else entirely, someone I didn't notice or the bald guy, who was now draped over the pinball machine, seemingly asleep.

Ike was talking, his Missouri yap a blur of motion. The cat sitting in my spot was listening raptly and didn't look up, but Dorcas did, showing me her teeth. I could picture her standing in the river, her skirts raised, the sun on her thighs.

"Hey," I said. "I just heard Kennedy was killed."

"No shit," Ike said. "The prince of frogs, back to the pond, silent as the water lilies."

Everybody looked at him and, for a moment, I think they were more entranced with what he'd said than what I'd said.

"JFK?" the other Jim finally asked. "The president?"

"That's what I heard. Shot, somewhere in Texas."

"Oh, God," the woman behind the bar said. "What kind of a country are we living in?"

Everybody turned to look at her. Tears suddenly stood out on her cheeks like warts, making her look ugly, misshapen.

"I don't think I want to live in this country anymore." She wiped at her face and shook her head, turning away.

"Jesus," one of the guys leaning against the bar said.

The guy with the crooked nose got up and leaned against the bar and I slid into the booth. We finished up the pitcher of beer and then a third one. Dorcas told a story about an Irish cousin who'd brushed up against Kennedy when the president visited Dublin the year before. There was a funny twist to the story at the end, and when she got to it she let her voice fall into a thick brogue that spilled out of her mouth like cream from a pitcher: "That's not my wife, it's the assistant secretary of commerce." We all laughed.

The guys at the bar drifted away. Someone else came in. The bald guy woke up and the bells resumed their chattering song from the pinball machine, like calls from distant birds. I was tired and the Eisenhowers said I could crash at their place, stay the night, too, if I wanted. I hadn't set anything else up and that sounded good. As it turned out, I wound up staying there two nights, and they even drove me up here to Grinnell. Nice people.

They took me a couple of blocks away to their place, two

rooms and a kitchenette in a rundown building webbed with tiny shoebox apartments like a rabbit warren. "Welcome to Cockroach Arms, home of dreams, dreamers, turquoise nights and Tiffany mornings," Ike said. The place seemed clean enough and I was too tired to be fussy. They gave me blankets and a sofa in the living room and disappeared while I stretched out. I fell asleep instantly, my face pressed against a rough, limp pillow.

In the evening, the Eisenhowers and I stopped to get something to eat and got to the bar about a quarter to eight. The guy who runs the place was pacing the floor because I'd forgotten to phone. But everything was cool. He was worried people wouldn't come because of the shock but I told him, no, people will want to flock together, for comfort and warmth, and I was right. We had a full house but people were quiet, subdued, and I did a strange set of songs, things I knew wouldn't break the mood, some stuff of my own but also "Masters of War" and "Blowin' in the Wind," Dylan songs I'd just learned, and an odd version of "The Bells of Rhymny" some cat in the Village taught me. They liked that. At the end of the final set, a woman with streaks of gray in her hair that seemed wrong for her young face asked for "The Star Spangled Banner." I didn't think I could do it and asked if "The Battle Hymn of the Republic" would do as well and she said it would. I sang that and, toward the end, everybody joined in. It was nice.

I went back to the Eisenhowers' after the bar closed up, which is at midnight in Iowa, and we smoked some grass Redbed had pressed into my hand before leaving me that morning. They'd never had any and it went right to work on them. Ike recited a long, Rimbaud-like poem he'd written that sounded wonderful, though I'm no judge. Nothing like the clean simple lines of the poems my cousin Rhoda writes. I crashed on the sofa again. Next thing I knew, there was a banging at the door and Ike's cursing. "Go away, infidels, the frog king's in his pond and there's no one to entertain the likes of mortals like you," he yelled.

But the banging kept up. I opened my eyes and it was light. Ike came out of the bedroom naked and scratching at the mat of hair running down his chest to his belly, like a smudged extension of his beard. I heard him muttering at the door and somebody outside said something I didn't hear and I rolled over. Then there was a hand on my shoulder.

"We're federal agents," a voice said. "Are you Frankie Stein, also known as Francesco Stern?"

I grunted and nodded, trying to untangle myself from the blankets Dorcas had thrown over me. "Sure. So what?"

There were two men standing over me, both with pistols in their hands, one looking at me, the other eyeing Ike, who was still by the door, and they didn't look like they were in the mood for kidding. The sight of those guns gave me a chill like I haven't had since I was in Cuba.

"Yeah, I am," I said.

"Maybe you'd better get up," one of the men said.

They were nice enough, as it turned out, nicer than I would have guessed, anyway. They put their guns away and we went into the kitchen and they let me put some water on for coffee. But when Ike tried to butt in, they chased him back to the bedroom.

I'm pretty groggy in the mornings until I've had my coffee, so I don't remember exactly how the conversation went, but it was something like this:

"What brings you to Iowa City, Mr. Stein?"

"I'm a musician. I had a job to play last night, and again tonight."

"Where were you before here?"

"Came in yesterday from Chicago. Before that, up in Wisconsin, Madison, Beloit, a couple of other places."

"You can verify that?"

"I've been playing gigs for the last couple of months, not every day but plenty of them. I get a *few* people out."

"We'll talk about that later. How did you come to town?"

"A guy I met gave me a ride."

"A guy you met. Where was that, and what was his name?"

"A guy I met in Madison. A bunch of guys. They were going to Chicago and they gave me a ride. One of them offered to carry me over here. I don't remember his name, don't think I ever heard it." I bit my tongue here. "No, they called him Red."

There were more questions like that, but I had already figured out where they were leading, so I wasn't surprised when they finally got around to it.

"At approximately ten minutes to 1 PM yesterday afternoon, 12:50 PM that is, local time, you told some people in Kenney's bar that the president had been killed." The man who was talking was tall and gaunt, almost bony, with shiny brown hair brushed sideways in the front, early fifties style, and a mole over his lip that made his face look lopsided. His neat brown suit was a size too big, as if he had recently lost weight. He looked like a druggist and he talked slowly and precisely. "How did you happen to have that information?"

They looked at each other when I told them about my phone call to Armand. The tall man's partner was a short, crewcut younger cat with bright green eyes, an eager punk. He didn't say much but he took notes furiously, as if he was a reporter and I was someone famous, giving an exclusive interview. The one thing he did say which I remember clearly was this:

"You expect us to believe that?"

I laughed. "Sure, why not? That's what happened." In the bedroom, Ike erupted into laughter, banging his head against the door where he was listening. The FBI cats looked over their shoulders, then at each other and shrugged.

"Your friend, he's got something against clothes?" the younger cat asked.

"It's the middle of the fucking night, man," I said.

"Some life you live," Green Eyes said. "It's past nine o'clock and to you it's the middle of the night. Some life."

"Hey, man, I *work* nights. *Work.*"

"And look at the friends you make. You know this guy, the guy with the hairy mask and the fabulous wardrobe, before yesterday?"

From behind the door, I could hear Ike killing himself with laughter. "Flying pigs over the garden at twelve o'clock high," he cackled.

"Jesus," Green Eyes said. "And this fellow with the car? Red, you said *maybe* he was called? Another guy you just met and took up with?"

"I didn't *take up* with him, or with anyone else. What're you getting at, man? I meet people, we become friends. What's the big fucking deal?"

"You were in Cuba in 1959," the bony man said abruptly, waving his hand impatiently at his partner. It wasn't a question so I didn't answer, just nodded my head. This didn't surprise me, either. I'd been waiting for it.

"Working for the Communists," he went on.

"They weren't Communists. And I wasn't working *for* them."

"No?"

"No. They were patriots, democrats. Maybe some of them were, so what? Some of them were probably Eisenhower Republicans, for all I know." I laughed. "The *other* Eisenhower. At any rate, that isn't what that fight was about."

"Oh? What *was* it about?" the crewcut asked.

"Hey, this is history," I said. "Ancient history, for me. You want to know what happened in Cuba, there's some good books on the subject, why don't you read one?"

"It's *you* we're interested in," Crewcut shot back. "Not Cuba."

"Well, maybe you should arrest me and I should get a lawyer. Then we can talk all you want." A couple trips South teaches a body *something* about his rights.

"Take it easy, son," the bony cat said. Cops always call you "son" when they're trying to show what nice, decent sorts they are. "Nobody said anything about arresting anyone."

"Then maybe you should get the hell out of here and let me have my breakfast in peace." I was on my feet, pouring boiling water into a cup with instant coffee.

Bony unwrapped his legs from around the kitchen chair he'd been making love to and got up. He really was tall, like a flagpole, with a knob of a head at the top of it. He looked like they'd pulled the flag up and down him too many times, skinning off the finish.

"Okay, son, we're about through. But let me tell you this: yesterday, someone shot the president of the United States. You knew about it, here, over a thousand miles away, minutes later, before it had been on any radio news in this town, in this state even. You said the president had been killed before he died. And the man who's been arrested as a suspect in the shooting of the president is a man who has very close ties to Cuba. And you were in Cuba, you fought there on the side of the people who have become the enemies of this country, regardless of what they might have been then. Now..." He stopped talking and spread his large, bony hands, palms up, like a supplicant in an Arab market, his head cocked to the side. "What would *you* think?"

Later on, laughing over all this with Ike and Dorcas, I couldn't bring myself to admit that I'd felt like crying then, not because he had shamed me or anything like that, but because I suddenly had this flash of how vulnerable we all are, how thin is the thread that keeps us this side of the jungle or madness or both. Our lives are so complicated, the truth so fragile, and it's so easy to misunderstand—like those trick photos where you look at them one way and see one thing and look at them another way and see something else entirely. Sometimes you can get locked on one side, and that's all you can see, try as you might. The other side is there, you just can't see it.

What I'm getting at is that you go through life trying to be a decent person, trying to do good, trying to keep your feet going in a certain way. But what if you're really doing bad? What then? I mean, doing bad and not knowing it. Or what if you really are doing good, but people *think* you're doing bad? What then? Like the good Samaritan who goes to help someone in a fight and winds up getting clobbered himself, just for butting in.

I mean, how do we protect ourselves from the lies we don't tell but people hear?

That's what I was thinking then as these two cops and I stared at each other in the Eisenhowers' kitchen, cracked plaster and all. I don't pray often, don't have anything or anyone to pray to, but sometimes you just can't help yourself. So I said a little prayer then, and this was it:

"Please, God, if you exist at all, please don't let me be misunderstood."

Then these guys got up and cleared out. I'd given them Armand's name and number and they said they were going to check. "You do that," I said.

"We will," Crewcut said, his bright green eyes crackling with something not quite anger, but not disgust, either. "We'll be in touch."

Of course, they haven't been. That was four days ago and there hasn't been a sniff of them, so I guess they got it all cleared up. It's really pretty funny, seems that way to me now, anyway. There isn't anything funny about what happened in Dallas but I guess my little part of it will make a good story a few years from now. It's nice to be able to say you were part of history, even if only a microscopic, inconsequential part. Someday, people will nudge each other when I walk into a room and whisper: "There goes the man who broke the news to Iowa City." They can't take that away from me.

Talk about your mystical moments.

I played another night in Iowa City, as advertised, although we didn't get such good houses this time around, and Ike and Dorcas gave me a lift up here to Grinnell in a battered old pickup truck with a "Vote for Hoover" sticker on its rear bumper. I played a couple of nights in a rathskeller in the student union and now I'm just hanging around until the weekend, when I have another gig, in a place called Cedar Falls, another little college town.

I'm disappointed I'm not going to be playing at Clear Lake. That's where Ritchie Valens and Buddy Holly and those guys died, in the famous aircrash—not for anybody's sins, though God knows we could use the help. It's not far, so maybe I'll hitch a ride up there anyway, take a look around. After that, other places to go, gigs to play. I forget where. I'm in no real hurry to go, or wasn't.

It snowed this morning—first of the season—and I went for a walk in it, getting my feet soaked. All sorts of things were running through my head, like Peanut Brittle, his hollow cheeks and the shiny spots on his suit, but clean and neat, no bum, and I sang the chorus of the song I'd written about him a couple of times, changing a word or two here and there. But the girl in the river kept elbowing him out of the way, asking why she's never made it into a song. It's not because I haven't tried. This town's pretty small so it wasn't long before I was *out* of the town, on a country road where the snow was falling thicker. I stopped to make a snowball and threw it without much force at an unsuspecting tree. Then I noticed my toes were freezing, so I turned around and headed back. Thinking about the girl on the river had reminded me of something else. Suddenly I was feeling anxious to be on my way.

This was on another trip, a couple of months ago. I'd been playing all over the map, college concerts, bars, coffee houses, some festivals during the summer, and, more and more, benefits of all kinds, either in the South or elsewhere to raise money to send South. I'd even played in Washington during the big march in

August, and I'd been in some coal mining town in Pennsylvania—
Sheppton, it was called—where people were trying to rescue three
miners trapped at the bottom of a collapsed tunnel. It had been a
crazy summer and I was a little weary and trying to take it easier,
just doing a couple or three gigs a week so I could clear my head
and maybe even write a song or two in between. But there's no
rest for the wicked. I was in Ohio, playing a college, and when I
checked in with Armand it turned out the bastard had got me into
a festival near Denver, a last-minute replacement. It was a good
kind of a gig to have, good people to be playing with, Judy Collins
among them, but it was crazy because I had to be back in Ohio
again a few days later, for some dates set up earlier.

I'd met these people at Antioch, real Beat types, not just
scruffy guys, a couple of poets, a quiet one named Karl and his
noisy pal called Leadbelly, and a weird political-mystical cat called
Philo who wore glasses thick as Coke bottle bottoms. Ike would
have fit right in. Leadbelly had this brand-new Chrysler that
belonged to his dad, a guy with a real belly who owned half of
some Ohio town, and they were keen to show how hip they were
by getting a lot of mud and miles on the beast. So I had a ride.

I was booked in for the final day of the festival, Monday, in the
afternoon, and we left Antioch Sunday morning, so we didn't have
much time to spare. Philo and Karl and Leadbelly took turns driving and we all passed around some wine that must have been
made from squeezing the feet of the peasants who stomp on the
grapes, it was that sour and thin. We made good time and were a
happy crew.

At dusk, we crossed the Mississippi at Rock Island, and I told
Leadbelly to drive slow. I told them about her, about my vision, and
Leadbelly, who was a big, plump boy with an Allen Ginsberg beard,
said it was a wonderful vision, one to base an epic poem on. He
wanted to stop and search the banks of the river for her, sleep
along the river in hopes of seeing her at dawn, but Steamboat

Springs was still hours away so we just laughed, drank some more wine and drove on.

We drove through the evening, all across Iowa, and it was past midnight when we crossed into Nebraska. The wheels were singing on the highway and the headlights speared ahead of us into the darkness, pulling us along in their wake. There was staticky music on the radio coming from Denver and it seemed to get clearer and louder with each mile.

Philo was driving, squinting through those thick glasses, and he didn't notice the sign saying the freeway was ending, so when we came to a sign that said "last exit to Lincoln," he ignored it. After another quarter of a mile, there was a barrier closing off the road and a massive sign that said "Interstate Ends."

"The end of the road," Karl said softly, the first thing he'd said in hours. Philo stopped the car and we sat there in darkness that was total except for the Chrysler's headlights and the glow from the dashboard, bewildered, looking at the sign dumbly and trying to figure out where we were. We'd been driving all day, drinking that wine, and we were hypnotized, sort of, the way you can get.

"Where the hell are we?" Leadbelly said. Karl got out the roadmap and all four heads bent over it in the weak light from the overhead lamp.

And then a funny thing happened. The music on the radio stopped and the news came on, and it was about Birmingham. We'd had the radio on and off through the day, but for some reason we'd never caught any news, so we hadn't heard this yet, even though it was old already. Birmingham, Alabama—that beautiful name. It's got the sound of poetry in it, but I've been there—just last spring I sang to a crowd of, I don't know how many, a hundred or more at a Negro church, and the next morning most of them were in jail—and it's not really a very nice town. This night, the news was about a bombing in a Negro church that morning, maybe the same one I'd played at, and some girls who were killed, and then two boys, one by a policeman, another by two white boys, for no apparent reason, and the governor sending in state troopers to keep the peace, though it seemed a little late for that.

Keep the peace. That was what the voice on the radio said.

"How can there be any peace?" Leadbelly asked.

He turned off the radio and Philo turned off the ignition. We sat in the car for a long time, the headlights the only break in a darkness that was complete, without a star or a glimmer from another car or a building anywhere in the distance, a darkness that wrapped around us like God's breath. I was thinking, for no good reason, about the girl on the river, her thighs flashing white, her face hidden by flowing hair, her head lifted to the sun. I was wondering if I had ever really seen her, and if I would ever see her again.

And in the silence, the only evidence available to our senses that an intelligent life was present among us was the sign illuminated by our headlights: "Interstate Ends."

"The end of the road," Karl had said, but I swear, it felt more like the end of the world, like we were the only ones left, hurtling through space and eternity until the end they said would never come hit us right in the face.

11. Three Women

It's finally happened, the moment I've dreaded: I'm in love.

And with a girl called Molly Bloom, no less.

That's not really her name, it's Margaret Reagan, but she calls herself Molly, and I call her Molly Bloom, after my own fancy, because she truly is blooming within me, and I in her.

This girl is a reincarnation of someone from an earlier life— my own, that is. I was an itinerant folk singer with barely a change of strings to my name and she was an earnest—oh, *so* earnest— student at Goddard College, where I played once, back in those good old days when the world was new and there was so much that could be done.

Then there was a Woolworth's in a city nearby, a picket line. Me cooling my heels in a jail cell waiting for a judge, cursing her for having dragged me along, she and her pretty ass safe and sound back in the dorm, hitting the books, not even knowing I'd been busted.

All that is forgiven now, of course. Love bears no grudges— that part, Pops used to say, comes later. Right now, I'm just in love, for real, and it's unlike anything else I've ever done or saw or thought about. It isn't bells ringing or violins playing or angels singing in the leafy bowers overhead, nothing like that. And it isn't a high, like the kind you get from drinking vodka martinis at those New York literary cocktail parties my cousin Rhoda has become so fond of, or beer in some low dive (we put tomato juice in it here in Iowa and call it a Bloody Nose), or the kind you get from smoking grass (which I've been doing a lot of lately). It isn't anything like that. It's more like the feeling a snake must have when it's shed its skin and a new one is growing: raw and sensitive to every touch, every breath and sound, and everything is new, undiscovered.

Stags must have that feeling when their antlers fall off, except they don't just *fall* off, they batter them off, knocking their heads against trees and the heads of other bucks. *That's* what being in love is like, wanting to knock your head against trees, not because you want to bash your head in (that comes later, if I remember Pops on the subject right, when everything's gone bad and sour), but because you want to experience the tree—all feelings I never had with anyone before, not even Ana, who I used to think was the one true love of my life.

"It's a damn shame fucking takes such a short time," I remember telling Ana once. "We think about it, scheme about it, plan it, look for it, work up to it, sweat and cry for it, and then— poof—it's over, and the whole thing starts up again."

"Well, tha's okay," she said, snuggling her nose in beneath my chin, doing her patented little girl imitation, "but it would be nice, now wouldn' it, if it went on a teensy bit longer?"

I'll go her one further.

I've been thinking lately that it's only while fucking that we are truly alive—I mean *alive*, not just living, *open*, wide open to the universe and what it has to offer—so the orgasm, when it comes, because it's an end to that rhythm, that openness, is like a door slamming shut. Oh, lovely door, oh, sweet slam.

And it suddenly becomes clear to me what all the fuss about virginity is, although it's upside down or inside out, maybe because it comes from old women and men with collars turned around and other people who have either forgotten or never knew. It doesn't matter whether you're a virgin when you're in love because the loving makes you into one, regardless of what's gone on before, and every time *is* the first time, brand new—not just the making of love but the things that make *up* love, every touch, every laugh, every sight of her, every word, all new, every time. How else to explain the way the world turns, why people don't fall off when they're on the down side? You can't. You just sit back and let the world turn. Maybe, if you're lucky, you can watch. Maybe, if you're *really* lucky, you don't even fall off.

I mean, everything with Molly and me has been exactly the opposite of how love was supposed to be. I always thought it would be the pizza-pie-in-the-face thing like in the songs—hell, even in *my* songs.

That's the way it was with me and Ana, the old "some enchanted evening you will see a stranger."

I'd been playing that evening at the Cafe Au Go Go, at a fundraiser, something to do with a bunch of people getting busted the day before in a big protest—Johnson had just sicked the B52s on the north—and afterwards some of us wound up at a party over in the East Village, blowing some dope and ogling the chicks, and there she was, a fucking vision, an apparition in a sailor suit, white bell bottoms and a kind of middy top, navy blue. I shook my head, rubbed my eyes, but she didn't go away, and it was love at first sight, just like in all the stupid songs. She must have felt the same thing, or something like it, because she started weaving across the room toward me, just as I was heading toward her. We met in the middle and I said to her—I swear this is true—"This is it, isn't it?" and she said "Yes." Just like that, one word, fitting like a key into a lock I'd put around myself for no good reason, just because it had fit.

Rhoda, always my confidante, didn't think so, but Ana is striking, which I admit is at least part of what I liked so much about her, since she wasn't really my kind of girl. Four years at Bennington and two on her own in the city had brushed a lot of the

Midwest off her, but at heart she's still a square. A beautiful square, though. She's fair, part Swedish and all Indiana. Even when she was tired, her skin glowed with electricity, and that night she was positively giving off sparks. Her honey-colored hair was freshly washed, and in the odd light at my place, where we wound up, it had a kind of halo around it. Her eyes are the clearest blue I've ever seen, not so much like sky as the transparent blue you see on some kinds of porcelain, and her nostrils are the clean, sculpted kind that hair could never grow in. She's ridiculously short, which had kept her off the cheerleading squad back home and made our embraces absurdly awkward, and, if she has one real fault, it's her determination to overdress—she even had a little white cap to go with that sailor suit, though she wasn't wearing it then. I thought she looked awful damn cute in it that night, although I came to hate that outfit, all her outfits, in fact—that was Rhoda's sarcastic term for the way Ana dressed: "Your Barbie doll doesn't have clothes, Frankie," she said after Ana had moved in, "just *outfits*." She pronounced the word like it was a mouthful of slightly sour milk.

I was a little low that night—lonely—and having my usual case of self-recriminations and self-doubts. *Why can't you get along with another human being?*—that sort of thing. And, of course, it was spring—just about this time, in fact, just about a year ago—and we all know about a young man's fancy. And then, all of a sudden, there was Ana, washing over me like some sort of cool sailor-suit balm.

We spent that night together—came together like animals, yeah, more like animals driven by instinct than human beings working out a centuries-old tradition of courtship and dance. She was gone in the morning and I hesitated for a day or two before pursuing her, although I wanted to badly enough. In my way was a sort of distrust, suspicion—not of her, of myself. I resisted, told myself, well, that was nice, but no big deal, just another in a long line of well-that's-nice nights but what can you do, that's life on the road, after all. Except I wasn't on the road anymore. I went over to the cafe where she was a sort of glorified waitress called hostess, not sure what I had in mind. I took one look at her and the suspicion was swept away.

Next thing I know, we were in a fever, Rock Hudson and Doris Day in some Technicolor Saturday matinee. "Que sera, sera," Doris was singing in the background as Ana and I took in ball games at Yankee Stadium, ate hot dogs at Coney Island, rode the boat to the Statue of Liberty.

"This is a brand new experience for me," I told her the day we lugged three suitcases and a cardboard box of her clothes over to my place, her pillow and a ragged teddy bear stuffed under my arm.

"Moving in together?" she asked, looking up at my elbow.

"I never even went steady in high school. Move in? I've hardly ever even *known* a girl longer than a weekend."

To Rhoda, I went even further. "The whole thing is a brand new experience. How the hell am I supposed to know I can trust what I'm feeling?"

"You mean wanting to live your life horizontally?" Rhoda sneered. Now that she gets her poems published in *The New Yorker*, she can be impossible sometimes.

"I mean wanting to *cling* to someone, not just touch and pass on." I was finally, at the ripe old age of twenty-four, what Rhoda's father, my uncle Nate with his sad eyes, would call a *mensch*. I had a place of my own, a chick, and sort of steady work—the holy trinity that signifies to anyone interested enough to care that a boy has grown up to be not just a male, but a *man*.

"Why are you telling *me* all this?" Rhoda wanted to know. "People in love are supposed to talk to each *other*."

It was true, Ana and I didn't talk all that much. We had other preoccupations, slippery skin and crevices and protrusions, sweat and fever. But until Rhoda pointed it out, I hadn't noticed.

When we did talk, it often wound up being about me.

The Statue of Liberty! The closest I'd ever been to that tourist trap was the deck of a ferry heading to Staten Island. Now I was up in the torch, gazing out at the entire known world, the prettiest girl in that world clinging to my waist. It was a Tuesday afternoon and we had the place to ourselves.

"I can't believe how this is going," I said. What I meant was I couldn't believe any of it was actually happening to me.

"People do fall in love," Ana said, standing on tiptoes so to be closer. "Some of them even live happily ever after."

"Yeah, but me?"

"Why not? You're not immune from life, Frankie."

That stopped me, just for a second or two. Of all the girls in New York, I have to pick a philosopher from Indiana. Across that dazzling stretch of blue water and sky, the Manhattan skyline was shimmering in the May sunshine, the Empire State Building pointing its finger to heaven. Somewhere behind it, out of sight, Harlem.

"Maybe this is hard to understand, Ana. Look, when I was a kid, I used to go to the movies Saturday afternoons, over at the Apollo or the Rialto on 116th Street, or even sometimes to those big cool palaces on upper Broadway, and I can remember watching people up there on the screen kissing each other and then crying when they were torn apart."

"Hmmm, Van Johnson and Claudette Colbert in London during the war," Ana said, her eyes going mock dreamy. "Making love in the air raid shelter." She put her hand on my thigh.

"That's the one. I would always be wondering what those images meant, the giant faces, the mouths that took up half the screen as they embraced, the enormous wet eyes, the giant tears trickling across the screen."

"What do you mean? They were what they were."

"But *what?* That's what I couldn't figure out."

She looked at me thoughtfully, pursing her lips in a way I found delightful. "Frankie, it was just the movies."

"Sure it was. That's not the point. What I'm saying, there *I* was in my seat in the dark, and there *they* were, up there on the screen, bathed in light. What the hell did they have to do with me? And even to each other?"

"They were connecting to each other," Ana said.

"Exactly. But not to me. The screen was close enough that I could have thrown a spitball from the balcony and hit it, maybe, but the people on it were a million miles away. There wasn't any way they could ever touch me."

Ana didn't say anything. She squeezed my hand.

"Nobody could," I blurted out, without thinking.

She looked at me but I turned my eyes away. I looked south, past the curve of Brooklyn and out to what I imagined was the sea, toward the Old World. I waited for her to say something but she was silent, remembering her own movies, maybe.

"That feeling of distance stayed with me," I finally said, "long after the images faded. Not only were people that far away from me, so too was my own body from myself."

"And?"

"And nothing," I said, shrugging it off, and the next thing I knew we were making love, standing up, my hands behind Ana's back to protect her from the rough concrete of the torch wall, her hair whipping against my face in the wind, the dizzying porcelain sky swirling above us.

"*And nothing*," I said, but what I meant was that she brought me up to myself, like when you press your face right up against a mirror. I looked at Ana but I saw myself. I was in the way.

Our fever didn't last long. We'd met in early April, she moved in late in the month, and by June, just around the time the big bombers began to unload on Hanoi and people were going nuts in the city, things were already starting to unravel. I had been feeling it, but I wasn't sure if she did, which shows how little I know about women.

"What's wrong?" she said one day. We were in the sunny room that led out to the garden in the Village apartment Rhoda had helped me find the previous fall. It was the ground floor of a Victorian and I had the run of the yard, which was paved with grass-cracked bricks and bordered by an aggressive assortment of overgrown trees and flowering shrubbery. The kitchen looked out on the courtyard, and the room next to the kitchen, which would have been a dining room if I'd had a table and chairs, opened onto it. I spent a lot of time out there at a white iron table with a tattered old Cinzano umbrella, reading or fooling around with my guitar, but if it was too hot, or the flies were getting to me or one of those ballerina rain showers they have in the city in spring was passing overhead, I'd sprawl out on the blonde-as-butter hardwood floor in that room.

I'd heard her moving around in the bathroom, then the kitchen, but I was trying to write, the guitar cradled in my lap and a notebook by my side, and hadn't stirred myself to get up and kiss her good morning. I'd been busted in a big demo just a couple of days before and spent the night in the lockup, so you'd think I'd be writing about war or injustice, but no, the song was about her, and it wasn't coming. Then she was standing at the kitchen door, a cup of coffee in her hand, smiling down at me. I felt the question and, since there never seems to be any point in lying, I said: "Restless, I guess. I'm used to being on the road." If there was deception there, I wasn't aware of it, and it didn't even occur to me that it had been months since I'd been out of the city.

She sat down on the floor next to me and stretched out her legs, which were in tight, silvery bell-bottoms that made her thighs look like smooth, rounded sheets of tinfoil. With her hips right next to mine, her feet came only to about halfway down my calves. "I can feel it," she said.

We sat there for a long time in the sunshine and I laid the guitar on the floor beside me.

"And there are other things, too," I said, immediately regretting it. If someone had asked me at that moment if I loved her, I would have said yes, but I would have hesitated.

The album I'd been working on during the winter had come out and everybody I knew in the city had bought a copy but I don't think anyone else had. It was looking like this one wasn't going to do any better than the other two had. I'd only had two gigs in the Village, a few days each, since we'd been together, and I'd had a few session jobs, including one with Phil Ochs and another I'd like to forget, but that was about it.

"Like what? Tell me, Frankie." She put her hand over mine and squeezed, just the way she had at the Statue of Liberty.

"There's the little matter of the rent and our next meal."

That made her laugh. "I bring home a paycheck every week. It's no fortune, but I was living on it before I moved in here. You don't have to hustle for gigs if you don't want." She leaned forward so she could face me, her breast pressing against her arm in a way I always found exciting. "Really, honey, you could stay here and write, or go back to school like you were talking about. I don't mind supporting us."

"I do."

She laughed again, a silvery laugh, like water running over shining stones. A few weeks earlier, that laugh would have melted my heart—now it scraped against me, chalk on a blackboard. "You don't like a woman supporting you." It wasn't a question.

"I guess not." I shrugged.

"It would be far out, you know? I mean, really." After a few seconds, when I didn't say anything, she added: "That's bullshit, you know that, don't you?"

"Maybe so. But it's more than that. I feel like being on the road. I'm comfortable that way. I've been sitting here on the floor almost every morning this week and I don't have a line written that I like. I'm just not thinking too well."

She didn't say anything for awhile, but I could feel her shoulder and arm, which were against mine, tightening, the physical space between our bodies growing.

None of this means anything, I thought.

Then she said a funny thing: "This is it, isn't it?"

It took me a second or two to understand, then I said "Yes." She got up after a minute and went into the bedroom and closed the door. If I'd gotten up and followed her, maybe things would have worked out differently, but I don't think so. At any rate, I didn't. I sat there in the sun and in a few minutes a cascade of notes came into my head and I wrote them down. I didn't have to play them to know what they sounded like.

That conversation sticks in my mind like a burr. It's amazing how the smallest tear can start the edge of something to go ragged. The stupid thing—the *stupid* thing—was that we didn't admit that we recognized it, and do what we should have. But we kept right on. Ana kept going every evening to the cafe and I stayed home and wrote music, more or less falling into the pattern she had suggested and I'd so vehemently said no to.

I'd come back to New York the fall before in a state of confusion. I was exhausted, for one thing. I'd been on the road for over two years—altogether, for almost seven years, off and on, but two years solid that last time around.

But there was more to it than just that. All during that time, I'd been on my own, traveling alone and playing alone, and I'd gotten a little ingrown, like a toenail you forget all about. My songs had always been a little vague, but now even I sometimes had trouble penetrating them, the lyrics flowing out of my pen like a mess of voodoo mumbo jumbo. And, worse, they were all starting to sound alike. I'd realized that when I was at Newport that summer. I was one of the morning acts, second stage, so there wasn't exactly a huge crowd, but what bothered me wasn't the numbers of people, it was the expression on their faces. They looked bored, dozy. They clapped when they were supposed to, but there wasn't anything remotely resembling electricity in the air.

Later, when I heard the tape of my set, I was appalled—it wasn't bad, no, not that, it just all sounded the same, like one long song with pauses along the way, or the same song done over and over again in different keys, different tempos. Even worse, it all sounded familiar, just like the stuff I'd been doing a year before, even though the songs were almost all new.

So, when I came dragging into the city a few months later, I was all wired out and looking for a chance to get my head together. What I really wanted was just to sit someplace quiet, hibernate and listen to the sounds of the universe—the *silence* of the universe. My ears hurt from hearing so much of myself.

But I couldn't have come at a worse time. The city was full of noise. Uptown, where you could almost smell the smoke of Watts, everybody was into soul, which is a little too brassy for my tastes. And downtown, the Village was crawling with cats carrying electric guitars, just like Dylan, who had electrified Newport, me included, and the streets were just blaring with music. Most of it was good stuff, rock with a lot of blues mixed in and a hell of a lot of flash, and louder than some of Ana's outfits.

I cashed in, of course, with all sorts of gigs, but I was never really happy about it. And by spring, around the time I hooked up with Ana, I was starting to feel like a child whose body was growing faster than his skin. I wasn't satisfied with the same old songs I'd been writing for years but I wasn't really moved to write rock. I'd *been* there. I was listening to jazz, even classical, and my mind kept taking me along stretches of melody I'd never been on before, with loops of notes that didn't seem to fit the terrain, that I didn't recognize. It was the beginning of something for me, although I didn't fully realize it then.

Ana worked nights, and I would be at home in our cozy pad, spinning out notes, or I'd have a one-night gig at Folk City or someplace else or, like as not, I'd be prowling around the Village, taking in the bands, or up in Harlem, digging the street sounds, hearing things I hadn't before. Ana would come home at three or four and I'd still be up and we'd make love, though sometimes she'd be too tired, but we didn't talk much, and what we did say sounded stale to me, lines from a play we'd rehearsed too many times. She'd sleep most of the day, then get up in late afternoon and pad around, sit silently in the sunny room with her coffee listening to me doodling, then get ready to go.

"This is crazy," I said one day as she was getting dressed. She was wearing a long flowered skirt left over from Bennington and a peasant blouse with lace around the collar, the kind of stuff Molly wears but more expensive, more deliberate.

"It's just life," Ana said. Again, the philosopher. "A little backwards because it's *me* working, and it's at night instead of the day. Do you think it would be any different if you sold cars or wrote TV commercials or drilled people's teeth, or drove a bus"—this a reference to my father, who she hadn't met but had heard plenty about—"all day long while I stayed home? Would that *not* be crazy?"

"Maybe it would," I said, "except that I'm *not* a car salesman or an ad writer or a dentist. *Or* a fucking bus driver."

That was as close as we ever came to fighting, and maybe that was part of the problem. We never scraped each other raw, never really got stuff out on the floor where we could both see it. Ana was too civilized, and I was too stupid. Instead, she took off her long skirt and the blouse, folding them neatly and laying them over a chair, and we gravely made love on the floor, in the pool of yellow sunlight pouring in from the garden. Then she put her clothes back on, leaned over and kissed me, and went off to serve coffee through the night. I lay naked in the sunlight until it faded away, hearing bursts of notes that went nowhere.

Later that summer, I took a composition course at NYU and, just for a lark, freshman English. I was really digging the music and was seriously thinking about going full-time. My classmates in the English class were five or six years younger than me and I kind of dug being the wise old man. For the first time in years, I was keeping some sort of normal hours, getting up in the morning and going to a regular place, coming home in the afternoon when Ana was getting up. Sometimes we'd make love then, but usually she was in a rush. I was in bed asleep when she came home, and she was asleep when I got up.

Then things started seriously falling apart.

Being with Ana—any woman, really—on a regular basis had made me start thinking about my mother in a way I hadn't for years, made me start wondering again about my parents' marriage. When I was a kid, that was always a sore point between me and Pops—I wanted to talk about it, he didn't. Guess who always won? That year in New York, I would occasionally get a telephoned invitation from Ruth, the woman he was living with, to come over to her place on 85th Street for supper, and I'd dutifully go. At one of those evenings we had a blowout that convinced me I had no business being anywhere near him.

I was taken by surprise a little because having a live-in lady friend has mellowed the old man a lot. The year before, he had thrown in his bus-driving job for a regular gig with a funky Latin band, at a restaurant on upper Broadway, Friday and Saturday nights. Sometimes there's other dates too. It's not enough to live on but Ruth is a school teacher and brings in a nice regular, if small, loaf of bread, and she likes to indulge him. She is a righteous—but not *self*-righteous—Negro lady, no black broad, with a whole life already behind her, a run-off man, grown kids, a couple of kitty cats, the whole bit, and I dig her. I wish she'd been around years ago. The whole thing—her, the steady gig, the no-more-transfers-and-exhaust-fumes—has had an incredible effect. I mean, Pops is practically a new man, mellow. Not entirely, though. Not that he and I could ever conduct ourselves like grown-up human beings when we were together, no, that would be asking too much. There's been too much noise over the years for there ever to be a real quiet. And, sure enough, one summer night when I was over at their place, everything cozy and copecetic, I crossed over some invisible line by asking him a question about my mother. He looked at me like he was the junkyard dog and I was an intruder, with a "bite-me" sign pinned on my ass. I could feel the heat start to radiate off his skin.

"Why do you wanna rake up the past, Frankie?" he growled. It wasn't just a question, not even just a challenge. It was a line drawn in the dirt. "She's dead, that whole life is dead. Let the past be the past."

He's gone gray and, instead of becoming plumper, like most aging people do, gaunter than he ever was, like something has been eating him out from the inside. I guess that's it exactly. He was looking at me with such intensity I had to turn my eyes away, letting them fall on Ruth, who immediately got up from the table and began banging around in the kitchen.

"That's just it," I said. "It may be past for you, but not for me." I mustered up all my resolve and looked directly at him again, determined to win the staring-down contest for the first time in my life. "She's my mother, for God's sake. She isn't dead for me. She never will be."

"That's good, Frankie. The two of you can be very happy together."

I just got up and left. What was the point? I told myself I wasn't going to let the bastard get to me, but the exchange kept festering under my skin, keeping me awake, nagging at me like a sore tooth, adding to the general sense of displacement I was feeling. *I don't belong here,* I kept thinking. Not that I knew where else might be better.

The next week, I was busted at another demo and spent a couple of days in jail. A good place to think, jail. That is one place for sure you know you don't belong.

And all the while, I could feel Ana moving further and further away from me. Or maybe it was me who was moving—like sometimes, in the subway, when two trains are at the station at the same time, one of them starts to move, but so slowly, so smoothly, you can't always tell if it's your train that's going or the other one, the one you're staring at with dull eyes through the smudged window.

I was pretty sure there was another guy, and when I asked her she didn't deny it. Some guy from the cafe, someone who'd seen her across a crowded kitchen maybe.

Ah, what the hell difference did it make?

"You don't own me," she said, and *I* had to laugh, because she sounded like someone in a movie, not Doris Day and not Claudette Colbert, either, someone in a movie I likely hadn't seen. I laughed, but I felt like crying too.

And we didn't make love after this argument.

So I fled. What else could I do?

I'd heard about this new music program at Iowa and I called to see if there was a chance of me getting in. There was, so I didn't fool around. Six years on the road, I know how to travel light, with my duffel bag and my guitar to hold me up straight.

Gone.

I roamed the dark pizza streets of this little town. Lived for weeks in a tiny, piss-stained room in a crummy hotel, worse than some of the dives on Broadway, going to classes, listening, *listening*, walking the streets at night, keeping myself to myself, not touching anybody, like a shell-shocked soldier, singing myself to sleep at night.

After awhile, I started to come out of the stupor. I found a decent little pad not far from the campus. I started to play again and got a weekend gig at a bar, which is how I met—or re-met, I should say—Molly. She had come into the bar a couple of times and I'd noticed her looking at me, a tall, gangly girl with straight yellowish brown hair and clear green eyes, an "I-know-what-I'm-about" expression on her face like my cousin Rhoda's. Not a beautiful girl, but something about her stirred me, pleased me. I didn't recognize her at first.

She came up to my table between sets one night and sat down. "Hello, Frankie Stein or Stern or whatever you call yourself these days," she said. "I still think you took a Jewish name for effect."

It all came back then, of course. How can you forget an accusation like that? "You shaved your legs," I said, although she had jeans on and I couldn't have known that. I just knew.

We laughed and that was it, a beginning, that's all. We had a beer, talked, then I went back on the stage. When the set was over, she'd already left, smiling to me from the door.

I saw her a few other times between then and Christmas break, but there wasn't anything special happening, she was just a groovy girl who came to hear me play or who I ran into with other people I knew at the student union or a bar I go to a lot or at a rally on campus.

At Thanksgiving, Iowa City closed down the way a summer resort does after Labour Day, the students hissing out of town like air from a punctured balloon. I stayed, enjoying the solitude, and feeling like a survivor in one of those awful sci fi movies where most of the human race gets blotted out by invaders from Pluto or a nuclear war. On the day after Thanksgiving, the Friday when most people are looking forward to their first helping of leftover turkey dinner, I wrote the first piece of *real* music of my life, a sonata for guitar and cello and violin. I felt like I had been in a deep sleep and I was waking. I felt like I was coming back to life. One day in early December I was walking across campus to a class and I passed Molly. It was snowing and there was a biting wind, so we didn't stop to talk, but we both slowed down as we approached and recognized each other. We didn't speak—it was too cold to open your mouth—but her smile warmed me. I think something happened there, some chemical sprang loose and started flowing through my body, setting off triggers and other chemicals racing to other relay stations, setting off other triggers, opening doors. These things take a long time, maybe. It's not like being hit on the head, more like spreading the word. I hadn't heard yet.

At Christmas, I came to New York to play in a recording session I had promised Eric Andersen months before. The money was good and it was nice to get away, anyway, a good excuse. I played the session, which went a lot longer than it should have, and I saw Rhoda and a few other people.

"I'm thinking of giving Ana a call," I told Rhoda.

My cousin has let her thick brown hair grow into a kind of sculpted afro and she shook it vigorously now. "Do you ever listen to a word I say?" She blew thin trails of smoke through her nostrils toward me. She's taken to smoking Gaulois.

"I listen to everything you say, Road."

"Yeah, but do you understand? Or, more to the point, have you ever learned a single thing about women?"

"Oh, I understand everything there is to know about women," I laughed. "It's *me* I don't understand."

Also found the time to see my old man, which went better than I had feared. We managed to have a civil visit, and a good hug when I left. My living a thousand miles away is bound to be good for our relationship, I guess. "You take care of yourself, Frankie," he said. He's let his gray hair grow long in the back, making him look like an aging hippie, a gaunt Timothy Leary. He gave me one of those trademarked lopsided looks of his that I knew was a grin. "For God's sake, stop trying to be me."

"Is that what I'm trying to do?"

"Sometimes." He gave Ruth a quick glance and I realized she probably knew things about Pops and me that I didn't, maybe he didn't either.

I gave him a grin back. "Yeah, you stop trying to be you, too."

Ruth walked me down the hallway to the stairway of her third-floor walkup. "Your daddy's all tangled up inside about you, Frankie," she said.

"You're telling me?"

"I'm giving you a different perspective. I'm not saying he's right. From what I can translate for myself, he hasn't been much on that score. I'm not taking sides at all, though if I had to it would be *his* side—you understand what I'm saying? But right or wrong, it's the way he is now, and trying to change him would be like going against nature, like telling cats not to chase birds or a cockroach not to crawl."

"I appreciate your metaphors," I told her, thinking about working them into a song.

It was my last day and I had to go to Jersey City to meet the cat I'd driven east with, a guy improbably named Glenn Miller Goldberg. I went down to Fulton Street to catch the ferry right from Ruth's place. It was a gray, snowy day but not too cold and I was walking slowly along Fulton digging the junkstores and the pushcarts. I hadn't been down there for a long time, hadn't been on the ferry to Jersey since I was a kid and had gone with my father to a gig when he couldn't find a sitter. I remember perching myself on the rail and staying there for the whole windy ride so I'd have something to hold onto in case there was a crazyman on the boat who tried to throw me over. That was something Pops was always talking about, "Watch out for the crazyman." And then, at the gig—it was a dance of some sort in a hotel—there was this big fat woman with perfume on her breasts who took charge of me, gave me something to eat and put me in a bed in this tiny little room somewhere behind the bandstand. I forced myself to stay awake because I was afraid Pops would leave without me—now *there* was a crazyman to look out for—and so I saw when two girls came in and changed their dresses and kissed each other.

I was remembering some of this stuff and taking it easy because I had time till the ferry. I went into an army surplus store and looked at some of the junk and bought a strap that would be good for my guitar, a green web thing made for holding ammunition, and out on the street again I stopped at a cart and got some chestnuts. There was smoke rising from the cart and a smell like the inside of some happy home in Iowa on Thanksgiving Day, and the chestnuts were hot on my hands. There was a clock in a window on the corner and I saw I had fifteen minutes to catch the ferry so I started heading that way.

There was a girl walking toward me up Fulton. She was wearing an olive carcoat and black tights and boots, a Village chick with long straight brown hair that she flipped away from her eyes as she walked and the hem of a short skirt just visible beneath the coat, which was fastened with toggles. When she got close enough, I could see that her eyes were dark with mascara and shadow. She was looking right at me, so intently that I thought maybe she was someone I knew, and I slowed down.

There was something in the air I can't describe, a mixture of smoke and snow and desire that made the street and the cars parked along it almost translucent. There was a dusting of it in the girl's hair. We kept looking at each other and, when we drew abreast, I saw that her eyes were brown, deep chocolate brown with flecks of green and amber, and her face was hard and cold and perfect, like a crystal of snow or ice, like porcelain, light visible just beneath the skin. I could see myself in her eyes.

We kept walking, until we had passed each other, moving so slowly we seemed like creeping boats, shouldering themselves through fog. The sleeves of our coats brushed, and I turned my head and so did she. When we were about ten feet apart, we both stopped, as if some cord between us had grown taut or a whistle had blown, but there was no sound except the crunching of our feet in the snow. The chestnuts were hot in my hand and I would have offered her one except that we were too far apart.

We stood like that for, I don't know, no more than ten seconds, but it seemed like forever and, though we didn't say a word, I swear there was a message going back and forth between us. What it was was this: there is so much desire here in the space between us that it will consume us if we allow it to, suffocate us, swallow us whole. I knew, with a certainty you don't argue with, that all it would have taken was a word and the ferry and the guy in Jersey City could go on without me, that whatever world this girl was on her way to or from would have a long wait before it saw her again, that I could have reached out, stepped forward, taken her hand and the touch of her would have been like an electric shock, that we would have melted into each other. We could have made love right there in the street, with our clothes on, cars passing, people stopping to watch, the snow falling gently on our faces. We could have done that, or we could have called a cab and gone to the Ritz-Carlton and ordered the bridal suite, or to the Statue of Liberty and made love in the torch. All those things were possible, and it wouldn't have made any difference, because between us, within us, all things were possible, if only for that moment.

The girl smiled and the spell was broken, the moment gone. It was an incredibly sweet smile, filled with promise and regret, the kind of smile you save for when you meet a former lover on the street. If I were to meet Ana, I would smile like that, I think, to show her there is still tenderness between us, still some love that will never completely burn away.

"I'm sorry, I thought you were someone I knew," the girl said. Her voice was both musical and oddly anonymous, like that of a telephone operator in a Southern city. "I am," I said, nodding my head, but I mumbled and I doubt if she heard me. I shrugged and we both turned and walked on. If I hurried, I'd still be able to make the ferry. At the end of the block, I looked back over my shoulder, expecting she'd be doing the same, but all I saw was her back, receding into the haze.

I didn't see Molly for almost a week after I got back here, but when I did I believed that Ana was out of me, finally, as out of me as someone you once loved or thought you did can ever be. And there was a door open in me.

It was January and bitter cold but we went for a walk by the frozen river and talked for a long time. Afterwards, I was thinking about her all the time. We saw each other a few times in a more formal way than we had before, me taking her places, almost like we were squares and dating. But it wasn't for a few weeks till I kissed her—for the first time, I thought, but she reminded me that we had kissed in Vermont.

"Is that all?" I said, and she laughed.

"I should hope so that was all, Mr. Stein. Not that I didn't want there to be more. But I would never speak to you again if there had been and you didn't remember it. I'm sore enough you don't remember the kiss."

It got to be spring. There never was a moment when I said "This is it, isn't it?" and she said "Yes." It didn't work that way. We grew on each other, something grew in us. Somewhere along the line, I said "I love you," and she said "I know, I know, I love you too. I thought I would die if you didn't see it soon."

I lay there in the darkness with tears in my eyes, more frightened than I have ever been in my life, frightened out of my wits. I kept thinking about Van Johnson and Claudette Colbert kissing on the screen while London's fog pressed in on them and the world fell apart all around them, the tears in Claudette's eyes filling the screen. For the first time in my life, it made sense.

Spring is here in this funny little town, but winter hangs on, too. Lilacs are out, and today it snowed, turning the flowers to porcelain.

12. Push Comes to Shove

Did I ever tell you guys about the time Miles Davis hustled my date?

It was 1963, I think, maybe '64. I was in Chicago, playing a club in Old Town, the Plugged Nickel, I think it was, and Miles and the old quintet, with Hank Mobley and Wynton Kelly, were playing the old Sutherland Lounge, in a groovy old hotel on the South Side. One night after my gig I went down to see them, me and this chick called Judith Heart, another folkie, with big brown eyes and long, raven-black hair that went straight down her back clear to her ass. She was some cool chick.

We were the only honkies in the place but, you know me, I don't really think of myself as white, so I barely noticed. These four cats at the next table started jivin' us—"Heyyyyyy, my maaaannn, cool to see you, you lookin' *gooood*"—buying us drinks, and I was trading them shot for shot, playing the dozens, you know? Thinking I was real cool and impressing this chick, who started out a little scared but after awhile got to be too drunk to be anything but flattered by all the attention.

I knew what was happening all along, I mean I knew I was going to lose it if I wasn't careful, but somehow I just got carried along with it, the booze and the chick, who'd been making those beautiful brown eyes at me all evening, and the delicious tension racing back and forth along my skin as these dudes kept pushing their faces closer and closer, their eyes big, their foreheads wet, and the music, Miles and Hank trading those incredible solos through the smoke and heat and noise—suddenly, I knew I was going to be sick and lurched up from the table, making it to the men's room just in time.

I was gone about ten minutes, probably, washing my face and cleaning up and smoking a cigarette to get the awful taste out of my mouth, and when I got back to the table they were gone, of course, the chick and the four jivecats, and I wasn't so much surprised as I was disgusted with myself, and just a little bit scared. The band was taking a break and there were people milling around and I couldn't see a sign of any of them, or even of the people who'd been sitting at tables nearby, who I could have asked. I sat down and finished off the watery remains of a bourbon and ice in a smeared glass and slumped my head down, feeling about as shitty as I could remember.

I sat there for five or ten minutes, I guess, my head in my hands, fantasizing all sorts of horrible things happening to that chick: rape, disfigurement, dismemberment, murder, white slavery, the works, and wondering what I'd say to the club manager the next day when she didn't show up for work. I was just at the point where I was figuring I should get up and borrow somebody's gun so I could shoot myself, or call the cops, or *look* for her or, at the very least, go home to the pad on the north side where I was crashing, when I heard a noise and felt someone sliding into the chair next to mine. I looked up—moving slowly because my head was already starting to split, you understand—and there she was, those big beautiful eyes a little glazed but otherwise none the worse for wear, not looking it, anyway.

"Judith!" I said. "Jesus, girl, I've been worried sick about you. Where've you been?"

She gave me a funny look, as if reassuring herself I was who she thought I was, and gave her head a little shake that made her hair swing. "I've just been having the most wonderful conversation with Mr. Davis," she said in the same sort of stagy, breathless way she sang. "We're having lunch together tomorrow and he's going to show me his collection of trumpets."

I stared at her for a second, and then, because there was a little shuffle on the bandstand, swung my eyes up to where the band was ambling back, Philly Joe Jones just starting to settle himself behind his drum kit, the cymbals tinkling. "Whadya mean, Mr. Davis? You mean Miles?"

"Sure. He's really cool."

"Yeah, I know that, but ... what happened to those cats who were at the table with us?"

"Merle and his friends? I don't know. Mr. Davis—Miles, I mean—came over and they just sort of vanished. We went to the bar and he bought me a drink, then we went to his dressing room. I was looking for you to have a drink with us but you'd vanished too. *Say*"—she leaned forward and gave me a serious look—"you don't look so hot. You okay, Frankie? Where *were* you?"

"Tilting at windmills," I said. Miles was just coming onto the stage, shaking his horn with that sideways wrist flip of his, and his mouth was screwed into what on anybody else would be called a grimace of pain but on him was a grin. I swear it was aimed at me.

This story comes across better—juicier—told than written, and I put a lot of spit on it and have them all laughing the last thirty miles or so to the shrink's place. Roger's driving the Jeep wagon, both hands rigid on the wheel, Dusty pulled over close beside him like a high school date, Molly and me sprawled out on the back seat.

The Jeep's big enough to hold the entire dues-paid SDS membership of Iowa City, with a couple of FBI rats thrown in for good measure. It's a boat, with a V-8 engine and more horses than race at Aquaduct in a season. There's even a winch. Roger bought it used for as much money as he made last year tending bar at The Mill and, though he doesn't say so, I think what he has in the back of his mind is that, should push come to shove, he and Dusty could live in the thing, back in the hills somewhere.

"Did she have lunch with Miles, then, Judy Heart?" Dusty asks. She's a solemn-faced girl with a purple scar running from her scalp, across her left eye and down her cheek all the way to her chin. She got it from an automobile accident that shot her through the windshield on the night of her high school prom.

"Judith. Always Judith, never Judy. I guess so. We didn't spend the night together, if you were wondering"—Molly gives my ribs a grab and I have to finish the story through our giggles—"so I wasn't with her the next day at noontime. Hey, really. I saw her that night at the club, but she didn't say anything about it. When I had a chance, between sets, I sat down with her. She seemed okay, just a little cool, maybe. 'How's Miles?' I asked. 'Fine,' she said, and started talking about something else. I didn't push it, so I never did find out about his fabulous horn collection. Couple days later, I split and I never saw Judith Heart again, or heard about her, for that matter. Another voice in the crowd, just like me."

"Proud Mary" comes on the radio, Creedence, and we laugh, then fall silent. All morning on the trip up, the deejays seem to be playing it every other song, every station Dusty tunes to, those incredible guitars pushing us along the highway like a tailwind.

Roger's draft notice arrived a couple of weeks ago, like a snake popping its head up out of the weeds, just a few days after a mob of us were busted for closing down the student union when recruiters for Dow were trying to do interviews. Just a coincidence, I'm sure.

"What are you going to do?" I asked him.

"I'm not going to go, that's for damn sure." We were sitting in the Hamburg Inn, trying to see our future in the bottom of our coffee cups.

"That's what I'd do," Rory said. He and Roger have been pals since even before politics—what Molly calls BV, Before Vietnam. "Christ, this is a chance of a lifetime. I mean, they're dumb, man. They think they can shut people up by drafting them. That's just opening the door to us. I mean, think about it: if an organizer from the coal miners' union, say, went and applied for a job at some non-union mine, think they'd take him? Don't be fucking crazy. But here's the army saying, 'Come on in, guys, the water's fine. And here's our nice soft belly to cut while you're at it.'" Rory grinned, his nose wrinkling like a prize fighter's when he's taking aim.

"Nice soft belly, bullshit," I said. This is Rory's favorite theme, but he's a navy veteran, in and out in the early sixties before any of it really mattered very much, a veteran of the brig, too, for taking a swing at an officer. "You make it sound like the army's just this big soft berry, waiting to be picked. But once you're in, you're their nigger, they can do with you what they will."

Nobody else sitting at the table—Roger or Rory or Dusty— would dare use the word "nigger," but I have special dispensation from the pope, since I can prove an inside track.

"Anyway, I'm not going in," Roger said. "You go in an' orga- nize the so'jer boys, Rory. I'll stay here and organize the civvies. And I'll meet you at the wall when the time comes."

Roger is no pacifist, that's not it. If anything, he's the other way around, and I think he's right that if he went in he'd likely wind up fragging an officer or switching sides somewhere in the jungle. In an earlier life, he spent a year in Bible college in Dubuque, and there's one thing he learned for keeps: an eye for an eye. And, like Molly, he's pretty sure he knows which side he's on.

It's been a year since he's seen the inside of a classroom, though he swears he means to go back, that he wants to go to law school, if his arrest record doesn't keep him out. But the truth is, other than Dusty, his only passion these days is politics.

Roger's a big, rawboned Iowa farm boy with hair and eye the color of sand and a sense of humor almost as dry, still wrestling with the change from home. He quit Bible school when word came that his brother had been killed in Vietnam, one of the first marines to make the big body count, went bumming around the country and wound up on the docks in San Francisco. He started hanging around North Beach and at City Lights, reading poetry and some politics, and falling under the wing of some lefty dock union guys, Rory among them. When he came back to Iowa, Rory tagged along and they took classes and drifted around the edges of student politics for awhile, all of this before I came out here. Then, when SDS got going, they were in the middle of it, along with Molly and her pal Dusty. Molly and Dusty are very tight. They're both into sisterhood, whatever the hell that is.

Getting out of the draft isn't as easy as it used to be, but where there's a will, there's usually a way, right? I know a couple of guys who convinced them they were fags, and a couple of others who got so speeded up before their physicals they just whizzed by faster than the eye could see. One cat I know, who really is a little strange, beat up his girl and got himself busted and sent to the bughouse for observation so he'd have a good case for talking them into thinking he was nutty. Poor bastard did such a good job of convincing them at the hospital, they kept him an extra thirty days.

Roger has the same sort of plan, minus the beat-up, the bust and the bughouse. He already had the name and the number of the Chicago shrink, which is where we're headed today, not to his office but his home, up the lake in Highland Park, one of those fancy-assed suburbs where the servants have to commute to work from the next town over, inland. He likes to do this sideline work on the weekends, he told Roger on the phone, so his nurse won't get wise, we figure. We have a hell of a time finding his place. It's on a narrow road that winds along on a ridge of land above the lake, past houses big as airplane hangars with stone fences that look like the kind of things you see in movies about the South during the Civil War, high fences designed to keep soldiers out and slaves in.

His house turns out to be a brick and cedar thing full of unexpected angles and planes, like a cardboard box that's been ripped open and partially flattened, situated at the end of a crushed-stone driveway on a bluff and surrounded by windblown and stunted pines. Roger has a much-folded slip of paper with penciled directions that he keeps referring to, but he drives past the entrance to the driveway twice before deciding to try it. There's no name at the gate, no number, no mailbox.

"The good doctor likes his privacy," Molly says.

"This may turn out to be worse than the army," Roger says, grinning. "Maybe he does experiments on innocent little boys who wander in off the beach."

"Don't worry," I tell him. "You're not out of there in three days, we call in the marines."

A black maid answers the doorbell, giving Roger a saccharin smile. She looks at the rest of us suspiciously, especially me. "We're the cheering squad," I say, but it doesn't soften her.

The shrink comes out of the living room and meets us in the hallway and immediately leads us down a carpeted stairway to the basement, which is just as elegant as the little glimpses of house we've gotten above. He's a fattish man with a Peter Ustinov beard and glasses, wearing blue jeans and a cashmere sweater and hush puppies. He nods at us and shows his teeth in a curiously bashful smile, but he doesn't shake hands. He clearly doesn't want us in his living room, where someone coming by might see us.

He ushers Roger into an office and asks us to wait in what is sort of a den, with comfortable leather chairs and couch, over-flowing bookshelves crowding the walls, a fireplace and, in a few places where the books haven't taken over, small paintings on the walls, including something Dusty, who's an art major, says is a Chagall, maybe an early version of one of the Jerusalem windows, and a striking black and white print of an excruciatingly depressed looking man crouching in a field of daisies. Just the thing for its owner.

"You know, don't you, that when the revolution comes, the good doctor will be among the first to go," Molly says. She says that sort of thing a lot lately, and I'm never sure if she's kidding—I don't think she knows herself.

"Naw, not this guy," I tell her. "He's building up credit in heaven."

Molly's not the only one talking like that these days. Sometimes we have to remind ourselves that this is called the peace movement, and this is a sore point with Molly and me, one which I'm afraid is going to get worse.

I'm no more of a pacifist than Roger but the more I see of ugliness in the world, the less I want to have of it—no, that's not right: you can't help but *have* of it, and maybe you need to, as long as it's there. But I don't want to contribute to it. It's bad enough if somebody wants to hurt me, but I don't want to hurt him. Maybe I've been listening to my own songs too much. Or maybe that's not really all that far from where I always was, but didn't know it. I can remember telling my father after I came home from Cuba that war is one thing, a kind of flirtation, but peace is an entirely different thing, that peace would be my passion. He laughed at me, and I laughed too, at how serious I must have sounded, but I don't think I really understood what I'd said. Not then.

Every once in awhile, my doubts turn to flesh, like this guy I communed with when we were barricading the union last month, forty or so of us, our arms linked and chanting "How Now Brown Dow?" and saying "uh uh, buddy, no sir," stuff like that, to the earnest young men who came to the fringe of the line, pressed up against it like lovers and asked to be let through.

"What does all that have to do with us?" this guy said to me. He was a big, tough-looking guy with short hair and a fraternity jacket. "What does all this have to do with *me*?"

He had the look of a football player, but one who hadn't made the team. He had a thick, muscular neck and shoulders but lacked the necessary firmness in the jaw. His eyes were bright and he looked like he'd like to kill me—hurt me, anyway, flatten me the way a linebacker does a quarterback getting set to snap the ball— just because I was in his way. He didn't want an interview with Dow Chemical, he just wanted to go into the union and have a burger and a Coke and watch the chicks in their short skirts. And it didn't matter that there were a couple other entrances—he was at this one, and I was in his way.

"What does it have to do with you that your country is dropping napalm on civilians, on women and children, in Vietnam in *your* name, on *your* behalf? You shittin' me?"

I learned long ago that there's no percentage in talking nice to tough guys. They don't even hear it. But that doesn't stop me.

"Hey, well, maybe those gooks deserve it, didja never think about that?" the linebacker shot back, and what do you say to that? It's not exactly the time or the place to launch into a discussion of Marxist politics, or even good old Fulbright-Gravel-Bobby Kennedy liberalism, or into philosophical raps about the oneness of the universe or even religious trips about the sacredness of each individual, the purity of each individual soul, and all you *really* want to say is, "Naw, we just don't want to waste the stuff over there when we could be pouring it on pricks like you," but you can't say that because you're supposed to be nonviolent, and passive resistance is what this morning's bit of theater is all about, anyway, right?

And if you said, "Hey, listen, even if those people *were* communists and enemies of America and just plain evil people—which they aren't, but let's not get into that—even if they *were* all those bad things, they still don't deserve napalm, to burn to death in that horrible, incredibly painful way. Even you don't deserve napalm." If you said all that you'd just confuse things.

"Hey, fuck off," I told him instead. "What do *we* have to do with *you*? Maybe you don't give a shit, but *we* do. Dig?"

He stood there looking at me, and Molly tightened her arm around mine, as did the girl on my other side, and I braced myself, because a swing at my face could have been the next word in this exchange, I knew that. But the guy just grinned, shrugged and turned away, his sense of bravado impressed by mine, maybe. He stood on the sidewalk, looking up at the steps we'd completely mobbed, and I could see he was thinking. Who knows, maybe there'd be another convert. Stranger things have happened.

But the sidewalk was lined with people, two and three deep, and every couple of minutes one or two or three of them would come up to challenge our line, jocks mostly, guys in frat jackets with big shiny teeth and jaws like the front of Mack trucks. So talking down one of them was only a very small victory.

"You're crazy," Meredith, the girl on my left, said. "He could have knocked your head off."

She's a tired-looking girl with a baby at home and no alimony. *She's* the crazy one, if you ask me, because even without tempting fate or tough guys anyone could have gotten hurt, from the jostling alone. It was only 10 AM, just an hour since we'd swooped down on the doorway, and the crowd cheering every time someone tried to crawl over us was twice our size now, getting bigger all the time. Sooner or later, most likely, they'd rush us, and we'd either have to give way or someone would get hurt. And we'd already decided we wouldn't give way.

"Naw, his heart wasn't in it," I told her. "He was just testing."

"Testing us or himself?" Roger asked from behind me.

"Both."

"And who won the test?"

"Both, right?"

We laughed at that, then braced ourselves. Two guys with noses like linebackers' chins had started to climb over us, just three people down the line to my right. "You're not walking on us. You're walking on the bodies of dead Vietnamese children," Molly yelled at them, but there was too much shouting and I don't think they heard her. There was a scuffle, a jostling of arms and flying legs, and one of the jocks retreated, nursing his elbow and cursing, but the other one was over us and through the door, laughing uproariously. The guy on Molly's right had a bloody nose, someone else had a sore ear from the victorious jock's big, brown shoe. He was standing inside the door now, making faces at us and yelling, and wondering why he bothered, maybe, except that he'd done it, he'd *done* it, and wasn't that reason enough?

I looked over at the sidewalk where the guy I'd challenged had been standing, watching us, but he was gone now. I wondered what *he* was thinking.

But if moments like that make me less interested in hurting people, it has exactly the opposite effect on Molly.

She says she isn't in this so somebody can beat on her and she'll smile and they'll beat on her some more. "I'm not *against* the war," she said one day. "I'm *in* the war. *I'm* on the other side. I'm behind enemy lines."

"Does that make me the enemy?" I asked her. "I mean, if I won't go that far?"

"No, of course not."

"But isn't it 'You're with us or against us'?"

She frowned. "It's only like that when things get very tight, Frankie, when push comes to shove."

"Okay, let's say things get very tight." We were in bed, sitting up, and I gave her a little nudge with my shoulder. "Push comes to shove. Now, am I the enemy?"

She didn't answer right away, she didn't like this—and I can't say that I did, either. "I *love* you, Frankie," she said after a while. "Please don't be my enemy."

I had planned, as my next move in this discussion, to pop her on the head with the pillow, but Molly doesn't have much of a sense of humor these days, so I put my arms around her instead.

But the question stayed unanswered, hanging in the air above the bed, like a nightlight someone forgot to turn off.

They're in there for over an hour, Roger and the shrink. I have my ear to the door occasionally, but I can't hear anything. Dusty keeps frowning at me whenever I go near it, which may be what keeps me going back since, I have to admit, I find that frown particularly attractive, sexy, as I do with many of Dusty's expressions, gestures and parts, even the scar.

When Roger comes out, the doctor doesn't come to the door with him. "Hey, guess what?" he says. "I'm crazy."

The maid meets us at the top of the stairs, almost as if she'd been stationed there to make sure we didn't wander into the house proper, and leads us to the door. "Good afternoon," she says when we're safely outside, but I don't think she means it.

"It has been," I say, grinning at her.

We drive in silence till we're out of Highland Park and heading north, toward Milwaukee, as planned. "I guess you don't want to talk about it," Dusty says.

"It's okay, but there isn't anything to talk about, really," Roger says. "I'm crazy, that's all. Ain't that great?"

He doesn't smile and we don't say anything. The lake is on our right, sneaking into view once in awhile. I can see him glancing over at it, and gradually the tension drains from the muscles in his neck and his hands loosen their grip on the wheel.

"*I'm* crazy," he says, shaking his head slowly. "*That* guy is *crazy.*"

"What happened, Honey?" Dusty asks. Roger is exceptionally tall, about six-six, and she's five feet tops, so even sitting down she has to tip her head back to look at him, baring the smooth skin of her throat below the scar when she talks.

"Nothing *happened.* He asked questions and I answered them. But funny questions, you know? No hocus pocus, though, and everything straight out, I give the guy that. He never winked at me or said excuse me while I go through this little charade to make my Hippocratic oath happy or anything like that, and I never said 'Okay, let's get right to it.' Nothing like that. Straight business, like maybe he's afraid the FBI has the place bugged."

"Maybe he's smart," I say from the back.

"Maybe he is. I don't know. If there was someone listening, he made it sound good for them. He asked me questions, I answered, and I didn't lie. That was the first thing he said to me, 'It's important that you answer all my questions as truthfully and honestly as you can.'"

"Is there a difference?" Dusty asks. "Between truthfulness and honesty?"

We all laugh and Roger shakes his head. "They were funny questions, though, you know?"

"Like what?"

"All sorts of stuff. How'd I get along with my mother, my father, that sort of thing."

"A Freudian," Dusty says brightly. "Did he ask about toilet training?"

"No, everything but. A lot of stuff about my brother, how I felt about him at different times, stuff like that."

"When he was killed, you mean?"

205

"Yeah, but other times, too. Like when we were kids and he'd get something I didn't, or I had to wear clothes he'd outgrown, stuff like that."

"A *real* Freudian," Dusty says. She glances in the back at Molly and me, as if confirming her position in a dispute.

"And authority. How do I feel about authority?"

"Politics?" Molly asks.

"No, never directly, but a lot of authority sort of things, like how do I feel when I pay the rent or apply for a phone, things like that. How do I feel about cops and judges and train conductors? And then, at the end, he asked me if I'd be upset if I went into the army. 'Yes, I would,' I said. 'Very upset?' 'Yes, sir.' And he wrote something down on his pad—he was taking notes all along, scribbling like crazy on this long yellow pad. Then he said, 'Son, I'm afraid I'm going to have to recommend to the draft board that you are emotionally unsuitable for military service.' That's what he said, 'afraid I'm going to recommend you're emotionally unsuitable.'"

"And he called you son," Dusty says, smiling.

"Yeah, and he called me son." Roger pauses, thinking, his eyes darting to the right, past her to the gently rolling waves of the lake. "And he said, 'I hope your parents won't be too upset.'" He shakes his head. "Emotionally unsuitable. Crazy guy. And then he wrote out a bill for a hundred bucks, and I gave him a check. He gave me a receipt, look."

Roger takes a slip of paper from his jacket pocket and waves it at us.

"Tax deductible," I say.

"Sure. Well, this is to show this was a real visit, you know, a pro-fesh-un-al con-sul-ta-shun. He's got the check to prove it, I've got the receipt."

We drive on in silence, the lake blinking in and out of sight like a star behind a floating cloud. "So I'm crazy," Roger says as we approach Milwaukee. "Certified. Signed, sealed and delivered."

"Proud Mary" is blaring out of the radio speakers all around us, *"rolling, rolling, rolling on the river."*

"Say, you think the Viet Cong's gotten this far?" I ask, invoking a joke that's become a touchstone. An Iowa politician, complaining about the protests on campus, had told the legislature there had to be vigilance at home or the Viet Cong would be coming up the Skunk River, which ran through his area, before we knew it. Everybody laughs, but nobody's heart is in it.

We have a marvelous meal of wiener schnitzel and sauerbraten at a German restaurant, drinking a lot of a bubbly local beer the waiter recommended. We're belching and laughing and Dusty bends her finger and pushes it up under her nose and does a hilarious imitation of Hitler addressing a group of fat burghers at a Munich beer hall until people at the next table begin giving us dirty looks.

We've all brought sleeping bags and had planned on sleeping in the wagon but it's too cold, a heavy snow starting to fall. We feel good after the meal so we splurge on a motel, even get separate rooms, somewhat to my regret. I tell them about sleeping four or five or more to a room during my old rock and roll days, two to a bed, head to feet, but nobody's impressed, and we turn in early. Molly and I make love and lie on our backs afterwards, smoking cigarettes and listening to the blood race through our temples, the snow gently falling outside.

"God, I'm glad you don't have to go through that," she says.

I whisper a little prayer of thanks to my lucky stars for the old subversives list and my limp. "Why do you think I married you?" I say. And I tell her a great story about my cousin Rhoda's grandfather—this is my Uncle Nate's father—about how, when he came to the States, they asked him if he was a communist or a subversive or a revolutionary, and he said, "God forbid, no." But when he'd tell this story to Rhoda and her brothers, they'd protest because their grandfather was famous in the family for having been deported from three countries, and escaping from prison in a fourth, and they would say, "But Grampa, you *were* a revolutionary and all those things," and he'd laugh and say, "Sure, sure, but the first thing a revolutionary learns is to lie when they ask you about it."

"And not feel bad about it," I have him add, although that's not really part of the story.

"Well, I'm glad anyway," Molly says.

She hasn't met any of my relatives, Rhoda and her folks or any of my other cousins or aunts and uncles, who I barely see myself anymore, or Pops, but she enjoys hearing me talk about them. I haven't met any of her folks either. They're all mad at us for getting married on the quiet. We've been talking about getting to New York this summer, but, to be honest, the thought of Molly meeting Pops gives me the willies. I know there isn't any woman he'd think was right for me, even if she was the spitting image of my mother, which Molly definitely isn't.

The next day, we drive over to Lake Geneva and go skiing. Molly has done some, when she was going to school in Vermont, but the rest of us haven't, and Dusty and I are chicken, going up a little beginner hill on a towrope and snowplowing down. Molly and Roger go up a chairlift after they get the feel of the skis and Molly comes halfway down on her ass, but Roger does great, staying on his feet all the way and blazing past us, his teeth clenched into a grin against the cold.

"He really is a jock," Dusty says, shaking her head, her scar white from the cold. "You'll kill yourself," she calls after him. "You're nuts."

"Sure," Roger says, wiping snow from his face, "I'm certified, haven't you heard?"

His words hang above our heads like snow caught in wind, swirling up and over, around and around, afraid to touch earth.

"I'm freezing," I say. "Let's get something to drink."

"You go on," Roger says. "I want to go down one more time." Molly goes with him and Dusty and I hustle into the lodge and have something called a Broken Leg, hot apple juice with bourbon and a twist of lemon. "He'll be okay," I say, though I'm not convinced. Dusty looks at me and the corners of her mouth soften. I feel like leaning over and kissing her, and think she probably won't mind, but something as strong as the wind on the ski hill holds me back, squinting up my eyes.

"Sure," she says, lifting her glass. "To broken legs."

"That's what the actors say."

Across the room from us, on a small makeshift stage, a young woman with honey-blonde hair in a ponytail is playing a guitar and singing a Judy Collins song. The guitar is one of those big-bodied Gibsons, highly polished and with a nice rich sound. It makes me feel homesick, but I'm not sure for what.

"Maybe that's your friend Judith Heart," Dusty says, raising her chin, which is small and pointed.

"No, I don't think so."

"Because there is no such person? Because you made that whole story up?"

"Why, Dusty, I'm surprised at you, doubting me that way." I rear my head back, feigning offense. "I may embellish, but I do *not* invent."

She grins at me, and again I find myself thinking how nice it would be to cover her mouth with mine.

"Well, I *beg* your pardon. That's not her, though, you sure?"

"Positive. Her hair was black, she didn't sing as good as this chick and she played a Spanish guitar, a Flamenco style."

"Too bad. I thought maybe we could ask her about Miles Davis' trumpet."

"Yeah, I'd kind of like to know about it myself."

They come in soon, shaking snow from their parkas, Roger leaning on Molly.

"What happened?" Dusty runs over and helps him into a chair.

"I came down on my ass again," Molly says, laughing, "and Roger broke the sound barrier."

"I'm a fucking madman," Roger says, but he's laughing, and it's okay.

His ankle is sprained, so Dusty drives. We head down to Beloit, where I played once, years ago, and then across the bottom of Wisconsin and cross the river at Dubuque, where Roger spent that year at Bible college. We stop there, at a place he knows, and have some burgers and coffee, then drive on through the darkness. It's getting late. Dusty works in a bookstore and has to be there at nine in the morning, and Molly and I both have early classes.

We head southwest toward Cedar Rapids, then cut off on Iowa 1 and head south toward Iowa City. We've been quiet for awhile, even Dusty, Roger sitting straight and rigid beside her, staring through the windshield at the high beams and white line rushing toward us, Molly dozing in the backseat beside me, her head on my shoulder. The Mamas and the Papas come on the radio, "California Dreaming," and because they remind me of Peter, Paul and Mary, I'm back a few years and thinking of that weird chick Judith Heart.

There hadn't been anything between us—I only knew her for those few days we were both playing at the Plugged Nickel—and I can't say I've thought much about her after that, although I guess I've told that story, about Miles Davis and his trumpets, a few times. But I find myself now thinking again how I gleefully led her into that situation with those jivecats, who maybe were harmless but, hey, I know better, fucking well weren't. I don't mean they were necessarily going to rape her and perform all sorts of depraved acts on her lily-white pure body, brutalize her and sell her into bondage, dope her up and put her on the streets for them, murder her and cut her up into pieces—that isn't what I mean, although who can say one or another of those things might not have happened. It's a dangerous world and we all have to take our chances. But that isn't what I mean. I asked this girl if she'd like to come down and hear Miles Davis with me, down on the South Side, territory that was as good as home to me but was a foreign country to her. She was not exactly a born-yesterday country girl, but she was not particularly hip, either. She had heard of Miles, but just barely. She came down there with me and, I mean, that was it—we weren't just together, she was *with* me. I had her under my wing, I was responsible.

If *I* had taken her home afterwards and done unspeakable, depraved acts on her lily-white pure body, that would have been one thing, bad enough. But what I did was put her in jeopardy, and that was worse, that was inexcusable. I don't know what would have happened with those guys if Miles hadn't come along, no doubt because he had his *own* evil intentions, but *something* would have, something that probably shouldn't have, something that only would have been able to happen because I thought it would be cool to play some word games, some head games, with those cats, because I thought it would be cool to show this little chick how perfectly, utterly, unspeakably cool I was, how *easy* I could take care of her.

There was one of those cats, I remember, who had a gold tooth—his name was Merle and seemed to be the main man. They were all well dressed, these cats, in sharkskin suits and tight collars and narrow ties and gleaming black shoes—if they hadn't been down at the table with us, they could have been up on the bandstand with Miles, they were that slick, that hip. They were just as friendly and polite as you could hope for, but there was a smell of menace about them, clear as garlic on the breath of someone who's had sausage for lunch, and there wasn't any doubt, not to *me*, that it wasn't me they were interested in. But this Merle, he was probably a doctor or a lawyer, for all I know, his hands were so smooth, he kept slapping hands with me, kept thrusting his face close to mine, his mouth open just enough to show his teeth, that gold tooth flashing like the point of a dagger. "Beeoootiful, man, that's beeeoooti*ful*," he'd say in response to everything I said. "You are *some* beeoootiful cat." And that's what it was, beautiful, my head was spinning with it, and all the while there was the smell of menace, clear as that flashing tooth, and I ignored it. And then I lost control and went away, and left her there in its circle.

It's past midnight when we come to the Cedar River, and it must be getting warmer because there's fog in the valley. The road is dark and empty and the wheels of the Jeep rattle like chattering teeth across the wooden boards of the old bridge.

"Wait a minute," Roger says. "Stop the car, will ya?"

Dusty stops in the middle of the bridge and Roger gets out. It's okay because we haven't passed another car in a hell of a long time. "What is it, Honey?" she calls after him.

He hobbles to the rail and drapes himself over it, staring into the darkness below.

Dusty starts to get out but I put my hand on her shoulder. "Let me." I get out and walk over. "What's up, man?"

"Nothing's up. Why does something have to be up?"

"Okay, take it easy. I thought maybe you were sick or something."

"Naw, I'm okay. I'm sorry. Listen."

He cocks his head over the railing and I look down. The sky has cleared and there's enough moon to light the river. Snow is piled over most of it, but there's one narrow clear channel where water rushes with a black hiss, like air coming from the belly of God.

"Listen," Roger says again.

"Must be the Viet Cong. Is this the Skunk?"

"No, really," Roger says. His voice is lean and tired, like the answer of someone who's been asked too many questions. "Listen, you can hear the fish."

"You're shittin' me, man," I say.

"No, really." He looks up—he's three or four inches taller than me, but because of the way he's standing, draped over the rail, he has to look up to face me. "Listen, man, I'm a farm boy, a *country* boy. Fish is something I know about. No shit. Just listen."

We stand there in the fog and the darkness, the Jeep humming behind us, its lights stabbing the dark, empty bridge and the road beyond, and I bend further over the railing.

And I swear, I can hear them, leaning into the current of the rushing river, their mouths open in silent laughter at the darkness.

13. Another Woman

Please don't say I told you so.

It looks like Molly and I have split—for good, I guess.

Anything can always happen, so it's possible we could patch things up and try again, but the slam of that door when I went through it had a firm ring of finality that even someone with a tin ear for things like that, someone like me, couldn't help but catch. We ran into each other at a hasty demonstration over Cambodia today, after word broke about the invasion, and the strongest feeling I had, I was shocked to realize later, was embarrassment, because she was with a bunch of people we both know and everybody seemed tongue-tied.

This is something that's been coming on for some time, I think, although it's taken both of us awhile to catch on to it—Christ, we've only been married two and a half years and together for only three. But the end came, the tears-and-shouting, door-slamming end, two weeks ago, and I've been doing a lot of thinking since, about that scene itself—going over every second of it, everything I did, everything I said and she said, trying to figure if there was something I could have done differently, the way a boxer must pore over the TV footage after Muhammad Ali's knocked his stuffing all the way to Thanksgiving. But also about our whole marriage, trying to figure out if I could have seen trouble coming months ago, if I could have predicted what was going to happen, and done something to avert it. Yeah, sure I could have, even with my eyes closed.

Things came to a head when Molly accused me of fooling around with another chick which, I had to admit, I had. Her name is Penny, but I call her Petunia, a sweet, all-Iowa church-going girl, a teensy bit on the pudgy side—not my type at all. She's in my geology class and I met her when we were thrown together on a class project. I can honestly say she didn't mean any more to me than a couple of hours of sweet giggling and jiggling and ego-stroking—she kept telling me how *wonderful* I was: wonderful musician, wonderful singer, wonderful lover, wonderful person. Molly was up in Wisconsin somewhere at an SDS meeting, one of about a hundred she's been to this year, which has been at least part of the problem between us.

My few hours with Penny were more or less unplanned, and weren't going to be repeated. I don't know how Molly found out, except that this is a *small* town, we know everybody and I stupidly brought the girl to our place—she lives in a dorm—and God only knows who might have seen us. On the Wednesday after the Saturday night in question, Molly came home in the evening spitting nails, slamming the door, the pupils in those lovely green eyes slightly smaller than normal, as if she were strung out on something, although she's given up all that shit.

"You bastard," she said.

I didn't have to be Einstein to figure out what she was talking about but—again, stupidly—I hadn't given a moment's consideration to this happening, and I was unprepared, so, for a couple of volleys, I played dumb, which just made things worse.

"What's eating you, babe?"

"Don't babe me, you bastard. You know what's eating me."

"No, I don't. If it's cleaning up the place, I was going to get to that this evening when...."

"Fuck cleaning the place. Don't play games with me, Frankie, please. I hurt. How could you?"

"Oh," I said stupidly. "That." Then, because I have worse secrets to hide, I fessed up. "You mean Penny."

"Penny!" Molly said. "Is that what's she's called? Your fat-assed little farm girl?"

Petunia is all sweetness and light, like one of those packaged desserts you churn air into with an eggbeater and chill, all teeth and fluttery eyes, and if I didn't know it first-hand, I'd swear there was nothing between her legs but cool, smooth Saranwrap, she's that pure, although, to my surprise, she wasn't a virgin. Making love to this girl was like lying in a field of soft grass on a July day, the sun and a gossamer breeze licking at your body as you fall into a strawberry-and-fresh-cut-hay-smelling sleep filled with angel dreams—it was that easy, that sweet, that uncomplicated.

Making love to Molly, by contrast, is often like playing chess or running a political campaign—contemplative but vigorous, intense; exhilarating but exhausting, filled with false moves, strategy, little defeats, decisive victories. But, oh, shit, I don't want to be thinking of that.

"Hey, Penny's no sillier a name than Molly," I said quickly, again stupidly, digging my own fucking grave.

"Molly's what *you* call me, you bastard. My *name* is Margaret."

I started to protest that she called herself Molly when I first met her, back in Vermont, years ago, but she was already crying, which always undoes me, her face twisting and sort of caving in, like one of those photo sequences you see in the newspapers of a building being demolished, not *exploded* but *imploded*. She flopped onto the overstuffed couch our cats have been tearing to shit and I sat next to her with my hands on my knees, afraid to touch her, like she was a boil about to burst.

"Molly," I said, "Molly." Then, after a moment, a little lamely: "I love you," because it was true, although I realize it may have sounded hollow. Between the sobs she coughed out something that sounded like a bent-out-of-shape laugh. I twisted around and put my hands on her shoulders but she shook them off. "Listen, Molly, it doesn't mean anything. I swear. She's just a goofy kid I took a little liking to because she seemed to like me so much, and ... I guess maybe I've been feeling a little neglected or something because you've been so busy, and...."

"This is *my* fault? Is that what you're saying? Because I wasn't around every precious minute to hold your fucking precious hand?"

"Damn it, Molly, that's not what I mean. It's just ... oh, shit, I was just lonely while you were gone, that's all."

"Horny, you mean."

"Okay. What difference does it make? The point is you weren't around and I was drifting. So I spent one lousy night with this chick. That's all. There isn't going to be any more. It doesn't *mean* anything."

Molly took her hands away from her face and looked at me. Her eyes were red and puffy and I wanted to lean over and kiss them but I didn't. "It *does* mean something. It means you broke a promise to me. It means you have no self control, no respect for yourself, no respect for me. It means I can't trust you. It means you put your arms around someone else, it means you put your body into someone else's body, in *our* goddamned bed ... Jesus, Frankie, are you *stupid*? It means all sorts of things. How can you say it doesn't?"

There wasn't any answer to that so I just sat there, numb. I was starting to realize that I had done something more than merely stupid, and that there wouldn't be any talking around it.

Molly is a bundle of contradictions, of course, as are most people I've run across. On one hand, she's a revolutionary (and into some things, I think, that she doesn't tell me about) and a radical feminist—and I have to take her word for that, not knowing one kind from the other myself—but in some things she's conservative as they come, and has never been able to get over a childhood filled with Catholic dogma and ritual. She doesn't believe in God, or so she says, but does believe in natural grace, in holiness of the spirit.

I had to talk her into getting married—and what I was thinking of I can't imagine now, except that I truly did love her—but then she took it more seriously than I ever did. She talks about the sacredness of the family but she can't get along with her own family, especially her father, who she's also half in love with, if you ask me. She's always on about artificiality, how the capitalistic system has cheapened life because it puts so little value on natural things, and she herself is preoccupied with naturalness, tries to avoid eating anything with chemicals in it, has even dabbled with giving up meat, but, at the same time, she's shy and won't wear clothes that show off her body. She won't wear makeup but changes her earrings every day. She believes in people doing their own thing but she also believes in the good of the many coming before the good of the few. Sometimes I think she isn't really sure what she means.

"I told you the one thing I wouldn't be able to stand was your being unfaithful," she said, just as I was thinking about those contradictions in her. "Remember? When we got married? I *told* you that, Frankie."

"Molly, for Chrissake, I haven't been *unfaithful*."

"What would *you* call it?"

"All right, so I slept with another girl, I had sex with another girl. Okay, I screwed her, I *fucked* her—that specific enough? I'm sorry, I shouldn't have, it was stupid of me."

I started pacing around our living room, which is filled with frayed, spring-broken furniture that comes with the crummy place and stacked orange crate book cases, painted half a dozen shiny colors. There are brightly colored posters on every wall, one of Che above the desk Molly and I shared, a psychedelic sunburst with Tim Leary's prescription about dropping out over the sofa. I stood in front of the desk, staring at Che's burning eyes. It was tempting to blame the whole thing on him—on politics, anyway. The truth is, though I keep getting involved, I never have been too interested in the finer points, or crazy about a lot of the people you wind up rubbing shoulders with. That goes all the way back to when my cousin Rhoda dragged me in with the crowd of Trots she hung out with in high school. Everything she said about the state of the world and the divisions between *them* and *us* made sense, but soon as some of her pals started yapping off I was lost, and happy to be. And that's the way it's continued, more or less, right down to now, all those benefits I've played notwithstanding. The only politics I'm ever really comfortable with is banging on my guitar and leading a singalong of "This land is your land," the way my Uncle Nate taught it to me when I was twelve. Uncle Nate, who died last year, poor bastard, was a communist, so the story went, but he never said a word about it to me, never tried to push an idea on me, just tried to be a decent man.

But that's not the way it is with Molly. She's always been a partisan, someone with a definite point of view and not a hell of a lot of tolerance for different points, even if they're aimed in basically the same direction. This made loving her easy, of course—her love was so intense, and didn't have room for any doubts, long as it lasted. It's a good way to paint yourself into a corner, which is sort of what was happening with us. We'd go off to a meeting or a demonstration and, out of twenty or fifty or five hundred people there, Molly would just naturally be part of a group or faction that kept getting smaller, with less and less room for anybody else to scramble on board. Fine, except the small group was starting to exclude me more and more and I'd wind up being not only on the outside but dangerously close to being one of *them*, rather than one of *us*.

"But that doesn't mean I've stopped loving you," I said, "or that I love you any less than I did the day before, or the day we got married. I did something with my body that I shouldn't have but that doesn't mean in my *mind* I've been unfaithful. I screwed her but I didn't make *love* to her, if you see the distinction, I swear. I love you, Molly, and I haven't been unfaithful to that."

"Yes, you have, Frankie, don't you understand? You said you

wouldn't do something, and you *did*. That's what being unfaithful means. Don't twist words."

"And that's it? Simple as that? The twig is broken so the whole tree has to be cut down? That doesn't make any sense."

"I didn't say anything about cutting down the tree," Molly said miserably.

"You didn't *say* it, but I hear what's in your voice, Molly, I know you." But the thought pierced my mind, with a swiftness and sub- tlety that took my breath away, that it was me, not her, who had introduced that idea, who saw the rightness of it.

She hit her knees with her fists. "Fuck, Frankie, I *hurt*."

"So do I, Molly, so do I," I said, but my voice sounded hollow, even to me. I turned away and went to stand by the open window overlooking the alley, where lilacs were already in bloom and small green fingerlings of what I hoped were the marijuana seeds I'd scattered there last fall were pushing through the patchy soil around the house. Dusk was coming quickly, robbing the blos- soms of their color but not their scent.

"*I* haven't done anything to hurt *you*," Molly said angrily.

I shrugged. "I hurt myself, I guess. It hurts just the same."

In the silence that followed, I thought I could sense her soft- ening, her resolve to be angry melting like caked summer mud under rain. Then, like a kid picking at a scab and staring in won- der when the blood starts to flow again, I said: "Maybe it wouldn't have happened if you hadn't been away. I mean, if you weren't *always* away, at this rally or that meeting, in *jail*, for shit's sake, or this...."

"Jesus," Molly said.

But I had started and I guess there was more resentment or dis- satisfaction bottled up in me than I had realized, and it all started to pour out of me, not only resentment over the sort of wedge I'd seen coming between us, but anger over some of the things I'd heard her say and, Jesus, suspicion over this guy called Pat Ryan,

a red-faced former marine from Detroit who's big in the movement and holds Molly in some kind of thrall.

"Pat?" she exploded. "He's a *comrade.* I *respect* him. He's got
his shit together. *You* like him, I've heard you say so."

"I didn't say I *didn't* like him. I said I didn't like the way the two
of you look at each other some times."

"Oh, for Chrissake, Frankie, this is lower than I thought you
could go. Who's the injured party here? Me or you? I haven't been
holding hands with anybody, let alone screwing them, Pat Ryan or
anyone else. *I* was knocking myself out all weekend trying to work
out some strategies for the good of *all* of us against the common
goddamn enemy—that I've heard you say you hate just as much
as me—while *you* were home with your goddamn school books
and your precious music and being cozy with a little farm girl. So
don't give me that injured party bullshit."

"Jesus, Molly, you're so smart, you're so fucking smart, but
you don't understand shit, do you? You want to save the fucking
world and you can't even look out for your own life." I shouted
that, and I don't know why—why I was shouting, or what I meant,
although the words "precious music" had stung—but my head
was spinning, and people say crazy things sometimes. But as
soon as I did, in the silence that pounced on the room like a cat
on a bird before the last word had died away, a silence that was
filled with the sound of Molly's crying again, in a moment, I realized that it was all over, that one or the other of us, maybe both,
had crossed over an invisible line from which there could be no
going back. It wasn't just that a twig was broken, something in the
tree itself had gone wrong, cancerous, twisting it so it was growing away from the light instead of toward it.

The fight wound up with me leaving. *I* left, *I* slammed the door,
feeling like *I* was the aggrieved party, and convinced at the moment
that I was. And the slamming of that door was as awful a sound as
any I've heard in my life, like the crunching of bone.

I clattered down the porch steps without stopping to smell the lilacs, which I like to do, and across the street and up two blocks and around the corner to Kenney's Bar, where "Light My Fire" was blaring from the jukebox. That was dumb because the last thing I wanted to do was see people I knew, we both knew. I sat at the bar and ordered a dark draft, and stared at the mirror running along the wall above a counter littered with jars of pickled eggs and beef jerky. In the little bit of mirror Irene Kenney hasn't covered with postcards from former patrons, I saw the one person I least wanted to talk to, sitting at a booth behind me and two down to the right, with a bunch of people, most of whom I knew, all music students.

She was looking past the guy next to her, at my back, and I wondered if there was something written there, between the shoulder blades, that she could read, some tightness of the muscles she could sense. Then she shifted her glance and caught my eye in the mirror and smiled. I gave her a tight, closed-mouthed smile back and looked away, down at my beer.

The truth is, I had a deeper secret to keep than Penny, and this was her. Her name is Diana and she's something really special. She's black, married, a PhD student in the music school and a violinist with the university orchestra, pretty good. Her husband is a white cat, a writer of some sort, a drunk and a creep. They're a classic torch song couple—he ignores her, abuses her, shits on her, runs around with other women, disappears for days on end without word, and she takes it, sheds a tear and turns the other cheek. "I love him, Frankie, I can't help it," she tells me when I harangue her about him. Molly, for all her talk of sisterhood, would have nothing but contempt for Diana, for the shit she willingly takes. I have to smile at the thought that comes to me just now, even though it hurts—is that why I like her so much? No, I know that isn't it.

She's in the composing course I've been taking, and somehow we gravitated toward each other—maybe because I'm the closest person to a black in the class besides her, although she's pure ebony, not weak café au lait like me, or maybe it's my soulful eyes, I don't know. At any rate we've become friends. She is a very classy broad—she's from Kansas City but *ought* to be from New York, and she's been around some. She's about thirty-five, married once before and has a kid who lives with his father and stepmother back in Missouri. All the weight of her life has settled on this creep she's married to now and she can't be shook from it.

I haven't done anything with Diana—that is to say, I haven't slept with her, even kissed her, though certainly not for not wanting to. She's loyal to her man and, up until my slip, I was loyal to my woman, so it just hasn't happened, although the chemistry has been right more than a few times. We've spent afternoons after our class walking along by the river or in the Hamburg Inn over thick white mugs of coffee, talking and talking, the elements in our bodies letting each other know the circuits were open, if only our stubborn straight-jacketed brains would give the word. But it hasn't come. Even so, I have to say that, on any realistic scale, I've been more unfaithful with her than I was in my jolly couple of hours of tickling and bumping with Penny.

Petunia's a sweet girl and I really like her, but she rarely enters my thoughts when she isn't actually within my sight, and if I never saw her again it wouldn't hurt me, but I believe I *love* Diana—I emphasize that word to indicate I'm using it not necessarily in a different way than usual, but more thoughtfully, which is to say I don't know *what* it means. I know I love Molly—I *still* love Molly—but I love Diana too, if that's possible. In my *mind* I've been unfaithful. But that doesn't seem to count, does it? Funny what people will put up with from the ones they love, and what they won't.

I knew I should have left as soon as I spotted her, that I wouldn't be able to get away with not talking to her, but it seemed awkward, after we'd both noticed each other, to just turn around and walk out. Sure enough, I was just halfway through my beer when I saw her disengage herself from her booth and step over to the stool beside me. "Hey," she said. She was smiling, her teeth brilliantly white, and I think I could be forgiven for thinking it was a *hopeful* smile, one aimed just at me.

"Hey yourself. Afraid I'm not very good company tonight, though. Lousy, in fact. I don't...."

She waved off any further explanation. "Shhhh, Frankie. I've been there, more times than I'd like to remember. Don't give it another thought." She put her hand lightly on my upper arm, as lightly as if my arm were a violin she were about to play, and the hopefulness in her smile transformed itself into something more like regret. A moment later, she was back with her friends, and I was alone again, second-guessing myself.

I finished my beer and left without looking at Diana again, and went to another bar on the next block, the Airliner, where I hardly ever go and the chances of my running into anyone I knew among the frat boys and sorority girls in their dyed-to-match sweaters was slim. I had a sandwich and some more beer, then went on to a friend's place, not because I wanted to talk but because it was getting late and I needed someplace to crash, and he was decent enough to keep pouring the suds into me without asking why and we both got stinking. But before I left Kenney's, I had this moment when two separate feelings were racing through me, vying for attention. One was that, despite what had happened, I was glad Molly didn't know about Diana, or at least hadn't brought her up, because I really wouldn't have known how to handle that—though how anything could have been worse than what *did* happen I don't know. The other was I was wondering, feeling the heat of her eyes on my back, if *Diana* knew about Penny, if she too felt somehow betrayed. I hoped she didn't. It wouldn't be long before Diana heard about me and Molly, and maybe she'd hear that the blowup was over, as they say in the funny papers, *another woman*. But she wouldn't necessarily hear Penny's name, since Penny isn't part of any of the crowds I hang with, neither music nor politics. That pleased me, somehow, that and the thought that, perhaps, she'd think it was her.

What I keep hearing is that door slamming. Sometimes, it's like the chilly thud of a hatchet on a butcher's block; other times, more like the percussive splash of a bucket hitting water after a long descent into a well. But, final as that sound always strikes me, I think the end had come a long time before that; I just didn't realize it, and neither, I guess, did Molly.

I remember one night, in February, I think—it was still deep winter, I know that, bitter cold and snow piled like heaps of dirty laundry on the streets—when I came home and found Molly already in bed, asleep. I'd been to a concert—in the audience, not playing—and afterwards a bunch of us had gone to a party. I'd been with Diana, drinking a little and talking, listening to the rumblings of our chemistry, and it was about two in the morning when I pulled in, aching like a sore tooth. Molly had been out that evening, too, to one of her meetings—she hasn't been in school all this year, so that's never a hindrance—but, usually, if one of us got in before the other, we'd stay up waiting. We had the habit of having a cup of tea and toast before going to bed—the flaming radical and the brilliant musician cozy at home!—and talking about what we'd been up to, which, more and more, was different for the two of us. It didn't surprise me that she'd gone to bed this night, though, because it was so late. And, truth was, I felt a little relieved because I was full of Diana, and couldn't share that. And, of course, as soon as I realized I was feeling relief, I felt a little guilt.

I took off my boots and padded around the place for awhile, putting away some junk while the water for the tea boiled. Then I had my toast, feeding crumbs to one of the cats, which had curled up on my lap vibrating like an engine, and scanned through the paper, my mind not on anything in particular. By the time I got to bed, it was almost three. Our place was really just two rooms, a long one that's living room at one end, kitchen at the other, with a bathroom extending off the kitchen, and the bedroom, not much bigger, at a right angle off the other end. There's a door on the bedroom, so anyone in there sleeping isn't likely to be bothered by someone puttering around in the kitchen at the other end of the apartment. So I assumed Molly was still asleep.

I undressed in the living room, Che's eyes on me, hung my clothes on a hook behind the bedroom door and turned out the last light. We had a big down quilt, an heirloom from Ireland that's been in Molly's family a few generations, and she was scrunched up beneath it like a question mark. I got into bed, shivering a little until the warmth from Molly's side crept over me, and I put my hand on her back, just to make sure she was asleep. There wasn't any reaction.

After I warmed a little, I lay on my back, letting my mind wander, the way you do just before sleep, little strands of music flickering against my inner ear like flames, faces taking shape, then melting away to be replaced by others. The face that took hold was Diana's, and I was listening again to something she'd said and my response, wishing I'd phrased it differently. All of a sudden, I became aware that Molly was awake and I drove Diana from my mind, as if afraid that Molly could somehow peer inside me and discover her. She had made a sound or moved against me in a way she wouldn't have if she were asleep—I know her that well, old married people after all. As I lay there, slightly tensed, listening to her breathing, I was certain she was awake. Other times, if I'd awakened during the night, say, and sensed that she was awake, I'd have taken her hand, murmured "hello" and we probably would have rolled against each other, maybe to make love, maybe not, but either way to touch and share each other's warmth. But this time I didn't do that. I lay there, listening to her breathing, wondering if she was doing the same, listening to mine, knowing I was awake, but lying silent, separate, untouching.

I think *that* was when our marriage was over, that shared moment when neither of us had anything they wanted to say to the other, when we lay as strangers—no, *less* than strangers, because there was actually something, some force, between us—in the same bed, enclosed by an indifferent darkness. After awhile, I remember, I grew uncomfortable lying on my back and I rolled over onto my side, facing away from Molly, and stared open eyed into the darkness. Just before I fell asleep, Diana slipped quietly back into my mind.

14. The Children's Hour

Marcel, the guy upstairs, was in an accident tonight and killed a man.

His wife, Anne-Marie, is a civil servant, an overseer of a small section of the welfare department, I think, and she has to travel out of town occasionally. She's been away for a couple of days, and tonight Marcel came downstairs and tapped on my door shortly after I got home from the cafe, my hands still redolent of garlic and basil. It was around two in the morning.

"Hi, Marcel, come on in," I said in French, glad to see him. "Want a beer?" The hour or so between coming home and going to bed is always the emptiest, the hardest to get through, so it was nice to have a visitor. It wasn't until he'd stepped inside and my lights fell on him that I saw his pale face, the red puffiness around his eyes that comes not from crying, but from holding it in. "Jesus, man, *qu'est-ce qu'il ya?*" The first thing that came to my mind was Anne-Marie, that something had happened to her.

He shuffled into my little sitting-room and let himself collapse onto the sofa. He was wearing his cabbie uniform but not the cap, and his hands, which he rested on his knees, were shaking. Marcel is a thin, weedy man a few years younger than I am, with a full, black beard and hair that comes to his shoulders. He doesn't talk about it much, but I gather he was some kind of a radical—and in some kind of trouble—at university, which may explain his difficulty in getting a teaching job, even though he has an education degree. He talks rapidly, with a slight lisp, and he's interested in all sorts of things, science to poetry, but mostly he and Anne-Marie are preoccupied with *la mouvement independence*, the Parti Québécois and some other group they're hush hush about. He says he likes driving cab because of the people he meets, and I can believe it, because he loves to talk, though you don't notice it so much when he and Anne-Marie are together because she does too.

"*Qu'est-ce qu'il ya?*" I repeated. "What's the matter?"

He made a funny sound in his throat that was half laugh, half sob. "I'm, I'm okay, François, just a little shook up. I had an..."— his voice stumbled for a moment—"...an accident, eh? With the cab."

I stood in front of him without saying anything, waiting. When he didn't go on, I said: "*Ça va?*"

"Yeah, sure, I'm fine. Just a little shook up."

"Do you want a beer? Or something else? I don't have any booze, but there's some wine."

"Yeah, yeah, I'll have a little wine."

I turned toward the kitchen but he stopped me, holding up a hand. "Maybe in a little while, François, eh?"

I sat down on the chair across from the sofa. "There's something wrong, *n'est-ce pas?* Something bad?"

Marcel shrugged.

"You were in your taxi?"

"*Oui.*"

"Is it damaged?"

Marcel smiled weakly. "*Un peu.* The bumper and the fender, and the radiator. All in the front end, eh?" He croaked a dry, twisted laugh and gestured with his hand. "And the fuckin' windshield, too. It's cracked." He stared at his hands.

"Did you have a passenger?"

"No, no ... I was on my way to pick one up." He raised his head, the muscles around his mouth tightening, as if he were interested in explaining the process by which taxis are dispatched. Then the light went out of his eyes and his head slumped again.

"There was someone hurt, though, wasn't there?"

Marcel laughed bitterly, a strong, clear laugh this time, and shook his head, staring at the hardwood tiles of the floor. "No, no one hurt." He hesitated. "They said I shouldn't think about it, eh? That he didn't feel a thing."

"Jesus, Marcel."

He put his head between his hands and shook it violently. "I keep thinking it's a dream," he said suddenly, the words spilling out of his mouth like vomit. "You know what I mean, François? That I'm asleep and having a nightmare, eh? And if I shake myself hard enough I'll wake up, or I'll disturb Anne-Marie and she'll reach over and wake me up. And it'll be over. But it doesn't work that way, eh? I shake and shake—I even hit my head against the wall a little while ago, upstairs, but that didn't help, it just hurt my head and cracked the plaster." He laughed again. "I don't wake up. I just keep sleeping, keep dreaming. I keep on seeing him staring at me."

Marcel put his hands on his knees and looked up at me. "He's sleeping, too, eh? But he doesn't dream." His face contorted into something that was like a smile and a frown pulling his mouth in different directions simultaneously, and tears started to flow down his cheeks.

"I can't help it, I keep laughing," Marcel said. "I keep wanting to laugh, eh? It isn't funny, I know, but he was looking in at me, and he had the most comical expression on his face, like Charlie Chaplin, eh? Or Jerry Lewis or somebody when they slip on a banana peel, and I keep wanting to laugh. It isn't right, but I can't help it."

"It's okay, Marcel," I said. I got up and sat beside him. I raised my hand to his shoulder but hesitated. I couldn't bring myself to touch him—I was afraid he would burst, like a boil or a blister swollen too large, too tender to handle. "It's natural. You're in

230

shock and your head doesn't know how to handle it. It'll go away after a while."

"I'm not in shock," he said quickly, as if that were a possibility he had already considered and dismissed. "I know about shock. This isn't it. But this is something, man, this is something."

We sat silently for a moment, rigid and untouching. I was staring at his hand, which was lying motionlessly on his knee, a thin but strong-looking hand, with wisps of dark hair swirling from the wrists toward the knuckles, and I could see it resting lightly on the steering wheel, then tightening suddenly, the knuckles going white.

"Do you want to tell me about it, Marcel? Maybe that will help, if you talk about it."

"Yeah, sure." He turned to me, gave me a suspicious glance, as if I were a ghoul licking my lips for the details. "No, I don't want to. I've been talking about it all night. In my head." He smiled weakly and shook his head, turning off whatever sounds were going on inside. "Maybe I'll have that wine, though, François. Just a small glass, eh?"

I fetched it, and one for me, too, waterglasses filled with some cheap local *plonk*, and he took his with both hands, holding it in front of him like a chalice.

"I was in the old city," Marcel said, "going up St. Louis, toward the Chateau Frontenac." His voice was tiny, distant. "There's an intersection right before where the road angles, it's the Rue Ste. Ursule, eh? There's a gas station on one corner, a drugstore on another."

"Yeah, I know it," I said.

"The light was red when I came to the intersection and I stopped, then the light turned green and I went across. There wasn't anyone there and I started to speed up, eh? I was changing to second when suddenly he was there—he just walked out in front of me from between two parked cars. He wasn't there, eh? And then he was." Marcel's voice trailed off and he was silent.

"And you hit him? I asked stupidly.

"Sure I hit him." Marcel's head rolled back and he screwed his eyes tightly shut, his teeth gritted. "He went flying up onto the hood and his head went bang against the windshield and I saw him looking in at me, eh? His eyes were open and he had this ... this *surprised* look on his face, like he'd just slipped on a banana peel, like he was saying, well, whaddya know, fancy meeting you like this. Then he just sort of slid off the hood backwards, in slow motion, eh? I stopped the cab and just sat there for a second or two. All I could see were those eyes pressed against the windshield, wide open and surprised. His nose was kind of bent and his mouth crooked, a sort of Charlie Chaplin lopsided grin, *whaddya know*. I swear, François, I'll see that face for the rest of my life. I'll see those eyes forever."

He drained his glass and put it on the floor. We sat there without moving for a long time, beside each other but not touching, each of us separate and whole. I was thinking about Molly, our last months together, when not much was happening between us, and about my father, how, when I was a kid, he used to sit at the kitchen table in his undershirt, his elbows propped up on either side of his coffee cup, and I would come in sometimes and sit down across from him and the muscles around his mouth would tighten into some kind of a sign of recognition. Just when it seemed we were about to say something to each other—well, we wouldn't. Suddenly I was thinking about all sorts of people I'd known whose hands I'd almost touched but, for some reason, I couldn't bring myself to, because they were boils, ready to burst, or I was. Finally, I lifted my hand and put it down on Marcel's. His eyes shifted slightly and his head seemed to waver, as if he were counting the fingers he saw on his knee. "Well, whaddya know," Marcel said softly, "fancy meeting you like this."

Our place is in an older section of the city, on a quiet, shady street called Rue St. Leon, not too far from a hospital, a *riviere* called St.-Charles and a park called Victoria—a name that seems to pop up on half the geographical points in this country, even here in Québec City. My suite—*logement*, my elderly landlady, Madame Leclaire, calls it—is the bottom floor of the house, with a little porch and even a garden, with roses growing on vines like the ones Molly and I used to have outside the kitchen window on Capitol Street in Iowa City. Marcel and Anne-Marie live upstairs.

There's a fence around the garden and a flowering tree, a crabapple, although I arrived too late to see the blossoms and there's no sign of any apples yet. There's an old wooden table in the garden, actually a big spool that wire must have been wrapped around at one time, and two ancient lawn chairs, the green paint peeling off them in strips. I like to sit out here in the mornings and read or fool around on the guitar, coffee cooling at my elbow, sunshine streaming down through the leaves of the crabapple tree. There's a bit of traffic on the street, and a lot of it on a bigger street a block away, but in here, among the flowers Madame Leclaire spent so many hours on in the spring and the tall grass I've neglected to cut, the most that can be heard of it is a beelike buzz, broken only by the chirping of a bird on the fence. I don't know the names of the plants, except the roses, nor of the birds, and I've been thinking about getting some books from the *bibliotheque publique*, where I've become a regular, on the local flora and fauna.

Before I got the job at the cafe, I used to hang out at the library a lot or chat with people at bus stops, anything to practice my French without being too conspicuous. Actually, it's gotten pretty good—a lifetime of speaking Spanish without thinking about it has made slipping into the language a lot easier than I feared, except for the peculiar idioms that abound here and which I keep stumbling over. I find new ones every day in the newspapers, which I devour from first page to last, trying to ingest as much of this place as I can, as quickly as I can.

The papers are filled with politics, and news of bombs in letter-boxes, and everybody is wrapped up in the argument over Québec independence—which I hadn't even heard about before—but it's different politics, of course. There's plenty of stuff about Vietnam and Cambodia too, of course, and there's been some demonstrations, which I've studiously avoided, but that all seems very far away now—not only the countries themselves, but the sense of urgency and passion which seemed to make the war itself seem very close, just outside the window in Iowa.

But I haven't been involved in anything, or even talked about politics very much. I've been lying low. There are quite a few Yanks around, especially in Montréal—including a few draft dodgers who Molly and I helped bring up—but I've decided to stay away from there, at least for awhile. I just want to stay out of trouble and work on my French. Marcel says I practically speak like a native, which is what I'm aiming for, but I think he's just being kind. I try to make sure that whatever little bit of accent does sneak through is Spanish, not English, to go along with my story that I was born here but raised in France and spent a lot of years in Spain. Nobody bats an eyelash at that.

I'm calling myself Sterne now, the name I started out with but with an added "e." My father always used to say he changed it from Stein to Stern when he went to Spain in 1936, as a *nom de guerre*, but I always thought it had more to do with my mother and her family, or maybe to keep his own family off his track, after he split with them. I used to be accused of taking the name Stein so people would think I was Jewish, and I look more Latin than Jewish any day, so, who knows, maybe I can pass here, people might think I'm a light-skinned Haitian, or from Algeria. At any rate, under the circumstances, it seemed like it might be a good idea to muddy the waters, at least a little. And the French comes so easy to me, I figured I might as well make use of it to blend into the woodwork— the other Yanks I've run across in Québec, dodgers and deserters, all speak English, of course, and stick out like sore *heads*.

I arrived in Montréal in mid-May, just a week after that stupid snafu in Ames, that damn demonstration that went so wrong, with enough money to get settled and keep me going for a little while. I'd gotten to New York and up to Canada and over the border all without the slightest twitch of interest from the fuzz—their absence just made it all the more excruciating for me, so sure was I that they were watching from the shadows. No sign of them as I left Iowa City in a sweat, but I figured I might get picked up on the road (rousted for illegal hitching by the locals somewhere in Illinois or Ohio, taken down to the lockup where some sharp-eyed sergeant looks me over and says "Stein, Frankie Stein, now where've I heard *that* name lately? Oh, I remember, that APB the FBI put out..."). But, no, not a whiff, even the highway patrol cars that passed me by once or twice as I stood with my thumb drying in the breeze didn't seem interested. So, naturally, I figured they were waiting to take me down in New York, hoping I'd lead them first to others in the underground. But nothing happened there, or on the way up through New England, so I was all braced for it at the border, Mounties in scarlet tunics surrounding me with their dogsleds, making the big gesture for international cooperation. But no, again nothing. Not a sniff there or in Montréal or here, where the local gendarmes are all jolly *bon jovi*.

Of course, it's easy being paranoid these days—some of us have paid the admission to that show, and then some. There was a bomb scare at the student union last year that set something off in me, I don't know what, but it more than just jangled my nerves that day. It seems like I've been nervous ever since. Looking over my shoulder comes natural now. I was always embarrassed to say anything about it, and Molly didn't notice anything, but my friend Diana picked up on it one night in the bar after we'd all been to a demonstration and there'd been some nasty heckling. I remember she put her hand on mine and looked at me with those eyes of hers that could see through Superman's kryptonite shield—"What is it, Frankie?" she asked me, "You're vibrating like a tuning fork."

Funny, all the demonstrations I've been in, picket lines, sit-ins, people snarling, crawling over me, the cops' sullen faces, the yank on the collar, mace in the face, even the billy club on my shoulders and head—even all that didn't really bother me (though it was building up, maybe, especially the billy clubs), but that bomb threat seemed to go further. There was no bomb, but there *could* have been. And if it had gone off? Somebody wants to kill somebody, I remember thinking, *anybody*, and why not me? "A fella could get dead in this line of work," my pal Roger said once, and we all laughed, but, Jesus, what the fuck were we laughing at?

But bomb scares is one thing, real bombs are another. A big noise in Ames there was, most certainly, even if most of it's been drowned out by the Kent State clamor.

And yet at first there was all that shouting from the cops and that stupid state senator, and when I phoned from New York Roger said it looked like the DA was going to the grand jury, talking about conspiracy indictments.

Conspiracy! That's a big one. And guilty as hell, I confess. I *did* conspire, to make a better world, to bring some rays of sanity to the madness darkening the fucking place! Yes, Your Honor, guilty as charged to that one. But the big boom in Ames? Well, I don't know about that. Yeah, I *heard* it, Your Honor, I was there, but light the match? No.

I knew—*know*—I hadn't done anything wrong, but guilt by association is usually enough. And the thought of going to jail or of being tied up in a court case for months, *years*—win or lose—just does not turn me on, not now. A few years ago, when I dug soapboxes more, I might have thrived on it, maybe. But not now, not when my head's more into music than politics or anything. Sure, I'm still (well, *was*) a ready and willing soldier—call me to Ames, I go! But that's as far as it goes.

Skedaddling from Iowa City, I was running on pure adrenaline, sheer panic, sure that the long arm of the law was going to swoop down and snatch me up any second. I calmed down a bit after I hit New York—my cousin Rhoda always calms me down, made being on the lam seem almost natural. "You don't want to be arrested, that's for sure," she said, matter-of-factly. She has a good editing job at a publishing house and lent me some money without batting an eyelash. I'd been unsure whether to head to Montréal or Toronto, and she cast the deciding vote. "Montréal's great—you'll love the women there, Frankie," she said straight-faced, and that settled it.

I couldn't resist taking the time to drop in for a quick visit to the old man, to see his eyes pop out when I told him I was on the run. "What'd I tell you about not trying to be me, Frankie?" he said, shaking his shaggier-than-ever head.

"Believe me, Pops, I'm not *trying*."

But we had a hug and I was just nicely humming, sort of like a tuning fork, on the last leg of the trip, knapsack on my back and my guitar in its battered old case, just like in the old days, and wearing this absolutely wild shirt I'd picked up that morning as a final gesture at one of those raunchy men's shops on 42nd Street: a weird floating red-and-black design on top of a deep purple background. I had the sleeves of this goodbye-to-the-good-old-USA shirt rolled up to the elbow, and the tails, which were long, hung out over the jeans, covering up frayed spots on the thighs and ass. I guess I could have passed, except for that shirt, for a Basque sheepherder, which was a childhood daydream of mine, back when I was forever running away from home, heading for Montana.

At any rate, I stuck my thumb out like always and motion took me. Considering I feared I was on the most-wanted list, I don't know what the fuck I was thinking, sticking out like a sorehead that way, just like those Yank soreheads I now disdain. But the next day I was in Canada, over the border without a blink or any of the formalities. The end of one life, start of another, just that easy.

A draft dodger outfit helped get me oriented and within a week I came up here, calling myself Donaldo Cervantes, with a tip of the old chapeau to the old scribbler, who I'm sure would enjoy the joke, and claiming to be from Chile. That gave me the chance to butcher the *français* as much as I wanted without attracting undue attention, and it only took a couple of weeks with that identity, in a furnished room, before I felt confident enough to find this place.

Not so confident that I'd take on a gig at a club, though, even if I could find one. I'm not sure that's what I want to do, anyway. I couldn't just take the kind of stuff I used to play and plunk it down here in Québec City and expect people to buy it, even translated. I'd have to rethink my whole songbook, come up with a whole new approach and I'm not sure I can do it. Not just like that, anyway. Before I had to wrestle with the problem too seriously, however, it got short-circuited by my getting an unlikely kind of job and easing the money pressure I was feeling.

Marcel had offered to let me work for him, driving his cab evenings, but I've been afraid to apply for a driver's license or have any kind of connection with bureaucracy until my French is perfect. I told him and Anne-Marie I can't drive, which isn't entirely a lie, since I've never done it very well. But they came through by steering me to a job as a salad chef in a cafe owned by a friend of theirs. I've only been at it a few weeks, but it's okay—fun, actually. It's easy work that requires little thought and little talking, yet I can listen to the steady stream of bantering among the other chefs and kitchen help, which I like. They treat me well and have been scrupulous about not asking any questions—they know about fugitives here.

Last weekend, Marcel and Anne-Marie took me on a picnic in the hills west of here, to celebrate my new job. It was sweltering in the city and it was a good excuse to get away. They've been living in the cramped quarters upstairs for over a year, saving every penny like mad for a downpayment on a house, and they grab any chance they can to get out of the place.

It was a beautiful day, one of those simmering July days when the air closes in around you and you can actually see the heat rising, when something that's been lying in the sun for even just a couple of minutes becomes too hot to touch. We crossed a bridge over the little river and drove through a part of the city I hadn't been in before, and then onto a highway that was straight at first but soon began to wind as we entered the rolling countryside dotted with tiny towns with names like St. Charles de Bellechasse and St. Lazare, real French territory, a country of saints.

I was in the back seat of their car, not the taxi but Anne-Marie's little yellow Renault, and I was hugging my knees to keep my legs from going through the floor boards. Marcel was driving and Anne-Marie was beside him, half turned around so she could talk to me. She was telling me a story about Trudeau, the prime minister, who is still relatively new and somewhat mysterious, "*et trés excitante,*" Anne-Marie said—very sexy—but also "*un maudit batarde.* That man doesn't mean well for people like us," she said, shrugging. She didn't have to explain, even to a newcomer like me.

Anne-Marie was laughing and the wind was blowing in through the open windows and tearing at her hair, which is dark and cut in a style I never saw in Iowa, in layers like a mane. She had one hand to her forehead, as if she were afraid the wind would blow her hair away. She looked very lovely, but I was thinking not so much of that, or even of her femaleness, but of her place in the car, I mean her actual physical location, between Marcel and me, not only in the actual physical space of the car, but in the mystical space that envelopes us all, separates us.

But she was with him, of course, and I was alone. There was no changing that. And I felt not only apart from her but from him as well, apart from *all* the people I've known in my life, all the people in the world—like some rock-jawed character in an Ayn Rand novel, alone and defiant, baring my teeth at nature's tyranny.

We arrived at a small provincial park and picnicked on the grass under a maple in full leaf. I've never seen anything quite like it, even in my logging days—a tree like a tall, dignified man with his arms raised to the sky, his cloak spread to shelter all that lies beneath it. We ate cold chicken Anne-Marie had fried the night before, and potato salad and sliced pickles and crusty French bread, and drank beer and *cidre*, and lay on the grass with our faces in the sun. After awhile, I excused myself and went for a walk so they could be alone.

But I was the one by myself, utterly. I was thinking of Molly and all the things we had done wrong—*I* did wrong—and all of the wasted opportunities, the chances thrown away. We were so busy fighting the fucking war we never gave ourselves a chance—but that isn't the way to look at it, is it? There was something that had to be done and we were not so much victims as casualties along the way, that's all.

I have to admit that I'm lonely here, sometimes out-and-out miserable. I think about Diana and how it looks like nothing's ever likely to come of that, me up here, her so far away and nothing ever really happening anyway. But more often, I find myself thinking about Molly and I feel a stab of physical pain that draws my shoulder in tight. I wonder what would have happened if she and I had still been together last spring: would I even have gone to Ames, been around at the bombing? That was always the last thing I wanted to get involved in but suddenly I was acting recklessly. And, even if I had, would she have come here with me, or would we have fled somewhere else entirely? Or held our ground and stayed to fight the charges? Or, if it had only been me they'd been looking for, would she have stayed or come with me? It's all academic, of course, and I know there's no going back, but it's an irresistible thought.

I've been thinking a lot about relationships between people and why they always seem to go sour. Is there something in our psyches, our chemistry, that rebels against the combination of minds? I think of all the relationships—not just Molly and me, but ones each of us had before, our friends, or just read about in the newspaper—relationships that start out so well, seem so perfect and ordained, and then see what happens to them. There seems to be only one logical explanation: that men and women were not really meant to live together.

But that's nonsense, isn't it? Before I got my job, I used to spend my afternoons walking, usually in the old part of the city, with winding cobblestone streets and tiny shops that specialize in everything you can imagine, and churches and cafés everywhere. Wherever I'd look, there would be couples, boys and girls, young men and women, old men and women, everywhere you go, on the street strolling hand in hand, lining up at the movies, at the markets, in the parking lots, at restaurants and bars—everywhere there are people living under the tyranny of the idea of the sexual couple, some kind of an inner law that forces us to reach out, to try to cancel our singleness, our *alone*ness. It's as if the hardness in men, the straight lines, calls out for the softness of women, the curves, and the other way around too, of course, so that both can somehow deny their own uniqueness and blend into some shapeless whole, like pieces of a puzzle that drive you wild with contours that never seem to fit anywhere, then suddenly give up their angles and projections and gaps to snap mysteriously together, surrendering their own life to become part of the whole picture, complete.

But it isn't just male and female, either, is it? On one narrow stretch of the old city I've seen couples of boys and young men walking, even couples of girls occasionally, and their hands seem to be just as tightly clasped, their eyes just as steadfastly on each other. And I don't know how these people fit in, whether they are true rebels or merely perverse, or whether the biological equation doesn't have anything to do with it anyway, not even the *sexual* equation, that it is merely the tyranny of the *couple* itself that drives us, the awful fear of being alone, nature's damnable compulsion for symmetry.

The stream I was walking beside grew wider—it was a river, I guess, shallow and rocky but with a deep channel in the center where water rushed through gaps in the rock with a roar. A couple of kids came floating by on inner tubes, cool and ecstatic. One of them shouted something at me but I couldn't hear what it was.

I came to a spot where I couldn't walk beside the river without getting my feet wet, the foliage pressed so close to the bank, so I ducked into the trees and crashed through for a hundred yards, swatting at tiny bugs which suddenly descended on me, then followed the trail of sunlight through dense bush to the river again. When I stepped out of the trees onto the rocky bank, I was surprised to see a group of people on the other side of the river, a bit further downstream. I could hear snatches of laughter over the roar of the water. Upstream, the foliage still pressed too tightly against the bank, so I had no choice but to pick my way downstream, in the direction of the group across the river—either that or turn back into the buggy woods.

When I drew a little closer, I saw that the people across the river were all women and children, lounging on what looked to be a sandy beach. They were all in swim suits, stretched out on folding lawn chairs and inner tubes, four women who must have been in their thirties, all gleaming with suntan oil, and five or six kids, the oldest no more than twelve, a skinny girl with blonde pigtails who stood up and pointed at me as if I were a bear that had come crashing out of the woods. I was shirtless and I suddenly felt very self-conscious—I'm not in the best of shape, and my belly was hanging over my belt like a sausage. I sucked it in till it hurt and raised my hand when one of the women waved to me. But I hurried on, averting my eyes, picking my way along the rocks till my back was to them and I could let out my breath. I heard a shout that was unintelligible and I turned and the women all waved to me, laughing, then the children joined in. The woman who had waved, a deeply tanned brunette wearing a green bikini and a short terry robe, got up and the others followed, all waving with both arms now. The brunette took off her robe and put one hand on her head, the other on her hip. The skinny girl with pigtails parroted her. Then all the women and half the children were posing and pirouetting, swaying their hips, cocking their heads, curtsying. A blonde, slightly pudgy woman bowed deeply toward me, jiggling her breasts. Laughter danced across the river toward me in the spray, blending in with the shards of sunlight.

I stood there for a minute watching, my belly hanging over my belt, my jaw loose, like an idiot. I wanted to go, to flee, but my feet wouldn't move. And the strangest feeling washed over me, as if I were a child who had sneaked down the stairs to peek at his parents' party—there they were in all their splendour, adults, swathed in a mystery I could never hope to fathom, could never penetrate, and there I was, hidden in the darkness beneath the banister, so far away from the light and noise of the living room that a river might be flowing between us.

As if to put form to my thought, I noticed then a little boy who was wading in the water, slightly apart from the others, and staring at the women and other children as if thunderstruck. He was brown as a squirrel and naked except for a pair of yellow trunks that had slipped halfway down his hips. His head bobbed on its springy neck, turning first to the crowd of waving, laughing people on the beach, then across the river to me, then back again. He seemed to set my feet free. I smiled at him, waved at him—at *him*, not them—and then bolted into the woods. My face was burning with shame—but why? My belly? Being a child in the presence of grownups? Being a man in the presence of a group of women? Or of being alone in the face of their togetherness?

I crashed through the woods till the elms and maples thinned out and I reached a clearing, passing through it into a wide rocky channel undulating through the trees. It seemed to be a dry river bed, a flood plain of the main channel. The floor of the bed was littered with stones of all sizes and large outcroppings of rock from a shaley cliff that ran along one side of the channel, with slim, twisted trees growing from the thin soil above the rock. I walked in the direction I thought I had come from, picking my way carefully along the rocks, pretending that there was water below me I must be careful not to step into or be swept away, devoured by sharks. Everywhere, there were wildflowers, little yellow star-shaped flowers, and stalks of purple petals, groups of bluebells growing tenaciously from cracks in rocks so minute I couldn't see them until I bent over to look closer.

I trudged on, my head down, lost in thought. I was thinking of Molly and, inexplicably, of LBJ on the flickering television screen at the student union the night he gave it up a couple of years ago and the way she turned to me, her face open and filled with a kind of light of victory that thrilled me, and of Ted Kennedy and the girl who was killed when his car went off the bridge in Massachusetts, not so far south from where I am now—now why the hell did I think of *that*?

It wasn't the first time since I've been in Canada that I felt lost and adrift, totally and completely apart from every other living thing, but this time I was frightened. If I died right then, if I slipped from those rocks and was swept away, no one would ever know, let alone care. Marcel and Anne-Marie would wonder what had become of me, waiting longer than they'd like, but then they'd go home, shaking their heads, *"Those crazy Europeans."* At the cafe on Monday evening, they'd look at the clock, make a telephone call, curse me, then fill the job with someone else. My elderly landlady would be forced to clean my few possessions from the suite— some clothes, my guitar, books I've bought, notebooks—and find another tenant. All traces of me would be gone. And people in the

States, Molly and my cousin Rhoda and my father, everyone I've ever known, maybe, would sometimes wonder whatever became of Francesco Stein, the promising young musician, son, cousin, friend, husband, Cuba veteran, freedom fighter, antiwar activist, fugitive, refugee.

"Say, whatever became of Frankie Stein?"

"Stein—didn't he go off to Canada a while back? On the run? He was in the wrong place when a recruiting station went blooey in some hick town in Iowa, remember?"

"Yeah, sure—say, he wasn't involved in that, was he?"

"No, but people he was with were."

"No one was killed, though."

"No, but someone might have been. People were hurt."

"Jeez, man ... what's become of him since?"

"Gone underground, I guess, like those Weather Whatchamacallits."

Gone underground.

I stopped, suddenly. At my feet, growing out of the conjunction of two rocks and a sliver of gritty soil was one perfect flower, five minutely veined pink petals on a stem no more than four fingers high and barely thicker than a thread. It bobbed in the wind the way the little boy's head had, its petals gently fluttering like the waving of arms viewed from a vast distance. It stood totally alone, stubbornly clinging to the meager soil, surrounded by lifeless rock, refusing to bend to the wind, its face lifted hopefully to the sun. I bent down to look at it closer, dropping to one knee in the rough pebbles. I could see the thin, variegated veins in the petals, their design a reflection of some cosmic command. I reached out my hand and lay a finger against one petal, then another, but there was barely a sensation, like laying a hand against a cobweb or into the lightest stirring of air.

I put my finger on the stem, intending to pluck it up, a gift for Anne-Marie, but that didn't seem right. I left it to fend for itself, alone with the rocks and wind and sun, battering its fragile face against the tyranny of nature that held it aloft, that sought to pound it down.

───────

I think of that flower now as I sit beside Marcel in my sitting-room, my hand on his. It's been some time since either of us have spoken. The rigidity has drained from his shoulders and his breathing has become regular, as if he might have slipped into sleep. Outside my window, the reaching arms of the crabapple tree are beginning to take shape as the light of dawn filters down. In a moment, I'll get up, make some coffee. I should make an attempt to locate Anne-Marie.

Returning to the picnic ground, I remember, I was awfully glad to see her. "Oh, here you are. We were starting to worry," she said, in French. She half smiled, half frowned at me the way a mother might at a child. "*Ça va?*"

"Sorry. Just walking. I guess I got a little lost."

"*Ah oui?*" Marcel said. "We should be getting back to town." They had gathered up the remains of our picnic, tucking it all away into the basket.

"First come look at the children," Anne-Marie said. She took me by the hand and led me as if I was a child myself across the meadow to a slight rise. We scrambled up, followed by Marcel, and at the crest we could see another expanse of grass where a dozen kids of all ages were playing. They were tossing Frisbees and balls, and some of them were wrestling or rolling in the grass. Two big dogs were yelping happily among them, running this way and that. There wasn't an adult to be seen, except for us.

"Now isn't that your idea of perfect bliss?" Anne-Marie said, using the expression "*beatitude parfait.*" She was eager to have a child, I knew, but they had decided to wait until they'd bought their house. "Pure, unadulterated bliss. Little mindless animals playing in the sun."

"They could as well be wildflowers," I said, in French.

We looked at each other and Anne-Marie smiled, obviously pleased. Marcel was right behind us but, for that brief moment, I was with her. We were together.

Two children came running up the hill toward us, shrieking. One of them was the skinny girl with pigtails I'd seen before by the river. They turned their faces toward us as they ran by, wild, open, naked faces, filled with light and savagery, but she didn't recognize me.

15. Montana

When he was ten or eleven, the pressure cooker of his hormones just starting to simmer, Frankie ran away from home, lighting out for the West—Montana, he hoped—and got as far as Pennsylvania, he thought, spending two nights on his own before being picked up by the police and brought home.

It wasn't the first time he'd run away, or been brought home by a policeman.

When he was nine, for instance, the copper who picked him up at Coney Island, where he'd gone by subway hoping to run off to sea on a tramp steamer, called him a "dumb nigger" but later made up for it by buying him a frozen custard while they waited for his father to come home and answer the phone.

"Don't be stupid," a social worker at the station told the cop, but he just shrugged his big Irish shoulders and went out to get the cone.

"I ain't no nigger," Frankie sulked, and the social worker laughed.

"You're right, but don't say ain't." She laughed again, but she was frowning, too.

Another time, another police station, to help him while the time away, another cop gave him paper and pencil to draw with. Instead, he began to write about the horse he knew he'd have some day. "That's not bad," the cop said, looking over his shoulder. "Why don'tcha write a letter to your dad, tell him you're sorry for running away."

"I'm not," Frankie said, "and he don't care." But he obediently set pencil to paper. "Dear Poppy," he wrote, "I'm sorry I ran a-way agan."

This time he meant not to get caught. He had a plan, some money, more nerve. All that worked and he was miles away, out of the city and short-hopping through New Jersey before lunch time. Late in the day, he got a ride from a friendly man in a Cadillac and had an adventure he more or less forgot about in later years—forgot about the whole thing, really: the running away, the plan, Montana, the man in the Caddy, what happened afterwards, sleeping in a hobo shanty the second night, getting picked up by the state police the third day, *letting* himself get picked up.

More than twenty years later, and just a year before the automobile accident that took his life, Frankie, calling himself François Sterne now, finally found himself in Montana. It was the first time he'd been back in the States since fleeing to Canada a few years earlier, when the whole world had seemed to be falling apart after Nixon sent the troops into Cambodia. He'd been involved in something in Ames, Iowa, that had gotten out of hand and he'd thought he was a fugitive, and maybe he was, so coming back now he was nervous at the border. But the customs man, the holstered pistol belted high on his waist, barely gave him a glance in the back seat of Dave's car. He'd been in Canada long enough to be legal and his ID was good, but no one ever asked to see it.

His new friends Dave and Ilya had a cabin at a place near St. Mary, a village just outside Glacier National Park where the road leading over the mountains and the Continental Divide is called Going to the Sun Highway.

Frankie found himself drinking strong coffee at a picnic table in the sun on a deck looking out over a lake called Lower St. Mary, rolling both those phrases around in his mind: *continental divide, going to the sun.* "The address here is Deck, Cabin, Stone's Throw from Lake, Montana," Dave said. "Don't know the postal code. In case you were wondering where you were."

"I usually am," Frankie said.

Then Dave and Ilya went for a walk, leaving Frankie alone. As he often did those days, he was soon thinking about his father, who had suffered a stroke a few months earlier and was only partly recovered. There was a portable typewriter inside and he lugged it out and set it up on the picnic table, which had peeling blue paint and knife scars across its top, making it look like one of those high altitude aerial photos of Vietnam after a bombing run he'd seen in the papers and on TV. He meant to write his father a letter.

From where he sat, he could see the lake, long but narrow, and the opposite shore, which was fringed with evergreens. Behind them was a road, the highway they'd come down on from Calgary, where he'd been living the past few months, and behind the road there was an open meadow sloping up toward a thin belt of brush and then a dense forest of evergreens again that appeared to be as high as the upper half of his thumb, viewed with his arm extended. The whole thing was level at the top, making it more like what's called a ridge than a mountain, he supposed. To see real mountains, the kind with pointy crests and massive sloping shoulders, he'd have had to get up and walk down to the beach, looking south or to the west, behind the stand of poplars bordering the cabin. On the drive down, he'd seen some of them, mountains that looked like something on a postcard from Italy or Switzerland—massive and blue, a discolored tooth in the open mouth of some fearsome giant. There was something frightening about them.

"What you're supposed to feel, I know, is *awe*," he had told Dave and Ilya, "because you're reminded of the majesty and power of nature and the insignificance of man, on the scale of things. That sort of thing."

"And you don't?" Ilya asked. She was a slim, dark-haired woman who reminded him vaguely of his cousin Becky, who he hadn't seen in years. Except for his father, who he got news of from his live-in friend, Ruth, and his cousin Rhoda, he'd lost touch with what remnants of family he had. There'd always been something unreal about them anyway, coming into his life late, and tentatively.

"Nothing like that. What I feel is the same sort of tightening in the pit of the stomach you get when you turn a dark corner and the street ahead of you is completely empty—no shoppers, no cars, no lighted windows—except for three big guys walking shoulder to shoulder down the sidewalk toward you, like a tidal wave about to engulf you and half the world beside."

They'd all laughed at the intensity of Frankie's description and he soon forgot about it. Just the same, he'd passed up joining his friends for a walk to the high meadow behind the cabin, where the mountains would leer down all around them. And from where he was sitting now, his vision focused on the gentle blue undulation of water and sky, the feeling seeping through his veins was more one of peacefulness than dread.

The previous evening, after a chili supper, they'd gone for a short stroll along the beach, which was covered with a foot-trapping mixture of sand and small stones and all sorts of greenery he didn't know the names of. Ilya pointed some of them out and he tried to remember those names now, something to catalog in his letter. There was a red-osier dogwood directly in front of him, its branches spilling over onto the deck, and, to his right, a little birch, and, just past it, an alder which he had thought must be a cherry because of the white markings on the smooth dark bark. All around the deck and cabin stood massive cottonwoods, their branchless trunks huge arrows pointing toward the sky, and slender, girl-like aspens, their leaves trembling like scarves and hearts, and just before the beach, a spruce, its flanks bristly as a three-day beard. It surprised him, considering he had once cut trees down for a living and would know a lodgepole pine or a black spruce anywhere, even in the dark, how little he knew about trees, plants in general, the outdoors.

He rolled a sheet of paper into the machine and began to type, starting off by describing the scene, the way he used to when he would write imaginary letters to his father in his head. "All of these things I've been mentioning are called *trees*," he wrote, "that's what they are, different types of trees. I mention that because I know, while you've never seen anything like these, you probably have heard of trees, perhaps have even seen one or two, in a park or a museum."

He pulled the page out of the typewriter, crumpled it and rolled in a fresh sheet. "Dear Pops," he wrote, though he knew that might annoy the old man. "Guess where I am? Montana, of all places. I'm visiting some friends, at a cabin on a lake. My hosts have gone off to pick berries that my hostess promised to bake into a pie for me this evening, and left me here with the typewriter, the picnic table, the deck, the trees, the lake—and you, somewhere over there, far behind that ridge, way out of reach."

He had been thinking all morning, and the day before, as they'd driven down through the brown, rolling Alberta hills, and when they'd crossed the border and the green and brown mountains began to open up ahead of them, that he was here, finally, that he had finally made it to Montana.

"Do you remember how I used to talk about going to Montana and having a sheep ranch?" he wrote. "Having one or working on one, I don't remember. God only knows where I got the idea, or how I knew they raised sheep here. You used to call me the little Basque sheepherder, remember that? I remember I thought it would be quiet—sitting in the mountains, watching the sheep eat grass—and I could think. There was always such a racket at home in those days, people coming and going, all your committees and political work, there wasn't any place I could get away from it."

When Frankie had asked about sheep, Dave said he thought there were some in the state, but further to the east, where it's flatter, more like prairie. They'd seen huge herds of cattle grazing on the brown, sloping meadows as they drove south, strikingly different terrain than that of his boyhood daydreams, in which he had always seen himself riding a horse through flocks of sheep stretching out before him like a white sea, with high, straight pine trees and brooks all around him, and snow-capped peaks of mountains in the not-very-distant distance.

"I used to think about it a lot, and talk about it a lot, too," he typed out. "It must have been the sound of the word, *Montana*, that Spanish sweetness on the tongue, that attracted me, that and the incredible distance—to me, it wasn't a real place at all, but a magical, mythical place of possibility, a Camelot. But I had forgotten all about it, that childhood daydream, I mean, not the actual state itself—and this is weird, in all the traveling I've done, back and forth across this country, hitchhiking and in buses and trains, I think there's only half a dozen states I haven't been in, but Montana is one of them, like fate was saving it for me, for the right time. Forgotten, I swear, until yesterday, when we were driving down and the word *Montana* kept coming up, flying around the interior of the car like a moth batting itself against the windows trying to get out, and suddenly it caught hold in one ear and clicked—Montana! Oh, you mean we're going to *Montana*."

Then it had all come flooding back.

Not just the shepherding daydream, but the running away, the heading out after it.

"It was gone completely from my memory," he typed, "and now it's back, bingo, just like that, almost as if it had happened last week, some of it anyway. I remember I wrote you a letter from a sort of railroad shack in New Jersey where I spent a night and almost froze my ass off, and I remember the New Jersey state police picked me up and brought me home."

253

Actually, the state policeman had taken him to the Holland Tunnel and turned him over to a Port Authority policeman, who'd driven him through the tunnel and turned him over yet again, to a city cop who brought him home. He remembered the Jersey trooper because he got to ride in the front seat of his car, the radio crackling, all the way from Cherry Hill, where he was picked up, to the tunnel, a couple hours' drive, and he listened to the police radio and thought that was kind of cool, even though he didn't like cops any better in those days than he did now. He remembered the Jersey cop as being pretty decent, though.

"I remember he talked to me like I was a real person, a human being," Frankie wrote, "and we stopped somewhere on the highway and he bought me something to eat and a cup of coffee. That's the thing I remember best about him—that he bought me a coffee without batting an eyelash, without asking if I was allowed. We went into a diner and sat down at the red formica counter with the truckers and he ordered two coffees, just like that. I'd already been drinking coffee for awhile—you never cared one way or another—so it wasn't like it was any great treat or anything. I was just impressed with the way he did it."

He had been thinking all morning about that runaway trip because he had a feeling that he had learned something then that he'd forgotten, just as he'd forgotten the runaway itself, just as he'd forgotten Montana, and that it was something of value, something he ought to know, now. "In the strange way that fate works, it's almost as if things conspired to bring me down here," he wrote his father. "Writing the sonata, having it performed in Calgary, the university job, making friends with these people, them inviting me down here this weekend."

He stopped to light a cigarette and pace around on the deck. "Did you know that I'm smoking again, or that I'd quit?" he thought, addressing himself to his father, but he didn't bother to type that. He sat at the picnic table again, one leg curled under him, smoking and watching the lake. A wind had come up and the water was moving in lazy curls toward the north, whitecaps breaking occasionally through the rippled blue like little tongues. A yellow canoe was overturned on the beach and Dave had said perhaps they'd go out in it later, but the lake didn't look very inviting now. The night before, when they walked on the beach in the pale moonlight, the lake had been like glass at their feet, smooth, shimmering, silent. Now it was making a chopping noise along the shore, like a heavy rain.

"Things change here quickly, unexpectedly," he typed. "All morning, Ilya was trying to find some kind of bird to show me, a certain type of bluebird peculiar to the mountains, but one would not appear. Now, since I've lit this cigarette, two bright blue blurs have flickered by and one is perched on the little birch by the steps—or is that an alder?—singing at me. I know you can't see, can't hear, but perhaps you can remember hearing of such things in your youth, of birds and of singing."

He kept going over that runaway trip in his mind, turning it over and over, looking for something, amazed at how well he could remember it—and new pieces, like chips from a broken vase, kept surfacing, falling into place, as if the whole thing was seared into his memory like the brands he'd seen on the flanks of cattle alongside the road the previous day—although, funny, he couldn't remember if he was gone for two days or three.

"I left one day," he typed, "April or May, maybe, and I don't remember specifically why—maybe you do—but I was sore about something and determined to really do it. I had run away a couple of times before, and when I came home you always seemed almost indifferent, as if you'd been just as glad to be rid of me, which is something I always believed, true or not. But this one was going to be different. I wasn't going to chicken out and come back, I was going to make it out to Montana, get a job on a sheep ranch as a herder or whatever they do, and ... well, I don't know what else. I must have had some idea then, but if I did I've forgotten it. As you can see, I don't remember *everything*."

———

He hadn't known about bindles, and didn't have a bandana, anyway, so he stuffed a few things into a paper bag along with three peanut butter sandwiches wrapped in wax paper and an apple, put that under his arm and walked across town and took a bus up to the George Washington Bridge. He had a few bucks that he'd scooped up from the cookie jar in the kitchen where his father kept change, and a ten-dollar bill he'd found on his father's dresser months before and hid away for a rainy day.

He had thought he'd take a bus across the bridge and start hitching in New Jersey but they cost more than he wanted to pay so he stood on one of the curving ramps leading up to the bridge with his thumb sticking out and someone picked him up right away, a woman with bundles piled all over the back seat. Of course, he lied—a ten-year-old couldn't say he was running *away* from home, he had to say he was going back. Frankie had figured it all out beforehand, and that's what he told people all that day as he moved west and south through New Jersey—that he'd run away, gone to the city, but had changed his mind and was heading home.

It worked great—people smiled at him, told him what a sensible boy he was and didn't give him any lectures. One man even gave him a five-dollar bill. He had to keep the rides short, though—he quickly figured out that if he said he was going to a place the drivers were going, they'd want to take him right to the door, and if it was a town further than theirs, they might want to drop him off at the police in their town. He had to quickly figure out where they were going, then name a town before that, so he'd be left off on the highway, at the outskirts. He didn't know any of those places, of course, but he memorized the names of towns and their distances apart from the road signs. Remembering it, more than twenty years later, it seemed hopelessly complicated to Frankie, beyond the abilities of a ten-year-old, but it hadn't seemed that way then, and it worked. He'd wave goodbye to those nice people, then stick his thumb out again as soon as they were out of sight. He had a lot of short rides and it took him most of the day to get across New Jersey, but they came one after another with no long waits, no hassles. A couple of times, he spotted a police car and dove into the bushes.

He'd just done that, and was coming out of the bushes, when he got his last ride of the day, from a small white-haired man in dark glasses, driving a pale-blue Cadillac. He was quite sure he had seen the Caddy drive past a few minutes earlier.

"No, you're not," the skinny driver said as soon as Frankie started to spill out his story. "Don't make me laugh. You are *so* running away." He swiveled his head toward him and puckered his lips into a kind of frown that caused his glasses, which had bright tortoise-shell frames, to slide forward on his nose, almost toppling off. Frankie had already had nine or ten rides, and this man was the first one to see through his story, and it surprised him, but there was nothing menacing about the man, who looked like a drawing of Ichabod Crane in a book at school. Even his frown was only half-hearted.

"Where are you really from? New York?"

"Yeah." Frankie had the feeling he wouldn't be able to lie to this man, so he didn't try.

"Uh huh. And heading west, no doubt." The man had already looked Frankie up and down several times, his eyes dark and sly beneath snowy white brows, but he gave him a quick once-over again, smiling a little at the pointy tips of his boots—cowboy boots his father had given him, along with a pair of jingly spurs, for Christmas after Frankie begged and pleaded—sticking out under the folded cuffs of his jeans. "To be a cowboy?"

"Not exactly," Frankie said. Without making a conscious decision about it, he suddenly trusted the Caddy driver. He told him about Montana.

"Sheep, huh?" The man smiled and made his eyes roll up, the way Frankie had seen Milton Berle do the couple of times he and his father had gone across the hall to their neighbour's place to watch TV. Frankie laughed. The man was wearing a tan tweed sports jacket with leather patches at the elbow and powder-blue slacks, almost the color of the Caddy, with a razor sharp crease. Tufts of milky white hair poked out from beneath a matching tweed cap and a dark blue scarf was wrapped around his neck. He looked like a slightly dissipated version of a grandfather on a *Saturday Evening Post* cover, someone old enough to have used up all his violence and meanness but not so old the cunning's been ground out of him, a man who likes to take small boys fishing and impress them with his skill in putting worm to hook. "And you had a fight with your folks, I suppose."

"I don't have any *folks*," Frankie said. "Just a father. And there wasn't any fight." What he had done, though he couldn't have put it into words, was quit trying to bear it.

"Ran out of steam, eh?" The white-haired man looked at him over his sliding glasses and Frankie felt like he knew exactly what he meant. There didn't seem to be any point in lying to him, nor to tell him anything, either, because he already knew.

They drove along for awhile, talking a little, and Frankie loosened up and cozied against the window, his head bouncing lightly on the glass. They grinned at each other as they passed by the town Frankie had said he was going home to. The telephone poles racing past them outside ran into a blur and the Caddy hummed like a cat being stroked. It was painted to the highway, it ran so smoothly, and it was cool inside, like the lobby of a movie theater, a relief after the heat of the sun outside. Frankie was certain they crossed a bridge into Pennsylvania, but then he slept a little and the next thing he knew it was dark and the Caddy was slowing down, stopping.

"Where are we?" He had been hoping to see the Pennsylvania Dutch country, which one of the kids at school had talked about during a show-and-tell, and now he was sure, suddenly, that he'd missed it.

"We're stopping for supper. Hungry, aren't you? Your stomach's been singing to me for awhile."

The peanut butter sandwiches had long been eaten, and he was ravenous and wide awake. He had no idea where they were— no sense of city or country—but they had pulled up along a driveway lined with crushed stones to a magnificent white building fronted with arches and pillars and surrounded by dense shrubbery highlighted by hidden lights. The Caddy stopped beneath a canopy that was fluttering in a light breeze and a black man dressed like a general in a movie about Napoleon Frankie had seen at the Apollo was coming through a broad, double glass door and down a set of low stairs toward them. Behind him, the windows of what appeared to be the lobby of a hotel glittered and Frankie could see smart-looking people moving about with grace and dignity. He pressed his nose to the Caddy's window until the doorman swung it away from him and he realized with a start that he was the first Negro he'd seen since getting off the bus at the George Washington Bridge that morning.

They went into the lobby and his new friend took him by the hand in a proprietary way. Frankie had only seen him seated until then, and he'd had the sense of him being a small man, so he was surprised by how tall he actually was, almost as tall as his father, and how limber. Despite his white hair and lined face and the almost comical way his glasses rode along his lengthy nose, he moved with precision and grace, easily, like an athlete. His hand, Frankie noticed, was cool.

The only hotel Frankie had ever seen was the Theresa, on

Amsterdam Avenue, and it was nothing like this. His eyes were wide as they walked through the lobby toward the front desk, past furniture that seemed to be made of thick, cream-colored clouds. A woman with enormous blue eyes and wearing a long silvery-blue dress with a scooped neckline was standing at the desk, chatting with the clerk behind it, and she smiled at Frankie, an amused, delighted smile, as if she had never seen a ten-year-old boy in dungarees and cowboy boots in a hotel lobby before and was relishing the idea.

"Is Mr. Faust around and about?" the Cadillac man asked the clerk, taking off his cap and nodding his head in the direction of the woman. His blowsy white hair formed a peak at the top of his head and he ran a hand through it, patting it down.

The clerk was a skinny boy with a large Adam's apple and pimples not very well concealed beneath caked ointment. He pulled his eyes reluctantly away from the woman in the long dress. "Sure," he said diffidently.

"Tell him Mr. Polite is here."

Frankie let himself be led to a sofa within sight of the desk and they dropped onto cushions that threatened to engulf him. The clerk stood behind the desk hesitating until the woman, leaning forward, whispered in his ear, laughed and walked away. Then he disappeared behind a partition. Frankie let his eyes follow the woman, who was absolutely the most beautiful creature he'd ever seen, until she was lost from view down a short flight of carpeted steps and behind a pillar, then kept himself busy examining the plush lobby furniture, the potted plants and the rich carpets, so he didn't see the clerk re-emerge, nor did he see the extremely fat man until he was upon them.

"Mr. Polite! What have we here?"

The Caddy man got up grinning, his hand extended. "Have someone here I'd like for you to meet, Mr. Faust. Frankie, say hello to my good friend, Mr. Faust, who is going to be, I certainly hope, our host for dinner."

The man who stood towering above Frankie was hugely, monstrously, grotesquely fat, but there was, oddly, nothing menacing about him, just as there had been no apparent sense of danger about the man in the Cadillac. Frankie was sure he'd never seen anyone even nearly as fat and he was, simultaneously, repelled, amused and fascinated. He was still seated in the deep cushions and the man stood so close to him that his belly, dressed in the thin, whitish material of a seersucker suit, seemed to loom even larger than it really was, all but obscuring his upper body and face. Frankie scrunched back into the sofa, as far from that floating white balloon of fat as he could get but, at the same time, he wanted mightily to stick his finger into it, to see how far it would go, the way you stick a finger into rising dough to see if it's ready for the oven. He did not say hello, as he'd been commanded, or anything else.

"Well, hello there, boy," a voice boomed down at him from somewhere north of that giant belly. "Frankie, is it? Welcome, Frankie, most pleased to meet you." A huge, soft-looking hand, white and puffy like the gloved paws of Mickey Mouse and Bugs Bunny, descended and waved in front of Frankie's face. He stared at it dumbly.

"I think the boy is impressed, *most* impressed with you, Mr. Faust," the Caddy man said.

"I believe you're right, Mr. Polite." The hand withdrew, and the belly retreated by perhaps a foot, giving Frankie breathing room. He wriggled to his feet and looked around. To his left, around the obstacle of the fat man, was the front desk, where the Adam's apple of the skinny clerk floated like a buoy in a sheltered pocket of water, his runny eyes casting nervously in their direction above the pimples. To Frankie's right, past the powder-blue knees of his companion, was the double-doored entranceway through which they had come. He was not considering bolting, but he felt more comfortable on his feet, knowing the lay of the land.

"The boy is terribly hungry," the man called Mr. Polite said. "And I could do with a bite to eat myself." The white brows above his eyes arched like caterpillars stretching themselves in the sun. "And he is tired, too, the dear boy. He's been traveling all day long and has come a long way. And the same for me, I might add." He got up suddenly, his long, lean legs raising his body effortlessly, like a pneumatic jack. "I had hoped, Mr. Faust, that we might be able to avail ourselves of some of your deservedly famous hospitality."

The fat man beamed, his face breaking into a patchwork of thick lines and folds, his lips parting to reveal teeth large as kernels of candy corn. "Of course, of course. How rude of me not to have offered immediately. I'll see that something is prepared at once." He put a puffy hand on Frankie's shoulder. It felt soft and weightless, as if it were a balloon. His voice dropped, almost to a whisper. "Are we not being a bit indiscreet, however, Mr. Polite?"

"Not at all, Mr. Faust." The Caddy man laced his fingers together and pushed the palms away from him. He raised his voice. "My nephew and I will be delighted to join you for a late snack. How gracious of you to offer. Come along, Frankie."

Frankie *was* hungry, and very tired, and he let himself be led along. He registered Mr. Polite's reference to him as his nephew, but it didn't alarm him and he didn't question it.

The fat man stopped to quietly say something to the desk clerk and then they were standing before the ornate brass doors of the elevator. An ancient mulatto with a toothless grin and cheeks wrinkled as a roasted turkey's skin sat on a low stool inside the elevator. He gave Frankie a sharp glance. "Seventh floor, Mr. Faust?" he asked cheerfully.

"That is correct, Charles," the fat man said. He winked at Frankie, a big, thick eyelid drooping down over one jade-green eye, then springing back up like a window shade with a tight spring. His voice was elegant but weary, as if he had engaged in this particular exchange hundreds, perhaps thousands, of times and was bored with it. As the door slid closed, Frankie could see the woman in the long dress resume her position at the front desk, waving a gloved hand gaily at them.

The elevator creaked and moved slowly upward. There were no electric numbers to indicate the floors, but Frankie could actually see them through the grating of the folding door as they rose. At a few of the landings, he caught glimpses of faces through the glass triangles of the outer doors, but the elevator didn't stop. No one said anything until the elevator slowed and came to a jerking halt. "Here we is, Mr. Faust," the ancient man said, opening the inner door.

"Ah," said Mr. Faust. They stepped out into a long carpeted hallway lined with closed doors. A cart with the ruined remains of someone's dinner on it sat beside one door, a soiled napkin hanging listlessly from the handle. Mr. Faust shook his head disapprovingly and led Frankie and Mr. Polite down the corridor. Behind them, the elevator began its creaking descent.

At the end of the hall was another elevator behind a door marked "private" and barely wide enough for Mr. Faust to squeeze through. He inserted a key and the door instantly slid open. He waved the others in ahead of him, then cautiously negotiated his own way in, scrunching up his shoulders and laughing an embarrassed titter. The elevator was tiny, but padded with velvet quilting. The ceiling was a mirror. Mr. Faust pushed a button, the door slid silently closed and the elevator slid silently up. Frankie couldn't actually feel it move, but the door opened again and they were on a different floor, stepping out into a dimly lit foyer lined with mirrors and leading to a carved wooden door. Mr. Faust opened the door with a key. "Welcome to my humble home, gentlemen," he said grandly.

"Ah," said Mr. Polite. "At last. I'm famished."

"There will be just a short wait," Mr. Faust said. "Please, make yourselves at home."

Nothing in his short life had prepared Frankie for the opulence and mystery of the hotel. Mr. Faust, despite his great size and elegant way of speaking, was just another person, not so much strange as *different*, which was a quality Frankie liked and admired. So was Mr. Polite, different, and pleasantly so. But the hotel, with its doorman and desk clerk and elevator operator, its lobby and plush sofas, its carpets and mirrors and carts, its elevators and women in long dresses, was more than just different, it was totally beyond his experience, another world.

The apartment Mr. Faust led them into was the most elegant thing Frankie had ever seen. The foyer opened onto a living room-dining room combination, an open gleaming kitchen at the far end separated from the main area by a long floating countertop lined with open-back stools. The creamy white walls were thick with framed paintings and photographs; large drape-lined windows dominated one side of the living room, a fireplace made of pink, irregularly shaped stones the other. The apartment was cluttered with furniture covered in leather and fur and Oriental rugs of various sizes, between which gleamed thin slices of hardwood parquet floors. Vases, gold cigarette lighters, ashtrays and small statues were scattered about as if on display at an antique shop.

"Please make yourself at home," Mr. Faust repeated. "Go on, Frankie, look around all you want. It will be a few minutes, I'm afraid, until our supper is delivered. Mr. Polite and I will just sit here and chat and you go on, make yourself at home. My home is your home, young sir." His big wide face cracked open into a watermelon smile and he bowed ceremonially, his belly contracting like a folded pillow. "Go on, don't be shy." He made a shooing motion with his hands, as if he were talking to a cat that had gotten on the sofa.

Frankie wandered around the big living room, examining the photographs and paintings. The latter had that textured nubby feeling of oils but otherwise made no impression on him; the glassed photographs, though, were of people who looked familiar and he peered at them with curiosity while Mr. Faust and Mr. Polite conferred in whispers. Several of the photos were of actors he recognized, including one of Gary Cooper wearing shorts and a T-shirt and a baseball cap, a tennis racket under his arm, and looking impossibly young. There were two baseball players, a football player grinning toothily over massive shoulders, and a black prize fighter whose picture Frankie had seen before, on the sports pages of *The Daily Mirror*, his arms glistening with sweat, nostrils flared with menace. Over a long, chocolate-brown leather sofa was a large framed color photograph, the pink of flesh so bright it looked more like a painting, of the Pope, his face almost gaunt, his arms spread wide, speaking to a crowd in an ornate, baroque square.

Frankie edged his way cautiously toward a corridor leading to the rear of the apartment. When he got there, he studied a painting closest to the doorway with great interest, observing Mr. Faust and Mr. Polite out of the corner of his eye. The two men were seated on a pink velvet love seat, their knees touching, heads close together, speaking seriously in whispered tones. Mr. Faust's back was to Frankie, and the fat man's bulk blocked him from Mr. Polite's view. He slipped quietly out of the room.

He went past a bathroom and a book-lined den to the door at the end of the hallway, beyond which was a bedroom with its own small bathroom and dressing area, a massive, canopied bed and French doors opening onto a balcony overlooking the grounds of the hotel. Frankie quickly retreated and went into the large marble bathroom, dominated by a built-in stepdown tub big enough for half a dozen people, and urinated as quietly as he could into a glistening blue bowl. It had been hours and he was bursting. The toilet flushed with a soft vacuum swish rather than a splashing and gurgling of water. He washed his hands in a marble basin cool and smooth as glass, the water hissing from a gleaming, arched faucet controlled by glass and gold handles. The smell of the bathroom was a combination of talcum powder and spices like those he had caught whiffs of in bakeries and in a woman's handbag he once stole.

He was in the study, reading the titles of books, when he heard a soft chiming he knew must be the doorbell. A minute or two later, Mr. Faust called. Frankie had a leather-bound copy of *The Arabian Nights* with beautiful colored illustrations in his hands and he quickly shoved it back on the shelf.

"Where's Mr. Polite?" he asked when he came back into the living room. Mr. Faust was leaning over a cart like the one they had passed in the hallway, a silver tray cover in his hand and a pleased look on his face, but the white-haired man who had brought Frankie here was not in sight. For the first time since arriving at the hotel, he felt a twinge of panic, like a finger of chalk running up his spine.

"Our mutual friend has had to run off, I'm afraid," Mr. Faust said, shaking his head slightly, just enough to set his cheeks shaking. "It was quite unexpected, since I know he was looking forward to a small repast and an evening of conversational cheer with us. When our supper arrived, there was a note for Mr. Polite that had just arrived downstairs. Some urgent business, I imagine, or a family matter. Mr. Polite's mother lives not too far from here, and she is elderly and not all that well, poor dear. He didn't confide in me. He did assure me, however, and ask me to assure *you*, that he would return to collect you, my boy, and made me promise to look after you in his absence, as if such a promise were necessary." He snorted, making his nostrils flare like those of the prize fighter in the photo on the wall behind him. "It will be a pleasure. Now, come look at how much food there is for us. I had ordered for three."

Frankie was starving, so he came into the room, but slowly. Mr. Faust was taking the covers off the trays on the cart and he could see piles of neatly quartered sandwiches, bowls of pickles, potato salad, potato chips and pretzels, stacks of cheese and deviled eggs, a platter of pastries oozing red and yellow fillings, glistening with icing. There was an ice bucket filled with bottles of beer and pop, cold steam rising from the glass like a beckoning, ephemeral hand.

Mr. Faust observed him, his thick lips puckered into a rosebud. "You're not frightened of me, are you, Frankie?"

"No, sir."

"Ah, you say that with conviction, young sir, but something about your demeanor belies that, I'm afraid."

"Sir?"

Mr. Faust showed his marshmallow teeth. "I mean, you *look* like maybe you are."

"No, sir, I'm not afraid." To prove it, Frankie stepped up to the cart, smiled at Mr. Faust and let his eyes feast. His stomach was growling.

"Well, good. You're obviously a young man who knows his own mind and is not afraid to state his own case forcefully. I like that in a man, young or old. Keep true to that, Frankie—it will serve you in good stead in the world so loudly advertised as cold and cruel but most notable for its subtlety, its penchant for irony. Let's eat then. Here's plates. Help yourself, don't be bashful, I know you won't be. Everything has to be eaten or it will be thrown away, those are the rules in a hotel just like in a restaurant, wasteful but hygienic and hygiene must be served, God knows. Don't be polite—our friend *Mr.* Polite wouldn't be, of that you can be sure. That's right, have more of that. This salad is a specialty *de la maison.*" He beamed, his small green eyes shining. "That means it's our chef's special pride. Now, sit down here, beside me. Soda?"

The fat man kept chattering on while they ate but Frankie was too intent on the food to pay much attention. "Mr. Polite tells me you're off to see the world," he said.

Frankie nodded, his mouth full of soft bread and creamy chicken salad. "Montana," he mumbled.

"Ah, yes, the life of the cowboy. Very romantic. I know a few cow-boys, real ones, I mean. Rodeo cowboys. They do the same sort of thing that men before them did every day to earn a living, and a mean living at that, but they've mastered the techniques and made them into a sport. Most fascinating to watch. Most fascinating men."

Crumbs cascaded from his mouth and clung to the nubby fabric of his suit jacket and tie. He excused himself and went into the bedroom to change, returning in a tentlike satiny smoking jacket and ascot, both the pale orange color of salmon flesh Frankie had seen in the window of the fish store on 125th Street.

"Most commendable, taking off on one's own to see the world and make one's own way in it," Mr. Faust said, resettling himself on the leather sofa, which let out a sigh beneath his weight. "You might not believe it, to see me now, but when I was your age, or perhaps just a little older, I was a cabin boy on a merchant steamer, plying the North Atlantic."

Frankie looked up with interest and the fat man winked, the loose flap of his eyelid coming down like a window shade, then springing up.

"The things I could tell you about *that*. But it makes no difference how one goes about it, running off to the sea or to become a cowboy or to join a circus, for that matter, as a dear friend of mine did, the important thing is to *do* it. To run off."

He beamed, wiping the watermelon smile with a linen napkin. Mr. Faust's face was something like what Frankie would have expected Santa Claus to look like, with red cheeks that seemed to be puffed out, dark eyes made small by the rolls of flesh pocketing them in, a nose like a walnut, bloated and veined. His chins cascaded into themselves, like a Chinese box set. The mouth, pink and soft, was strangely small—much too small to have consumed all that must have been required to build the bulk of the body which depended on it.

Frankie ate and ate until he was stuffed, the variety and idea of the food pushing him on way past hunger. He was tired, and the exertion of all that eating now made his head begin to fill with cotton, his eyes to sag. He didn't know what time it was, but it had been dark for awhile and, through the thin white curtains blowing airily over the bay window, the lights of what appeared to be a city spread out in the distance, blinking, the occasional burst of neon color punctuating the generalized glow of streetlamps. He wondered idly where Mr. Polite had gone and when he would be back. His friend hadn't actually said so, but he had given the impression that he was traveling west, and that Frankie could go with him as far as he went. With the ignorance and confidence of a ten-year-old, though, he wasn't worried. The Cadillac man would either come back or he wouldn't. If he didn't, there'd be other rides. Frankie was too sleepy to think on the problem for long.

He stretched and yawned, juggling his shoulders into the firm leather cushion, and Mr. Faust, who had been watching him intently, put the watermelon to work.

"Ah, Frankie, have enough?"

He nodded, eyelids drooping. "Yes, sir. Thank you."

"Good, good." Mr. Faust selected a tray at random—it contained several quarters of sandwiches—and waved it at Frankie. "Sure now? Don't be polite. Your stomach will never thank you for a nicety of the intellect like that."

"I'm not, sir. I'm full, honest. Thank you."

"Good, good." Mr. Faust put the tray down and looked at his bloated hands, which had neat, smoothly filed nails, each one big as a quarter. For the first time since they'd begun to eat, he was silent. He took a long cigar from a glass-lined silver humidor and rolled it appraisingly in his fingers before putting it into his mouth and reaching for a silver lighter in the shape of a goose touching down on water. The cigar, unlike Mr. Faust, was long and slender. He licked the length of it, his tongue pink as a cat's and surprisingly dainty, just before lighting it, and then it was sleek and dark, like the body of a cat in flight.

"Frankie." Mr. Faust said the name quietly, then repeated it with more precision, breaking down the parts, as if it were a foreign word he had just heard for the first time. "Frankie. It's a nice name, rich in meanings." He squinted through the cigar smoke, which smelled rich and exotic, not like the awful stogies Frankie's father used to smoke occasionally, when he was feeling chipper. "Many layers of meanings. Frank. Straight-forward, no beating around the bush, uncompromising. Strong. But, at the same time, suggesting something of the French, something subtle and continental, full of flavor and history." He shrugged, rolling the cigar between pudgy fingers. "And Frankie, of course, Frankie, *Frankie*, the color that name conjures up, the romance." He tilted his face up, eyes raking the ceiling, the pudding of flesh that was his neck pulsing. "*Frankie and Johnny were lovers*," he crooned softly, "*lawdy, how they could love.*"

Frankie closed his eyes and let his chin drop into the hollow between his collar bones. The fat man's voice was soft and filled with moonlight, filled with the light of the streetlamp which poured into the window of his bedroom at home, filled with the sounds of the street where he lived.

"My name is John, you know," Mr. Faust said suddenly.

Frankie opened his eyes. The fat man laughed in a way he knew was forced, without real mirth.

"Johnny. Lord, it's been years since anyone called me that. Frankie and Johnny, that's us." Mr. Faust lifted the great weight of his haunches, tilted his hips and let his body descend closer to Frankie on the flattened leather cushions, which hissed beneath him. He put his hand on Frankie's leg, patting it, then squeezing the knee. "Yes, yes, Frankie and Johnny." He laughed again, this time with more conviction.

"Frankie. Is it Frank? Or Franklin? After our great, much mourned president? Or short for Francis? The great saint who the birds took for their own? Or what?" A cloud of bluish smoke hung around his head like a swarm of tiny flies, but behind the pockets of flesh his eyes swam like green moons in a buttery sea.

"Francesco," Frankie said with distaste, grudgingly. "But I don't like that. Everybody calls me Frankie, even my father."

"Ah, Francesco. Now *there's* a name with magic in it. Magic and romance. Spanish, you know, is the loving tongue."

He pronounced the last two words with a reverence that made Frankie look at him more closely. Spanish was a language that he knew, but he was sure he had never heard that expression before. It made him think of his mother, who had died the day he was born. Spanish had been *her* language.

"It's okay," he said, perhaps to hide his shame.

"Okay?" Mr. Faust smiled. "I understand. It sounds ... *foreign*, doesn't it? Someday, I assure you, you'll appreciate it. Take my word for it, young sir. And your father, is he a poet? An admirer of Garcia Lorca, no doubt. Only a poet would bestow on his child a name with such poetry in it, such *fragrance*."

Frankie giggled. "He's a mailman. He plays the trumpet and he likes to think he's a jazz musician, but he's only a mailman, he delivers the mail, that's all." He said that in a burst, with such bitterness he surprised myself.

Mr. Faust observed him thoughtfully. "Ah, a mailman and a musician." He peered at Frankie, puffing on his cigar, while he rolled those words around in his mind. "A *messenger* and a musician. Then I was right. He *is* a poet. But not one who meets with your whole-hearted approval, that is plain to see for anyone who has eyes. Is he aware of your disapproval?"

It seemed like such a silly question that Frankie couldn't think of anything to say in response. He shrugged. Mr. Faust studied him, then sprang to his feet with a surprising agility.

"Well, no matter, none of my business, anyway, is it? And it's getting late, there can be no denying that. We should be thinking about getting off to bed. You've had a long day, so Mr. Polite tells me, and you must be tired. No, I can see you are. And here I am, babbling on, keeping you up when there's nothing you'd like better than to slip into dreamland, am I not correct?"

Frankie stretched his arms but wouldn't let himself yawn. "No, that's okay. I'm not so tired."

The split watermelon flashed in Mr. Faust's face. His belly jiggled right through the tent of his smoking jacket. "Good, good, that's what I like to hear. Never give in to the weaknesses and demands of the flesh. Very commendable. Still, the flesh must be served. The mind is king, but the body is the palace in which the king lives, and it must be maintained, so that the king should not be seen to be in even the smallest way shabby. Isn't that correct, Francesco?" He grinned, the grin turning quickly into an expression that was almost sly. "Now, what do you say to a bath? Something to spiff up the old palace with, one might say. A nice, warm sudsy bath to relax us, then it's off to bed. Did you see the, *ahem*, swimming pool in the bathroom? It's a delight, let me assure you."

Ordinarily, the idea of a bath wouldn't have appealed to Frankie and he would have protested, but that gigantic marble tub conjured up such an exotic world of decadence and sweetness he couldn't resist. He had decided, much earlier in the day, to go where the adventure took him. "Okay," he said, and he let Mr. Faust lead the way down the corridor.

One whole wall of the bathroom, behind the massive tub, was glass, and it joined a hinged skylight directly above. They stood for a moment in the doorway of the dark room, staring out at the night, stars twinkling above them, sparse city lights below. "Isn't that a lovely sight?" Mr. Faust said simply.

He turned on a dim, blue light and set water flowing in the tub. It gushed out of a dozen spouts set in the marble sides and in a thin, delicate stream from the penis of a bronze angel the size of a cat standing on a pedestal in the very center of the tub. "My, my, but this cost a terrible fortune, but it's worth every penny," Mr. Faust said. "Every penny, every day."

"It's swell," Frankie said. His eyes were open wide and he couldn't take them off the bronze penis, that delicate arch of bathwater.

"Well, shall we?" Mr. Faust unbuttoned his smoking jacket and took it off, fastidiously hanging it on one of a dozen hooks beside the door. Beneath it, he wore a sleeveless undershirt and his arms were pale, hairless, sagging.

"You're going to take a bath, too?" Frankie asked. The notion didn't so much surprise as amuse him. The tub was certainly big enough for both of them, but he had never heard of such a thing. Shame filtered through him for a moment and he hugged his arms, as if he had a chill. He had a dim memory, suddenly sharpening into focus, of standing with his father in a public changing room at Coney Island, each locker attended by a naked man and boy like strangely defrocked priests and altar boys performing some obscene ritual of a dark religion. He had been sickened—actually nauseated—by that endless row of flashing buttocks, the men's hairy and wrinkled, the boys' smooth and lean, like the flanks of cattle in a barn, the penises and scrotums hanging like vines and clusters of grapes from each body, waiting for some vile hand to pick them. He hadn't wanted to take off his clothes, to expose himself, to become part of that vulnerability, but his father was already out of his shirt and pants, oblivious, his socks drooping, his shorts baggy and torn in spots, hair curling out from under his arms like licks of flame. "G'won, take off your stuff," he'd snarled, the words cracking down at Frankie like a slap on the ears. He had closed his eyes and fumbled for his buttons, taking off everything in a burst of speed, the way you jump into cold water to get it over with quickly.

He remembered all that while Mr. Faust was taking off his silk ascot and struggling the undershirt over his head.

"Don't you think the tub is big enough for the two of us?" the fat man laughed. "Damn this thing, why does it always have to catch on my elbows. There." He gave Frankie a sharp glance, saw

273

his hesitancy and discreetly turned his back. "Go on, get undressed, Frankie," he said in a surprisingly gentle tone. "Don't be shy. We're men of the world, you and I, don't forget. We're runaways, men who run off to see the world, men who aren't afraid of life, who seize it and drink it up, down to the very bottom of the cup, then demand that the cup be filled again, right to the brim. Now ... last one in is a rotten egg." Mr. Faust giggled and began to huff and puff his pants off.

Another memory broke the surface of Frankie's mind, like a fish in a lake breaching the calm of the water with a roll of flashing side to catch a fly. After the swimming that day, splashing through the waves in their trunks, he and his father had gone back to the locker room and taken them off, then sat naked and streaming sweat in the Turkish bath at the rear of the bathhouse, men and boys with their heads lowered like supplicants in *shul*, hair plastered to their bodies in thin, dark rivulets, sharing their vulnerability, drawing strength together from it.

He took his clothes off and lay them in a neat pile on a glass magazine table. The underwear was dirty and he stuffed it into one of the legs of his jeans, where it wouldn't be seen. He extended a toe into the frothing water that had filled a third of the tub. It was warm and sleek with soap and oil.

"I just remembered something," he said, trying not to look at the huge pendulous moons of Mr. Faust's ass. "I thought I never took a bath with anyone else, but I just remembered I did, a Turkish bath. Does that count?"

Mr. Faust turned around and beamed at him, the watermelon splitting across his face. He was incredibly fat, with a roll of flesh like an inner tube around his middle. He wasn't circumsized, and his penis was like a thick sausage or a hank of rope hanging from the untidy package of his belly. There were hairs scattered across his chest and belly like weeds in a lawn and he was pale as the underside of a fish. A vague feeling of sadness for the fat man washed over Frankie, as if he had just heard of a death in his family or some other great loss.

"Does that count? Why, it certainly does. A Turkish bath is one of the most delicious inventions of mankind, and it certainly is a bath. But"—he stepped toward the tub and put the toes of one swollen foot into the water—"there isn't anything as delicious as this, not in heaven *or* on earth."

There were steps going down into the tub and Mr. Faust negotiated them gingerly, then settled like a great walrus into the suds. He sat crosslegged, like a Buddha, the water lapping at his knees. "Come on in, Francesco. Tell me about this Turkish bath of yours. *This* city isn't sophisticated enough to have one, but I've been in many of them in my time. Tell me about yours."

"Look out," Frankie yelled, holding his nose and jumping into the water, sending balls of suds flying into the warm air above the tub. The water was actually deep enough for him to swim in and he splashed around for a moment, then claimed a spot across the tub from where Mr. Faust lay, grinning. He propped his neck against the rim of the tub, the water all the way up his skinny chest, slippery and warm, thick with bubbles that hid most of his lower body and made him feel at ease. He had a sudden image of himself curled up like a baby under his desk at school during an air raid drill. Miss Murphy, his teacher that year, said the children should have clean, pure, gentle thoughts so if the bomb really fell they'd wind up in heaven. Tiredness wound its way through him like a lazy cat stretching in the sun, and he felt, inexplicably, *natural*, and content, as if he'd been traveling for a long time but had finally come home.

He told Mr. Faust about the Turkish bath, and about he and his father changing to their trunks in the locker room—telling him details of feeling that he could never have told his father, but somehow had no hesitancy in pouring out now, to this stranger—and the fat man listened intently, with the kind of narrow-eyed interest adults don't usually waste on children.

"Thank you for sharing that with me," he said when Frankie finished. "I think I understand. I *know* I do. A similar thing happened to me." He moved his bulk slowly, edging closer to Frankie.

"Oh, yeah?" Frankie said, only mildly interested, he was so sleepy. "To you?"

Mr. Faust nodded solemnly, looking slightly comical, since a puff of suds was on his nose. "My father was a physician, in a very prosperous community in Indiana. Do you know where that is, Frankie? A few states to the west—you'll pass through it if you continue your travels in that direction. He was an educated man, a refined man from whom, I'm happy to say, I acquired many of my tastes, but he was, ah, shall we say, just a touch arrogant? Pompous? Do you understand those words, Frankie?"

"Arrogant, I think. Not the other."

"Pompous. It means sort of what it sounds like: pomp, pompon. Puffed up." Mr. Faust laughed. "Not like me, I mean puffed up inside, thinking that you're very important. Have you heard the expression 'stuffed shirt'? That's what it is to be pompous."

"Oh, yeah." Frankie let himself slide deeper into the soothing water, right up to the crown of his head. Mr. Faust edged closer, moving his bulk slowly and sending small waves rippling against the walls of the tub.

"Of course, my father was important, and he knew it. He was an extremely capable physician, and by far the most experienced one in our community. And he had business interests as well that made him quite influential. People sought out his advice, not only on medical matters, but on affairs of business, and even of the heart." Mr. Faust winked, and he extended one plump hand in Frankie's direction as if to tousle the damp hair on his head, but they were too far apart in the huge tub for him to reach.

"So he was important, but there is *so* much difference, isn't there, Francesco, between being important and *thinking* you are, even if, in fact, you are—if you see what I mean."

"I think so," Frankie said, although he didn't really. The warmth of the water was conspiring with his tiredness and the food to make him sleepier than he could ever remember being.

"Well," Mr. Faust said, waving his hand and stirring the suds, "pompous, he was that, surely, Father. But the point is, the reason I'm telling you this, Francesco, is that because he was so pompous, so arrogant, he was also intolerant of weakness, in himself, to be sure, but in others as well, including, all too often, his patients. Not a particularly sympathetic bedside manner, no, no, that was certainly not Father's way. Gruff, strict, demanding. But effective. He refused to let people lie back and feel sorry for themselves, refused to let them give up. None of my father's patients was ever sick a day longer than they *had* to be. None of them ever died unless the good lord absolutely insisted. Yes, effective, to be sure, but not very tolerant. No, no, not Father."

Mr. Faust's voice trailed off, and the sudden silence in the bathroom startled Frankie awake. When he looked up, he found the fat man staring at him as if surprised to have found a stranger in his tub. But, after a moment, Frankie realized he wasn't really looking at him at all. The puckered green eyes were unfocused, directed ahead but not seeing anything. Frankie made a little splash and Mr. Faust shook his head, like someone coming out of a doze in the back seat of an automobile.

"What was I saying, Francesco?"

"About your father...."

"Ah, yes. I started to tell you about being ashamed of being naked. I was. *Me.* Can you believe it? A fine figure of a man such as myself!" The folds of flesh on his face and chest shook as he laughed. "Of course, when I was your age, I was more of a slim little charmer like you, and had no good reason to be ashamed to be naked. I don't know if I'd always been so, but all of a sudden I was. And it happened that the time came for our annual checkups, which Father performed himself on his children, boys and girls alike. Yes, I have three wonderful sisters as well as two loyal and brilliant brothers. And it was my turn. *Take off your clothes*, Father said." Mr. Faust made his voice go low and gruff as he imitated his father, then spring back to his natural tones, like a ball being forced beneath the water then quickly rising to the surface. "But I felt I could not. *Take off your clothes, I said,* Father repeated, and I said to him, 'Father, I am not being willfully disobedient, but I feel I cannot.' *You cannot?* he exclaimed. *And why is that?* And, listen to this, Francesco, you may find this hard to believe. I started to tell him. I said, 'Father, I'm ashamed to be naked in front of you.' And, instead of dropping to his knees and enfolding me in his arms, murmuring to me, reassuring me, explaining to me how silly I was being, how natural it is to be naked—in short, acting like a civilized man, acting the way you would expect a father to act toward his beloved young son—now, wouldn't you, Francesco? Instead of doing any of that, listen carefully to this, he slapped me."

Mr. Faust brought his open palm down hard on the surface of the bathwater, producing a sharp cracking sound that startled Frankie.

"Slapped me," Mr. Faust repeated, as if his face still tingled from that sudden blow. "Me, his son, his beloved son, eight years old. How old are you, Frankie?"

"Eleven. Almost eleven."

"Ah, yes, eleven. A good age to be, young sir. I was eight." He blinked, his face blank. "And then, then—listen to this very carefully, Francesco—then my father tore my clothes off me. I don't mean undressed me, I don't mean helped me off with my clothes, I don't mean unbuttoned my shirt. I mean he ripped my clothes off my back, literally, buttons and strips of cloth flying around his examining room like feathers in a chickenhouse when the fox has gotten in. I mean tore off my clothes, every last shred, until I was standing naked in front of him, and then he said to me, *Ashamed to be naked, are you? Don't you ever say that to me again. And don't you ever be ashamed. Not of your body, or anything else that's part of you. Not ever.*

"And, do you know what, Frankie?" A smile suddenly spread across Mr. Faust's watermelon face.

"What?"

"I didn't cry. I imagine that surprises you, doesn't it? I wanted to cry, so badly, I think maybe you can imagine how badly I wanted to cry. Can you?"

"I guess so."

"Yes, I'm sure you can. I wanted to cry, but I didn't. I wouldn't let myself. I wouldn't give him that satisfaction. *Eight*, that's what I was, but I wouldn't give him that satisfaction. I just stood there, naked as the day I was born, and I held my shoulders straight and my head high, the way they taught us to at school and I'm afraid they don't anymore, and I didn't cry. And after awhile my father examined me—took my pulse and blood pressure, listened to my chest and tapped on my back, peered into my mouth and ears and eyes, pressed his finger beneath my scrotum and told me to cough. And when he was through he said to me, *You're all right, boy, now put your clothes back on.* And I said, 'I don't think my clothes are suitable for wearing anymore, sir,' and he went to a closet and brought me a dressing gown, the sort of thing he would give a woman patient to wear in the examining room, and said, *Here, wear this up to your room and get dressed.* And I said, 'That's all right, Father, I can walk naked through the house, because I'm not ashamed.' And he looked at me so hard it was like one of his scalpels going through me, and I thought he was going to slap me again, but he didn't. All he did was hand me the gown and say, *Put this on, son,* in a voice more tender than I could ever remember hearing him speak."

Mr. Faust took a purple washcloth from a hook and lathered it with a bar of scented soap. "And you know something else, Francesco?"

"What's that, Mr. Faust?"

"I never was ashamed again. Of my body, I mean. To be

naked." He laughed, making his cheeks jiggle. "Of course, there have been *some* things in my life I've been ashamed of. Not many, mind you—I've always tried to be a dutiful son—but some. And, please, Frankie, not *Mr. Faust*. Call me John, won't you? Or Johnny, better yet. Frankie and Johnny?"

Frankie nodded his head and they were silent for a minute. Finally, he said: "He never hit me."

Mr. Faust smiled. "Your father? He never slaps you?"

"No. Never. I don't think so."

"But he yells at you, I suppose. You said that's what he did in the locker room."

"It wasn't really a yell," Frankie said. "That isn't what he does. Mostly, he don't say nothing. Just nothing."

Mr. Faust considered this and his smile softened, his thick lips almost straightening. "All in all, Francesco, I'm afraid I'd have to say that was worse, far worse. At least when people yell they're talking to each other. When they hit each other, awful as that is, at least they touch."

He reached out to touch Frankie again, but they were still too far apart and he could only reach his foot. He patted it and, in the slippery water, it felt as if a fish were brushing against Frankie, nibbling at his toes.

After awhile, Mr. Faust withdrew his hand and rested it in his lap, with the other. He was watching Frankie, smiling, but he didn't say anything for a long time and his breathing grew heavier. Frankie thought he knew what the fat man was doing, although he hadn't ever done it himself. He'd heard other kids talking.

"Are you going to do something funny?" he asked.

Mr. Faust chuckled. "I'm doing something very funny indeed, but to myself, not to you. And you don't have to watch, if you'd rather not. Don't go away, please, but you can turn your head, or close your eyes, better. That's it, Francesco, why don't you close your eyes and just drift off to sleep."

"No, that's okay."

He didn't begin again right away, and, when he did, it was awhile before Frankie realized it. He was quiet, barely moving, his eyes never leaving Frankie, and the suds were thick around him. It seemed to take a long time.

"You can do it, too, if you'd like," Mr. Faust said. "I can see you're old enough. I could help you, or you could do it by yourself."

"No, that's okay," Frankie said. He would have liked to try, but he didn't want to, either. He watched for awhile, but then he made a boat with his hand and turned his attention to it as it skimmed through the water, like a sailboat on a windy sea. In a moment, he fell asleep in the warm water.

He woke up in Mr. Faust's arms, a towel big enough for the fat man wrapped around him. Mr. Faust was wearing a purple robe with satin lapels, and Frankie's cheek was pressed against the satin. The fat man lay him down on smooth, cool sheets and Frankie realized he was in the den, in a bed made from the sofa he had sat on earlier, reading *The Arabian Nights*.

"I'll just tuck you in and you can drift off back to sleep, Francesco," Mr. Faust whispered. "I'm afraid I don't have any pajamas your size, but would you like to sleep in one of my pajama tops?"

"Okay." He rubbed his eyes, sitting up, and put on the massive shirt. It was like a tent, but it was soft and he lay back again, snuggling into it like it was a cocoon that could keep him safe from everything, even being far from home, on his own, with a long way to go till Montana.

"You made me very happy tonight," Mr. Faust said from the doorway, just before he snapped off the final light. "Thank you."

"I didn't do anything," Frankie said, making a small shrug with his shoulders. "You don't have to thank me."

Mr. Faust smiled, his teeth a wide row of white seeds in the watermelon. "Do you have to *do* something to make someone happy? Can't you just *be*?"

Frankie was going to say something, but he was asleep before he could.

In the morning, he was awakened by Mr. Polite, tugging the covers and poking his knee.

"I brought you a present," he said, holding up a toothbrush. "The one you left in the car hardly had any bristles left on it. Your teeth will rot and fall out if you keep on brushing them with that dirty old thing, and you'll be a toothless old man before your time. Like me." He flashed a smile that showed lots of gum, but he seemed to have all his teeth.

"Come on, young man, we have to be on the road. The great vistas of the west call to us and time and tide wait for no man, or boy, either, I might add. By the time you're finished in the bathroom, breakfast will be ready."

In the bathroom, where Frankie broke in the toothbrush, he found his clothes neatly folded on a table, the underwear and socks and polo shirt washed and still warm from the dryer, which was good, since he'd drenched them with sweat the day before. There was a bowl of cereal, another of fresh strawberries and a pitcher of milk on a tray in the kitchen. While he was eating the cereal, the doorbell chimed and Mr. Polite went to the door, coming back with another tray, this one containing two dishes of scrambled eggs and bacon, a stack of toast and a pot of coffee for him, more milk for Frankie.

Mr. Faust was not in the apartment. "Oh, he's busy in the mornings," Mr. Polite said with a wave of his hand. He wore the same tweed jacket and blue slacks as the day before but his shirt seemed fresh. "You wouldn't believe the work involved in running a place like this. Now hurry up and eat. The sun is climbing in the sky and it will be hot on the road today."

Mr. Polite advised Frankie to go to the toilet before they left, so they wouldn't have to stop soon. "We're anxious to be on our way west, eh, Frankie?" He sipped delicately at his coffee cup, the rim barely making an impression on his wafer-thin lips, his fox like eyes darting over the edge of his newspaper. "And don't forget your new toothbrush."

They went down the private elevator to the floor below, where Mr. Polite steered Frankie wordlessly to the stairwell at the other end of the corridor. They walked down two flights to the fifth floor, then rang for the elevator. The young black man operating it looked Frankie over, then Mr. Polite, then looked away.

When the elevator doors opened, Mr. Polite took Frankie by the hand and they hurried through the lobby. There was no sign of Mr. Faust or the skinny desk clerk with the Adam's apple, or the woman in the long dress. Outside, the sun was dazzling, and Mr. Polite had been right, it was going to be a hot day. He gave his car keys to a shiny-faced kid decked out like the Philip Morris bellboy and the kid, who looked barely sixteen, tipped his red hat and said, "Yes, *sir*, right away, sir," and ran down the steps like he was on his way to a ball game.

A woman with two small dogs on a leash walked by, looking at them curiously. Then Mr. Polite's powder-blue Cadillac rolled up and they walked down the steps. Mr. Polite gave the kid a tip. "Thank *you*, sir, thank *you*," the kid said. They got in the car and Frankie was glad to see his crumpled paper bag on the front seat. Sure enough, though, the toothbrush was gone.

Mr. Polite turned on the air conditioning and a cool hand closed over them like a breath. He drove down the long crushed stone driveway and through what appeared to be grilled gates without saying a word. Then they were on city streets and, abruptly, after a sharp turn, on a highway.

"Where is this place?" Frankie asked.

"You should be thinking about where you're going, Frankie," Mr. Polite said, "not where you're been."

They drove in silence. The sun was halfway up to the centre of the sky, and it was ahead of them, a little to the left. Mr. Polite wore his sunglasses, and Frankie turned the visor down and squinted.

"Aren't we going to wrong way?"

"It's just the way the road goes, Frankie. It loops back on itself, like life. Sometimes you think you're going one way but really you're going another way."

They passed a bunch of signs for Philadelphia and then came to a big bridge over the Delaware and they were in New Jersey. "Just don't say anything, Frankie," Mr. Polite said. "Everything will be clear shortly. Did you have a good time last night?"

"It was okay."

He laughed and put a filter tipped cigarette between his thin lips. "Did you get hurt at all?"

"Who, me? No."

"So you haven't lost anything but one day of your precious time, am I right?"

Frankie didn't know what to say to that.

"And you've got your whole life ahead of you, don't you?"

Mr. Polite turned the Cadillac off the highway at Cherry Hill and stopped at a gas station. "We won't be able to stop for quite a long while after this, so why don't you go to the toilet?"

"I went already. At the hotel."

"We're on our way west, Frankie, and it's a long way to go. Better to be cautious at the beginning of a journey than desperate at its end, I always say."

There was a blast of heat like an oven door opening when Frankie got out of the car. He was pretty sure what was going to happen. "Should I take my stuff?"

"Don't be silly, dear boy. I'll be right here when you get back. I'm just going to fill up."

But the Cadillac was gone when he came out of the men's room, and his paper bag was on the pavement where it had been parked. He checked to make sure the new toothbrush was there, and it was, along with all his other junk and a twenty-dollar bill, neatly folded into thirds.

He bought a cold bottle of soda and asked the kid who was selling gas the way to the highway going west, then started walking, with his thumb out. He got a ride pretty quick, but it was going the wrong way and it took him awhile to figure that out. Then some kids in an old Chevy jalopy picked him up but they were just tooling around, so he didn't get anywhere. In late afternoon, he was still near Cherry Hill and his brains were frying from the heat. He got off the road at a bridge and followed a brook through some woods till he came to a place that looked safe enough, and went to sleep on the mossy ground, up against a dead, fallen tree, his bag for a pillow. Later, he walked along a railroad track till he came to an old shack where someone, hoboes, he guessed, had made a fire and left it still smoldering. He found some crumpled up paper and the stub of a pencil and, using the back of a rusted-out old wheelbarrow as a table, he started to write a letter to his father. As he'd done once before, he wanted to say he was sorry for running away, sorry he was always such a nuisance, sorry his father had to work those extra hours at Christmas, sorry about the lies he'd had to tell to keep his job.

He spent the night there, in the shack, hungry and shivering in the surprising chill, dreaming of the dinner cart in Mr. Faust's room. Next morning, he found his way back to the road and was just walking along, not even trying to hitch, when he saw the policeman coming. He thought to jump into the grass along the road, but it wasn't very high, and he didn't really want to.

Later, he remembered, his father had made a big deal out of his having been picked up there, in Cherry Hill. "Gone three days and you couldn't even get past New Jersey." His father said that often, hundreds of times, it seemed to Frankie, and he had burned to tell him that he had, but he couldn't, somehow, and he didn't. It wasn't merely that he sensed he had participated in something wrong—and he *did* feel some shame, though he remembered the advice Mr. Faust's father had given *him*—and there might be trouble if his father found out about it. For a brief moment, less than a day, he had slipped out of their world, his father's and his, not just its geography but its environment and its influence, and into another one, a world he hadn't even dreamed existed. For as long as he could keep it fresh in his memory, it would remain *his* world, completely apart from his father, and he wanted that, enough so that he was willing to bear the taunts.

"Here's the great adventurer, the Basque sheepherder, runs away from home for three days and can't even get past New Jersey." Frankie could remember his father telling people that, poking him and chuckling. Even now, sitting on the deck of his friends' cabin in Montana, the tips of his ears tingled with the memory flesh and blood carry of humiliation, long after heart and mind forgive.

"So I want you to know, finally, after all these years, that you were wrong," Frankie typed, "that I did go farther, not just past something as arbitrary as a river forming a state line, but past the kind of borders that men make for themselves, the kind of borders we create to define ourselves. I did go farther, and I guess I never stopped, even though I came home that time, and other times. Maybe once you start, you never do stop till you get to where you're going."

It had taken him a long time to get here, to Montana, wherever or whatever that place is, but he *was* here, and he kept moving closer to something else he just remembered—just that moment—something that his father, in his spiritual moments, used to call the *source*, the place we all come from and, some of us, if we're lucky, go back to.

"I did get farther," Frankie wrote, although he was pretty sure he wouldn't mail this letter either. "*I did*. I just wanted you to know that."